SPARKS OF DESIRE

"You're not a fool," Slade said evenly. "You are a pawn, and there's a difference."

"Fine difference, threatening to truss me up like a goose for market, if I tell anyone here who I am!"

" 'Twas for your own good, Bryony. There are some who might see the O'Neill's daughter as a rich prize to be used for their own gain."

"You mean besides yourself?" she snarled.

Slade took a single step toward her. Restraining himself at the last moment, he looked down into her flaming blue eyes and evenly stated, "The only gain you speak of is what's already mine by law. For I've a birthright to Clandeboye, and I mean to take it back."

"You!" Bryony exclaimed, understanding everything better now. She didn't know why, but the thought of Slade seizing Raven Hall hurt her more than the idea of some remote *Sassenach* queen laying claim to it.

"Well, I'll see to it the O'Neill won't surrender, not to any weak-kneed *Sassenach!"* she passionately vowed.

Hands on her hips and black hair swirling about her, Bryony squared off with Slade.

"Lafleur's right," he growled. "God's bones, but you're an insolent wench!"

Too late Bryony saw what he meant to do. Yanking her into his arms, he crushed her lips under his with a fervency that surprised them both . . .

* * *

"Sea Raven is a swashbuckling tale of pure Irish magic!"

—Colleen Faulkner, author of *Destined to be Mine*

TODAY'S HOTTEST READS ARE TOMORROW'S SUPERSTARS

SEA RAVEN

PATRICIA McALLISTER

ZEBRA BOOKS
KENSINGTON PUBLISHING CORP.

ZEBRA BOOKS are published by

Kensington Publishing Corp.
850 Third Avenue
New York, NY 10022

First Printing: February, 1996
10 9 8 7 6 5 4 3 2 1

Printed in the United States of America

Sea Raven *is dedicated to the grandmother I never knew, Margaret Jane Kennedy Howden, and all the brave women of Ulster, who seek an end to the Troubles through the power of Love.*

We must change Ireland's course of government, clothing, customs, manner of holding land, language, and habit of life . . . or it will otherwise be impossible to set up in them obedience . . .

—Sir George Carew
Queen Elizabeth's Advisor in Munster
1555-1629

Prologue

Raven Hall
Clandeboye, Ireland
Winter, 1559

Alanna O'Neill knew she was dying. Yet she clung with Irish tenacity to the last, thin thread of life. Her final moments would be content, knowing that at least she had not failed her husband in the end. For less than an hour ago, she was finally delivered of a healthy son for Brann, a squalling, black-haired boy who already favored his father in temperament.

She smiled even as another fierce, tearing pain ripped through her small frame, and blood gushed warm and red onto sheets the midwife could not change fast enough. Mab alternately pleaded and cursed at the younger woman to end the travail. But even the threats of her husband's dour old nursemaid could not force Alanna to rally again.

"Ye must bear down once more, colleen, and rid yerself of the afterbirth," Mab sternly ordered her. "Ye've a bit o' unfinished business left after birthing that laddie of yers."

"I'm too tired," Alanna murmured, when at last a brief respite in the torturous pain came. "All I want now is to see my son!"

Mab grumbled under her breath, but obediently gathered up the last armload of fouled linens and left her lady's chamber. Her coarse worsted gown stained with blood, Mab drew herself up with outrage when she emerged into the boisterous scene of laughing and drinking just outside the birthing chamber.

All had been deathly grim and quiet for most of the eve, when Alanna's rising shrieks had pierced the night air like a banshee's cries. Mab suspected even Brann O'Neill himself, that big brute of an Irish seaman, had muttered a mutinous prayer or two under his breath for his wife's sake, while he'd paced the Great Hall beyond.

Now, however, the O'Neill was apparently content to forget Alanna altogether. After all, she had finally done her duty by him and the clan, if a bit tardily. Brann was now sprawled beside Raven Hall's cozy winter hearth with a tankard of stout mead gripped in one hand, and a whimpering bundle in the other.

"My son!" Brann crowed again, holding the tiny swaddled infant high, so all present could admire his virility. The raw-boned Irishman grinned with satisfaction when the baby let out an indignant howl.

"Just born, and already a fighter like his Da! Aye, this one's me throw, all right. Though there's no doubt he's an O'Neill, he still must have a proper first name, as well."

While the others cheered him on, all but the silent and glowering Mab in the shadows, Brann went on to declare:

"He shall be called Brendan, the 'son of the Raven'! 'Tis only fitting that I honor our Raven heritage. 'Twill also appease Father O'Leary for St. Brendan was a sailor, too, and I've no doubt this little raven shall soon fly over the high seas with his old Da!"

Taking a great guzzle of mead, the O'Neill slammed down his empty tankard on the hearth and mischievously pinched the flaxen-haired lass who bent to fill it again. The other men present laughed at his bold antics, until one by one they noticed the glaring, bloodstained old crone who emerged from the shadows. An uneasy silence descended on the hall.

"Fer shame, Brann, ye that I raised from a scrawny pup meself!" Mab snapped, and to everyone's surprise the O'Neill flushed at the brusque reminder. "Have ye forgotten so soon that ye have a wife, as well? I might remind ye, ye great Irish oaf, that ye hardly bore that fine boy yerself!"

At barely four feet tall, Mab's tiny frame shook with suppressed fury. With a contemptuous snort, she came forward and tossed the bloodied linens at Brann's feet.

"That's what yer lust has wrought tonight, ye fatheaded Irish fool! Death has come to yer door at last, and now ye'll pay His price."

Belated alarm rose in Brann's dark eyes. "What babble is this, old woman?" he demanded. "The brat is healthy enough. Just hear his lusty cry!" He shook the little bundle nestled in the crook of his arm, and the newly christened Brendan O'Neill obediently let out a rousing wail.

"Aye, the boy, the boy, that's all ye think of now!" Mab said with disgust. "I speak of yer poor, wee wife, who has no more to give, I fear, and even now fades away before me eyes."

"Nay!" Brann shot to his feet with the babe in his arms, and defied the woman's ominous words with an angry roar. "God's bones, but I won't let her! She's to bear me a crew of strong sons, and I'll stand for nothing less!"

Mab knew the O'Neill's blustering was softened by genuine concern, for she had seen the love in his eyes when he had taken the fragile blond colleen to wife five years ago. Before Alanna came along, Brann had been content enough with the village whores and dockside slatterns. That he had wed at all gave much credit to Alanna, and their brief years together had been happy enough.

Brann's only disappointment had been Alanna's failure to give him an heir. Now that she had proven triumphant at last, he was assuaged, but Mab was not about to let him brush aside his devoted wife in favor of a peasant wench. She promptly turned an evil eye on the hopeful hussy lingering at O'Neill's elbow, and the young girl swiftly dropped her gaze and slunk away into the shadows.

Somewhat satisfied, Mab grudgingly said, "if ye hurry,

O'Neill, mayhaps ye can woo yer Alanna away from the final darkness. She's holding out to see the boy again, and 'tis only proper that ye be the one to bring him back to her arms."

Looking discomfited, Brann nodded. He moved to stagger a little drunkenly after Mab. Except for the crackling and snapping of the great hearth fire, silence reigned supreme now in Raven Hall.

Back in her lady's chamber, Mab moved to Alanna's bedside and held out a candle taper before the younger woman's lips. Relieved to see the flame flicker, if only a little, Mab gently shook Alanna O'Neill's shoulder and whispered, "Here now, colleen, someone's come and brought yer little laddie like ye wanted! Open yer eyes and see!"

Dark lashes fluttered against Alanna's pale white cheeks for a moment, and then at last she opened her beautiful dark blue eyes. Seeing her husband hovering protectively over her, Alanna smiled. With agony twisting his rough-hewn features, the O'Neill awkwardly settled the squirming infant boy in his young wife's limp arms.

Alanna glanced down at the baby, whose tuft of silky black hair poked up over the blanket. "He's perfect, isn't he?" she whispered.

"Aye, he's a strong, fine laddie." Brann's voice was husky now and quivered slightly. "Thank ye, Alanna Colleen."

"Have I made you . . . happy?" There was a wistful tone to the fading whisper, and the O'Neill looked desperately to Mab.

The old woman shook her head. Brann froze for a moment, big fists clenching and unclenching at his sides. Then, realizing his wife still awaited his reply, he whispered back, "Aye, me little Lana. Very happy indeed."

Alanna's smile widened with contentment, but this time it settled permanently in place, and an expression of utter peace and bliss stole across her lovely features.

Then abruptly the image shattered. Alanna went rigid and

let out a piercing cry that raised the hair on the back of his neck.

Mab snatched little Brendan away just in time, as Alanna suddenly bore down again, her frail white hands scrabbling for a hold on the sides of the bed.

"What is it? What's happening?" Brann demanded, but without answering Mab thrust his son back in his arms and briskly went to work.

A few minutes later, the old woman lifted another wet, slick baby up in her hands. She held it at a distance at first, uncertain if it lived. Then the miniature human face twisted as if in supreme disgust, or perhaps impatience, and a ragged cry arose from the newborn, easily drowning out the faint mewling sounds her twin brother was making in Brann's arms.

" 'Tis a fine wee girlie," Mab said.

The new father hardly spared a glance for the child Mab quickly washed and swaddled in warm linen. He stared instead at Alanna, a single tear frozen on his weathered brown cheek. His wife had fallen back against the bolsters, silent and stiffening now in death. Alanna's expression was twisted as if in terrible agony, and she looked more like a ghoul than the beautiful woman he had wed. There was no peace for her now, nor for him. And all because of a cursed girl-brat!

Awash in his own grief, Brann turned away from the sight of his dead wife, and roughly ordered Mab, "Away with that changeling, old woman, and cleanse this chamber of its evil stink!"

He pointed at the second lively bundle in Mab's arms, refusing to look directly at the girl-brat Death had spawned.

For once, Mab dared not gainsay him, not when the O'Neill's big frame fairly shook with fury. She saw the burning hatred in his eyes and hastily assured him she would comply.

Then, in a calmer manner, Mab drove the grief-stricken father from the room. Clutching his precious son like a lifeline, Brann retreated to the hall. When the door was safely barred behind him, Mab peeled back the blanket from the baby girl's face.

A ruff of raven black hair to match her twin's sprouted from the perfectly formed little head, and the eyes which blinked and stubbornly tried to focus on Mab were not the pale milky blue of a newborn's, but a deep blue color like the sea. No changeling this, Mab chuckled to herself, but a pure, ornery little dab of O'Neill blood. She was a qualified judge, having played nursemaid to two previous generations of O'Neill babes, and now beginning her third.

"Hah!" she said with satisfaction, bouncing the infant in her capable arms. The baby girl was already beginning to make greedy, smacking noises with her little lips. "We'll see how long it takes yer Da to come around, won't we, me bonny lass? Knowing that stubborn Irish oaf as I do, it might be a time. And in the while, colleen, ye must have a proper name."

Mab touched the petal-smooth cheek of the child, and the baby's flailing fist suddenly wrapped around her index finger. Surprised to find such a strong grip in a newborn, the old woman chuckled admiringly. "Sure, and there's no doubt at all in my mind that yer an O'Neill! Damme if we won't prove it to that ornery Da of yers, eh? With beauty like this, colleen, ye can be all that ugly old Mab is not. But ye must have a strong name to see ye through, something to protect ye from banshee, if nothing else."

Mab paused to think, gazing upon Alanna's cold, broken body one last time. And then suddenly, it came to her, though whether by providence or precognition, she would never know.

"Bryony," she murmured, and the little girl in her arms hiccoughed in apparent approval. "Aye, lovey, fer it means strong, and surely ye must be so, if ye are to force the mighty Brann O'Neill to see the error of his ways. Oh, aye, he'll come 'round. All men eventually do, sweetling . . . sometimes it just takes a wee while."

One

The Irish Sea, Spring 1578

"God's toenail! Be careful up there, Bry!"

Brendan O'Neill's anxious shout was torn from his lips by the brisk sea breeze, and the young man chafed with worry as he and the rest of the *Leprechaun*'s crew peered up at the tiny figure dangling from the crow's nest.

Standing beside Brendan, able seaman Finn O'Grady let out a long, low whistle of admiration. "Look at her, Dan! One slip, and she's a goner. If I didn't know better, I'd swear your sister's fey."

Brendan set his teeth and tried not to let Finn's words sink in too deeply. For though he loved his twin sister dearly, Brendan was wise enough not to display undue affection for her in front of the ship's captain. Brann was also watching the unfolding events with grudging interest from the ship's starboard. Thickly muscled arms folded across his broad chest, their black-browed and heavily bearded father scowled up at the lithe form now shimmying its way down to the deck.

Bryony O'Neill swung from the rope ladder over to the ratline, and executed a graceful fifteen-foot slide to land in catlike fashion on the deck beside her twin. Aware of their sire narrowly observing them both, Brendan's tone came out sharper than he'd intended.

"You could have broken your neck up there! Not that it would have done much damage, I'll be thinkin'!"

Bryony tossed back the wild black mane of hair blowing in her face and shouted right back at her brother, "Mind your own station, Dan! I'm only doing what the O'Neill ordered, and that's more than you can say!"

She stalked away from him, her slender figure rigid with anger and pride. Brendan glanced again at the O'Neill, who still leaned against the ship's railing, staring after his changeling child. There was resentment permanently etched into those craggy features, and mute fury in his eyes. Brann O'Neill was still a bitter man. Alanna's memory had seen to that.

In all these years, the O'Neill had never acknowledged Bryony, though he tolerated her presence at Raven Hall. Old Mab had worked that miracle, and even though Brann himself never referred to Bryony as anything other than the Changeling, the obvious resemblance between both twins and their father was startling enough to make his claim ludicrous.

All three of them possessed the same thick, blue-black, stubbornly wayward hair which glistened like raven's wing under the sun, and both twins had inherited their father's unusual height. Unlike the men, however, Bryony had her mother's deep blue eyes, hinting at a distant Viking ancestor who might have once plied the Irish Sea even as she did now.

But for those blue eyes, Brann O'Neill might have forgotten Alanna in time. Yet whenever he looked at Bryony, he was reminded of his gentle wife's death, and what he assumed was the cause of it. Brendan, the firstborn and his long-awaited son, could be forgiven his unknowing part in the crime. Not so Bryony, who with her cursed blue eyes was a constant reminder to him of the gentle, beautiful lady she had brutally destroyed.

Somewhere deep within his core, Brann recognized his own foolishness in publicly denying his daughter. But he was firstmost a proud man, and an angry one close on the heels of that. He had successfully managed to ignore Bryony during her early years, leaving her wholly in Mab's care, while he tucked tiny Brendan under one arm and set sail in the usual fashion.

A succession of ship's doxies had kept the boy from underfoot, while also providing an outlet for Brann's base needs. But even staying away for months at sea, and returning to Raven Hall only once or twice a year, had failed to make Bryony vanish, or turn into the changeling he still asserted she was.

And as the twins had grown, Brendan had shown a marked preference for the land, much to his father's disappointment. After being forced to live most of his childhood on a heaving deck, the lad longed for stability. Worse yet, Brendan had a weak stomach. This was unheard-of in an O'Neill, especially one expected to someday assume the position of clan chieftain. Humiliation had fired Brann's fury at his son, until Mab had finally devised a concoction of black horehound, chamomile, and meadowsweet, which settled Brendan's stomach enough for him to be able to sail with his father, but only as long as the seas remained calm.

Still, Brendan had never stopped searching for any excuse to return to shore. When he first took a stand, at the tender age of ten, Brann was at first outraged, then secretly pleased. Was it too much to hope the young pup was growing some backbone, after all?

Until then, the O'Neill had been terribly disappointed, and at times even ashamed, of his gentle-natured son. Meek spirits were acceptable in a girl, perhaps, but not for a lad of his own. When Brendan finally informed his father in a firm if quavering voice that he never intended to go to sea again, the O'Neill was almost pleased by Dan's unexpected display of bravery. Almost.

Then the boy's ulterior motive quickly surfaced. Brendan had seen how his twin sister was treated at Raven Hall, shunned by everyone except Mab, thanks to their father. He'd also seen his little sister gazing wistfully out to sea more than once. Knowing Bryony had a love for ships and sailing that he never would, Brendan vowed to change the situation if he could.

With Mab's help, he told the O'Neill he would only return to the *Leprechaun* with Bryony in tow. Brann was furious, but what could he do? He was anxious to teach Brendan the seafaring trade as his father had taught him, as countless generations of O'Neill's had done before that. Grudgingly, he gave into Brendan's demand, with the single, stony condition that the Changeling be kept out of his sight at all times.

That edict had not lasted long, however. It was soon apparent even to O'Neill that Bryony was born to sail, as her brother was not. On her first voyage, she had crept up from the below cabin to the rail, just a skinny little snip of a thing, her tangled black hair buffeting her face as the mighty galleon crested the waves. There she had cringed, fully expecting a beating from her angry sire, but willing to risk it just for the sheer joy of feeling the salt spray in her face.

In a rare show of generosity, Brann let her be. And as the years crept past, Bryony slowly matured into one of the best crew members he'd ever had. He was soon forced to grudgingly acknowledge the fact that she was of good sea-stock. The chit had an iron stomach and the will to match.

He gazed at his daughter now, while Bryony went unawares about the rest of her duties. She wore plain canvas trews and a simple white shirt like the rest of the crew. But for her long hair, she might have passed for a lad. She was lanky and reed slim, certainly no beauty in Brann's opinion.

Whereas his Alanna had been softly feminine from the start, Bryony still seemed to be all gangly limbs and awkward height. The O'Neill grunted as he continued to appraise the girl. She wouldn't even fetch a decent bride price, not that any sane man would have her. For one thing, she was too long in the tooth now, all of nineteen in a day when most girls were wed at fourteen or fifteen. Secondly, her unusual background would give any fellow pause. He knew their nearest rivals, the Magennis clan, openly joked about O'Neill's Cabin Boy. And his own crew had affectionately dubbed her Skinny Bones ever since she was a child. No, the Changeling would never be the feminine decoration on his ship that Alanna had once been.

But if Alanna O'Neill had been the masthead, Bryony was the bow. Brann could not deny the girl was sturdy and resourceful; she pulled her own weight, sometimes more. He had little complaint about the way Bryony ran her quarter at sea. *Leprechaun* was a three-masted, square-sailed galleon, and at full capacity she required nearly two hundred men on the oars.

Usually, the winds were sufficient enough to move the great ship at a fast clip, even through choppy channel waters. Most of their runs were made with only a skeleton crew. But when the sea was becalmed, everyone could count on Bryony to be the first to pick up an oar.

At first, O'Neill had hoped the rest of his crew would resent her presence, especially since she was a female and they were rumored to be unlucky on ships. But in a strange twist of events, *Leprechaun*'s crew regarded Bryony as more of a mascot, an inspiration to row harder or work longer. The O'Neill was puzzled and chagrined to discover his men seemed not to have the same camaraderie with his son. How could a mere chit, and a scrawny one at that, inspire such dogged loyalty?

Sensing the O'Neill's scrutiny, Bryony paused in the act of picking up a heavy coil of rope from the deck. Without a qualm, she turned and matched gazes with the man who had made her childhood a living hell. She knew better than anyone Brann's ill regard for her. How many days and nights had she sobbed in Mab's lap when she was little, cruelly and constantly reminded of her father's never-ending resentment?

Had she been any less an O'Neill, Bryony suspected she would have buckled under the strain of Brann's command long ago. He was harsh and overly critical of all the crew, but especially her, and oft as not she was the sole target of his furious disapproval. While Brendan, it seemed, could do little to incur

Brann O'Neill's wrath, except for his latest declaration of wanting to leave the sea, to become a farmer instead.

Once Bryony had resented her brother, and was bitterly jealous of the favoritism always shown her twin. But over the years, she had come to realize it was no more Dan's fault than her own, and the O'Neill's unreasonable grudge would only serve to alienate them from one another if they didn't stick together. Brann had never remarried after Alanna's death, so she and Brendan had only each other now.

So, for everyone's sake, but mostly her own, Bryony finally came to regard the O'Neill as an employer, not her father, for in truth he never had been. She maintained a cool facade that had finally even fooled her own brother into thinking she no longer noticed or cared how Brann felt about her. But deep inside Bryony, a remnant of the hurt little girl she had once been still cried, wanting desperately to be lifted up onto her Da's knee, hugged, and told she was loved.

Bryony quickly turned into the wind, letting the salty breeze sting her eyes and provide an excuse for the tears. Emotion was a waste of time and energy, as she'd learned long ago, and she had little enough of either to spare. They were sailing home at last after over eight weeks at sea, and everyone was exhausted. Trading up and down the Irish coast wore out even the most tenacious of men.

Finally Bryony felt the O'Neill's cool assessment shift from her to someone else in the crew, and she let out a small relieved sigh.

When they sailed into Clandeboye Cove later that afternoon, Bryony was up in the crow's nest again, and the first to spot Mab through a spyglass. The twins' old nursemaid was standing down on shore, waiting for them to row in from the galleon, anxiously wringing her gnarled hands.

Bryony knew something disastrous must have occurred to roust Mab from the household, for the dear old woman suffered from the ague now, and even walking proved a chore. And Mab couldn't have known of their arrival until just a short while ago. The O'Neill had no schedule by which he sailed, so that meant Mab must have implored someone with sharp eyes, a young lad perhaps, to notify her the moment the *Leprechaun* had been sighted.

Nimbly swinging on a ratline back down to the main deck, Bryony ordered Finn O'Grady, "Lower a rowboat for me. I'm going in ahead of the rest."

"What is it?"

It wasn't Finn who spoke so sharply, but the O'Neill behind her. Maintaining her poise, Bryony pivoted about and calmly faced the scowling captain. "Mab's down on shore. Something's wrong."

For once, Brann didn't criticize or countermand her orders to the crew. He nodded at Finn. "See to it, O'Grady."

As the young man hurried off to the task, Brendan moved up to join them.

"I'll go, Da—" he began to offer.

"Nay, Danny. I want you to sail her in. High time you took full command." At the O'Neill's gruff order, Brendan frowned, but obligingly moved astern to take the whipstaff.

Bryony quelled her own envy and hurried off after O'Grady, snatching up a woollen cloak and gloves as she went. It would be frigid on the water even in early spring, and she knew she mustn't let her muscles become chilled. It was a long row to shore, and she was running low on reserves as it was.

She waited while Finn and another deckhand lowered one of the small wooden longboats lashed to the ship's sides into the churning waters below. Fearlessly she climbed up and over the rail, and skimmed down the rope ladder someone had flung over the galleon's port side. Bryony had scarcely taken her seat, when another figure descended from above and landed heavily beside her. The little boat rocked dangerously, and she glanced up in annoyance at the O'Neill.

"It's a hard row in. You may need some help," was all he

said, and in response to that Bryony snatched up the pair of oars and rowed for all she was worth. As the longboat shot forward through the choppy gray waves, Brann was forced to quickly sit down, lest he topple overboard.

Bryony had rarely been in this close proximity to her father before, not under such isolated circumstances, anyway. It both irritated her and made her admittedly curious as to his motives for joining her. Certainly, he wasn't here through any sort of goodwill. She had long since given up trying to win his affection. She would settle for his respect instead.

So resolved, Bryony turned her concentration fully upon the oars. It was a good thing her hands were callused and her arms like whipcord, for she had to use every last ounce of her strength just to propel the boat inland. Her muscles blazed with pain, for she had rowed on the galleon twice in the last three days, and Brann's added weight did not help matters any.

The O'Neill turned his calculating eye full on Bryony. He knew they'd both drown in the cove before she'd ask him for any help. He almost admired her for it, yet he was still too upset over Brendan's recent request to undertake the life of a dirt-farmer, to show the girl any sort of approval. Damme, why couldn't his only son show such mettle? He wryly thought that Dan could take a few lessons from the Changeling, who had locked gazes with him now and set her straight white teeth. She grunted softly with the effort of rowing, but still refused to admit defeat.

Eventually the boat was barely crawling through the water, as Bryony gasped for breath and her teeth began to chatter from the cold. Enough was enough. Impatiently, Brann reached out and yanked both oars from her, leaving a bloody trail of splinters in her palms.

Too tired to feel the pain, Bryony collapsed against the bow, letting her hands fall over the sides and feeling the icy harbor waves slosh over her injured flesh. She was so cold now that the water actually felt warm. She knew she was dangerously close to exposure. The bitter spring wind sliced at them both, but Brann was at least fortunate enough to have his back to it. She felt her own cheeks burning, and her legs were numb and tingling by the time the longboat bumped the shore.

Mab hurried over to meet them as they came in, nearly falling and twisting her ankle between two rocks in the process. And as they both knew, the old woman was not one to hurry for anything.

"Blast you, old crow, it'd better be good!" Brann, too, was winded, and could scarcely manage his customary bellow as he threw down the oars and climbed wearily out of the boat. He stomped across the shore to meet Mab. Bryony had yet to rise, and was still absently picking the splinters from her palms. Then Mab's cry caught her attention, and hearing the O'Neill curse as well, Bryony hopped out of the boat and forced her rubbery legs across the ground.

"By all the bloody saints of hell!" Brann was swearing, smacking one meaty fist into the other. "I'll show those puking lapdogs of Her Majesty the Bitch a thing or two!"

Alarmed by Brann's words, as well as his open blasphemy against the English queen, Bryony demanded, "What happened?"

Mab's age-spotted hands trembled as she handed Bryony the same scroll of parchment Brann had read. It took some effort for her frozen fingers to rebreak the wax seal and unroll the paper, but after swiftly scanning the words there, Bryony loosed an involuntary cry of disbelief.

Unlike most females of the day, Bryony had learned to read and letter, and once again she had Brendan to thank. Her brother had secretly taught her during his own lessons, and though the O'Neill had been furious at first, he'd grudgingly admitted Bryony made good use of the skill by keeping his ship's ledgers at sea. When she wasn't serving on deck, Bryony maintained the books, laboriously recording each purchase or sale in a neat hand. Now she discovered her talent only made this moment harder, for the flowing script dancing before her eyes seemed to pound each ominous word into her head.

It was a royal edict, signed by Queen Elizabeth herself, though it had also been witnessed by the Governor of Ireland, Sir Henry Sidney. Sidney had apparently sanctioned the deed. Bryony shook her head as the meaning of the words finally sank in. The Tudor queen was laying claim to O'Neill lands!

And not only that, she saw, swiftly digesting the rest; the O'Neills were to be given only six weeks to evacuate Raven Hall before a "party of force" would be dispatched to see to it for them.

Besides Raven Hall and the land itself, any and all outbuildings had been confiscated. This meant the entire clan would be displaced. The reason for this, the proclamation droned on righteously, was the restoration of dormant English titles to Irish soil. Brann O'Neill apparently had the misfortune of owning a parcel of land the Crown coveted, and now saw fit to claim. The vague edict cited prior ownership dating from the time of the Norman conquest.

The tersely worded notice did allot the dispossessed Irish their personal effects, and "only such as can be reasonably carried upon departure." Therefore the livestock, as well as their homes, would be forfeit to the Tudor monarch.

"Why?" Bryony burst out. "What have we ever done to her?"

Mab just shook her head in a gesture of despair, and Brann seized the opportunity to swear again, using all the colorful adjectives unique to a life at sea.

"That skinny-shanked *Sassenach* whore can damn well come over here and tell me that herself! I'll not be movin' for the likes of her—" and here he paused and spat upon the ground. "And if that takes me to me grave, so be it!"

"Ye hotheaded fool," Mab hissed, "what of the twins? They can't fend fer themselves yet, and they have the most to lose of any of us! Will ye risk their futures so freely?"

"Brendan's a man now, even if not much of one," Brann muttered, and Bryony was not surprised when he did not address the matter of her future at all. "I'll not have his heritage torn from him, old woman, and if that means takin' on the whole bloody English navy, then I will."

Mab threw up her crabbed hands in exasperation, then hobbled over to Bryony's side. Leaning heavily against the younger woman, she said, "Come back to the hall, colleen. There's just no reasonin' with this fathead of a man. And ye look half-frozen, chick. I've a hot toddy that'll perk ye right up again."

Bryony hesitated, then nodded, and thrust the scroll back into the O'Neill's hands.

Brann stared at the edict long and hard, and as the two women moved off together into the growing twilight, he crumpled it in his huge fist and hurled it into the sea.

Two

"You can see it from here, *Capitan,*" Diego announced.

Slade Tanner reached out and accepted the spyglass from his first mate, holding it to a narrowed eye and focusing the lens on the single ship moored in the cove.

A muscle worked in his cheek as he surveyed the distant crew of men, no doubt in O'Neill's employ, who were visibly preparing the *Leprechaun* for future journeys. Slade took particular note of the number of hands scrambling about to clean the other ship's falcon cannon, and counted roughly twenty on the starboard side. With a soft oath, he snapped the spyglass shut and handed it back to Diego.

"Prepare to drop anchor," he told the Spaniard shortly. "I need to think about this some more."

Diego Santiago saw the concern written in his captain's green eyes, and fully sympathized. Slade Tanner was a merchant at heart, not a fighter, and it went against his grain entirely to force his claim to Clandeboye. The wiry first mate quickly passed the order down the line, and the *Silver Hart*'s crew responded with alacrity.

Fortunately, Slade Tanner's youth had never proven a deterrent where his command was concerned. Perhaps it had something to do with his size. Slade was half a head taller than the tallest of his crewmen, placing him well over six feet. Muscular, yet lean, he exuded a powerful presence which was impossible to ignore. While his size usually guaranteed him instant respect from other men, his unaffected air also gained him their admiration.

Slade favored practical garb at sea, unlike most of Queen Elizabeth's officers. Today he wore tan, knee-length breeches and nether stocks of thick yellow wool. A sleeveless, dark blue broadcloth coat was buttoned over his ruffled white doublet. He was also clean-shaven, flouting the current court rage of pointy beards and moustaches. His red gold hair was shoulder-length, and neatly tied back in a queue.

Diego grinned, wondering what the mighty Clan O'Neill would make of his youthful captain. Slade's seafaring skills had earned him the rank of first mate at the tender age of eighteen, and now at twenty-six he was already captain of his own vessel. Though chartered by Queen Elizabeth, he was solidly master of his own destiny. And no man alive was prouder of his ship.

Silver Hart was a graceful galley, whose four banners flying from the masthead and yardarm bore, respectively, the cross of St. George on a red ground, a golden fleur-de-lis on a blue field, the Tudor rose and dragon on a green and white ground, and a leaping silver hart, the Tanner emblem.

The vessel's high sides blended smoothly into the wales and skids of her structure. Her stern was square, the billowing topsail sheets and mizzen well distended in the crisp breeze. Spouts of iridescent spray rushed up against her sleek bow, as she plunged towards the cove. Slade stood on the foredeck, hands clasped behind his back, calmly surveying the enemy's realm like a Viking of old.

When Captain Tanner gave the signal, the huge anchor dropped with a mighty splash, and the chain clanked out rapidly behind them. *Silver Hart* groaned and shuddered like a living thing, as she ran up short on her tether. One by one, her sails began to droop, as the Englishmen swarming over her decks quickly and efficiently shortened and stowed her canvas.

With his calculating eye, Slade had brought them to a halt

right behind a massive outcropping of sea rock. From the cove or coastline, his ship would not yet be visible. He knew this particular mission would require extraordinary patience. He'd already been put to the test.

Slade had been notified several months ago by the Irish governor, Sir Henry Sidney, that the Tanner family had a valid claim to Irish soil. A Norman ancestor of theirs, under William the Conqueror, had originally owned Clandeboye and the surrounding lands. Though the Tanner claim was centuries-old now, it had been painstakingly researched, documented, and then ultimately approved by Elizabeth Tudor.

Being the youngest of four sons, Slade had naturally not inherited much upon his father's death. George, the eldest, had assumed the title of baron and the more valuable lands, as well as Cheatham Manor in Surrey. Kit received their mother's dower properties after her death, including a charming, little country estate known as Ambergate. Phillip, the third son, was presently away at Oxford. He had received a modest settlement upon the baron's death, and planned to secure a position as esquire in the Tudor court when he completed his studies. He was also betrothed to a young lady of good birth, and her dowry would be adequate enough for them to live quite comfortably after they wed.

Slade alone had been forced to learn a trade, but he bore no resentment against his elder brothers. Always drawn to the sea, he'd enlisted at age twelve with a merchant-trader, and it had saved him from total penury.

Later, he joined the queen's navy and considered it the wisest course he had ever taken. Besides his deep love for the sea and all things nautical, he had managed to amass quite a comfortable nest egg for himself. His first two ships had belonged to Elizabeth, but *Silver Hart* was his own.

The Tanners had always been a close-knit family, but the four sons had grown even more so since their parents' passing. Thus, when the news came of Tanner properties in distant Ireland, Slade's three brothers insisted he must be the one to stake the claim. He had earned a place of his own, and they wished him well.

The *Silver Hart* had made good time en route to Ireland during Slade's initial crossing, with favorable breezes and peaceful seas. But when he had first arrived two months before, Slade naively assumed that the O'Neills had already left. After all, Sir Sydney had assured him the native Irish tenants had been given proper notice.

But he quickly discovered that not only had the O'Neills not evacuated after the governor's warning, but they did not appear to have any intentions of ever doing so. Frustrated, Slade had sailed south to Dublin and contacted the governor again, in order to learn all he could about his adversary. Discovering the Irishman was a fellow merchant made Slade's task all the harder. But Sir Sydney logically pointed out that Brann O'Neill had enough family and funds to move on and resettle somewhere else. O'Neill was simply being stubborn, the governor said, as all the Irish were wont to do. He calmly advised Slade to drive them out.

"I can imagine how they'll feel, being ousted like that after so many years," Slade had pointed out.

"Feel?" Sydney chuckled, waving aside the captain's concerns. "They're only Irish, my boy, still savages at best. Why, they'll just roll up their animal skins and move on."

But Slade had reservations. He returned to England for a brief time, to consult his brothers and obtain the queen's advice. Elizabeth Tudor also airily dismissed the problem of the O'Neills, and granted Slade permission to force out the troublesome clan, if necessary. Though he easily obtained Elizabeth's approval of the deed, being one of her favorite captains, Slade realized he must go it alone. If he wanted Clandeboye back, he would have to take it himself.

His tall figure sketched against the setting sun, he now stood on deck and grimly waited while his crew prepared for confrontation. The two full tiers along *Silver Hart*'s sides numbered fifty guns, but her triple-masted design proclaimed her a merchantman, not a vessel of war. Her one drawback was that she was not quite swift enough to suit Slade, and as he and the O'Neill appeared almost evenly matched, he was taking a gamble on being able to overtake the older galleon.

As if reading his mind, Diego suddenly appeared at his side. "Having second thoughts, eh, *Capitan?*" the little Spaniard inquired.

"I don't want to force these people out, Diego, but it appears I have no choice," Slade replied. "Sydney said they've blatantly ignored three notices now. And while he's sympathetic to my dilemma, the governor says he can do no more. If I want my own lands, I'll have to take a stand."

Diego nodded. "First thing in the morning, then?"

Slade sighed, obviously reluctant to pursue this course, but seeing no other alternative. "Aye, we'll weigh anchor at dawn's first light. I don't dare give O'Neill a chance to man his ship. This way will be quicker, and hopefully we can capture the cove before there's any bloodshed." He reached out and absently skimmed his long fingers along *Silver Hart*'s graceful bow. She was a magnificent vessel, and he could well imagine O'Neill's consternation when the Irishman glanced out to sea and saw her entering the cove. Certainly O'Neill must see the legitimacy of his claim. Slade had never personally known an Irishman before, but surely they were every bit as reasonable as the next fellow.

Bryony heard the angry shouting coming from the hall, but paid it no heed at first. The crew was always a little extra boisterous after returning to shore, and the first night or two back in Raven Hall usually degenerated into a drunken brawl by the wee hours of the morn. Though the O'Neill had provided most of his crew with cottages within close range of his keep, Raven Hall was constantly cluttered with noisy kinsmen, yapping dogs, and dozens of children.

Bryony had sought out the privacy of her own small stone

chamber the moment she was home. Off ship, she socialized very little with anyone but Brendan and Mab. And when she was not outdoors, doing chores, she kept mainly to her room. For everywhere else in the keep, it seemed, there were constant reminders of Alanna O'Neill, from her mother's dower pieces of fine linens and silver, to the great oak-carved bed where she had died in childbirth.

The O'Neill had stoutly refused to surrender any vestige of his beloved wife, gone now nigh a score of years. Bryony still felt pangs of guilt and grief whenever she encountered these intimate items, blatantly left out for all to see. In her mind, she knew it was wrong of Brann to blame her for Alanna's death. But in her heart, she hurt as much as he, and so silently accepted the responsibility for the deed.

In her room, Bryony shrugged out of her soiled clothes and exchanged them for worn, comfortable buff breeches and a clean white blouse. She took a moment more to fasten her long black hair in a single braid, securing the end with a bit of leather. There were doubtless chores aplenty needing her attention. First of all, there was probably livestock to tend and water to fetch. Since Mab's joints had failed her, Bryony had taken over many of the onerous tasks, such as cooking and cleaning. She hated women's work with a passion, but realized it still must be done.

Bryony had made a few enemies, after forcibly recruiting the other women to help Mab with the chores whenever she herself was gone at sea. For too long, her kinswomen and the O'Neill's latest trollop had been content to lay about the chieftain's hall and be waited upon, hand and foot. Why should they bestir themselves or go home, they reasoned, when Raven Hall had better food and free service?

Bryony had brought a swift end to their laziness, by assigning each woman a specific chore in the large household. She knew she was not at all popular among her kinswomen, but cared little, as they had been equally unkind to her over the years. Since the O'Neill had never formally acknowledged her, there had been plenty of slaps, sneers, and catcalls when she was a child. Strangely enough, the womenfolk had been far crueler than the men.

But Bryony was nineteen now, a woman grown, and for the most part immune to the stares and whispers which still circulated whenever she appeared. She knew Brann's name for her—Changeling—produced as much uncertainty as contempt among the clan. But few dared to cross her anymore, for fear of arousing the Little People's ire. It might have been laughable, except for the loneliness she endured as a result.

Only Mab, bless her, had steadfastly stood by Bryony all these years. And Brendan, of course, though being a male he could not possibly understand the depth of her pain and confusion. Or could he? Bryony paused in the act of tugging her leather boots back on, in order to listen more closely to the yelling going on in the hall. Was that Dan's voice she heard? She shook her head, bending to lace her boots, but a moment later could not fail to recognize her twin's angry cry.

"No! I'll have nothing more to do with ships or the sea! I told you before, this was my last voyage, Da!"

Bryony heard something crash down upon the trestle table, doubtless the O'Neill's huge fist.

"What exactly are you sayin', boy? That you're willin' to trade the coveted position of the O'Neill for some foolish dream of becoming a sod-farmer?"

Bryony opened her chamber door and peered out in time to see her brother emphatically nod his head. Brendan faced the O'Neill across the vast expanse of the rough wooden high board, but judging by the fury in the older man's eyes, the distance between them might not be enough for Dan's safety.

Dan visibly tensed at his father's jeer, but did not back down. Bryony silently cheered her twin on, when he lifted his chin and softly but steadily replied, "No, Da, I'll always be an O'Neill, whether you like it or not. But as you've said yourself, it's high time I looked to make my own way in the world, and this is how I choose to do it."

Brann's nostrils flared. "Just what the hell do you think I've been tryin' to teach you all these years? I'm offering you the finest trade route north of Dublin, boy, something half the men in this hall would kill for."

Bryony glanced around at their kinsmen. Most hovered in the background in various poses of standing or sitting, and yet none of them looked particularly surprised or upset by Dan's declaration. She was aware of the general consensus among them: Brendan O'Neill was a fine lad, just not the stuff a leader was made of. Privately, they all agreed that Brann would do far better to groom some other man for his successor. After all, it was obvious enough by now the O'Neill would never have another son.

But Brann himself was not so willing to accept defeat. Wagging a thick finger at his son, he ordered, "I'll hear no more of this, Danny. Treason, that's what it is! Treason against me, and all the O'Neills who have sailed before us."

"Then treason it is," Brendan quietly replied with a shrug. "There's more to come, Da."

"Saints preserve us! What more could you possibly do to ruin me day?" the O'Neill swore sarcastically, slapping the table so hard the dinnerware rattled.

"I'm betrothed, Da. And I'll not hear another word about it," Brendan added swiftly, when he saw his sire's face begin to mottle with outrage. An uneasy silence descended over the hall.

Finally Brann spoke with deceptive softness. "Betrothed, ye say?" Bryony tensed, for she sensed what was coming. The O'Neill's brogue always thickened in a prelude to an explosion of rage.

Brendan nodded, relaxing a little. Apparently he thought his father was going to be reasonable, after all. Bryony knew better, but there was no way she could forewarn her twin.

Uncertainly, but eagerly, Brendan offered, "To Glynnis MacDougal, Da."

The O'Neill thoughtfully rubbed at his bristly jawline. "The Scot's daughter?"

"Aye, the pretty little redhead from up Glen way. As you know, I've been courting her properly for over a year now, and we've finally decided to wed. Her father's offered us a small homestead, near Ballycastle. It's good farming land, Da. The best in the north."

Brann's bloodshot eyes narrowed dangerously. Bryony knew he had been drinking heavily since their return to Raven Hall. There was no telling what he might do. She stepped cautiously into the hall, trying in vain to get her brother's attention. But Brendan was too anxious to share his good news with everyone. He stood there gazing hopefully at his sire.

"Well," the O'Neill said at last. He shook his shaggy dark head in amazement, but looked somewhat pleased. " 'Twould appear ye have a man's needs after all, Danny boy, for all your mealymouthed ways." Brendan flushed as his father continued in an increasingly louder voice, "Aye, I'll drink to that much, laddie!" Brann's fist swiped up a jewel-studded goblet resting on the table. With an uneasy smile, Brendan reached for his own.

As the two goblets crashed noisily together, Brann cried, "Here's to me lusty son, and the next O'Neill!"

"Da—" Brendan began to protest.

"Hear me out, lad. I'll let you wed the Scot's little pigeon, as ye seem to have the hots for her; hell, I'll even give you Raven Hall as a bridal gift. Just agree to take me place as the O'Neill. And when you do—why, I'd saved the other as a surprise for later, but you might as well have it now."

"Nay." It wasn't Brendan who spoke so forcefully now, but Mab. The old woman pushed through the crowd and stepped between the two, as if to protect the younger. "Leave him be, Brann O'Neill. Let the boy go his own way."

As if Mab hadn't spoken at all, Brann continued eagerly, his dark eyes shining, "She's moored a short ways down the coast, Danny. Just waitin' for you to climb aboard her, for like all spirited wenches, she secretly craves a master. And she's as sleek and fine a caravel as you ever did see. I bought her from a Portuguese, who couldn't pay his debts. Been hidin' her half a year, waiting for the right time to hand her over.

"Mind you, Danny boy, she'll need a stern hand; she's a bit of a frisky filly on the high seas. But a finer-looking lady isn't to be found in these parts. That's why I named her for me beloved wife and your own Mum, God assoil her sweet soul; she's been christened the *Alanna Colleen.*"

Brendan paled. The goblet slipped from his fingers, and with a metallic crash spilled a froth of brown mead across the table. Then, a moment later, a bright flush crept up his neck. Furiously, he shouted, "God's blood! You'll never understand, Da! What must I do to break these damned chains?"

With an angry curse, Brendan turned and stalked from the hall. Bryony rushed after him, trailing her twin through a pair of open wooden doors he had crashed between. Both of them emerged beneath the dusky blue of a twilight sky.

Bryony cupped her hands to her mouth. "Dan!" But her brother kept right on walking, fists clenched rigidly at his sides. She was forced to break into a run to catch up with him, but finally gained his side at the crest of a saucer-shaped hill.

She reached out and touched his arm, but Brendan jerked away, so angry and hurt that when he glanced at her, she could see tears glistening in his dark brown eyes.

"Why?" he whispered. "Why won't he let me go?"

Bryony had no answer for that, but when Dan squatted down on his heels overlooking the cove, she knelt close beside him and offered the simple comfort of her presence. Her twin was still shaking with fury. Staring out over the darkening water, he reflected stoutly, "I hate it, Bry. I've always hated the sea, and the way the O'Neill worships it. You and I have never meant anything more to him than a burden."

"Not you, Dan. Just me," Bryony murmured, and suddenly his hand dropped down, caught hers, and gripped it tightly.

"I hate him, you know, for the way he's treated you all these years," Brendan said fiercely.

"You mustn't. He's still your father."

"Yours, too, and everyone knows it! Ah, Bryony. What a fine bit of God's jest we two are. You're everything I'll never be; O'Neill's prodigal son, if only you were a boy."

"Well," she said philosophically, with a touch of irony, "there's probably been some Magennis rumor to that effect, too."

Despite his anger, Brendan chuckled. "No chance of that, Bry. You're nineteen now, and you won't pass for a cabin boy anymore. Sure, and that's the truth of it," he added when she looked dubious. "Believe it or not, plenty of fellows have noticed you, and some would have acted on their interest by now, if you weren't so set on scaring them off."

Bryony scowled at that. "I don't have any desire to get married."

"Neither did I, until I met Glynnis." Brendan smiled at her. Loyally, he considered his sister quite lovely, if in an unconventional sort of way. Those sea blue eyes and raven black hair never failed to attract male attention. In fact, he had caught Finn O'Grady speculatively eyeing her more than once. It would delight him to no end if Bryony eventually married his old childhood friend, their second cousin, but he wouldn't force matters. Aloud, he said, "I only want the same happiness for you, Bry."

She sighed and snuggled against him, resting her head for a moment on his shoulder. She and Dan had never been this close, even though the bond between them had always been strong. Ironically, she also realized she was about to lose him forever.

"You're going north soon, aren't you?" she whispered sadly.

"Aye. Glynnis is waiting for me. I had planned to wait until the morrow, but considering the O'Neill's position, I may as well leave tonight. Come with me, Bry! There's surely a place for you on MacDougal's farm. Better yet, come live with Glynnis and me after we're wed!"

She shook her head. "Bless you, Dan, but I can't leave. Mab sorely needs my help, and you know the other women will stop working altogether, if I go. Besides, leaving the *Leprechaun* means leaving the sea. And sure as shillelagh, I would be miserable if I ever did such a thing."

Brendan smiled with resignation at the truth of that. The sea was as close to a lover as his sister would probably ever come. "The offer still stands if you change your mind, or ever need a safe haven. But before I go, there's something I must give you."

Brendan reached down into his leather jerkin and withdrew a familiar object. He drew the sinew cord over his head and passed the amulet to her without a word. Immediately, and emphatically, she shook her head.

"No, Dan. I can't!"

Instead of taking back the amulet, her brother reached out and firmly wrapped her fingers around it. "Hist, now. It's your heritage, as well as mine. I'll never have a use for it. Remember how Mab once let you hold it, when we were little? Faith, I'll never forget how your eyes sparkled! And when the O'Neill took it away and gave it to me instead, you were pea green with envy."

Bryony opened her fingers and gazed for a moment at the ancient disk cupped in her palm. Splendidly crafted of Irish red gold, it was about three inches around with a small hole drilled on top to fit a cord. Legend said the amulet had originally belonged to one of their ancestors, Airdi O'Neill, who had served under Brian Boru at Tara. It had been a gift from the High King of Ireland, who saw fit to reward loyal service. Boru was also rumored to have bestowed the original clan symbol upon the O'Neills.

Because he considered Airdi O'Neill particularly clever, the story went, Brian Boru had given their kinsman a pet raven. The live mascot had traveled at sea with its owner until the

O'Neill's death, at which time it was said the bird screamed three times and vanished into thin air. The sea raven had remained the O'Neill motif ever since. The amulet Bryony held had the image of a screaming raven in flight, deeply etched into the gleaming gold.

Running her fingers lovingly and longingly over the imbedded bird, she repeated softly, "No, Dan, I can't take it. The amulet belongs to the next O'Neill of Clandeboye."

"Who'll not be me," Brendan stated with finality. He took it from her only long enough to slip the amulet firmly over her head. The gold was still warm from her twin's skin, and nestled gently in the valley between her breasts. Bryony gasped softly when she felt a strange sensation ripple through her, reminiscent of the electricity in the air before a storm.

"What is it?" Brendan wondered aloud, also feeling a faint but definite jolt of hidden power.

Bryony tilted back her head and gazed at the clear, dark blue sky above them. She sniffed the tangy brine of the sea. " 'Tis odd, but I sense there's a storm brewing nearby. The likes of which we haven't seen in awhile."

Brendan didn't doubt his sister's prediction. Where weather was concerned, her talent was infallible. He swept out a long arm and hugged her close. Cheerfully, he said, "Then it's a good thing we're off the ship. Although there's never been a gale yet you couldn't ride out, Bry."

Bryony smiled, but she was troubled. Something was wrong. All her senses screamed there was an incoming storm, but the sky was clear, the sea smooth and shimmering like cut sapphire under the last rays of the dying sun. She wondered if she was unsettled because Brendan was leaving. After all, her brother had finally cut the ties binding him to the O'Neill and the legacy of the sea, and she felt as if she'd literally watched a boy turn into a man tonight.

"I'll miss you, Dan," she said, wondering why the words leaving her lips rang with such finality.

Her brother reached over and playfully tugged on her long

braid. "None of that now, Skinny Bones! Our parting must be swift and merry, for I'll accept nothing less. Sure, and by this time next year, I'll likely return to Clandeboye to find you happily married, with a passel of brats hanging on your skirts."

"Hah!" Bryony swatted him and leapt quickly to her feet. Whirling about, she dashed along the cliff's edge with Brendan in hot pursuit. Outwardly she laughed, but inwardly she cried, realizing that come tomorrow, she would be well and truly alone for the first time in her life.

Long before the first rosy blush of dawn stained the sky, Bryony was already up and tending the livestock in the yard. Wearing a comfortable ensemble of old clothing Brendan had left behind, she went about her familiar chores. After milking three cows and slopping the pigs, she methodically forked hay to the small herd of calves and goats. The O'Neill didn't have horses, as he claimed only the *Sassenach* had need of such fancy pieces to "trundle their fat arses about."

As Bryony absently tossed scratch to the chickens, the first pale fingers of dawn stretched up over the soft green hills. Brendan was long gone. He'd left late the night before, after gathering up a single satchel of his worldly goods. Although obviously reluctant to part from his sister, Dan couldn't keep the eager anticipation from shining in his eyes as he'd hugged her farewell. The young woman he loved was waiting for him, as well as the lifelong dream of working his own land. It was impossible to begrudge Dan his happiness, so Bryony shooed him off on his grand adventure with laughter, not tears.

The O'Neill had not appeared to wish his only son god-speed. Bryony was not surprised. Although it was not hard to imagine Brann's fury, temporarily bottled though it might be. Sooner or later, it would explode again, and she fully expected to be the recipient when it came.

Pitching the last handfuls of grain right and left, she set down the feed pail and crossed through the yard. Chickens clucked and scattered before her, as she trudged back up the hill where Dan had given her the amulet. She halted on the narrow rise, her hand seeking out the smooth disk at her throat. It was comforting to know that the amulet had seen generations of O'Neills safely through the worst storms life had to offer. All of her ancestors had been long-lived, and, except for Alanna, most had come to relatively peaceful ends. Of course, there had been a pirate here or there; what Irish clan didn't have them? But for the most part, her kin had been honest folk, and she was proud of the spirited people who had preceded her.

Bryony was musing upon her own empty future, when a distant glimmer in the water below caught her eye. The sea always mesmerized her, even in the worst of weather, but this morning she nearly choked, seeing a stout galley bearing down on the cove. In a flash, she recognized the white and green forked pennants flying gaily from its masthead and yardarm. She knew it was customary for all Tudor vessels to carry along their rails rows of shields; those on this ship were placed in groups of four, each bearing the royal arms of England, borne on gold-tipped lances.

Beautiful sight though it was, Bryony wasted no time in whirling about, and ran shouting all the way down the slope towards the hall. It was early yet for her kinsmen to be up and about, but Mab came outside, obviously fresh from the kitchens, as she hastily wiped her hands on an apron tied to her waist.

"What's wrong, colleen?"

"It's time to pay the piper," Bryony gasped, pointing back out to sea. "The Virgin Queen has sent her navy!"

Mab paled, realizing her dire warnings to the O'Neill had all been for naught. She began to wring her crabbed hands.

"How many ships, could ye tell?"

"I saw only one. But the others are probably close behind. Where the devil is the O'Neill?" Bryony demanded with exasperation. She peered past the old woman, expecting Brann to burst from the keep at any moment.

"Och, he's already up and left. Down in the cove with the *Leprechaun*, I think. Only he and a handful of the others could hold their drink last night. The rest of them are still passed out snorin' in the hall, lolled about like a pack of lazy curs." Mab effectively snorted her opinion of Brann's crew. "Precious little use they'll be to him now, eh?"

Thinking hard and fast, Bryony came to a decision in a matter of seconds. She knew their ancient galleon would stand little chance against the impressively armed English navy. Though by now the O'Neill had surely seen the enemy rapidly closing in, he would be hard-pressed to get the *Leprechaun* underway before a battle would ensue. And in the shallow cove where neither ship could maneuver well, the costs in terms of lives would be terrible.

"Where's *Alanna*?" Bryony asked the old woman.

Mab shook her iron-grey head emphatically. "Nay, lovey! 'Twill do no good, I tell ye! The O'Neill's made his own grave, and must lie it now."

"Where is she, Mab?" Bryony reached out and lightly grasped the old woman's arm. "We may have a chance yet, but only if I can get to the other ship." She knew the sleek caravel her brother had refused last night might be just enough to make the difference in the battle's outcome.

"Curse ye both!" Mab cried. "Proud and ornery, the pair of ye. Yer both cut of the same stubborn cloth, and I can't bear to lose either of ye." She wiped at her misty eyes with the edge of the apron, then took a deep breath, and reluctantly murmured, "I didn't want to frighten ye, lovey, but I've sensed trouble comin' fer some time now. And I feel if ye leave us now, our paths will nay cross again in this time."

Bryony paused to consider Mab's words. Everyone at Raven Hall took her predictions seriously. "But I've no choice," she said at last, searching the old woman's faded blue eyes. "You know that as well, don't you?"

Mab nodded wearily. "I doubt 'twill do ye any good, but . . . she's moored at Airgialla, just a wee jaunt down the coast."

Bryony nodded, giving Mab a quick kiss of thanks. "Find Finn for me!" she ordered, already reverting back to the crisp tones she used on her crew at sea. She dashed past the old woman to the main hall, where she threw open the double doors and lustily shouted a wake-up call.

Startled to life, the various bodies sprawled about the Great Hall on the floor and benches began to stir. The stench of liquor was enough to rouse Bryony's disgust. Without undue compunction, she kicked the nearest behind.

"Get up, the bloody lot of you! There's a fine Tudor lady bearing down on our cove, and I would guess she's not here to pay her respects." Stomping past the groaning men, she entered her own chamber and took only a moment to stuff her long braid up out of the way under a knitted cap. Then she grabbed her new black frysdown cape and tossed it about her shoulders, tying it firmly in place with a double knot.

When Bryony strode back into the hall, she found most of the men shuffling about and sheepishly awaiting further orders. Finn O'Grady also stood there with a bewildered expression on his face. He alone of the crew was not moaning, groaning, or clutching his pounding head. But then her cousin had always been reliable. Short, stocky, and serious, Finn was a confirmed teetotaler, and considered by all to be a lifelong bachelor at the greatly advanced age of thirty. Bryony also knew he happened to be the only fellow in the vicinity with his own horse.

Briskly she informed him, "We're under attack by the English."

Finn merely nodded; he, too, had seen the mighty vessel bearing down on them. Though the ship would not arrive for some time yet, there was little question as to what would happen when she did.

Bryony turned and briskly instructed the other men to report at once to the *Leprechaun*. Then, taking Finn aside, she said in a low voice, "O'Grady, you're one of the few here I can trust. I'm going to ask you to obey me as you would my brother, if he was here. Will you agree to that?"

Finn hesitated. Not that he wasn't loyal to the core where Bryony was concerned; after all, she was his own second cousin on his mother's side. But the fierce brightness in her blue eyes worried him. What on earth was she planning? Even the O'Neill weighed anchor to meet the *Sassenach* in battle; his equally willful daughter obviously intended to tackle an even more formidable feat.

Bryony sensed his hesitation, and reached out to touch his arm entreatingly. "Please, Finn. It's not for myself, or even the O'Neill that I ask this, but for Brendan. He stands to lose his heritage today, and though he claims he doesn't want Raven Hall now, maybe someday he shall, or wish to pass it on to his sons. Besides, I'll not allow our land to fall into *Sassenach* hands. But I can't do it alone. I need you and as many other men as you can find in an hour."

"The O'Neill's claimed most of the sober ones already," Finn said, not without a twinkle in his eye. "He sent me back to shore to rouse the rest." He saw her frown, and hastily added, "But there are surely some others I could round up, if I head out now. Where are we to go?"

Bryony leaned forward and pecked the first mate's cheek with pure gratitude, not seeming to notice how he blushed. "Bless you, Finn! You and the others meet me down at Airgialla bay. Mayhap together, we can yet save the O'Neill from his folly."

Three

Slade swore under his breath when he saw the Irishman's galleon coming slowly but surely about in the cove. He knew O'Neill had seen them long before now; there was no way to hide a ship bearing full down until the last moment, but by all his calculations the *Silver Hart* should have been swift enough to cut off the other at the narrow inlet to the cove. As it looked now, O'Neill's slower vessel still might be able to slip past them out to sea. And the worst news was yet to come, he thought, just before Diego's shout from the crow's nest confirmed his suspicions.

"Capitan! They are manning the cannon!"

"Keep us out of range!" Slade ordered, his powerful voice carrying to the far ends of his own ship. He heartily regretted his last-minute decision to leave his extra hands behind in London; he could sorely use them now, for as it stood, he had barely enough men to see to the sails, much less the cannon.

If it came down to an act of desperation, Slade would send all hands below to man the cannon, but he still hoped it would not erupt into an all-out battle. Not only would it be foolhardy for two merchant-traders to engage in war like a pair of undisciplined pirates, but in this case, it also would solve nothing.

Part of Slade cursed Brann O'Neill for forcing a confrontation, while the other half grudgingly respected a man who refused to surrender so easily. As Slade understood it, most of the native Irish detested their English overlords, and if Governor Sydney's attitude was any example, they could hardly be blamed. But it still didn't excuse O'Neill from behaving like a gentleman, and it was becoming readily apparent that Slade's adversary had no intentions of doing so.

Diego soon slid down one of the ratlines and landed beside his captain. "I still think we can cut her off," the Spaniard said a little breathlessly.

"Aye," Slade agreed, judging the distance remaining between the *Leprechaun* and the open sea, "if it comes to that. But I think we should give the fellow one more chance to change his mind."

Boom-boom! Diego's reply was drowned out by a sudden puff of smoke and the resounding roar of cannon. The Irishman's galleon was turning to full bear on them, and though she was still out of range, her whistling cannon shot rained with definite menace before the *Silver Hart*'s bow.

"Damme!" Slade cursed, leaping up a few stairs to the forecastle for a better view. "He's forcing my hand!"

Diego trailed his captain up the steps. "You bear the queen's charter," he reminded Slade. "By firing on us, O'Neill has just committed treason."

Slade nodded grimly as he began to pace the deck and think. There was not much time in which to choose a course. While by all rights he could sink O'Neill's ship—and probably even earn a commendation for doing so—his conscience balked at the idea. He would not choose the path of wanton death and destruction, unless there was no other course left. But neither would he forfeit his mens' lives, merely for the sake of foolish Irish pride.

Setting his square jaw, Slade said over his shoulder, "Fire a single warning shot across her bow, when she's in range."

Diego nodded and scurried off to collect the hands necessary for priming and firing the cannon below. Slade heard the running feet on deck and the enthusiastic shouts of his crew. He knew they were fiercely loyal to him, but then he'd made a conscious effort to treat them fairly in a trade renowned for cruel captains. His slightest wish was their command. Especially when it came to a battle for a righteous cause, and this was one they obviously believed in.

The *Leprechaun* still bore down on them, showing no signs of hesitation as she sailed boldly to meet them in battle. Slade shook his head in exasperation at O'Neill's pride, before he finally signalled Diego to make the warning shot. He knew his expert gunners would give the other vessel a wide berth, for he'd already told them he wanted no bloodshed this day.

Silver Hart's cannon boomed, and a single ball arched a perfect path over the Irish galleon's curved bow. Slade expected to see the other ship veer off course, or at least slow in her determined plunge towards certain disaster. But there was no sign of O'Neill's surrender, and with resigned fury, Slade turned to his crew.

"All hands below to man the cannon!"

Lusty shouts of aye, aye! greeted his order, and soon Slade was left standing sentinel on the forecastle. His eyes narrowed as the tiny figures scurrying about on the *Leprechaun* came into view. He could make out a tall, dark-haired man pacing the deck of the other ship even as he did his own.

No doubt it was Brann O'Neill. But what kind of madman would sail a merchantman into battle over a mere scrap of rocky land? Slade shook his head in amazement, then tensed when he heard Diego's muffled shout from belowdecks.

"Ready for your order, *Capitan!*"

"Hold!" Slade hollered back. Against his better judgment, he would give O'Neill one last chance. He waved his right arm in a visible signal to the *Leprechaun*'s captain, clearly indicating he wished to break off the attack. But to Slade's outrage, O'Neill's craggy face broke into a bray of mocking laughter. He saw the Irishman's lips form a single word: *Coward!*

After his anger subsided, Slade decided O'Neill was only trying to bluff him with this outright display of madness. He didn't doubt the Irishman was perfectly sane, simply determined to make Slade appear the fool. He half-turned to the open hatch to shout his orders to fire, then caught sight of a second ship bearing down hard on *Silver Hart's* port side.

The third vessel was a solid black caravel of sleek Portuguese design, four-masted with a square mainsail and topsail. Her lateen sails had captured the wind, and she was closing fast. Slade had just enough time to make out the name carved on the bow, *Alanna Colleen,* and the fact she flew a standard which matched O'Neill's—a flying black raven on a blood red ground—before she swept grandly past.

Before Slade could even think to swear, the caravel had tacked hard right and slid through the narrow channel of water separating the two other ships. At her closest measure, barely a plank's length remained between her bowsprit and that of *Silver Hart's*. Slade might have leaned over the rail and touched her high bulwark, had he the inclination to do so.

"What the devil . . . ?" He glanced over at the captain of the *Leprechaun,* surprised to see O'Neill looking equally astounded and outraged. The Irishman had barely enough time to correct his own course, and ploughed sharply starboard of Slade's ship as the caravel sailed blithely between them, leaving the two merchantmen to helplessly ride out her wake.

Slade burned with newly kindled rage, when he considered the recklessness which had nearly rendered them all afloat. Sweet Jesu, who the devil would even risk such a thing?

Diego had returned above deck to see what was happening. He, too, had seen the black hull of the caravel glide past *Silver Hart's* open gun ports, as if daring them to fire. He found his captain cursing and fumbling about in his coat to find the spyglass, and promptly pulled it from his own pocket.

Slade remembered Governor Sydney telling him that Brann O'Neill had a son, just come of age. It could be none other than the Irishman's brat who had nearly rammed a caravel down his own father's throat.

"Another crack-brained O'Neill!" he roared. "That's all I need now!"

He steadied the spyglass to his eye and focused the lens. But all he could make out were a few small figures climbing about the caravel's after castle, hastily adjusting her sail. The *Alanna Colleen* was headed out to sea. Slade quickly realized that Brann O'Neill would have to bring his own galleon full circle in the cove, skirting dangerously close to the rocky coastline, before he could come about to do the same. *Silver Hart*, by contrast, was already primed for pursuit.

Slade decided to take the bait. He ordered Diego to return all hands to their stations, with the obvious intentions of capturing the caravel instead. The first mate glanced at him as if tempted to inquire about his captain's mental stability, and for the first time that day, Slade grinned.

"If we can catch O'Neill's pup, Diego, then we'll have a valuable bargaining chip with him."

The Spaniard's dark eyes twinkled with mirth and approval. Diego put two leathery fingers to his lips and whistled sharply. Within seconds, the crew was swarming above decks again, hoisting all sails to the breeze, while Slade drew the whipstaff about.

By design, the caravel was lighter and swifter than his merchantman, but Slade also suspected that she was grossly undermanned. He hadn't seen more than a handful of bodies on the vessel, and unless O'Neill's brat had an army hidden somewhere below in her narrow hull, she'd be no match for a more experienced captain and crew.

"Ready the grappling hooks," he told Diego. "The minute we're in range, you're to board and disarm her."

The little Spaniard grinned in anticipation. "Sort of like piracy, eh, *Capitan?"*

"Sort of. Except I have no intentions of cutting our young captain's throat. No, Diego, just shaking O'Neill's daft lad until his teeth fall out will provide me with quite enough satisfaction for one day!"

* * *

From where she leaned into the brisk wind, Bryony patted the *Alanna Colleen*'s sleek hull. "She cuts a mighty clean wake, doesn't she, O'Grady?"

"Aye, that she does. She's a pretty enough colleen on the high seas to attract a score of admirers, too!"

Bryony caught the meaning of Finn's words as she glanced astern. She noted with consternation that the Tudor ship had turned from its inland course, and now was headed back out to sea. Also coming around was the *Leprechaun,* foundering a bit in the shallower waters of the cove, but equally determined to pay her respects. Bryony wet her salty lips a little nervously.

"Can they catch us, O'Grady?"

"Not the *Leprechaun*. But the English ship's another matter. She's a merchant, too, but see how high she rides in the water? Her hold must be empty. Without all the bulk, she's fast enough."

Bryony motioned him back to his post. "Keep an eye on both of them. We're not changing course now. I'll sail her all the way to Scotland, if need be."

Finn knew she meant it, and wisely made no comment. But privately he thought that Bryony was either incredibly brave, or foolishly naive. In less than an hour she'd managed to infuriate both a queen's captain and Brann O'Neill, who was not notorious for having a good temper even in the best of times.

Finn hadn't believed it himself when Bryony first declared her intention to sail the *Alanna Colleen* right between the two merchantmen. He assumed the idea was only borne from desperation when they'd stood helplessly by, watching the O'Neill egging the Englishman on.

But the hastily christened first mate of the *Alanna Colleen* vowed never to doubt Bryony's word again, for not only had she guided them through that narrow wedge of water with barely a handspan to spare, but she'd informed her cousin that she had absolutely no intention of surrendering, not to Brann or the English captain.

Before he climbed up to the crow's nest to resume his lookout, Finn ventured cautiously, "Remember, Bryony, we've no ammunition below."

She nodded. "But *he* doesn't know that." She indicated the three-masted *Silver Hart*, still in hot pursuit. Her initial disappointment had been wrenching, finding the caravel's hold devoid of any cannon fodder. But their gun ports were all in place, and she was counting on the Englishman's wariness to keep him at a safe distance.

To Bryony's further dismay, the *Alanna Colleen*'s hold was also empty. Not even the most basic provision—fresh water—was in ready supply. She could only assume the O'Neill had intended to keep the ship safely stowed away until Brendan changed his mind about going to sea. Obviously, the stubborn old goat had never given up his dream that his son would someday take over his trade and follow in his footsteps. But Brendan had called the old man's bluff. And now so had she.

One look at the stunned expression on the O'Neill's face as the *Alanna Colleen* sailed by had made Bryony want to laugh with triumph. She could almost read his mind in that moment: *"Curse that Changeling!"* And then, close on the heels of that thought, perhaps one of wry admiration: *"By all the bloody saints, why couldn't* she *be the boy?"*

Bryony knew the word reckless wasn't sufficient to describe her actions back in the cove. They had been outrageous! Yet, she had loved every moment of that fleeting glory. Aye, she'd been born to the sea, and it owned her fully, heart and soul. She touched the amulet at her throat, wondering if perhaps the sea raven wasn't responsible for her newfound courage and convictions. She felt as if she no longer sailed alone. For somehow, in the last hours, the *Alanna Colleen* had become her own ship.

If not for her faithful Finn, though, Bryony suspected her crew would have mutinied. The only "sailors" her cousin had been able to round up on such short notice were green lads, most of them never having been to sea. Half of the youngsters had cowered with terror when Bryony sent their ship flying into the fray, and the others deserted their posts to huddle under the mizzenmast like a pile of whimpering puppies.

Well, Bryony decided, she could make do with them 'til Scotland, then send them home and hire on fresh crew. Her own life savings, earned from her cut of the profits since she'd first gone to sea with the O'Neill, were securely hidden in the small cabin below. All that remained now was to escape Tudor justice.

But she soon saw it wasn't going to be easy. The farther they went out to sea, the more doggedly the Englishman pursued them. Instead of giving up, the other captain seemed all the more determined to trap his prey. Cat-and-mouse, they threaded the churning green waves of the channel, until even the *Leprechaun* finally gave up the chase and returned home, leaving the other two to press on.

And of all her miserable little crew, Bryony discovered that only she and O'Grady had any navigational experience.

On top of that, they had no compass. So, until darkness fell, they could not even hope to find Scotland, and even that would ultimately depend upon a clear starry night.

"How much longer?"

Slade hadn't meant to snap at Diego, but the game was beginning to wear thin. He'd never expected O'Neill's spawn to be a first-rate sailor, and the hours they had wasted in pursuit of the impudent lad were nearly enough to see them home again.

"Not long now," Diego replied, trying to pacify his irritated captain. "The wind's beginning to die. Before long they'll be becalmed, and then we'll have them."

"You said that an hour ago," Slade curtly reminded his first mate, then pivoted on his boot heel and crossed the main deck. It was getting late in the afternoon, and the sun was an orange burst of fire, rapidly sinking on the western horizon. Soon it would shrink out of sight altogether, and then they would be at the mercy of the dark. No doubt the caravel would slip easily enough away then, perhaps hiding somewhere among the many tiny islands dotting Scotland's shores.

Silver Hart's sails billowed one last time, then fell limply against the masts. Slade glanced up hopefully, just as a ragged cheer arose from his weary crew. The wind was gone. But did they have enough daylight left?

He sent all hands below decks to draw out the mighty oars, reserved for moments of emergency such as this. Only Diego stayed above to ferry Slade's orders to the men, and with slow sure strokes, they began to advance upon the other ship limping towards the eastern horizon.

Aboard the *Alanna Colleen*, Bryony was in her first genuine panic since she had sighted the Tudor vessel that morn. She had her makeshift crew turn the sails this way and that, but it soon proved an exercise in futility. The wind was gone, they were becalmed, and the enemy was fast closing in.

At the last moment, Finn O'Grady came to her side, devoted as always. "You go below, when they come in range," he advised her. "I'll hold them off as long as I can." He nervously fingered the cutlass at his side.

"Don't be a fool. You're no match for all those men, and this is my fault anyway. Nay, Cousin, I want you to look after the lads instead. Poor little mites, this has been a long and frightening day for them."

"What will happen to us?" Finn wondered aloud. He was himself frightened to the core at the thought of crossing Elizabeth Tudor. He'd heard of men being keelhauled for simply failing to speak of her with respect.

"I don't know," Bryony had to admit. "But it's my responsibility, and I'll stand fast to accept it. Go back to your station and stay there. We'll not turn tail and hide from a cursed *Sassenach.*"

They both turned to look one last time at the ship ominously bearing down on them, before Finn reluctantly moved off to his post.

Left alone, Bryony took a moment to regather her courage. She realized she'd been foolhardy, but she hadn't expected the Englishman to pursue her so relentlessly. All she'd sought was the chance to defend their cove and the clan's holdings.

Mayhaps the O'Neill had never acknowledged her, but Raven Hall was still part of her heritage. She felt obliged to defend it from the enemy, real or imagined. But now the enemy was real, definitely *here,* and she knew she'd best plan how to greet him right quick.

Slade followed the pacing figure on the *Alanna Colleen*'s deck with his spyglass. The lad was young, all right, but he'd proven more than the fact that he was a reckless fool. He was a damned good sailor, Slade had to admit. He wondered if he himself had ever shown such mettle at that age.

Surely O'Neill's brat knew he was facing treason, at the very least. That charge alone could call for the block, though the queen might temper her justice by considering the impetuous nature of youth. At any rate, the lad was certainly an O'Neill. He had not one single drop of common sense!

"Board her," Slade ordered his men, almost wearily. Everything seemed anticlimactic after the high seas chase and capture. The *Silver Hart* brushed up with a groan of wood against the caravel's stern, and then Diego and the others tossed out the grappling hooks.

The *Alanna Colleen* was unceremoniously hauled over to the merchantman's main deck like a snagged whale. Slade's crew laid down the boarding planks and crossed over to the smaller ship, while he himself remained behind.

Some moments later, Slade heard a surprised outcry from his first mate. Expecting trouble, he reached for the thin rapier strapped to his waist. Then Diego reappeared, dragging by the shirt collars what appeared to be very small sailors indeed.

"Niños!" the Spaniard cried, in amazement or amusement, possibly both. Diego threw back his shaggy dark head and roared with laughter. The two boys, not older than eight or ten, squirmed helplessly in his firm grasp.

"*Capitan*, the ship is manned by children!" Diego gasped out between great guffaws of laughter, but Slade was not nearly so amused. He stared at his first mate in disbelief.

"What about her captain?"

Diego shrugged. "There is only one even old enough to grow a beard on this ship."

"Bring him to me!"

Slade's snarl caught everyone off guard, but Diego obediently dropped the two snuffling lads and went in search of the culprit. Moments later, Finn O'Grady was forcibly prodded across the planks to face the stony stare of Captain Tanner.

"So," Slade rapped out, taking narrow measure of the man standing before him, "you're the cause of all this trouble today."

Finn opened his mouth to speak, but another voice cut in. Bryony fought free from the restraint of one of Slade's crew, and dashed across the planks to the *Silver Hart* before anyone could think to stop her.

"Nay! You're looking for me."

"Bryon—" Finn began in alarm, giving her a fierce glare which told her to stay quiet.

It didn't work. Bryony stormed over to stand before the English captain, a little daunted by his height, but nonetheless defiant. Planting her hands on her hips, she looked up at him and squarely stated, "I'm the one you're looking for. I'm captain of the *Alanna Colleen*."

Bright green eyes burned her to the spot where she stood. The queen's captain was much younger than she'd expected, tall and lean and broad-shouldered, a veritable giant among men. Bryony was accustomed to looking down on her crew, being unusually tall for an Irishwoman, but this man's great size gave her considerable pause for thought.

"Bryon, is it?" Slade snapped to disguise his own confusion. There was something very odd about the lad, though he couldn't say what it was. A few loose strands of jet black hair dangled from beneath the rim of his knitted cap, framing an oval face bronzed golden by the sun. By comparison, the light blue color of the boy's eyes was almost startling.

"Do you claim to captain this vessel in your father's name?" he growled at O'Neill's pup.

"Nay, not his, but my own! I'm an O'Neill in my own right."

"Amen to that," Slade muttered, remembering the rash display of courage he'd witnessed earlier.

Bryony stared up at the *Sassenach,* feeling the deep tones of his voice reverberating through her. Her heart pounded in mixed anticipation and dread, as somehow she found herself locked in an inadvertent struggle of wills with this man. Their gazes had locked, each one trying to glare the other down. It was therefore impossible to ignore his appearance.

He wore no beard, though a faint golden stubble on his jaw showed he was slightly overdue for another shave. His hair was reddish gold, mirroring the hues of the sunset behind them. The eyes which coldly scrutinized her were a moody emerald green.

"Captain O'Neill," he began, giving the title a faintly mocking emphasis, "I am Capt. Slade Tanner, in Her Royal Majesty's Service." He did not bow, but simply continued to pierce her with that hawklike stare.

Bryony had no way of reading Slade's mind, but she did read the growing wariness in his eyes. And she was right.

O'Neill's brat has a damn effeminate voice, Slade suspiciously mused. It occurred to him that the boy's bone structure seemed much too fine for a male's. And the loose cape the lad was wearing obscured any detail of the figure beneath, so Slade decided to seek some answers on his own.

Reaching out, he abruptly whipped the knitted cap from the

other's head. A long black braid tumbled down, before the girl could hide it from him.

"What charade is this?" he demanded, and when the little chit wouldn't answer him, he seized the front of her cape with both hands and wrenched it apart. "Aye, I thought as much! You've a mighty admirable chest for a captain, wench!"

Bryony flushed, much to her mortification. And Slade's crew sniggered until he threw them all a quelling look.

"Now," he began sternly, releasing Bryony and turning slightly to include Finn O'Grady in his glare, "just what the devil is going on here?"

Bryony swallowed hard and began again. "I didn't lie. I'm the captain."

"Nay, I am!" Finn countered desperately, and in turn each received a hard stare from Slade Tanner.

"That's enough from both of you. You know, I could find out the truth of this matter very quickly, by stringing up your motley crew over there . . . all ten of them, from the yardarm."

Bryony gasped. "You wouldn't dare. They're only children!"

"That's Captain Tanner to you, Mistress Bryon, and you should have thought of that possibility long before you signed them on as able crew!"

"It's Bryony . . . Bryony O'Neill," she corrected Slade furiously, "and you've no right to treat any of us badly. We've done you no harm."

"No harm?" Slade stared at her incredulously a second before a short burst of laughter came from his lips. "You nearly sunk three ships today, girl, and all hands with them! Whoever taught you to sail should be soundly flogged."

"You'd best get out the cat, then," she shot back, "for I taught myself."

Slade gazed at her in obvious disbelief, until Finn put in, " 'Tis true enough. The O'Neill would have none of it."

"Then the man has at least that much common sense," Slade said, trying to tear his gaze away from the burning blue one of his female adversary.

God's bones, he thought, *but there's something about this young woman . . .* He'd seen his share of beauties at Court, yet there was some greater substance to this proud Irish wench which captured and held his attention. With belated shock, Slade realized he was feeling the first faint stirrings of desire.

Suddenly he couldn't imagine how he'd ever mistaken Bryony O'Neill for a boy. Her skin might be tanned, but her face was softly rounded, as only a woman's could be. Those beautiful sea blue eyes sparkled and snapped with keen intelligence. Feathery, expressive dark brows highlighted each fleeting emotion upon her face—anger, insolence, pride; each was a part of Bryony O'Neill's complex mantle, and one she wore with definite flair.

But a second later, Slade denied his own fanciful thoughts. Tired, that's all he was. Tired and disgruntled after a long, relatively worthless day. Seeing a slim but definitely curved female figure in tight breeches was enough to distract any man from his duties.

"Diego," Slade said, pausing to clear a sudden thickness from his voice, "please escort our Irish friends below. Secure them in the cargo hold for now, and make sure they're adequately guarded."

"What do you mean to do with us?" Bryony demanded.

Slade Tanner paused to regard her with a smoldering green gaze. "You should have worried about that, m'dear, long before you committed treason against Elizabeth Tudor."

Four

Night fell suddenly, like a black velvet cape dropped upon the Irish Sea. Stars bristled high above the dark waters, but no hint of breeze disturbed the sails. Even the Irish Sea, which so often displayed a Gaelic temperament, slapped peacefully against the hulls of the two vessels still linked together.

In the *Silver Hart*'s cabin, Slade picked at the remnants of his late supper. The salt pork and hardtack were no longer appetizing. Instead, he found himself musing upon the matter of a fiery blue-eyed wench, one safely sequestered in his hold below, but doubtless not one whit penitent over her actions.

Slade frowned when he recalled Diego's report on the condition of the *Alanna Colleen.* Not only was the caravel bare of ammunition, but she was shockingly devoid of even the most basic supplies. The lack of food could conceivably be explained away, even excused, but no water . . . if not for his timely intervention, Bryony and her young crew would have perished at sea simply due to thirst. And all because of one overproud, impudent chit!

With a snort of displeasure, Slade rose from the table, flinging his linen napkin aside. He left the cabin and went to the main deck, where he found Diego calmly awaiting further orders.

"All quiet?" Slade asked his first mate.

The Spaniard nodded. "Food and water were given to our guests about an hour ago."

"A good thing we brought extra rations. I never expected

I'd be forced to play nursemaid to a shipload of somebody else's brats."

Diego chuckled, then said admiringly, "That Irish *chica,* she has *muy fuego*—much fire—in her eyes! She'll be a lucky catch for the right man."

"Then best count your blessings you're already married, old friend. I'll wager you she'd put a man through hell."

Diego glanced shrewdly at his captain. "My Maria Elena was much the same. *Si,* she fought me tooth and nail at first, but the final victory was all the sweeter for the many battles."

Slade chuckled at that. Diego Santiago and his wife had been happily married for many years, and had nine children to prove it. It seemed each time they returned to port, Maria had another fat, black-eyed baby bouncing on her hip. Diego obviously didn't shirk his shore leave duties.

With a slightly envious grin, Slade left Diego and moved on. He dismissed the posted guard and then moved to lift the iron grate which secured the hold below.

Darkness enveloped the narrow stairs, for fire was the nightmare of the sea, and Slade forbade his men to smoke while on duty. Except for the stern lantern, lights were usually not permitted, but he had taken into consideration the youngsters' fear, and so allowed them a single lantern.

The sound of his approaching footsteps caused a shuffling of bodies below, and Slade heard a hushed murmur of anxious voices echoing off the ship's hull. He descended to the hold, and there took the lantern off its secure hook and flashed the light over his huddled prisoners.

Bryony sat back against the hull with her knees drawn up under her chin. He noted with some consternation that she'd given her warm cape to the children, arranging it over as many of the small bodies as she could. The rest were squeezed between her and Finn O'Grady, and she had a protective arm draped around a little lad on each side. With her braid tumbled down and her great blue eyes, she looked much like a orphaned waif herself.

But Slade didn't underestimate Bryony's backbone. He noted the untouched plates of food neatly arranged in a line upon the floor, and felt the silent daggers in her gaze. When she spoke, her musical lilt was deceptively soft.

"So, Captain Tanner, I trust the wee ones are behaving themselves to your satisfaction?"

"All but one," he shot back. "One who certainly knows better, and one whom I feel obliged to punish. Merely as an example to the others, of course."

Her eyebrows arched defiantly, and Finn quickly interposed, "Bryony's not the one who ordered the fast, Captain Tanner. 'Tis an old O'Neill tradition, whenever one of the crew is taken by the enemy."

"But you're an O'Grady, aren't you?"

There was a definite twinkle in Finn's eyes at Slade's impatient question. "Only by marriage, sir. My dear mother, God assoil her soul, was an O'Neill born and bred."

Slade waved the lantern slightly, indicating the children. "And all these brats? Who do they belong to?"

"Oh, whoever'll have them, I suppose. Most of 'em are O'Neills as well, though there's a MacQuillan here or there, and even a Maguire or two—"

"Enough." Slade spoke abruptly, shaking his head. "I see there's little to be gained by keeping you prisoners down here. If I let you all come up on deck, will you promise to behave yourselves and even eat a sustaining bite or two? I'll not have any undue deaths on my conscience."

"Faith, Captain, I didn't know you had one," Bryony remarked as she rose to her feet, and in a catlike fashion stretched the kinks out of her back and legs. Slade's eyes flashed at the challenge, and she bit back a satisfied smile. She knew she irritated him more than the others did, and assumed it was because she was female. Men didn't like to see women in positions of power, Mab had once told her. It was the same reason Elizabeth Tudor was both duly admired and secretly despised by her own people, Bryony supposed.

Instead of reacting to her comment, Slade merely gestured to the open hold. "Why don't you all come above deck and get a breath of fresh air."

He didn't have to suggest it twice, for though the ship's hold was empty and cleaner than most, it was stuffy and still reeked of fruit and spices from the last voyage.

"Come along." Slade beckoned them with his lantern, and following Finn O'Grady's lead, the children fell into line. There was no way they could escape him, Bryony realized, even though Slade looked weary. There was no place for them to go. Without further ado, she followed the others out of the hold.

As they ascended the steep stairs single file, with Bryony ahead of him, Slade couldn't help but notice the unconscious swing of her hips in the tight breeches she wore. He would have to do something about that, he thought, and the sooner the better!

The entire party trooped out on deck, and Slade watched from a distance as Bryony moved swiftly to the rail, breathing deeply and almost reverently of the salt tang. The crisp sea air visibly revived her flagging spirits. He studied her closely, marvelling that a young woman could be so obviously devoted to the sea. She gazed out over the dark deep waters, with no sign of fear or uncertainty on her face. Slade was struck with the thought that it was like the calm and loving gaze of one old friend upon another.

He understood her obvious fascination with the ocean. Many were drawn to it. But Slade sensed there was something virtually binding Bryony O'Neill to the sea. For him, it was simply an occupation. For her, he sensed, it was more of an obsession. When she turned slightly to face him, the emotion in her deep blue eyes told him it was true.

"Do you have any news for me?" she inquired.

"Aye," Slade replied, coming a few paces closer, where he

casually hooked a boot heel over the lower rail. "First, there's the dispensation of your ship. Of course, you realize she's now forfeit to Queen Elizabeth."

Bryony stiffened in outrage, but said calmly enough, "No, that can't be. In the first place, she's not my ship to surrender."

"Do you expect me to believe that?"

"Aye, I do."

Frustrated, Slade said pointedly, "But you claim to be her captain."

"And so I was, for a day. But the *Alanna Colleen* is not mine to give."

"Then how about to take? You certainly seemed to accomplish that task with ease!"

Under the pearly white moon, he clearly saw the angry flush rising on her cheeks. But Bryony stubbornly replied, "Much as I might wish it otherwise, Captain Tanner, that ship is not mine. She belongs to the O'Neill."

"Your father?"

"Brann O'Neill," Bryony added curtly, without further elaboration. As if suddenly agitated, she spun away from the rail and folded her arms across her chest. Slade thought he saw her shiver.

"You're cold," he said, giving her no opportunity to argue. " 'Tis probably wisest that we discuss this further in the warmth and privacy of my cabin. That is, if you can accept the word of a gentleman not to take advantage of the situation."

"Were there a gentleman present, I certainly should," Bryony retorted a little caustically, "but in any case, I'll take it your word's as good as the Virgin Queen's."

Before Slade's eyebrows could drop again, she pushed off from the rail and stalked across the desk, headed straight for the captain's quarters. She would let Slade Tanner and his nasty-minded crew make of that what they would!

* * *

Bryony had no opportunity to regret what she'd said. Slade quickly joined her, shutting the cabin door behind them. She had enough time in those few seconds to note the room was much like the man who occupied it.

Spacious and clean, Slade's quarters were nonetheless spartan by the standards of the day. Aside from a mahogany map desk secured in one corner and a window seat of gilded rose leather, there were no luxuries to be seen. There was a makeshift wooden table, small and square, with two chairs. At the far end of the room was a purely functional, double-sized bed; the linens were white, the wool blankets brown.

When Slade suddenly chuckled, Bryony tore her gaze from the bed back to the man, and found to her chagrin that he was looking at her with one golden eyebrow cocked.

"You seem to have quite a fascination with my quarters, Mistress O'Neill," he observed with a hint of mischief.

"I've never seen the insides of a merchantman before," she hastily replied.

"Then feel free to explore her. I only ask you don't wander about unescorted."

"Why? Don't you trust me?" As she flung out the challenge, Bryony couldn't help but notice the single lantern in the cabin was turned down low, far too low for her liking. The warm golden glow it cast on Tanner's hawkish features made her suddenly feel like a fluttering little bird, securely trapped in a pair of sharp talons. At the moment, she felt far more a juicy pigeon than a fierce sea raven.

It's the air, Bryony decided. It was too close, too intimate. She was suddenly warm, and cast a longing glance back at the door, which was hooked securely shut. Every nerve in her body seemed to vibrate as it never had before. Then again, perhaps the one she really didn't trust was herself.

Slade shrugged and finally answered her challenge. "Trust you? Don't forget, m'dear, we're supposed to be age-old adversaries." He gestured to the table, then pulled out a chair for her.

Surprised by the gentlemanly act, Bryony hesitated.

"You have my word not to harm you," Slade said. "But we've an urgent need to discuss various matters."

Bryony obediently sank down into the hard wooden chair. She was tired, hungry, and admittedly frustrated. When she leaned forward to rest her elbows on the table, she felt as if a leaden weight had been temporarily lifted from her shoulders. Every inch of her ached with pain and weariness.

"What will happen to us?" she quietly asked Slade. "To me and my crew?"

He didn't bother to reply until he had settled back in the chair across from her, and slung a long leg off to one side. Linking his arms comfortably across his flat middle, he said, "I'll be blunt with you, Bryony O'Neill, which I'm sure you'll appreciate. You did a very foolish thing today. Were it not for Lady Luck, you would be in deep waters indeed."

"I know sailing between the two ships was reckless," she muttered.

"Not just that. Were you aware the *Alanna Colleen* has no provisions, not even water, on board?"

She didn't answer him, and Slade pressed her. "Well, Mistress O'Neill? Had I not managed to waylay you, thanks to the wind stopping, you might have handily perished with all hands aboard. And most of them young children. Did you never stop to think of their kin?"

Her eyes widened. Sweet Jesu, she really hadn't considered such a dire fate. But now she could imagine poor Tommy Maguire's widowed mother, weeping and wailing over her only son's death, or Uncle O'Grady drinking himself into a stupor to quell the pain of losing Finn. Briefly, she closed her eyes, and when she opened them again, Slade was watching her, rather soberly and expectantly.

"I thought we'd make it to Scotland," she whispered.

"Aye, I suppose you might have. Had you stopped sailing in circles."

"What!"

"There's no mistake about it. My first mate, Diego, made careful record of the *Alanna Colleen*'s movements with a compass."

"We were not so fortunate to have one ourselves," she stiffly retorted.

"That doesn't strike me as a particularly good excuse, m'dear, especially if you were raised at sea, as you claim."

Bryony's chin shot up, and her blue eyes shot sparks at him across the table. "I'm not a child!" she exclaimed, slapping the table with her open palm. "Will you stop treating me like one?"

"Then grow up," Slade retorted sternly. He heard her chair scrape loudly against the floor as she leapt up and began to pace the narrow confines of his cabin. He had a sudden suspicion.

"How old are you, Bryony O'Neill?" he demanded.

"Old enough to captain a ship!"

"Just barely, I'll wager. And how is it you came to be allowed to sail with your father?"

He saw her fists suddenly clench at her sides. "I never said the O'Neill was my father."

"Uncle, then? Damme, wench, I've had enough of your games," Slade said with exasperation as he came to his feet. "What I want to know is how you came to be sailing at all. Why weren't you raised at home and taught proper domestic arts, as befits a female?" His gaze dropped pointedly to her breasts. "You're obviously no child. How it is that you've managed to escape marriage for so long?"

"I . . . I just have, that's all. Most men wouldn't have me."

"And why not?"

Alarmed by his persistent questioning, Bryony changed her tact. She stopped pacing and faced him as calmly as she could. "I thought I came in here to learn the respective fates of me and my crew. Not to discuss my marriage prospects!"

"Very well." A tic worked in Slade's left cheek, showing

Bryony he was extremely annoyed with her, but to her relief he seemed willing to overlook that detail in favor of business.

"I think that, given the unusual circumstances, I can forego punishment of your young crew."

When she relaxed, he added sharply, "But your first mate—O'Grady, is it?—and you are both clearly of an age to know better. Some sort of example must be made here, and I'm afraid I have no say in the matter."

"But—" Bryony began.

"Hear me out." Slade raised a hand, and she noticed that his fingers were long and slender, but also callused. The previous image she'd held of a queen's captain was of some prissy English nobleman, or a daintily mincing fop inclined to take snuff. Slade Tanner perplexed her with his aristocratic posture and working-class hands. Which was he, rake or dandy? And why did she even care?

"Perhaps you're not fully aware of the circumstances yourself," Slade continued, his stern voice bringing her back to attention. "Brann O'Neill is refusing to relinquish lands previously titled to another family."

" 'Tis true the O'Neill won't hand over anything without a fair fight," she replied. "And in that much, I agree with him. Like the ship, the land's not his to give."

Slade looked exasperated. "Quit speaking in riddles, Bryony. Explain yourself!"

"Aye, aye, Captain." Slade was surely mistaken, but he thought he saw a dancing mote of laughter in her sea blue eyes before she continued. "It's really very simple, you see. The O'Neill is only guarding the land for his rightful heir, Brendan."

"So Governor Sydney didn't lie. Brann O'Neill does have a son."

Bryony nodded in the affirmative. "The same lad I would defend with my own life."

"I see. I'd heard tale you Irish were clannish folk, but

this . . ." Slade shook his head and sighed. "You deliberately intended, then, to commit treason against the queen?"

"No." Bryony surprised him with her calm defiance. "But I would do it again, if my hand was forced."

"Little fool!" he exploded. "You're too damn young to risk yourself like this. You have too much of your life left to live."

Bryony chuckled a little, her voice laced with irony. "Tell me what great adventure I could possibly imagine that I haven't lived already, Captain Tanner."

Slade was honestly shocked. "Don't you know? Marriage, a home of your own, children . . ."

"All of which would require I give up the sea. I don't consider it a particularly tempting trade."

"Come now. You're surely no different than any other female beneath those devilishly tight breeches and that prickly name of yours."

She simply raised an eyebrow, mocking him.

"You've never been good and thoroughly kissed, have you, Bryony O'Neill?" he demanded. "No man has ever dared try to ford your defenses, because you're too damned set on scaring them off."

Bryony shifted uneasily on the balls of her feet. His remarks were getting dangerously close to the truth. Defiantly, she retorted, "And I suppose your wife sits home, properly pining for you to return from sea, saddled with a dozen of your mewling brats to keep her company!"

"I have no wife as yet," Slade snapped back. "But if I did, she would certainly mind her lord and master."

"And what, pray tell, if she defied your orders, Captain?" she taunted him, her blue eyes flashing.

"Then I'd decide upon a proper course of punishment, one very much like this." Slade suddenly reached out and yanked her into his arms, pinning her in a powerful embrace as his lips sought out hers and staked an irrefutable claim.

Surprised, Bryony struggled a moment, but discovered her strength was inconsequential against Slade's. The realization was as shocking and heady as the passionate kisses he rained upon her lips and neck. With a moan, she briefly surrendered the fight, leaning fully into Slade as his warm tongue began to explore the sweet secrets of her mouth. His arms crushed her ever tighter, molding her soft curves to the lean angles of his hips and thighs, and letting her feel the hard edge of his arousal.

"This is why life is worth living, Bryony O'Neill," he whispered, brushing his lips against her tingling earlobe. She shuddered in his arms, not trusting herself to speak. Slade was right. She'd never been properly kissed before, and though she knew she should fight off the handsome Englishman with every last breath of her being, some traitorous part of her didn't want him to stop. It was madness, and well she knew it, but Bryony clung to Slade and began to return his wild kisses measure for measure, with all the inadvertent passion he'd unleashed.

Slade groaned low and deep in his throat. How long had it been since he'd had a willing woman in his arms? No lady he'd ever known had displayed such honest ardor as this. He was buffeted by a mixture of denial and desire; this beautiful Irish vixen was like nothing he'd ever encountered before, wild and defiant and as much a part of the sea as he was. There was nothing at all proper or predictable about Bryony O'Neill. Suddenly he wanted to know more, much more, about the fascinating firebrand in his arms.

Slade stepped back and gazed for a moment down into Bryony's lovely face. Her sea blue eyes were wide, he hoped with wonder. Her lips were slightly swollen and berry red.

"Your hair," he said a little roughly, and without further explanation took hold of the thick braid and began to unravel it. When her tresses were freed, they spilled down over her shoulders like shimmering, blue black flames. Beneath that callused facade, she was more beautiful than he'd dreamed, more feminine than he could have asked.

Grasping her chin lightly in his hand, he said huskily, "You can deny anything and everything to me, sweetheart, except for the plain fact that you're a woman. A woman badly in need of both a stern hand and some gentle loving."

Bryony gasped. The spell between them was shattered. His words had wounded as well as shocked her. Slapping his hand aside, she passionately cried, "I'm not one of your damned English doxies, Tanner!"

"Hush. Listen to me." His voice was so soft, she had to fall silent and strain to hear the words. Her hesitation gave him the opportunity to wrap her even more securely in his arms.

"I have nothing but the greatest of admiration for your sea-faring skills, Bryony. But surely you realize that ships and the sea are not all there is to this world of ours. There is base lust, aye, and plenty of it, but also the honest and enduring love between a man and woman."

For some reason, his words set her to trembling. She'd never thought much about it before; no man had ever spoken to her of love, and there had been little enough of it back at Raven Hall. Mab loved her, she knew, and Brendan in his own brotherly way, but that was not the kind of love Slade spoke of now.

"I'm afraid," she inadvertently whispered, then flushed with shame and began to struggle when she realized she truly was. Slade only held her tighter, soft laughter rumbling through his broad chest like thunder. It was a comforting sound, though she would have fiercely denied it.

"Aye, my little Irish vixen, love is both terrifying and wonderful. But love shared between the right two people can be the most magical thing in the world." As he spoke, Slade began casually unbuttoning her blouse. Frozen with indecision, and admittedly curious, Bryony didn't protest, and a moment later his large warm palm slipped inside and gently cupped her breast.

Lightly raking a callused thumb over her nipple, Slade smiled with triumph when he felt it respond. "You're no different than any other woman, Bryony O'Neill," he repeated, nuzzling her neck beneath the silky curtain of her hair.

How she wanted to deny his words! Yet Bryony couldn't restrain a small hungry moan as his fingers flicked and teased her pointed little nipple. The power he possessed for disarming her was more than she could bear. But her body realized she was hungry for love, even if she did not.

Slade unhooked her blouse and slid it well back on her shoulders. Her breasts were fully bared then, framed by the inky waves of her hair. Sheltered between those pale peaks lay a softly gleaming, golden amulet etched with swirls and spirals, and the distinct image of a bird. Slade's breath caught in his throat. For a moment he envisioned standing before him not a woman like all the others he had known, but a fiercely proud and powerful Celtic priestess.

At his obvious hesitation, Bryony experienced a sharp pang of uncertainty. Was she too bony, too skinny . . . ? Her childhood nickname haunted her as his green gaze roamed over her figure, poised so rigidly in the soft light.

"Beautiful," he said at last, and the single husky word encompassed everything—his intense awe and wonder and pure delight. A moment later she felt herself scooped up in his strong arms and carried swiftly to the bed. There Slade deposited her gently and tossed the blankets aside, for the cabin air was close and warm. He lowered himself on an elbow beside her, as fascinated with her as she was with him.

Bryony waited with secret longing burning through her veins. Before she could speak, Slade reached out and brushed a finger across her trembling lips. Silently, he shook his head, and when she playfully caught hold of his queue and freed his hair as he had hers, they exchanged a sudden smile of camaraderie and something more.

Slade eased his body atop hers, his red gold hair lightly brushing the tips of her tingling bare breasts, as he settled himself in place. Leisurely he claimed her mouth again, and fire raced through Bryony, seeming to turn her blood to liquid molten lava. She trailed her fingers down Slade's cheek, surprised to feel a dimple there when he smiled at her. It made her think of the child behind the man, and she felt an unexpected tenderness well in her breast.

In her head Bryony knew it was wrong, but she couldn't stop now, and found to her own mixed fear and delight that she didn't want to. When Slade lowered his lips and feasted hungrily on her breasts, a ragged gasp escaped her lips. She had never imagined such delights existed. Gone for the moment was her fascination with ships, the sea, or anything but the golden man here and now. Her hands rose and entangled in Slade's hair, smoothed it back over his broad shoulders. His bronzed chest bore faint traces of blond and auburn hairs, which proved to be silky soft when she drew him back against her.

Strangely, Bryony felt no embarrassment when Slade began to touch her in places no man ever had before. Somehow it seemed so natural, so right, and the sensuous movements of Slade's hands upon her body seemed almost familiar, as if she had been with him before, in a misty dream or another life.

The passion which had leapt between them the moment their eyes first met was claiming a flesh sacrifice now. No words were needed, and the intense silence served only to bring them closer. Slade's own mind whirled with the image of the woman in his arms, her raven black hair, those stormy blue eyes. He suddenly knew he could never surrender Bryony O'Neill, not to her foolish cause, or even to his queen.

Slade moved to coax more sighs and moans from those sweet lips, amazed at the perfect fit their bodies had together. He knew he would curse himself forever if he let this rare woman go. Just a moment more, and she would be his . . .

Five

Neither one of them had heard the scratching at the cabin door, nor sensed someone else intruding upon their private paradise, until Diego Santiago coughed softly in apology.

The first mate stayed in the shadows, as acutely uncomfortable as the couple on the bed. But it wasn't so dark that poor Diego didn't have a very good idea of what he'd interrupted. The other two flew apart as if dashed with icy sea water. Bryony scrambled to rehook her shirt, as Slade leaped up like a nervous cat from the bed.

"Ah—*Capitan,* I am very sorry to have disturbed you, but you didn't respond to my calls, and I began to wonder . . ."

"Aye, Diego, what is it?" Slade's voice echoed in the cabin like a crack of a whip.

Though the Spaniard was every bit as embarrassed as Bryony, he regained his composure quickly and somehow managed to keep his gaze from straying to the captain's bed. Dutifully, Diego reported, "There's a bad squall coming in from the east."

Slade sniffed the air. "I should've noticed it sooner. 'Twas getting unusually warm in here."

Diego didn't take the bait. He reported matter-of-factly, "Not only that, sir. One of the men—Taylor—swears he saw a strange bird hovering over the main mast a little while ago."

"An albatross?"

Diego shook his head. "He says it was *todo negro,* all black." After a moment's hesitation, the first mate confessed,

"I think I saw it too, *Capitan.* A huge shadow over the ship . . . a bad sign . . . *Diablo Pajaro,* the Devil Bird."

Slade sighed and shook his head. "Sweet Jesu, Diego, I expect a little more common sense out of you." Without another glance at the woman on his bed, he motioned his first mate to follow him out on deck. "Let's go."

After the two men left and the door banged shut behind them, Bryony sat up and hugged a pillow to her breasts in disbelief and rapidly escalating fury. She was nothing to Slade Tanner! Nothing but a moment's casual distraction!

Furiously she blinked away an unfamiliar threat of tears, and scrambled off the bed. All the magic they shared had vanished like a leprechaun, when Diego had interrupted them.

Of course, it would soon be all over the ship that she was Tanner's new doxy. Bryony remembered the contempt she'd always had for the O'Neill's women, the endless parade of coarse jades back at Raven Hall, and felt her cheeks burning when she realized she might as well join their ranks. God's blood, what had she been thinking? Almost letting a *Sassenach*—the sworn enemy—make love to her!

Bryony loathed the thought of leaving Slade's cabin and facing down his crew's stares and snickers, but realized it would look even worse if she stayed put. It took her a moment more to remember what Diego had said. Something about a bird, and a squall. But what did one have to do with the other? She'd been too horrified at her compromising situation to pay much attention to the details.

Gathering her courage, Bryony finally decided to venture out on deck. She took the single lantern off its hook, and when she ducked back outside, she was relieved to feel the wind whip her hair into a sudden riot, giving some excuse for its tousled appearance. Then she also realized that Diego was right. The wind was a bad omen. It was coming from the wrong direction. It was warm, damp, and heavy, the most dangerous kind. When combined with the cooler air near the sea's surface, it could result in a deadly typhoon, a tornado at sea.

Glancing heavenward, she saw that in less than an hour, thick clouds had scudded over the stars and moon, and lacy white strands of lightning split the sky. The *Silver Hart* was beginning to pitch and sway, and Bryony glanced seaward with alarm to make sure the other ship was still lashed astern. She could just make out the dark hull of the caravel; its empty decks and skeletonlike masts thrusting skyward gave it a ghostly appearance.

Bryony shivered. She knew the *Alanna Colleen* would not ride out this storm with ease. She was too light, her hull as fragile as a bird's egg compared to Slade's solid merchantman. Keeping the two ships linked together during a storm would be foolhardy, if not downright dangerous. Their hulls could smash together, sinking them both. She resolved to warn Slade, and when she heard voices raised over the wind, she hurried to the foredeck to see what was going on. She reached the huddled knot of men just in time to hear what Slade was saying to them.

"We're in for a real ride, men," he said grimly, with a glance at the roiling sky. Every inch of him seemed cool and poised. Before she could speak, he added, "It's too dangerous to try and keep the ships together during the storm."

One of the crew spoke up. He was a big, rawboned sailor with a coarse thatch of straw-colored hair. "Then cut 'er loose, Cap'n. 'Tisn't worth our lives!"

Slade turned and coolly faced down the man. "I plan to, Taylor. Now, about all that bird nonsense—"

" 'Twasn't me imagination!" Taylor cried, clearly upset. "Diego saw it, too! Big it was, near big as the moon, and the black shadow fell all across the water." His roaming gaze picked out Bryony standing near her Irish crew.

Unfortunately, Taylor also spied the amulet about her neck, which she had forgotten to tuck back inside her shirt, and he recognized the design even by lantern light. He swiveled and pointed an accusing finger in her direction. "That's the same bloody bird, Cap'n, around the girl's neck! And we all know 'tis ill luck to 'ave a female aboard. 'Specially one of them pagan wenches."

Bryony almost laughed. She was surely as religious as any one of them! But the laughter died in her throat when she saw several of Slade's crewmen nodding in agreement, and heard them muttering nervously under their breaths.

Seeking to ward off further trouble, she stepped boldly forward and suggested, "Put us on the caravel and cut her free, Tanner. The loss of one ship is nothing compared to losing the loyalty of your men."

Under his deep tan, Slade flushed with anger. She hadn't meant it as a challenge, but he obviously took it for one. He turned on the big man. "Taylor," he said briskly, clearly a warning, "I'll hear no more about dark omens or devil birds or anything else, understand?" He rounded on Diego next. "Do we have enough crew to man both ships?"

The Spaniard considered it, then nodded. "Aye, I suppose I could handle the caravel, *Capitan,* though I'll need a few extra hands for the lines."

Bryony quickly pressed her advantage. "The lads know her from stem to stern by now. I'll go, too."

Slade paused to regard her a moment. His green eyes were cool. "That vessel is English property now," he said, "and you've been relieved of your command."

Outrage rose in Bryony, choking her long enough for another voice to intercede. Finn O'Grady stepped forward, announcing, "But there's nothing to stop me from going, even if Bryony has to stay. Besides, your man will need his own first mate."

"He has a point, *Capitan,*" Diego put in.

Slade slid a measuring gaze over the stout Irishman. "If you're thinking to escape English justice, O'Grady, you're sorely mistaken."

Finn's fists bailed at the insult. "I'll not run nor hide from the likes of any *Sassenach!*" he hotly declared.

"Finn!" Bryony's warning tone barely averted disaster, as

she stepped between the two men who stood glowering at each other. She turned to her cousin and said quietly, "I know can trust you to keep a ship and crew in tight running order. But remember, there can be no enemies in close quarters, especially during a storm at sea."

"Aye, I understand."

She patted him on the arm, then handed him the lantern. "Good man. You'll do right by me, I know it. But please keep an eye out for the lads." Then she turned to face Slade, adding coolly, "O'Grady here is as loyal as they come. He'll not let down Diego."

"Good," Slade said abruptly. Without another word he left them, in order to supervise the reefing of the *Silver Hart*'s sails and prepare for the full onslaught of the storm.

No sooner had Diego and his makeshift crew pushed off in the caravel and vanished into the thickening darkness, when the screaming squall hit the *Silver Hart* broadside. The gusts of wind and sheeting rain had only been a polite prelude; Bryony was nearly pitched overboard when the first standing wave hit, and water sluiced hip-deep across the decks.

Just in time, she grabbed the railing, but her footing was too precarious to last. As the ship lurched in the other direction, and the wave sloshed back across the deck, the force of the recoiling water spun her sideways and slammed her into the railing. The impact knocked her breathless, and the icy sea spray drowned out her cry for help.

Gasping, she shook the sopping hair out of her eyes and started to move across the deck to safety. Her aim was the rope ladder under the mainmast, where she might cling during the storm and also lend a quick hand to any of the crew.

Before she gained her goal, lightning cracked sharply overhead, its brilliance momentarily blinding her. When her vision cleared, she made out a beefy figure blocking her path of retreat. She recognized Taylor, the superstitious bosun who somehow attributed the storm's arrival to her. His ruddy face broke into a crooked grin at the sight of Bryony, and his eyes glistened with malice as he moved toward her. She saw the glint of something hard and metallic clutched in his hand. She knew, with a flash of sudden insight, that his intent was either to kill her outright, or force her overboard.

The drizzle had become a fierce downpour, and Bryony knew any screams would be snatched away by the wind. She ruefully sized up Taylor and decided her only chance was to run. Feinting to the right, she ducked and slipped past him just as he swung the makeshift weapon at her head. She heard a roar of outrage, or perhaps it was only thunder shaking the ship's timbers. Obviously, Taylor reasoned somehow that if only she were dead, the storm would miraculously disappear, and all hands would be saved. And when she was discovered missing, nobody would question the likelihood she had accidentally slipped overboard!

Bryony was quick, but the vengeful Taylor was crafty. He cut off her only retreat, then herded her towards the railing. As she bolted to the left, he lunged and finally caught her by the back of her wet shirt, flinging her bodily beneath his splayed feet. She was stunned by the hard impact of the deck; she found to her horror that she couldn't even crawl free. Taylor held her pinned down between his massive tree-trunk thighs, and when the lightning flashed, Bryony saw the object he raised over his head was an evil-looking, iron grappling hook.

Just before the hook came down, Taylor grunted and went flying sideways. Bryony thought a wave had hit him, until she saw two figures struggling by the railing. She came to her feet as the lightning cracked again, highlighting Slade's angry profile in eerie white light. The taller captain wrestled Taylor face-first to the ground, pinning the bosun's meaty arms behind him. The hook had been lost somewhere in the scuffle.

Seeing her standing there trying to stay upright on the slick deck, Slade jerked his head in the direction of his cabin, and shouted into the wind, "Get below!"

But Bryony had no intention of riding out the squall tucked away in that suffocating little box. "No!" she shouted back, getting some satisfaction from his surprise. Clearly, no woman had dared dispute Slade before, at least not where orders on his ship were concerned.

"God's nightshirt!" he swore, but apparently lost track of what he intended to say next. It didn't matter much, because they were all suddenly the recipients of another smashing wave from the starboard side.

Bryony went down hard, and the foaming water dragged her across the deck to hurl her against the rail. Slade released his hold on Taylor and caught her instead, just in time to prevent her from being washed overboard. One hand firmly wrapped around the rail, Slade held onto Bryony with the other, wrestling with the sea for possession of the young woman.

Finally, the huge wave shook free and dropped overboard, its curling spray like sullen fingers withdrawn into a hissing cauldron. Bryony half-sagged at Slade's feet, but as a bolt of lightning lit their world, she glanced up to see his scowling face.

"Get up!" He hauled her unceremoniously to her feet by the sodden lump of her hair, and steadied her briefly against his chest. "*Now* will you go below?" he demanded.

Bryony began to shake, and Slade thought at first that she must be trembling from cold. No wonder, they were all drenched to the skin . . . then he saw the empty space where Taylor had been, and shook his head with momentary regret, when he realized the fickle sea had claimed a flesh sacrifice.

Slade felt obliged to comfort Bryony, but when he glanced down again he saw that she shook not from fear or cold, but was laughing . . . laughing like a madwoman, or a drunk on a glorious binge.

"Go below? I wouldn't miss this storm for the world!" she crowed.

Stunned, Slade realized she meant it. There was no fear on her beautiful face, and her bright eyes reflected the blue lightning forks in the heavens above. She clung tightly to him as another wave hit, and the ship rose and plunged sickeningly. There was finally a moment's reprieve, and eventually Slade deemed it safe to loosen his grip on the rail and draw her to a safer spot on the forecastle.

Slade shook his head. "I can't believe you're not afraid," he said.

It was a statement, not a question. Bryony shrugged, adding softly, "Not of this."

He didn't pursue the matter. He already knew what genuine fear lay hidden behind her brave facade, for he'd touched upon it a short time ago in his cabin. Bryony O'Neill was more afraid of love than death. By all accounts, she was unlike any woman he'd known—or imagined might exist.

With the last of her strength, Bryony helped Slade hoist the *Silver Hart*'s foresail to the breeze. For over a day, the typhoon had battered and hurled them about like a child's toy on the water. Then, as abruptly as it had appeared, the storm melted away, leaving smooth seas and sunny skies.

At one frightening point, they had even caught sight of a thin, black funnel cloud twisting across the ocean's surface, sucking untold volumes of seawater up into its greedy maw. But though the typhoon swirled wildly past them, the ship had miraculously escaped being pulled into the churning whirlpool beneath it.

The crew was exhausted, having struggled with the lines and loss of sleep the entire time. Luckily, none of the sturdy masts had snapped, even though the mighty sea had plucked a few more hapless bodies to their fate. Besides Taylor, two more men had turned up missing after the storm. Worse yet, there was no sight of the *Alanna Colleen,* not even bits or pieces of floating wreckage, which would have told a story of their own.

Slade attempted to reassure Bryony about the fate of the others. "Diego knows enough to sail for the nearest port," he told her when they had finished securing the foresail. "I imagine he's nearing Scotland even now."

Bryony was not so optimistic. She better realized the limitations of the swift but lightweight caravel. "I hope you gave them plenty of provisions," was all she said.

"Aye, half of ours, which means we need to get ashore soon and restock the galley. The water's almost gone. I'm going to have to start rationing today."

Bryony nodded, well versed with the hard facts of life at sea. Later, as the wind picked up again and the sails billowed jauntily, she took a moment to collapse against the foremast and catch her breath. If she was not so bone weary, she would have frantically paced the deck, watching for any sign of the other ship.

Suddenly a tall shadow fell over her. "Come on," Slade said, his stern tone brooking no disobedience as he moved to lift her in his arms. "You'll be no good to me without some rest."

Bryony was sound asleep in the cradle of his arms, even before Slade managed to tug off her boots and lay her down on the bed in his cabin. He paused to tuck the blankets around her. Dark circles ringed her eyelids, and he smiled to himself as he brushed aside a runaway curl from her cheek.

In sleep, Bryony O'Neill looked like a child, but he knew better. She was more than most men could handle, and that included him, too.

With a deep sigh, Slade sat down to yank off his own boots and flex his aching feet. He wiggled his toes through the nether wool stocks, then started to pull off his damp shirt. Suddenly, even that simple effort was just too much. He fell back on the bed beside Bryony, and was fast asleep even before his head hit the pillow.

* * *

Sunlight streamed through the single port window, gently waking Bryony to a new day. She stretched and then groaned with pain, feeling every muscle in her body coming to life.

Vaguely, she recalled being picked up by Slade and carried off somewhere, but the rest of it was a blank. Her gaze gradually focused on the captain's cabin, and she forced herself up onto her aching elbows to look around.

Beside her, the bed covers were scraped back, but though the spare pillow bore the imprint of a head, Slade was long gone. He must have risen with the sun, leaving her to sleep half the morning away.

Bryony was still fully clothed, but she felt damp and dirty. She itched to get clean again. Her shirt was smeared with grease from the ship's chain plates, and her breeches were torn in several places. Glancing at her wind- and water-chapped hands, she winced. The skin had cracked, and dried blood dotted her palms. Her eyes felt raw, and still burned from the cruel kisses of saltwater and wind.

Crawling from the bed, she found her boots and eased them over her throbbing feet. Limping painfully to the door, she opened it a crack and let the blessed sunlight warm her aching bones. When she could focus her eyes against the glare, she gasped softly in surprise. The *Silver Hart* was no longer out to sea, but moored now in a small bay alongside fishing skiffs and smaller galleys. The deck appeared empty.

For a moment, Bryony was shocked. Obviously she'd slept far longer than a day. Then she felt annoyed, and wondered why Slade had chosen to leave her aboard ship, rather than wake her and offer to let her go ashore with the others.

She moved out on deck, but all she could see from there were tall, craggy gray cliffs. Above those, softly rounded green hills rose to embrace a misty sky. It wasn't Ireland, though the landscape was similar. She walked to the rail and looked about curiously.

She saw that the crew had taken both of the longboats, leaving her stranded. There was only a short distance to shore, and she eyed it thoughtfully, mentally weighing the risk. She gripped the railing and leaned forward, judging the drop of some thirty feet. She was a strong swimmer, and the current looked favorable. Maybe if she climbed over the starboard rail, and slipped unseen into the water . . .

"Good morning."

The deep voice startled Bryony, and she whirled about to meet those familiar green eyes straight on. Slade looked devilishly handsome, wearing snug black breeches and an open-laced white shirt. His red gold hair was loose and blew lightly about his broad shoulders in the morning breeze. He offered her a lazy grin, and she realized he had guessed her thoughts.

"I'd advise against it," he said. "There's a pretty treacherous undertow here."

To quell her pounding heart, Bryony quickly asked, "I thought you'd gone ashore, Tanner. Where's the rest of your crew?"

"I sent them in for a well-deserved romp and rest. No doubt they're drinking themselves under the table at the *Green Dragon,* thanking their lucky stars they didn't end up as sea fodder."

Bryony pulled a face. "I suppose you stayed behind to play the part of jailer . . . or is it martyrdom you aspire to?"

Slade smiled back at her without any rancor. For some reason, his easy manner irritated her more than if he had been cruel. His apparent kindness only made her suspicious.

"Are you up for a little shore leave?" he asked her.

"Do you mean it?"

"Aye. As soon as the first shift returns, we'll head ashore."

It sounded too good to be true. "Where are we?" Bryony demanded.

"The Isle of Man. It seems our luck has held. First riding out the storm, then ending up safely here."

She grimaced. "Her Majesty's territory."

"Aye, but 'tis most convenient for my present plans, and I'm well enough known here to sail by on credit." There was a twinkle in Slade's eye she couldn't miss, and she returned a grudging smile.

"Any sign of the *Alanna Colleen?*"

He sobered instantly. "No. Though I've spread the word, and everyone will be watching for her now. That's about all we can do. Did you get enough rest?"

"More than enough. I wish you'd woken me earlier."

"You were utterly exhausted and in no shape to keep pushing yourself like that."

"What about you?" she challenged him.

"I slept a little. But I'm the captain, and it's my responsibility to see to the welfare of the crew. Not that I don't trust them, but with Diego gone, they require closer supervision." He paused and eyed her with concern. "You look miserable."

"I am," Bryony confessed, self-consciously pushing back her mass of wind-snarled, matted hair. "I'd give anything for a hot bath."

"Anything?" Slade teased her. One golden eyebrow was cocked, and he watched her reaction with obvious interest.

"Within reason!" Bryony's cheeks burned as the memory of their closely intertwined bodies flashed in her head. "Tanner, about what happened in your cabin . . ."

"Say no more." Slade waved his hand in dismissal. "I can assure you, the incident is already forgotten."

But the way in which he studied her with those bright green eyes, told Bryony it wasn't true.

Six

When the first handful of Slade's crew returned to the ship, the two of them rowed ashore in a longboat. Slade claimed oar duty, much to Bryony's relief. She was so weary, she didn't even protest when he suggested she conceal her unruly hair under a high-crowned felt hat, topped with a jaunty orange plume.

Pressed as they were like a pair of young bloods, nobody gave Bryony or Slade a second glance when they entered a seaside establishment called the *Green Dragon.* Slade had offered to buy his captive a hot meal, and Bryony was too hungry to care that the offer came from the enemy.

The busy atmosphere of the place caused Bryony to relax. Nobody would notice, or even suspect, that a female lurked beneath her cape and breeches, and all the generous grime. Slade guided her towards a crude plank table at the rear of the ale house.

As they took a seat on a wooden bench, a redheaded ale girl hurried over in their direction. Recognizing Slade, she squealed with delight and literally flung herself into his lap. Bryony's eyebrows rose.

Obviously embarrassed, Slade pried off her clinging arms and said, "Molly, you're looking well."

The girl's freckled nose wrinkled with disgust at his formal greeting. In a thick Cockney accent, she pertly quipped, "Is that all ye 'ave to say to yer favorite tumble, luv?" She playfully pinched his cheek and added, "Too fine now fer the lot of us at the pub 'ouse, eh?"

"None of your impertinence, wench," Slade said gruffly, pushing her off his lap. "Bring us two full trenchers, and tankards of Gordo's best brown ale."

Not to be so easily dismissed, Molly struck a pose with her ample bosom thrust aggressively in Bryony's direction. Brown eyes narrowed and calculating, she demanded, "Who's yer new friend 'ere?"

Slade didn't glance at Bryony as he stoutly replied, "I'm in need of a cabin boy. My young cousin here came along this voyage to try out his sea legs."

"Well now, that do change things a bit," Molly said as she leaned over the table and patted Bryony's cheek with a plump, freckled hand. "Sure now, and I can see the likes of our 'andsome Slade in you. 'E never told me 'e 'ad a cousin, and such a pretty, little blue-eyed lad, too."

"Knock it off, Mol," Slade laughed as Bryony reddened with fury and embarrassment. "You're scaring the poor boy half to death! Go on now like a good lass, and fetch us a couple of pints."

Somewhat miffed, Molly displayed a well-turned ankle as she whirled and flounced away. Staring after the girl, Bryony whispered fiercely under her breath, "She actually believed you!"

Slade chuckled and folded his arms on the table. "Aye, but you might give the wench a start, if you were to fling off that hat and cape of yours."

"More likely she'd scratch out my eyes," Bryony replied a little ruefully, as her gaze roamed over the crowded room. She was disconcerted to discover a man staring at them from across the inn. He looked big, bigger even than Slade, though it was hard to be sure, since he was sitting down. When she met his bold gaze, he conspicuously winked. She realized he had not been fooled by her disguise. She stiffened and looked hastily away.

"What's wrong?" Slade asked her, moments before a lusty bellow split the air.

"Quelle chance! Capitaine Tanner!" Bryony saw the big man had suddenly risen, dumping a buxom, blond tavern girl on the floor in the process.

Slade shot to his own feet with a joyful exclamation. "Lafleur! You old lecher, I see you're still harassing the poor wenches here." Grinning from ear to ear, he left the table and hurried over to greet his friend.

As the two men pounded each others' backs in a happy reunion, Bryony seized the opportunity to size up the Frenchman. Lafleur was big, at least six-foot-three, his head topped with a shaggy crown of thick black hair. His great size provided an amusing contrast to his name, a word she knew meant flower in French, implying something small and delicate, which he definitely was not.

Handsome in a sleek and oily sort of way, Lafleur reminded Bryony of a seal. Under black brows, his dark eyes gleamed like polished jet, and he wore a huge, elegantly waxed moustache.

"What's it been, *mon ami,* three years or more?" Lafleur exclaimed after he smacked his lips on both of Slade's cheeks in the Gallic fashion. "I just sailed to Cipango and back, and happened to stop here on my way south." He stepped back, and at arm's length eyed his old friend critically for a moment. "Ah, so that is what has changed, Tanner. You're far older than I remember!"

Slade chuckled at the friendly insult. "That's right, Giles. I'm no longer a callboy. I'm a queen's captain now."

The Frenchman promptly spewed out the ale he'd just chugged from the tankard clutched in his right fist. *"Tiens!* Whoring the high seas for old Bess?"

It was Bryony's turn to be amused, and the sound of her laughter carried over to where the two men stood. Lafleur glanced curiously at the slender figure perched on the bench. Slade stiffened a little.

"My cabin boy," he said.

Lafleur guffawed at that. "Cabin boy, indeed!" Slinging an arm companionably around his old friend, the Frenchman pulled Slade over to Bryony. When they halted before her, Lafleur peered drunkenly at her a long moment, and then threw back his shaggy head and roared with laughter.

"Ha! I knew I was right. What's this, Slade Tanner? Have you stooped to passing off your doxies as deckhands?"

"I'm no whore!" Bryony snapped, and Lafleur's eyes widened with surprise. "I'm this man's prisoner, not his trull!"

Lafleur tsked-tsked her, obviously amused by her spirit. "Such a temper! Simmer down, *ma petite!* You might attract the wrong sort of attention."

A swift glance about the *Green Dragon* proved the words true. The surprise and interest of the other patrons was squarely centered now on the slim young woman garbed as a lad. Slade swung a long leg over the bench and eased down beside Bryony again, discouraging further curiosity with his stony gaze. Across from them, Lafleur plopped down and continued to leer at her.

"Too skinny for my taste, *mon ami,* but you're to be congratulated on your prize." When Lafleur's big hand suddenly shot out and gripped Bryony by the chin for a better look, she ducked her head and promptly bit his knuckle.

"Oww!" The Frenchman withdrew and nursed his injury, though his eyes continued to sparkle with admiration and obvious delight. "Irish, is she? Tanner, what madness are you about? You know these Irish wenches can't be tamed!"

Instead of replying, Slade reached out and took a long draught of the cold ale Molly had plunked on the table before him. He reached out and grabbed the wrist of the retreating tavern girl.

"Another round for Lafleur," he said. "And tell your master we'll be taking rooms for the night."

"Aye, aye, cap'n," Molly coyly simpered, with a toss of her bright red curls. She'd obviously overheard a portion of their conversation, for she gave Bryony a knifing glance before she flounced off again.

When Molly was gone, Slade said, "Skinny or not, Lafleur, this lass nearly outsailed and outsmarted me. She led me quite a merry chase through the Irish Sea a few days ago."

Giles's eyebrows shot up in disbelief, but then he glanced at Bryony's hands and noted the raw callused skin.

"Faith, I've heard tale of such women before, but never quite believed it," he growled. *"La femme capitaine!* What next?"

"Perhaps a girl on the Tudor throne?" Bryony suggested sweetly.

"A sharp tongue, too," Lafleur chortled. "Watch out for this one, Tanner. I hear all the Irish have black magic in their blood!"

"Nay. Bryony O'Neill's got saltwater instead," Slade shot back good-naturedly.

"Did you say O'Neill?" The Frenchman narrowed his eyes, then swung a piercing dark gaze back on Bryony. "Not related to O'Neill of Raven Hall?"

"Aye," Bryony said reluctantly, before Slade could answer. "Do you know Brann?"

"Know!" Lafleur sputtered, ale spraying in every direction from his huge moustache. He slammed his tankard down on the table and snarled, *"Oui,* every man who's sailed the Irish Sea for any length of time knows of *Le Corsaire!"*

"Pirate!" Bryony half-rose from the bench, her voice strangled with rage, and only Slade's swift intervention prevented her from striking out at the Frenchman.

"That's my clan you slur, you—you French cur!" There was nothing of the soft woman in Bryony now, and Slade wondered if he'd only imagined the feminine creature who'd briefly nestled in his arms. A fierce challenge shot from her sea blue eyes into Lafleur's twinkling black ones.

Slade's old friend raised a hand in mock protest. "Simmer down, *tigre!* That's no black mark against you, just your sire."

"Whoever said the O'Neill was my father?" Bryony snapped

back, so quickly Slade was suspicious. She still trembled with bottled fury, but calmed down enough to speak in a reasonable tone.

"You slander the O'Neill's son, too, with such tall tales, Lafleur! I owe Brendan O'Neill my fealty."

LaFleur snorted. "Tales? No tale this, *ma petite,* but the truth. The whole clan is little more than a pack of bloody Irish pirates."

"You lie!"

The twinkle was gone from the Frenchman's eyes now, and he growled at Bryony, "Were you a man, *fille,* I'd have your tongue for calling Lafleur a liar."

" 'Tis a falsehood," she angrily insisted. "I've been with the O'Neill on nigh every voyage. All the O'Neills are honest merchants!"

"Mayhaps now," Lafleur said grudgingly, "but 'twas well known that Brann O'Neill was proud enough of ransacking ships on the high seas when he was younger. Perhaps the rumor I heard is true; that the old pirate mellowed with age and the loss of his wife."

At the mention of Brann O'Neill and his wife's death, Bryony suddenly sobered, a detail that did not escape Slade. What was her relation to the notorious O'Neill? She'd hotly denied he was her father, but she must be some degree of close kin to the man.

Before Slade could ask, hot food and another round of ale arrived, filling in the taut silence while the three hungrily devoured the offerings.

There was thinly sliced ham and sharp orange cheese on crisp, freshly baked rye bread, generous portions of a thick creamy porridge, and a flaky apple custard that melted in the mouth. Bryony was surprised Slade had ordered her a mug of the nut brown ale, but she didn't question her good fortune and sipped the foaming head off the drink with relish. She was famished, and even finished second helpings, to the amusement and admiration of both men.

"A wonder she's not as wide as the bow of her ship," Lafleur teased, nudging Slade. His good humor seemed restored as he watched Bryony reach for her third thick wedge of bread.

"She's earned a hearty meal," Slade replied.

Chewing and then pausing to swallow, she said to them, "You needn't talk about me as if I wasn't here." She nonchalantly wiped her greasy mouth on her sleeve. "And as for the food, Tanner, I'd be happy to pay for my portion, but I left my life savings on board the *Alanna Colleen*."

Slade looked directly at her. "This was my treat, Bryony O'Neill, so you can just swallow your cursed Irish pride for now. The same goes for the room and bath awaiting you upstairs."

Her eyes widened with mock surprise. "Why, Captain Tanner, best beware, or it might be said you spoil your captives," she sweetly retorted.

Slade refused to be baited. "If you've finished eating, I suggest you retire to your room and clean up a bit. We'll be leaving at dawn's first light."

"Aye, aye, cap'n!" Bryony mimicked Molly, the saucy tavern wench, before abruptly rising and taking her leave of the two openmouthed men.

The room Slade had rented Bryony for the night was spartan, but clean. At her request, a round oak tub was filled with hot steaming water, carried up in buckets by two stout lads who worked for the innkeeper. At long last, Bryony was able to strip and scrub herself free of all the dust and grime. She tossed aside her soiled clothing, all save the amulet, which she vowed never to remove.

After washing her hair twice with the bar of damask rose soap which came free with the bath, Bryony sank back, letting the hot water soothe her aching muscles and melt away the aches and pains. Her hunger sated, her cleanliness restored, it was little wonder she easily drifted off to sleep.

Sometime later, the sensations of a light breeze playing over her skin, and of bath water long gone cold woke Bryony with a start.

"Who's there?" she blurted groggily, struggling to sit up in the sloshing tub full of water. But the room was empty, save for a new outfit neatly laid across the bed.

Groping for a towel to dry herself with, Bryony carefully stepped out of the tub for a better look. Gone were her torn breeches and filthy shirt, even her seasalt-crusted boots. In their place lay a foam green gown of silky fine linen, with golden embroidery swirling across the hem and up and down the puffed sleeves. The long sleeves were also slashed to reveal golden silk inserts. The gown's underskirt was a paler golden silk, daintily stitched with daisies. Delicate undergarments edged with creamy lace and whisper-thin silk stockings were placed beside the dress. On the floor rested a pair of dark green velvet shoes with cork wedge heels.

After a quick, suspicious glance about the room to assure herself she was alone, Bryony walked over to gaze at the dress and hesitantly fingered the rich fabric. She'd never had a gown so fine; her best and only one at Raven Hall had been a Sunday dress of practical, but coarse gray worsted. Mab had tolerated Bryony wearing boy's clothes for the chores, but church was another matter altogether.

Bryony chuckled at the memory as she weighed the precious material lightly in her hand. What would her Mab make of this bit o' muslin, she wondered. The crusty old woman held a notoriously dim view of the English, and the Tudor court in particular. Mab often complained about its dire and evil influence on young people. Morals were all but nonexistent in Elizabethan England, according to her Mab. Bryony was curious to know if the gown had originated in Bess's court. It was certainly lovely enough to turn heads.

A brief search for her own clothing proved futile, and Bryony realized she had no choice but to try on the dress. But it proved more awkward to don than she would have guessed, and she struggled for some time to fasten the long rows of hooks down the left side of the rather low-cut, snug bodice.

Surprisingly enough, the gown fit perfectly once she secured the hooks and fluffed out the skirts. Tucking her amulet safely into the depths of the bodice, Bryony turned her attentions to her hair. It had dried during her nap, and she hastily combed out the curling black mass with her fingers.

She had barely finished sliding her feet into the strange shoes, when a scratching came at the door. "Who is it?" she called out warily.

"Molly," came the somewhat surly reply.

Bryony went to open the door, and was met by the red-headed ale girl, whose pretty face promptly soured once she saw Bryony's transformation.

" 'E wants you downstairs," Molly said without preamble, jerking her thumb in the direction of the common room.

Bryony didn't have to ask who. Picking up the wide skirts, she took cautious, mincing steps in the unfamiliar high shoes all the way down the stairs after Molly.

Slade was waiting for her by the door. Beside him, Lafleur stared a moment and then let out a low whistle of admiration. He nudged the younger man and said under his breath, "*Sacre bleu!* Under the filth . . . a woman after all!"

Though the remark annoyed her, Bryony also felt a brief tingle of pleasure. She'd never attracted much notice from men before, at least not the favorable sort. For a moment, she almost dared wonder if it was possible; was she really beautiful? Then she glanced at Slade and saw he was frowning. Her secret hope swiftly vanished.

"I suppose I have you to thank for all this?" she inquired a bit stiffly.

"It isn't practical to have you swinging your hips before my crew in tight breeches," Slade retorted. He wasn't about to admit that the sight of Bryony O'Neill in feminine garb was both intriguing and unsettling. Lafleur was right; it was almost as if an entirely different woman stood before them now.

It was not just that Bryony was lovely; so were many other women he had known. There was something different and enchanting about this blue-eyed siren, with her ebony tresses shimmering down about her shoulders. As he'd suspected, the sea green of the gown was perfect with her coloring. And thanks to Lafleur's expertise on female sizes, he'd been able to send Molly to find a gown that would fit properly.

With a glance at Molly hovering in the background, Bryony turned a level look on him. "Why did you call me down?"

"You're coming with us," he said, neither an answer nor an explanation. He reached out and firmly took her by the elbow, moving to guide Bryony through the inn door held open by Lafleur.

Bryony suddenly panicked. "Unhand me!" she spat, planting her feet as she normally would in boots. But the precarious cork shoes slid along the floor, and she soon realized any fight would be useless. Immediately she wanted to claw off the fancy garb. Females were far too vulnerable in such useless frippery! Lafleur grabbed her other arm, and between the two men she was swiftly hustled outside.

When she continued to struggle, Slade said in a terse voice near her ear, "I vow you'll not be harmed, but if you don't stop this little scene, I'll truss you like a goose for market and haul you over one shoulder to the wharf."

And she knew he would! Realizing they were destined for the waterfront, Bryony briefly ceased her struggles. Why such high drama, merely to escort her back to Slade's ship? She would never understand the peculiar minds of men, she decided.

When they entered the wharf area, Bryony was again surprised. Instead of returning to the *Silver Hart,* Slade and Lafleur escorted her to a merchantman nearly twice the size of Slade's ship. Bryony saw it flew the French flag, and she immediately tensed. Was Slade transferring her into Lafleur's custody? It didn't help one bit that the vile Frenchman, noticing her discomfort, grinned lewdly.

Lafleur finally shattered the tense silence by shouting lustily over the water for a pair of lads to row them out to the great ship. As the three of them settled into a longboat, Bryony burned with barely restrained fury. Lafleur kept leering at her suggestively, and Slade was no help at all, either unaware or unconcerned with his old friend's behavior.

After what seemed an eternity, they reached the French vessel, and a rope ladder was tossed down to them. Bryony realized with growing indignation that the men expected her to climb up the ladder in her gown. And when she did, she knew she would bare her charms for those below. In a tone of mock gallantry, Lafleur insisted she go first. Though she secretly burned with humiliation, Bryony refused to cause a scene. She mustered what remained of her dignity, and made the awkward ascent in the high heels and fine hose.

On deck, the French crew kept an ogling eye on her until Slade and Lafleur appeared. Once under their captain's critical eye, however, the men quickly returned to work.

To her further outrage, Bryony thought she detected a slight smile on Slade Tanner's lips. "You . . . you're enjoying this, aren't you?" she hissed at him under her breath.

Slade gave her a surprisingly boyish grin, which revealed his even white teeth. "If you're referring to seeing you dressed like a proper lady, and not some dockside urchin, then aye, I suppose I am."

"What did you do with my old clothes?" she demanded.

"I told Molly to burn them."

Molly! Bryony fumed at the memory of the sassy tavern wench who obviously preserved a special place in her heart—and bed—for the handsome Englishman. But why should his casual reference to the *Green Dragon*'s resident trull irritate her? She did not care one whit whom he chose to consort with!

During their exchange, Lafleur had rounded up a handful of his crew, and then herded them over to stand before Slade and Bryony. He said something in rapid-fire French to his men, then turned and grinned disarmingly at Bryony.

"Would you be kind enough to introduce yourself to my crew, *ma petite?"*

Bryony was still musing angrily upon the matter of Molly. Lafleur's request only annoyed her more.

"You great French fool," she snapped back. "Tell them yourself! Or better yet, ask Captain Tanner here. Though mayhaps he is too embarrassed to admit Bryony O'Neill is his equal on the high seas!"

The moment the rash statement left her lips, Bryony saw Lafleur smirk with the success of his mission. Aside to his crew, he said, "You see, *messieurs,* it came quite willingly from her own sweet lips." He suddenly seized Bryony's hand and placed a lingering, damp kiss upon it, before she could snatch it away.

"Merci beaucoup, my little tigress. I thank you most heartily, as does *Capitaine* Tanner here, for you have just brought the mighty Brann O'Neill within our grasp."

Seven

Bryony paled as she turned to look at Slade. He no longer smiled, but looked grimly resolved. Suddenly she understood their ploy. By admitting who she was to total strangers, she had given Tanner further ammunition against the O'Neill. Slade obviously considered her a valuable hostage in the struggle for possession of Clandeboye.

If the O'Neill demanded proof that she was a prisoner of the English, then here it was. Coming from Lafleur, a French captain with no claim to the disputed land, even Brann would likely not doubt Bryony's fate.

But for all his cleverness, Slade had not known of one very important thing. A cynical smile curved Bryony's lips, one which he quickly noticed.

"It won't work, Tanner," she told him. "Though, of course, you're welcome to try."

It was Slade's turn to be annoyed. "What won't work?"

"Forcing the O'Neill to surrender Raven Hall and the rest of his land by threatening dastardly acts against me."

"You're his kinswoman, aren't you?" Slade phrased it as a statement, not a question. "He'll be bound to come to your rescue."

She only chuckled at that. Slade's eyes flashed green fire. Reaching out, he grasped her by the elbow and demanded, "What tricks have you got planned, Bryony?"

She angrily shook off his possessive grip. "I don't need to

plan anything, Tanner. You're going to make a fool of yourself, without any help from me!"

He scowled back at her. "I've already figured out that you're O'Neill's daughter, so don't bother to deny it. You're the spitting image of the man."

Bryony didn't immediately reply. Finally, she sighed and said, "You're wasting your time, Tanner. He's never acknowledged me."

Lafleur, who had been listening to their exchange in silent fascination, loudly sucked in his breath. "You are illegitimate?"

Quick color rose in her cheeks. "No! But Brann believes it was my birth that killed my mother in childbed, and he's never forgiven me for it."

"Nonsense," Slade snapped. "I don't believe a word of this." To Lafleur, he added, "She's lying, of course."

"Why?" Bryony countered. "Why would I bother? I'm simply offering to save you considerable expense and trouble, if you're planning to send Lafleur back to Ireland with a ransom demand."

"We both know your worth to O'Neill," Slade abruptly reminded her. "You were sailing one of his ships, after all."

"Without his permission," Bryony said impatiently. "The ship really belongs to my brother, Brendan. The O'Neill could care less about my fate. He's well rid of me after all these years."

Was Slade mistaken, or was there a quiet note of painful resignation beneath her calm words? He hesitated. Was it possible that Bryony was telling the truth? But why would O'Neill deny his only daughter? It seemed unlikely the man would have permitted her on the deck of his ship at all, if he refused to acknowledge her birth.

"I'm sorry, Bryony," he told her a moment later, "but you obviously realize your value and are simply trying to discourage me from this necessary course. We all know the position this puts your father in." He pivoted to face Lafleur. "Thank you, old friend. I owe you one for this."

Giles nodded absently. He, too, was wondering if the feisty Irish wench possibly spoke the truth. Ah, well, they would soon find out. But until they did, Bryony O'Neill was destined to remain in English hands, under the judicious care of Captain Tanner, who, by the look of things, didn't resent the unusual assignment one bit.

When they arrived back at the *Green Dragon*, Slade firmly escorted Bryony to her room. Once they were alone, she jerked her arm from his grasp and rounded on him in a high dudgeon.

"I won't let you humiliate me like that again!" she cried. "Whatever devious plans you have in mind, whatever other indignation you intend to force me to endure, I swear upon the mighty Morrigan that you won't break me!"

Slade slammed the door behind them to cut off curious eyes and ears from the scene. "Keep your voice down, you little Irish savage." He was still nursing a deep scratch on his left cheek, where she had lashed out earlier. Though her nails hadn't broken the skin, it stung like all blazes.

"You'll keep to this room from now on," he said. "I'll have Molly bring up a tray."

His mention of Molly only infuriated Bryony more. "Don't bother," she sneered. "I'm sure your doxy has far more important duties tonight!"

Slade stepped closer to her, his jaw rigid, and spoke through gritted teeth. "Molly is not my mistress, but even if she was, I'd expect you to keep a civil tongue in your head. Obviously, nobody has ever taken a moment of their time to discuss the subject of manners with you, Bryony, but 'tis clear to me you're in dire need of instruction."

"Oh, am I now?" Her brogue thickened slightly, as she folded her arms and stared him down. "Then who's to correct *you,* Captain Tanner, when you try to play me for a fool in your sordid little plot against the O'Neill?"

"You're not a fool," Slade said evenly. "You are a pawn, and there's a difference."

"Fine difference, threatening to truss me up like a goose for market, if I tell anyone here who I am!"

" 'Twas for your own good, Bryony. There are some who might see the O'Neill's daughter as a rich prize to be used for their own gain."

"You mean besides yourself?" she snarled.

Slade took a single step toward her. Restraining himself at the last moment, he looked down into her flaming blue eyes and evenly stated, "The only gain you speak of is what's already mine by law. For I've a birthright to Clandeboye, and I mean to take it back."

"You!" Bryony exclaimed, understanding everything better now. It also explained why only one ship had appeared in the cove, not the entire Tudor navy. She didn't know why, but the thought of Slade seizing Raven Hall hurt her more than the idea of some remote *Sassenach* queen laying claim to it.

"Well, I'll see to it the O'Neill won't surrender, not to any weak-kneed *Sassenach!"* she passionately vowed.

Hands on her hips and black hair swirling about her, Bryony squared off with Slade.

"Lafleur's right," he growled. "God's bones, but you're an insolent wench!"

Too late Bryony saw what he meant to do. With an outraged shriek, she tried to duck under the long arm which shot out at her. Slade anticipated her move and cut her off at the door. Yanking her into his arms, he crushed her lips under his with a fervency that surprised them both. When Bryony's lips finally parted, the soft velvet of his tongue fiercely dueled with hers.

But even his lips could not continue meting out such sweet punishment. Instead of fighting him, as Slade had expected,

Bryony gradually relaxed, making no move to break free of his arms.

The moment she softened, he cut off the kiss and led her across the room. Bemused by this sudden change of tact, Bryony didn't flinch even when he turned to take her in his arms again, right beside the bed.

Then she shivered with the familiar fear she was still unwilling to admit, but Slade's strongly corded arms held her in place.

"I'm not afraid of you," she whispered, desperately.

"Then prove it," he murmured against her ear. "Prove to me you aren't afraid to be a woman, Bryony, and meet your adversary on equal terms." When he withdrew slightly, she saw his smile was both mocking and mischievous. How she longed to wipe that smirk from his lips!

Rising on tiptoe, she spontaneously pressed her mouth to his. She felt Slade stiffen against her, startled by her bold move and thrown off guard, as she had hoped. But before she could kiss him and flee, his fingers were pressing between her ribs to hold her in place, and coaxing forth a passionate response she never dreamed she was capable of.

No longer was Bryony in control. When at last she surrendered, he whispered, "There! Now I trust there's to be no more debate about who's the weaker of us!"

Slade saw her blue eyes shimmer with tears. He regretted what he'd done. He tried to take Bryony in his arms again, but she would have none of it. As she struggled in vain to get free, he stroked her head and sighed, "Ah, little sea raven, why do you provoke me so?"

The endearment sent shivers through Bryony, but anger still had possession of her heart. "Let me go," she demanded, but her voice shook with uncertainty.

Instead of answering, Slade's lips found hers again, and brushed light as a feather across her mouth, teasing. Bryony stopped struggling, too stunned to protest the tiny kisses trailing down her throat. Slade came to rest at the creamy expanse of flesh filling her low-cut bodice. A soft gasp escaped her when his finger unerringly located a nipple beneath the silk, and coaxed it to hardness.

Slade's passion became fiercer. His hands emboldened themselves to reach down and tug off her shoes. He sent them spinning one by one across the floor, then eased Bryony back upon the bed and kissed her again, long and slow and hard and deep.

Through half-closed eyes, Bryony gazed up at the golden man above her, her fury briefly quelled by a flurry of emotions she could not understand. Desire finally conquered the doubt as her arms linked around his neck, and Slade's low chuckle warmed her to the core. He began loving her then with a strong and gentle hand that made her blood burn.

With leisurely movements Slade unhooked the bodice of her gown, freeing her breasts to the admiring caresses of his bold gaze. "You're lovely, sweetheart," he murmured, and paid exquisite homage to each budding nipple, devoting equal time to each in order to ensure they were ruby-hard and throbbing beneath his lips, before he moved on to other, equally interesting areas.

When he moved to lift the amulet over her head, Bryony stayed him. He dropped the golden disk back between her breasts, where it reflected the red gold hues of his hair in its glinting depths. Slade realized the pagan symbol only highlighted her independence, her unique beauty, and left it where it lay.

Moving on, he found Bryony's skin a delightful contrast of pale creams and honey golds, baby-soft in some areas, pleasingly rough in others. Her hair framed her figure like a swathe of black silk, as he gently eased the gown from her shoulders and down over her hips. At last the frothy green material fluttered to the floor, whispering softly as a butterfly's wings.

Bryony lay before him then, unashamed, clad only in the glorious mantle of her hair, and a smile. Yet Slade knew she was no delicate court creature, no Tudor-bred tease. Nay, this

Irish vixen was pure unadulterated woman, and entirely unlike any other he had known. Part of her heart already belonged to the sea, but he silently vowed the other half would soon be his.

Bryony saw the glimmer of emotion in Slade's deep green eyes, and asked herself, *Can it be true?* Yet she could not deny the intense passion flaring between them, burning as strongly now as the first moment their eyes had met. Darker emotions melted to smooth hot passion, as Slade tossed aside his own clothing and brought his naked body into that first warm, fleeting contact with hers.

Bryony gasped as she felt Slade ease into place above her, lowering himself into the womanly saddle of her hips, and melding their flesh together in one continuous wave of pleasure. As her legs rose and locked around his, Slade looked deeply into her eyes, searching for something only she could give him.

"Aye, love," she whispered, or perhaps it was only her yearning heart which answered his unspoken question. Her lips trembled against Slade's throat, as he brought his maleness into contact with her womanly core, and she felt him seeking out the last sweet secret she hid from him.

She saw his eyes dilate with surprise, and perhaps a little regret. But then she urged him into the bewitching ancient rhythm of the sea, and with a ragged groan he drove deeply into her.

A brief flare of pain was quickly washed away by the burning urgent heat in her body, and Bryony moved instinctively to match his thrusts. Slade buried his face in her hair, inhaling the rich scent of damask roses, and her heart thudded with emotion when she heard him softly whispering her name over and over, like a litany.

Her own cries rose in crescendo, until she clutched Slade's shoulders for dear life, and a moment later she felt warm soothing waves of pleasure roll over her trembling body. When he made a noise, curiously like a sob, and went briefly still above her, she painted his feverish skin with tiny kisses. Though the pleasure they had shared was wonderfully sweet and poignant, Bryony somehow sensed he, too, ached for fulfillment of something neither of them fully understood.

Sometime later, she awoke to find herself tucked snugly under the blankets and curled under Slade's protective arm. When Bryony stirred, she realized he was awake. He murmured softly against her hair, "I'm sorry . . ."

"I'm not!" she whispered fiercely.

He kissed the top of her head. "Thank you, Bryony. But you don't need to soothe my male pride. I dishonored you tonight, when I knew better. Mayhaps we should—"

She quickly placed a finger across his lips. "Hush. I don't want or need any promises right now. Just you."

With one finger she lovingly traced the outline of Slade's square jaw in the deepening purple shadows of dusk, and when their gazes met, his green eyes held hers with such fierce intensity that she almost gasped. What was happening? Did her foolish heart mistakenly seek love from the one man who could never give it to her?

Or had fate chosen for them, and they were merely the unwitting players? Either way, Bryony knew she would never be the same again. When she laid her head against Slade's chest and heard his heart beating, strong and slow, she closed her eyes just in time to keep the tears from slipping down her cheeks.

When morning sunlight sprinkled across her closed lids, Bryony awoke with a soft contented moan. For a moment, she was disoriented, and was startled to feel the warmth of bare flesh pressed against hers. Then she raised her head and realized it had been pillowed upon Slade's broad chest all night long.

With a sleepy smile, she laid her head back down and listened to his deep rhythmic breathing. It was still early, and the lavender and pinkish colors of dawn slanting through the window in the room had fallen upon her entirely by chance. She didn't want to stir and break this precious moment. It might be all she ever had.

Bryony's thoughts roiled darkly onward as the true significance of what had happened between them slowly sunk in. She and Slade Tanner had become lovers—neither of them had bothered to deny the powerful attraction between them, nor had they tried to fight it.

Where had her common sense gone? Slade was the enemy, an Englishman intent upon stealing Clan O'Neill's land. But, she ruefully realized, it was too late now. Slade had taken her innocence, and her heart as well!

He must have sensed her restlessness, because a deep voice suddenly rumbled against her hair, "Good morning, my little sea raven."

The familiar endearment sent a flutter coursing through her. But Bryony steeled herself against the confusing new emotions churning beneath the surface of her heart. She hastily sought to divert him.

"Slade." As she spoke his Christian name, she realized with another pang that it was the first time it had ever crossed her lips. She raised her head from his chest to look into his smoky green eyes.

" 'Tis an unusual name," she faltered.

Slade smiled at her as his fingers lazily toyed with her hair, raising and then letting the silky black strands rain down on her back again. "Aye. 'Twas my mother's maiden name before she wed my father. There was little else she could offer her youngest son."

Bryony dropped her gaze and absently began tracing the whorls of golden hair upon his chest. "How many siblings do you have?"

"Three brothers, though none of them are as comely as I." Slade grinned, secretly flattered by her curiosity. Few women had shown much interest in anything save his coffers before this.

Bryony sighed. "I could do with a few more of those myself—brothers, that is. They could help me hold onto Brendan's legacy."

A tense silence spoiled the moment, as Slade silently debated his next course. He didn't want to break the fragile new bond forming between them, nor destroy the tentative trust he thought might be growing in her eyes. But he also knew that Bryony must accept the facts. He could not let go of the land he had worked so hard to claim, nor could he free her in good conscience, until Brann O'Neill surrendered Clandeboye.

A moment later, Bryony sat up on her own accord, her eyes unreadably dark as she moved to get dressed. Slade scooted up to sit against the pillows, watching her pull on her undergarments with noticeably shaking fingers. As she fumbled with the white ribbons decorating her corset, he moved to intervene.

"Here. Let me." Without giving her a chance to demur, Slade's suntanned fingers reached out and fastened each tiny bow with leisurely skill.

Bryony wryly observed that Slade was certainly no stranger to women's clothing. But she kept silent, even when his hands paused and slid down to grasp her waist.

Without a single word, he pulled her into his arms and gave her a slow, lingering, good-morning kiss that raised gooseflesh on her arms. Bryony's arms went around Slade's neck, and she ran her fingers playfully through the red gold waves of his hair. Her response was unchecked and passionate, and drew an enthusiastic moan from him.

"Witch," he murmured, when they parted for breath, "keep that up and you'll be abed all day long!"

She laughed with soft delight, nuzzling his chin where golden hairs had begun to sprout. "You need a shave," Bryony informed him, and when Slade growled with mock outrage and pulled her back on the bed beside him, she didn't protest.

They didn't straggle from bed until early afternoon. By then, both agreed another bath was in order for each of them. Slade departed to his own unused room to see to the task. While he was gone and Bryony was soaking in the tub, a scratch at the door admitted Molly with another armload of clothes.

"Where do ye want 'em?" the redhead demanded, a twinge of envy in her tone.

Surprised, Bryony motioned to the bed, and Molly sniffed resentfully when she recognized a few stray strands of red gold hair upon the pillows. Without another word, the girl dumped the clothes in an unruly jumble on the bed and departed with a crisp bang of the door.

Bryony quickly finished with her bath in order to satisfy her curiosity. This time her new outfit was comprised of two pieces, a doublet-style bodice of dark blue velvet with full skirts of cerulean-blue silk. The petticoat, called a farthingale, spread the skirts in a shimmering circle, so the fine silver-leaf embroidery between the narrow folds could be admired.

Sheer silk stockings and heelless black leather shoes completed the outfit, and once again she was amazed to discover everything fit perfectly. There was even a matching velvet cape with a detachable French hood, if she wished to protect her face from the sun or male stares. Bryony set it aside, not ashamed of the fact her face was already sun-kissed a rich golden hue.

A short time later, Slade appeared at her door, freshly shaven, with his hair still damp and curling from the bath. Seeing Bryony clad in the outfit he had sent brought a twinkle to his green eyes, and a wide smile of approval.

"You do much justice to the tailor, sweetheart," he said, raising her hand and kissing it with a lingering emphasis. The gesture did not revolt Bryony as Lafleur's had; indeed, it sent shivers up her spine. Slade's gaze locked with hers, and his eyes blazed with passionate intent.

"Thank you for the two gowns," she said in a low voice. "They're both lovely. Faith, I must confess I've never had anything so fine."

He smiled. "There's no need to thank me, Bryony. As you already observed, I don't ill treat my captives."

She stiffened, and abruptly withdrew her hand. "Are you telling me nothing has changed?"

Slade sighed. "If you refer to my intentions to keep you in my custody until O'Neill can be persuaded to be reasonable, then nay, nothing has changed."

He saw her blue eyes darken to black a moment before she spun away from him, quivering with outrage.

"Reasonable!" she spat at the wall. "And I suppose you think that taking my virginity was only reasonable, as well!"

His hands firmly descended on her shaking shoulders, and whirled her back around.

"I never planned that," Slade countered. "Besides, you came willingly enough to my arms, Bryony! D'you intend to deny it now?"

"Aye," she cried, "I'll deny it, because you are nothing more than a lowly, despicable *Sassenach* brute! You never intended to let me go free, and yet you let me think otherwise!"

"Assume, not think!" Slade corrected her curtly. "Are you so harebrained a wench you can't even admit to your own foolish assumption?"

"Ohhh!"

Bryony reacted with fury, her hand flashing up to slap him. Slade deflected the blow, knocking aside her smaller wrist with his own. She clutched her throbbing wrist with her other hand and stared at him in anger and pain, as he continued speaking in a reasonable tone.

"I'm sorry, Bryony. Truly, I never meant to hurt you. Neither one of us could have predicted it, and it seems we both briefly lost our sensibilities. But no matter how many times I say I'm sorry, it won't bring back your innocence."

"And I suppose you consider me a fallen woman now?" she mockingly inquired.

"Don't put words in my mouth. I certainly never meant to

imply anything of the kind. No, you're not a fallen woman, not in my eyes."

"What about my future husband's?" she spat back.

Slade's eyes darkened. "That's unfair of you. I won't let you make me feel guilty, because I saw firsthand how you responded to me. You're a strong woman made for loving, Bryony O'Neill, though 'twill doubtless take a stronger man than me to make you accept that fact. Besides, I might remind you, you were ill inclined towards the notion of any husband *before* this happened."

"It's true enough I've of no mind yet to marry," Bryony muttered, not letting Slade see how deeply his words had wounded her. But what had she expected? A marriage proposal? She shook her head at her own stupid folly. Of course, he had only been using her. Last night had meant nothing more to Tanner than a moment's ease. Why, when she looked at the hard cold facts, she was no better than Molly, the tavern trull.

The new gown seemed to burn into her skin, as her mind digested the real meaning of his gifts. Slowly raising her gaze to meet his, Bryony stated softly but firmly, "I'll not be your leman, Tanner."

He sighed at her sudden reversion to formality. "I don't ever recall asking such a thing of you."

"How else might this be interpreted?" She crushed the silk skirts of the blue gown in her fists, and lifted them slightly in a challenging gesture.

" 'Tis exactly what it appears to be; a decent outfit, nothing more. When I said you were badly in need of a few lessons, that included lessons in dressing as a female."

Bryony's eyes sparkled dangerously. "I'll not be ordered about like one of your scurvy crew, Tanner!" She dropped the skirts of the gown as if they suddenly soiled her. "I want my old clothes back."

Slade sighed again. How quickly they had returned to angry confrontations. In that moment he realized the chasm between them was wider than ever before.

"I'm sorry, but it isn't possible." He knew the futility of arguing with Bryony, and spoke more sharply than he'd intended. "I'm afraid you have no choice but to accept my hospitality in this matter."

"As you accepted mine last night?" she bitterly replied, but before Slade could answer, she brushed past him and stormed down the stairs to break her fast alone.

Eight

Bryony stood at the *Silver Hart*'s rail, bleakly watching the Isle of Man receding in the ship's wake. Though they were getting underway at a late hour, the wind and tides were favorable enough.

Slade had hired on extra hands, and restocked plenty of provisions for the trip to England. He had crisply informed Bryony that he was taking her to London, where they would await Lafleur's return from Ireland. His tone implied the O'Neill had better be reasonable this time, if he wanted to see his daughter again.

Bryony didn't believe Slade Tanner would really hurt her. Humiliate her, aye, as he'd already done in good measure, but injure her—she shook her head at the thought.

The man simply didn't have it in him. She'd already overheard the new cabin boy exclaiming with amazement over the fact that Slade refused to physically punish his crew. She suspected the incident with the bosun Taylor was the closest Slade had ever come to losing control. And that was only because Taylor had been intent on killing her, and the captain couldn't lose such a valuable pawn.

Pawn. Aye, that was all she was to him, she bitterly reflected. Though Slade had brushed aside Bryony's warnings against using her in his negotiations with Brann, his motives were still unclear.

Bryony shivered when she considered the very real possibility that Slade would turn her over to the English authorities when they arrived in London. One word to the Tudor queen, and her life was forfeit!

Yet somehow she did not believe he was capable of such cruelty. Perhaps her foolish emotions clouded her judgment, and if that was the case, then she must harden her heart and somehow lull him into relaxing his guard.

With a deep breath, she considered the possibilities. Too quick a turnabout in her attitude would merely raise his suspicions. She couldn't hope to slip free, until fate put better cards into her hands. For the first time that day, her fingers sought out the raven amulet at her throat.

Simply touching the amulet calmed her jittery nerves and strengthened her resolve. She must never forget that she was descended from generations of proud Raven clansmen. They had faced down centuries of greedy Viking and *Sassenach* conquerors, and still managed to master the sea. No Englishman on this earth was a match for an O'Neill!

Slade glanced over at the young woman standing at the starboard rail. He wondered what wheels were spinning in that lovely head of hers. An icy spring wind billowed Bryony's full skirts, yet she wore no cape. Her black hair was neatly braided now, and glistened with bluish highlights under the sunlight. He felt a sharp twinge of regret, remembering the wondrous night they had shared. He would not surrender that precious memory for the world, but he knew what it had cost them both. He could offer her very little, least of all marriage.

As soon as the fleeting thought occurred to him, Slade shrugged it aside. It was futile to plan any relationship with a woman like Bryony O'Neill. She was not someone a respectable Englishman took to wife. Too many years of bitter conflict with the Irish had soured Queen Elizabeth's opinion of that silver-tongued race, and he knew it would be political suicide for him to publicly court any woman other than the one Bess had already chosen for him.

Slade chuckled to himself, vowing both his parents would roll over in their graves, if they had the slightest inkling their youngest son had taken a fancy to a proud Irish wench. His brother George had married a sassy Welsh lass named Dilys, and that had been trauma enough for one generation.

When his ship was finally smoothly underway, Slade felt confident enough to leave the navigation to his second in command. A short time later he saw Bryony leave the rail and move towards the cabin, and he moved to intercept her as she crossed the deck.

A stray strand of jet-colored hair had escaped her braid, and blew across her left cheek. He stopped himself from reaching out to tuck it back in place.

But Bryony noticed the aborted gesture, and her eyes widened in surprise.

"Aye?" she inquired, admittedly curious to know what was on his mind.

"Before we left the island, I asked again if there was any word of the *Alanna Colleen*. I thought you had a right to know . . . nobody has seen her since the storm."

She swallowed hard and nodded once, looking out over the frothing waves left in the *Silver Hart*'s wake.

"That doesn't necessarily mean anything," Slade added. "The Irish Sea is a large body of water, and she likely went north to safely harbor somewhere along Scotland's shores."

"To get her bearings, maybe, but O'Grady would have found some way to get word to me."

"You're forgetting he's under Diego's command now."

Bryony shook her head. "Isn't your man as faithful to you as O'Grady is to me? If they survived the storm, somehow they would have gotten word to us by now."

Slade had to admit she was probably right. Diego wouldn't have settled for a strange port, not unless the ship had sustained grievous damage from the typhoon.

"There's no point in worrying," he said. "After all, both are grown men capable of handling a crew. Time will tell what happened to them."

"And the children," she whispered, with a pang of regret.

"Once again I need remind you, Bryony, that was your folly, not mine. And thanks mainly to my generosity, at least they won't starve or die of thirst."

"Aye, how could I forget the kindly Captain Tanner?" Bryony snorted with disdain, and suddenly turned on him with blue fire in her eyes. "How considerate you are to us poor Irish wretches! And so concerned with our welfare that you even took to comforting me in the most intimate manner possible!"

"At least you acknowledge the fact that I comforted you," Slade retorted with equal sarcasm. "Though I did have quite a devil of a time getting you into my bed."

At the reminder of her fatal weakness, Bryony stiffened and moved to leave his side. But Slade seized her by the elbow, drawing her close and out of the view of the rest of the crew.

"I'm sorry," he said. "That was unfair of me."

Bryony had to admit it really wasn't, but remembering her vow to harden her heart towards this man, she tried not to soften at his words.

"I suppose we must make the best of things," was all she said. A glance upward through her lowered lashes revealed Slade's relieved expression.

"Aye, you're right. I'd like to patch things up between us, but I don't know where to begin."

Neither did she. Nothing would ever come of their relationship, she knew, and for that reason she would be far wiser to deal with Slade Tanner on an impersonal level.

"I've a terrible temper," she admitted, with a reluctance that was genuine enough. "I fear I don't take to confinement very well."

"Neither would I, I suppose, if the circumstances were reversed." Slade paused, looking down into her deep blue eyes. Sweet Jesu, she was so lovely, a woman spawned from wind and sun and sea. He wondered if it was even possible to capture such a wild heart, or if it would only destroy them both in the end.

Bryony suddenly leaned into him, the brisk wind whipping the folds of her gown around his legs. With a low moan, Slade gathered her into his arms, pleasantly surprised to find her lips warm and willing beneath his.

Though her mind screamed a silent warning, her heart refused to hear it. Bryony's traitorous body didn't differentiate between this moment and the previous night. When Slade released one hand from her waist to fumble behind him for the cabin latch, she didn't protest. Nor did she stop him as he led her to the bed, and gently divested her of her clothing. All reason fled when Slade joined her on the bed, cradling her in his arms.

"Is it so wrong of us to share love, Bryony?" he murmured against her mouth, and the question hung in the air while he sought the answer in her eyes.

"Nay," she finally whispered, and then, without further hesitation, began to return his kisses measure for measure. Her heart sang as the burning fire in her loins reached a point beyond pleasure. When they were joined as one again, Bryony felt a startling rightness that made her gasp. *'Tis like coming home,* she thought, while all her five senses spun in confusion and delight. She wanted to lie there all day with Slade, not just making love, but simply held against his strong warm body, where she felt so safe. His magical touch drove all reason from her mind.

Slade's own eyes were wide with wonder as he plunged deep into her honeyed core. Never before had he felt so intensely perfectly whole as a man. Every inch of his flesh was finely tuned to this woman he loved. Aye, he loved her! Against all rhyme and reason and hope. Bryony tasted like seasalt and sunshine, and as he rode the stormy sea of her loins, he raggedly exclaimed, "You were made for me, sweetheart!"

"Aye," she sobbed in return, clutching Slade's shoulders as he groaned and flooded her with his hot seed. Her heart surged with hope when he held her close and gently kissed her cheek.

"This is how I imagine it should be between man and wife,"

Slade whispered, and she thought she detected a wistful note to his words. Did he want to wed her? What would she say?

But he didn't speak again, simply pulled Bryony flush against his side. Then he began to breathe steadily, and, after some minutes had passed, she realized with a mixture of annoyance and amusement that he had fallen fast asleep.

"Land ho! Land ho!"

The deck bell was clanging excitedly, and the shouts of the crew awoke Bryony from her sweetly wistful dreams. She was not surprised to find the spot beside her empty and cold. Slade had already slipped away to his duties.

She sat up and stretched, smiling a little as she caught sight of her reflection in the pier glass across the cabin. She looked well rested and well loved, with rosy cheeks and an unfamiliar sparkle in her eyes. Was this how it felt to be in love? Bryony hugged her secret happiness to herself, savoring the rare moment of contentment before it vanished again.

How could she have ever dreamed up the notion of tricking Slade, simply in order to escape English justice? Their hearts and their fates were inexplicably intertwined now. All thoughts of escape had promptly fled, once he took her in his arms again. Theirs was a love which had already survived stormy seas; what more could life throw at them that they couldn't overcome together?

Eventually she rose and went in search of her clothes. But before she chose either gown, she paused to consider Slade's sea chest at the foot of the bed. Tightly bound with cracked leather straps, it looked old enough to contain a few interesting tidbits. She'd seen Slade pull a clean if wrinkled shirt from it earlier, and she circled it a few times now with a devilish smile on her lips.

So, Slade didn't care for her wearing snug breeches? Bryony suspected quite rightly it was not the breeches themselves, but rather the curves they revealed which distracted him.

With a mischievous little laugh, she settled down on the cabin floor and sat back on her knees, reaching out to unfasten the straps binding the trunk. She struggled briefly with the heavy lid before it toppled back with a solid *thunk.*

Tucking a strand of hair behind her ear, she leaned forward and peered inside the chest. Folded in one corner was a simple coat of black cloth with sleeves, a silver whistle and chain coiled upon it. On the other side was a dark blue velvet doublet which looked new. Peeking under the clothes, she found two pairs of long hose, one green and the other blue, a white fustian jerkin and matching frieze coat, two pairs of white hose, one pair of long white breeches, and a solid black frieze mantle.

She also found the shirts, two of fine Hollands and four coarser cotton ones. She chose one of the plain variety, embroidered only with simple black-work at the neck and wrists. Bryony slipped it over her head and discovered it fell almost to her knees. It smelled of leather from the chest and the mild tobacco Slade occasionally indulged in. She delighted in the feeling of his shirt against her bare skin.

She reached for the matching white breeches, but as she tugged them out, she dislodged something else hidden beneath the clothes. A metallic flash caught her eye, and she set the breeches aside for the moment. She reached in to pick up the oval silver frame that had slipped from its resting place. Turning it over, she felt a stab of searing pain in her chest.

It was a painted miniature of an angel-faced young woman, garbed in sky blue silk. The artist had captured an expression both sweet and serene, as well as the perfect blond ringlets cascading over a pair of flawless ivory shoulders. The woman's innocent smile only seemed to mock Bryony's sudden bitterness.

Turning the miniature over, she found some words scrawled in ink. They were so faint she had to carry the frame over to the cabin window, so the sunshine could reveal the painful truth. The delicately looped letters seemed to leap up at her.

My beloved Slade—I count the days till we are wed.

With a choked cry, Bryony almost hurled the miniature aside. Then she forced the dagger ever deeper into her heart by turning it over and staring at the woman.

She was very beautiful, Slade's betrothed. Unless the artist had been overly generous in his representation, this English lady was hardly a hair short of perfection. The jonquil-colored hair, the lush figure, all these were what Bryony had heard men desired most in a female. It was obvious, too, the young woman did not lack for a generous dowry, judging by her silk gown and the glittering jewels dripping from her swan-white neck.

Who was she? Slade's fiancée? A courtesan whose affections he dallied with as casually as he did hers? Or—Bryony's heart began to thud painfully in her chest—perhaps she already was his wife? *Slade Tanner belonged to another woman.* Whether the lady in question was his or not, he devotedly carried her miniature while at sea. What more proof did Bryony need of his true loyalties?

The cabin seemed to spin dizzily for a moment, as Bryony clutched the silver frame to her breast. When she heard Slade's voice outside the door, she snapped into action and rushed to restore the chest to order. All except for the miniature. It was small enough to conceal in a clenched fist, and this she did before she whirled about and sat down on the chest, seconds before the door swung open.

Slade strode in with a broad grin slashing his handsome face, and shut the door behind him.

"So," he chuckled, his green eyes widening a little with pleasure and approval as he noticed Bryony clad only in his oversized shirt, "I must admit, love, that particular outfit becomes you far more than it does me."

He didn't seem dismayed that she had obviously been riffling through his wardrobe. Was he hoping to brazen it out? She managed to inquire evenly enough, "Can I assume we're in sight of land?"

"Aye, less than a day now to the mouth of the Thames.

We've made good time with that west wind." Slade hesitated, finally sensing something amiss. There was no warm welcome in Bryony's face, no hint of the passionate lady who had shared his bed last night. Too late he saw the dangerous spark in her sea blue eyes, seconds before she raised her fist and thrust a familiar object into his line of vision.

"What am I to make of this, Tanner?" she challenged him in a deceptively soft voice.

"Bryony—" he began, taking a step toward her.

"Don't!" She brandished the miniature as if she were tempted to strike him with it. "I see you recognize this. Tell me she isn't your intended, Captain Tanner! Tell me you haven't betrayed us both."

There was a deafening silence. A muscle worked in Slade's cheek, but at last he ground out, "I cannot."

Bryony felt her heart shatter into tiny fragments. A part of her had still dared hope for a rational explanation, some reasonable excuse for his deceit. Crushed to the core, she nevertheless held her head high.

"Do . . . do you love her?" she managed to ask.

"Would it make any difference to you?"

There was a peculiarly hollow sound to Slade's voice, and a swift glance revealed his green eyes were dark with pain. While she wondered at the source of it, Bryony was too proud to pursue the topic further. His confession was enough. When she silently moved to place the oval frame on the table beside his bed, Slade intercepted her with an angry challenge.

"What the devil do you think you're doing?"

"She's the one who should be at your side each morn, not me." Bryony's voice shook with emotion, but she would not look at him.

"Sweet Jesu!" he snapped, snatching up the miniature and casually tossing it facedown upon the bed. "Spare me this little drama, Bryony! You're a grown woman and unworthy of this. Don't you realize if I'd wanted her bloody portrait there, I'd have put it there myself?"

Her throat burned with tears, but Bryony was fiercely resolved not to cry. Slade's words seemed to echo as if coming from a great distance, and her heart steeled itself against any more lies.

"You can't deny her existence," she whispered at last. "She's standing right here between us at this very moment."

Slade gazed at Bryony, as he groped for an explanation, wanting to soothe away the hurt he had caused her . . . had caused them both. But there was nothing he could say which would ease the brutal sting of this discovery. Had he been able to deny it all, he would have. But he had too much respect for Bryony to resort to such lowly tactics. The truth might be crueler, but it was always best.

"Aye," he finally admitted. "Gillian is my betrothed."

There was no need to explain the unusual circumstances, which had led him down that path. Suffice to say he could not free himself of the lady, and at that bitter realization, it seemed as if Gillian's soft mocking laughter suddenly rang throughout the cabin. Aye, Bryony was right, the woman was standing there between them right now, taunting Slade that he would never be free of her. For Gillian Lovelle was the queen's ward, and to cross her was to cross the mighty Elizabeth Tudor herself.

Meeooww . . .

A faint, plaintive yowl distracted Bryony from her vigil at the ship's rail. She blinked into the brisk wind, wondering if she'd only imagined the noise. When the feline cry came again, she turned her head and looked around the deck for the source.

But the decks were mostly empty, save for the few hands swarming over the lines and trimming the sail, as they headed slowly toward the Thames. After she had confronted Slade in his cabin, he had left, and Bryony had dressed in her blue dress, then instinctively sought the comfort of the sea. But the open waters were receding behind them now, as they entered the narrow Strait of Dover. She felt suddenly claustrophobic, hemmed in on either side by the enemy, and her grip tightened on the railing in a futile search for an outlet for her emotions.

Meeeooowww . . .

The cat's cries were increasing in desperation now, and Bryony heard a flurry of claws raking wood. It reflected her own mood. She decided to distract herself by going in search of the other equally miserable prisoner.

The most obvious place to search was the jumble of loose boards piled and whip-tied near the main mast. The boards were kept mostly for repairs, though in harsher days one might serve as a walking plank in a pinch. Bryony ducked under the parrel and called softly for the cat. The mournful wails abruptly ceased, and she heard the boards rattle as the animal tried once again to thrust free of its makeshift jail.

When she saw a flash of tawny fur, Bryony grinned in triumph and pried two boards slightly apart to create a means of escape. Immediately, a huge orange cat squirmed free of its unhappy confinement, plopped down on one of the planks, and began to fiercely groom its dusty hindquarters.

"That's my thanks, I suppose," Bryony said, chuckling as she picked up the indignant cat. It was a homely thing, a tiger-striped tabby with an oversized head, short muscular body, and a stub of a tail. But its purr was gratifyingly loud, and rumbled against her chest as she cradled it in her arms.

"Milady?"

A hushed young voice startled Bryony, and she glanced down to see Slade's new cabin boy, a lad of about ten, who was nervously twisting a mariner's cap in his hands.

"Milady," he began again, pausing to clear his throat. He was nearly quaking in his too large boots. "I'm mighty obliged that ye rescued Lord Rumple fer me."

"He's your cat?" Bryony smiled at the boy, as she scratched the tabby behind the ears. "That explains why I haven't seen him before. You signed on at Man, didn't you?"

The boy nodded. “And I couldn’t bear to leave ol’ Rumple behind. ’E’s all the family I got now.”

“Why do you call him Lord Rumple?”

“Oh, ’cause of his rump tail, I reckon. And ’e’s allus carried ’imself so ’igh and mighty. Me mum named ’im before she died. But ’e’s no spring chicken, milady. Nigh ten years old, by me own reckonin’.”

Bryony gently handed Lord Rumple over to his owner. She saw love in the boy’s eyes, as he clutched the mangy old tom to his chest.

“What’s your name?” she asked the lad, impulsively reaching out to ruffle his red hair, as she often did the youths under her own command. When he cringed at the unfamiliar gesture, she laughed. “God’s bones, laddie, but I won’t bite! I prefer my meat well cooked first.”

He blushed. “Name’s Wat, milady. Only they all calls me Rusty, ’cause of me red hair.” He grinned an engaging gap-toothed smile at her then, encouraged by her kindness.

Bryony knelt and said, “Well, Rusty, I predict you’ll make a fine deckhand. Maybe even a captain of your own vessel someday. Just remember, as long as you run a tight ship and keep light of spirit, you’ll find nothing can sink you.”

Rusty gave her a serious nod, his gray eyes thoughtful. When Bryony rose, she found that Slade was also there.

“ ’Tis very good advice,” Slade said softly. “But I find that advice best comes from one who follows it, don’t you?”

His dark green eyes challenged her, and Bryony felt a flush of rage and then cool resolve settle over her.

“Aye,” she agreed, meeting his steady gaze with her own. “I’ll work on being more lighthearted, Captain, if you’ll attempt to run a tight ship from now on. Is it agreed?”

The double meaning of her words was obviously not lost on him, for Slade’s mouth tightened. He curtly addressed young Rusty instead. “I thought I told you to leave that old moggie behind.”

The boy's ears reddened with guilt. "Aye, Cap'n. But e's a good mouser, and won't trouble ye none."

"Let the lad keep his pet," Bryony put in.

Slade wondered at the sudden fierceness to her tone, but gave a resigned shrug.

"Just so long as he pulls his weight," he gruffly replied. "Now get along to work, lad. Time's a wasting."

"Aye, sir. Thank ye, sir." Rusty flushed with relief, before he ducked past Bryony and scooted off with the cat protectively clutched under one arm.

Slade took a step closer to Bryony and saw her stiffen. But there was nowhere for her to flee, so she bravely faced him down.

She groped for words. "I assume I'll be transferred into protective custody once we reach shore."

"Aye," Slade replied. "Mine."

Bryony looked startled.

"I haven't quite decided what to do with you yet," he admitted.

"And I suppose freedom is out of the question?"

"It is until Brann O'Neill comes around to my way of thinking." Slade paused, then added abruptly, "I'm sorry, Bryony. Sorry that you had to get tangled up in all this."

Was he also sorry for the brief, magical moments they had shared? She shook her head, cutting off the wistful thoughts before they began. She wouldn't gain anything by ruminating on her loss. All she could do was acknowledge the pain and go on.

"How long before Lafleur returns from Ireland?" she asked him in a resigned tone.

"A few weeks, I imagine. In the meantime, you needn't worry about being mistreated. Nothing will change in that regard."

Bryony gave a short laugh. But there was no humor in it.

"Oh, I daresay you've already done your worst, Captain Tanner." The beautiful blue eyes fixed on Slade were now remote, as if Bryony gazed right through him. He felt a corresponding pain so keen it knifed his heart before he knew it.

He realized there would be no easy amends made with this rare woman. Perhaps he was a fool to even try. But his heart—or more likely his masculine ego—still insisted that Bryony O'Neill was his woman, that she always would be a part of him—whether she liked it or not.

He asked her quietly, "I trust there will be no scenes on shore?"

"If you're referring to female hysterics, rest assured I'll not lower myself to such theatrics," she retorted. "I have no desire to call attention to myself, especially dressed like this." She indicated the blue gown she was wearing, the soft folds of which only emphasized the femininity she was still trying so hard to deny.

"Why are you ashamed of being a woman, Bryony?" Slade demanded.

She looked at him directly then, and too late he saw the blue fire smoldering in her eyes.

"After the past few days, Tanner," she replied, with a slow and bitter emphasis, "d'you really have to wonder?"

Nine

When he heard rumor that the *Silver Hart* was back in port, Christopher Tanner saddled his fastest horse, a high-spirited blood bay named Queen's Folly, and left Whitehall at a full gallop.

Kit didn't even stop to retrieve his beaver hat, when a sudden gust of wind sent it spinning from his auburn head. With a rueful glance over his shoulder, he saw a handful of street urchins explode into a violent quarrel over possession of his lost hat.

Reaching the wharf, he drew Queen's Folly down to a brisk trot that still sent sailors diving out of the way. For a moment, Kit Tanner felt young again, not like the jaded court dandy he had become. He even envied his little brother the cheeky catcalls from admiring maids along the row, mistaking him for Slade.

"Slade, luv, stop an' visit a bit!"

"Don't ye 'ave a kiss fer yer sweet Catlin today?"

With a good-natured grin, Kit spared a passing wave for the girls, indicating he couldn't spare the time. When he finally drew his fractious steed to a prancing halt on the docks, he was relieved to discover he hadn't missed Slade's arrival after all.

Standing at the *Silver Hart*'s rail, Bryony gazed down on the docks and marvelled on the unlikely coincidence. Slade must have a twin, as did she. But when the other man leaped down from his saddle and stood waiting with reins in hand,

Bryony saw he was half a head shorter than the captain, and his hair was a truer red. Still, he cut quite a dashing figure, garbed in a forest green doublet and black velvet breeches, with green Venetian hose clinging to his sturdy legs.

Bryony turned to see that Slade had already noticed the other man, and he crossed the deck to her side in several brisk strides.

"Who is he?" she asked, gesturing toward the red-haired man standing on the dock.

"My brother," he answered. She wondered at the tight lines near Slade's mouth.

"Best stay in the cabin for now," Slade said to her.

"Very wise of you, I'm sure. We can't have your betrothed hearing rumor of the captain's new doxy!"

Slade shot her a dark look before he turned and called out for the crew to lower a longboat. Bryony sighed, regretting she'd let her temper get the best of her.

Shaking her head in frustration, she left for the cabin, but not before Kit Tanner had already noticed the slender, dark-haired young woman on his brother's ship. His brow furrowed thoughtfully, but he was not one to jump to conclusions. He waited until Slade rowed in to meet him, and then helped his brother secure the boat to the dock.

"Thank God you're back," Kit began without preamble.

"What's wrong? Where's Gillian?" Slade quickly turned and scouted the milling sea of bodies surrounding them, somehow not surprised to discover his betrothed was absent. Gillian had never before shown any interest in his comings or goings during their acquaintance, so there was no reason she should start now.

Still, it was a tiny stab in Slade's heart each time he came home and the docks were filled with loving wives and devoted fiancees, all eagerly waiting to embrace their men. There was never anyone there for him, and for the first time he consciously resented that fact.

For some reason, Kit looked uncomfortable at the mention

of Gillian. "I'm sorry, Slade. She said she wasn't feeling well. I invited her to come along, but you know how women can be sometimes."

"Indeed. I know only too well."

Kit cleared his throat. "I didn't intend to waylay you like this, little brother. But this is important. The queen's asking for you."

"Why?" Slade frowned. "Bess knew I'd be gone a month or more. Don't tell me my title to Irish lands has already been revoked!"

Kit shook his head. "I don't know. But whatever the problem is, Bess is fit to be tied. You know she's usually cordial enough with me. But when she heard your ship had been sighted, she said to me, "Master Tanner, if you know what's good for you, you'll find that scoundrel brother of yours and bring him here right quick!' ""

"God's blood!" Slade swore explosively. "That's all I need right now." He gestured to his travel-soiled clothes. "Bess'll be even less amused by my appearance."

Kit suddenly grinned. "Don't worry, I already thought of that myself." He moved to pat the bulging saddlebags on his horse's saddle. "I've brought along some finery from my own court wardrobe. Mind you, the fit might be a bit snug, but it should squeak you through the boundaries of acceptability this time."

"Bless you, Kit," Slade said absently, and Kit caught the worried glance he tossed back at his ship.

"Who is she?" Kit asked his brother.

Slade hesitated. "An Irish rebel under arrest in the name of England."

"Ah." Kit nodded a bit too knowingly for Slade's liking.

"Don't 'ah' me. I'm only seeing to her welfare, until I get my lands back. She's the ornery cub of the same stubborn Irishman who refuses to relinquish Clandeboye."

"I see," Kit said. But he wondered why Slade sounded so defensive, and why the last look he gave his ship before they left for Whitehall, was one which was curiously close to longing.

Slade held his position before his monarch with uncommon grace and stamina for several long minutes, before she deigned to speak.

"La, Captain Tanner, but you give an elegant leg," Elizabeth Tudor said gruffly, admiring the golden-haired man kneeling at her feet.

"Doesn't he, Dudley?" The queen turned slightly and addressed her favorite, seated on a lesser chair to her right. The affirmative noise made by the Earl of Leicester was all she seemed to expect.

"You may rise," she granted at last, and Slade rose to his full height to regard the woman on the throne. Though she was still relatively young, the Virgin Queen's manner of dress and formal coiffure better resembled those of an aging matron. Not for Elizabeth the gay bright colors favored by her ladies-in-waiting, nor did a single lighthearted frill or flounce lurk upon her person today.

Knowing her as he did, Slade recognized the queen's melancholy mood by her choice of attire. Elizabeth was clad head to toe in somber gray taffeta paned with black, the gown open in front to reveal a bejeweled stomacher strewn with onyx and tiny diamonds. Her ginger-colored hair was parted in the center, offset on either side by seed pearls woven through the strands. Fastened to her small ears were her famous pearl teardrop-shaped earbobs. Around her neck, long ropes of matching pearls and a large golden crucifix hung to her waist. The latter she twisted in her lightly freckled hands as she spoke.

"I like this not," Elizabeth said, meeting Slade's steady gaze with her sharp gray one. "You have always been one of my favorites, and it pains me greatly to be forced to summon you here."

She sighed then, glancing to Robert Dudley at her side. "I

think, Robin, that what passes here today in these chambers is meant for my ears alone."

With only a flicker in his dark eyes to betray his disappointment, the earl rose and graciously bowed out of the room, leaving the Tudor regent alone in the chamber with Slade.

"Help me up," Elizabeth said, impatiently motioning to Slade, who quickly moved to assist her to her feet. The queen's heavy ornate gown with its huge puffed sleeves and voluminous skirts seemed far more of a penance than a pleasure, and Slade dared make such a remark as the two crossed into an adjoining chamber arm in arm.

Unexpectedly, Elizabeth laughed. "Now you see what we ladies must go through to please our menfolk! Have you much sympathy for us, Captain Tanner?"

"Madam, I have a great deal of sympathy for one who bears so heavy a cross as you," he replied seriously.

The queen sobered, pausing to blink back the mist in her eyes. "Why, Slade, that is a kindness indeed coming from a man. I may call you by your Christian name, mayn't I? I still remember your dear mother with such fondness."

" 'Twas her lifelong wish to please you, Your Majesty, even as it is now mine."

Elizabeth playfully poked at his arm with a bejeweled finger. "La! A clever-tongued courtier like my Kit, when it warrants. We could use you here at Whitehall, Captain. Things have been so impossibly dull of late."

Slade smiled. "I think not, Your Majesty. You would doubtless quickly tire of seeing the longing in my eyes whenever I caught a whiff of the sea."

Elizabeth chuckled at the truth of that remark. She knew the saltwater ran thick in this handsome Tanner's blood.

"Then we must be content with dear Kit. He is a winsome scoundrel, that red-haired brother of yours. Too sad entirely that he wed such a sour wench."

Slade's eyebrows rose at the unexpected mention of his sister-in-law, Elspeth. But he could not deny Kit's wife had all the charms of the proverbial viper. He'd always wondered what his brother had seen in the Cornish-bred virago, when he'd wed her eight years ago.

It seemed Elizabeth Tudor read his mind. "Think you I cannot spot such an ill match from a distance? Our Kit was meant to have a spirited filly, not that sullen nag he is saddled with." She sniffed a little sharply. "Other men, though, know not what good fortune they have, and must needs be reminded of it at times."

Suddenly Slade knew the true purpose of this visit. His heart plummeted, even as he carefully replied, "Sometimes what seems bliss on the surface, might be peeled back to expose a black festering beneath."

Elizabeth halted and withdrew her arm from his, turning to face him directly. She was tall for a woman, and unexpectedly reminded him of Bryony, when he saw the fire in her gray eyes. There was no quarter in her voice, when she said sternly, "My dear foolish Slade, I do hope you have a very good excuse for deserting Gillian these past weeks."

Knowing Gillian was one of the queen's favorite wards, Slade trod cautiously. "Surely your Majesty is aware we have had our differences lately."

His red herring did not work. Elizabeth Tudor was too intent on her cause to be distracted from her course now. She raised her chin and stated coolly, "Which is perfectly understandable, given the nature of your business for the Crown, and Gillian's position in my court. 'Tis only natural that a young couple might drift apart under such circumstances. That is why the Crown is prepared to grant you a rare boon, one which will doubtless impress upon the both of you the wisdom of wedding soon."

Slade could hardly miss the warning in her tone. He stayed wisely silent, as Elizabeth continued.

"Gillian informs us that you are restless, Slade, not having a home of your own. I confess I had forgotten you were a youngest son, and left landless upon the baron's death. I fear the Crown has been selfishly using you for its own ends at sea, where you have certainly done us an excellent turn. Alas, I am given to regrets now, for I see your prolonged absence has broken my poor Gillian's heart."

Slade quickly swallowed a laugh. This was no moment for levity, no matter how absurd the queen's assumptions.

"So," Elizabeth continued in a grandiose vein, "I had Cecil search the Crown's vast holdings for a small parcel of land fit for a young couple in love. He offered up several choices, and at once I knew which would suit." She paused a moment to build the appropriate drama. "Something rather secluded, situated some distance from the tiresome stir and intrigue of Court. And something very suitable for children."

Slade felt his throat tightening, as if an invisible noose had just dropped around it. "Where, Your Majesty?"

"Dovehaven, in Kent." The queen's benevolent smile widened on him. " 'Tis not far from the quaint village of Canterbury, with Deal Castle and your beloved sea just over the next rise. We knew you should be pleased with our decision, dear Slade."

Should, not would, Slade wryly noted. With barely suppressed sarcasm, he inquired, "And when are we to depart for this little paradise, Your Majesty?"

With a sharp glance for his impudence, Elizabeth mused, "Gillian has so prettily begged to stay through the Season, that I could not turn her out. A Michaelmas wedding would be most charming, I think."

Slade debated whether or not to reveal the truth of Gillian's perfidy, but he realized with a sinking heart that his regent would probably not believe him. He cursed his own foolishness in becoming enamored of Elizabeth Tudor's ward during the previous Season.

Nobody could deny Gillian Lovelle was a stunningly beautiful creature, an icy pale blonde whose petite form gave her the illusion of fragility. Half-French, Gillian's charm came as easily to her as her beauty. Her appearance roused the natural male instinct to protect, and Slade had been no exception. It was her uncommon beauty which had, unfortunately, led to his present dilemma.

Gilly had been staying with a cousin at Court, when she overheard talk of an eligible, well-heeled baron. As it so happened, Slade's older brother, George, had been the topic of conversation, but Gillian had misunderstood. Upon meeting Slade, dashingly attired and obviously in Her Majesty's favor, she assumed he was the Tanner who was the rumored catch of the year.

Somewhat naive in the ways of Court, Slade had been awed that such a beauty even deigned to speak to him, let alone openly pursue his affections. It was only after their engagement was securely in place, and George had wed his Welsh Dilys, that Gillian finally learned the ghastly truth; Slade was a mere captain, nothing more, and not even destined for a small knighthood.

Furious, Gillian had shrieked all sorts of ugly things at Slade, accusing him of lying to her. It had taken all of his willpower not to throttle the greedy little bitch, especially when Gillian threatened to ruin his position with Elizabeth, if he did not quickly better his prospects in order to support her lavish lifestyle at Court.

However, after some swift calculations, Gillian had decided to wed Slade anyway. He was one of Bess's favorites, and hence might eventually come into a fortune or a title. The queen was also pestering her to marry, as she was nearing two and twenty. Since Gillian was an orphan, and her godmother the Queen of England, one in her precarious position did not dare disobey.

Long ago Slade had learned a bitter truth himself; Gilly had dozens of lovers in the Tudor Court, and she had apparently decided that an absent husband would be a great convenience. When he first heard the truth of it from her own lips, he was hurt and furious. Now he was numb and coldly resolved.

"Your Majesty," Slade said, even though he was aware the

queen's statement was final, "what of my lands recently granted in Ireland? What if I should wish to settle there instead?"

"In memory of your dear mother, Slade, I shall pretend I did not hear that last question," Elizabeth Tudor replied somewhat pompously, choosing a fig from a ornate silver bowl set upon a nearby table. Then he listened incredulously as she proceeded to tell him what might happen, should he fail to please her in this one "minor request."

Slade could not miss the distinct warning in Elizabeth's tone, nor her abrupt dismissal of him a few minutes later. With his expression carefully neutral to mask his deepening anger and despair, he finally bowed out of the chamber.

"Well?" Kit fell into pace beside his younger brother, forced to lapse into a trot in order to keep up with Slade's long furious strides down the hall.

"That little bitch!" was all Slade said, smacking his right fist into his palm. "Heaven help Gillian now!" He seemed barely aware of Kit tugging at his sleeve.

"Sweet Jesu, what happened back there?"

Slade suddenly stopped and turned to face his brother. His green eyes were bleak as he snapped, "Bess has suspended my charter. She won't renew it 'til I'm hobbled in matrimony to Gillian!"

"God's blood," Kit breathed, glancing about to be certain no one was listening. Whitehall was notorious for its spies. "Gillian obviously put the idea to Bess herself." At Slade's curt nod of agreement, Kit dared to ask the obvious. "But why?"

"Why d'you think, Brother? Gilly's bored with playing the court whore for now, and Bess is prodding her to marry. Gilly's also looking to punish me for leaving her without a word. She's always threatened to make me pay for allegedly tricking her into our betrothal. She's finally found a way to do it."

"But marriage? Gillian doesn't strike me as the sort to ever settle down."

Hollow laughter escaped Slade's lips. "Who said she has any intention of settling down? I'm merely a prop who'll offer Gilly the respectability she craves, and the freedom of a married woman." He paused, then added in a soft dangerous vein, "But that day will never come, Kit. I swear it."

Kit didn't quite know what to say, but he knew he didn't like exchanging confidences in the open halls. Taking Slade by the arm, he said, "Come on. Let's get you out of that ridiculous garb. You look like a damned peacock, and I confess it makes me uncomfortable."

Slade allowed himself to be led away, still too dazed and furious to demur. He didn't know how Kit managed to find his way down all the endless halls and multiple stairways, but finally they arrived at Kit's apartment, where they might be safely sealed away from prying eyes and ears.

While Kit dismissed his manservant and threw the bolt on the door, Slade collapsed into a thickly cushioned, somewhat worn velvet chair. Immediately he yanked off the too small shoes he had borrowed from his brother, then tore off the goffered lace ruff from about his neck. The tailored violet trunkhose, doublet, and plum-colored leather jerkin soon lay in a colorful heap along with the rest of the court frippery. Slade quickly slipped back into his own dirty but comfortable clothing, and let loose a gusty sigh.

"Kit, how can you stand it here at court? Mincing 'round like some addlepated popinjay, catering to that Tudor wench's every whim?"

Kit quickly raised a finger to his lips. "The walls here are thin, Slade. Be careful what you say. Men have been executed for far less in these times."

Slade gave a careless snort. "Nothing could be more dangerous than being forced to wed a snake named Gillian Lovelle. Damme! Why didn't I tell Bess the truth about the faithless jade?"

"Because you had no choice," Kit said, moving to pour them both generous goblets of a warm golden brandy. Handing one to Slade, he perched on the matching chair facing his younger brother. "Y'know Bess wouldn't have believed you. Gilly's the daughter of her girlhood friend, Catherine Montrossy, and that French viscount. Before their deaths, she promised to see to their daughter's welfare."

"Aye, Bess plays the dutiful godmother," Slade growled, "but I'd as lief she knew the truth about that little viper she so recklessly cradles to her breast!"

Kit sighed and took a sip of brandy. "Don't waste your breath. Bess isn't disposed to hearing any ill in regards to Gillian. She's dismissed two chambermaids already for spreading rumors of Gilly's evening entertainments. Y'know how strict Bess is with her wards. Admitting Gilly has found a way around her would be admitting to her own failure as the girl's guardian."

"And all the more reason for Bess to be so insistent that Gillian weds this year," Slade muttered.

"Exactly. As a married woman, Gilly becomes somebody else's problem, and Bess can convince herself in good conscience that she fulfilled her dying friend's last wish."

"Then 'twould appear I'm expendable," Slade said dryly, twirling the stem of the goblet in his hand before he tossed back the last of his brandy.

"Oh, I don't doubt Bess is genuinely fond of you, little brother, but she's a shrewd woman with a clear view to her own comforts. Politics take precedence over everything else in her book." Kit gestured somewhat ruefully at the small, shabby chamber he occupied. It was barely adequate for one person at court, but he knew Elizabeth had assigned it to him on purpose, intending to discourage his wife from accompanying him to Whitehall.

The queen needn't have worried. Of plain Cornish stock, his primly religious wife, Elspeth, never attended Whitehall with Kit, because she disapproved of what she termed the wasteful frivolity of the Tudor court, and also because Bess openly snubbed her. Elspeth Tanner had never made any attempt to disguise the fact that she despised their proud queen. For once, Kit was inclined to agree with his wife.

"I'm trapped," Slade said unhappily. "Trapped in London now for God knows how long. Unless Bess decides to be merciful, or Gillian changes her mind. What d'you think of my chances, Kit?"

"Not good," his brother admitted. Then Kit asked, "Where are you two supposed to reside after the wedding?"

"That's the richest part of all this. After these many years, Bess has finally granted my petition for land, on the condition that I take Gillian off her hands."

"I thought you desired land at any price," Kit mischievously reminded his brother.

"Did I really say that? Then the devil himself must be laughing at my predicament now. But mark my words, Kit, I'm not surrendering my ship. After all's said and done, at least the *Silver Hart* is still mine."

"You don't dare leave London now," Kit said with some alarm.

"Nay, I realize 'twould only bring disaster down on all our heads. But at least there's nothing to stop me from getting drunk on this woefully dark day!"

Kit took the cue to fill up Slade's goblet again, then settled back in the chair across from his brother. After a brief silence, he inquired, "What about the girl on your ship?"

"Bryony?" Slade moodily contemplated the golden liqueur through the thick crystal glass. "Aye, there's that little burr under my saddle, as well. I suppose she can stay where she is for now."

"I don't think that's such a good idea. Bess's spies will likely be watching you very closely over the next few weeks."

Slade exploded. "Why should the queen care if I've one Irishwoman on my ship, when Gilly's got a dozen bloody courtiers lining her bed?"

"Think, little brother," Kit warned him. "Passion can't overrule your common sense now. Bess is kindly disposed to Gillian, and no matter what happens, she won't believe the worst of the wench. And if Gilly hears rumors you've another female aboard your ship . . ."

"God's bones," Slade groaned, smacking his fist into his forehead. "You're right. There's no telling what the little bitch would do then."

"The girl can stay at Ambergate," Kit promptly suggested. "We'll say she's a distant Irish cousin of the Tanners."

"What will Elspeth think of that unlikely story?"

"Don't worry about my wife. Gillian is the one we need to be concerned with, in the event she finds out about the girl."

Slade gave a low sigh of surrender. "You're right, Kit. We'll have to be very careful. I can't risk Gilly exercising her twisted brand of revenge on another innocent party."

Out on the ship, another day slowly dawned, and Bryony awoke to find herself alone in the cabin. Slade had not returned for the night after departing with his brother. She didn't go hungry, however, for she was shyly attended to by the devoted cabin boy, Rusty. Saving Lord Rumple had obviously placed her high on Rusty's list of priorities.

Bryony noticed that the rest of the crew paid her scant attention during Slade's absence. What Bryony did not know was that Slade had threatened his crew with dire consequences should anything happen to her. He was accustomed to being obeyed, and the men knew his threats were valid ones. Henceforth, they avoided their Irish prisoner like the plague.

Bryony felt acutely self-conscious when she dressed in the blue gown and appeared on deck early that morning. She couldn't help but notice that the skeleton crew Slade had assigned to guard her in his absence made a point of refusing to speak or look at her. Was she so homely then, that even crusty sailors missing ears and teeth could hardly bear to glance at her?

She walked to the railing and concentrated fiercely upon the distant horizon. She felt something warm threading past her ankles, and chuckled to find Lord Rumple leaving great clumps of loose fur on her dark blue skirts. Bryony picked up the orange tomcat and cradled him to her breast.

"Poor old moggie," she said, noticing both his ears were torn and one was even missing a notch. "So you've sought out a kindred spirit, then? Ah, milord Rumple, I fear we're both doomed to be sad misfits in this quarter of the world."

Suddenly Bryony felt a hand touch her hair from behind, and she spun around with the cat clutched defensively in her arms.

"Slade!" She hadn't meant to sound glad to see him, but the relief in her voice was obvious to them both. Lord Rumple struggled unhappily to be free, for the old tom gave affection on his own terms, and Bryony absently deposited him back on the deck.

Slade reached out and wiped a betraying teardrop from her cheek. "Is this for me?" he asked her.

"Nay," she quickly lied. " 'Tis only the wind."

"Did you miss me?" he persisted playfully.

Bryony shook her head. Slade only laughed, and she thought with a pang of fresh pain that he had never looked more handsome to her. Simply clad in black canvas breeches and a white linen shirt with full sleeves, a silver scabbard buckled to his narrow waist, he cut a dashing figure.

"I'm glad you're on deck," he said to Bryony. "There's someone I want you to meet."

Who? Your betrothed? Bryony almost asked, but bit her tongue at the last moment. Slade led her to the foredeck, where the red-haired man she had seen the day before awaited them with a plumed hat in hand.

"Bryony O'Neill, I'd like you to meet my older brother, Christopher Tanner."

" 'Tis my distinct pleasure," the other man said, bowing low from the waist and sweeping his hat in an exaggerated gesture. His twinkling green eyes immediately put her at ease.

"Please call me Kit," he invited Bryony as he straightened and replaced his hat on his head. "Everyone does." Kit turned to Slade and exclaimed in a mock Scot's accent, "Fie, brother, ye never said she was such a bonny lass. No wonder yer so intent on hidin' her away!"

"Kit has a devilish sense of humor," Slade muttered, but Bryony could see the genuine fondness in his eyes for his irrepressible older sibling. "He's also agreed to help me out. 'Tis obvious to us both that a ship's cabin is no place for a lady, and Kit's kindly offered the creature comforts of his home to you until the—ah—little matter between the O'Neill and me is finally settled."

"I see," Bryony said, but she didn't.

"You'll be far more comfortable at Ambergate," Kit put in. "Especially with Elspeth for company."

"Elspeth is Kit's wife," Slade explained, seeing the shadow slowly darkening Bryony's blue eyes. "They also have three beautiful little girls."

"How long will I be staying there?" Bryony quietly asked.

Slade exchanged a glance with his brother. "Until Lafleur returns," he said.

"That could be weeks. Surely I'll overstay my welcome."

Slade sighed with frustration, sensing the tension in the air. "I'm sorry, Bryony, but there really isn't any other choice."

"I see," she said again. And this time, she did.

"Well." Kit cleared his throat. "I imagine we'd best be on our way. Elspeth will be growing worried."

"I'll have one of the crew bring your things later," Slade told Bryony. He didn't bother to tell her what things he meant, as her only other possession was the second dress he had bought for her on Mann.

"You're not coming with us?" The words escaped her lips before she could stop them.

"I'm afraid I have business to attend to on the ship."

"Very well," Bryony said, accepting Kit's arm without a single word of farewell. For all she knew, this was goodbye forever. As Kit escorted her to where a longboat awaited to take them to shore, she neither knew nor asked if she would ever see Slade Tanner again.

Ten

Kit Tanner hitched his blood bay gelding to the rear of a rented coach, so he and Bryony might journey to Ambergate in privacy and style. Bryony had never seen such a fine vehicle before; the plush velvet seats and elegantly scrolled interior astounded her. Was there no limit to luxury in the Tudor realm? She saw, too, that the houses they passed on the way to the Tanner residence were even finer than those she had glimpsed earlier along the Thames.

Other coaches passed them along the Strand, many crested with gold and coats of arms. At one point, Bryony was aware of openly gawking, but she couldn't help it. She felt like a country bumpkin come to the big city, and her eyes were wide with wonder as she peered out of the coach. Kit was a charming guide and pointed out many of the landmarks they passed, restraining his own amusement at her childlike enthusiasm.

Though he shared his countrymen's cynical opinion of the Irish, Kit had to reconsider as he listened to Bryony's comments, delivered in that enchantingly musical lilt of hers.

"Look!" she cried, pointing to an especially ornate coach rolling slowly past them in the opposite direction. Her eyes widened further with excitement. "Ohhh, surely that must be someone of great importance!"

Kit glanced at the other coach and gave a little chuckle. "Faith, no, that's merely the official Court painter, Nicholas Hilliard, on his rounds. He's made a tidy profit since his success with his portrait of Her Majesty. To have a Hilliard in one's home is to house a masterpiece." He grinned at Bryony's surprise. "But 'tis also rumored Master Hilliard takes a secret delight in showing up his artistic rival, Isaac Oliver. The two men maintain quite a lively competition at Court."

Bryony's smile faded as she remembered the miniature of Gillian Lovelle she had found hidden in Slade's trunk. Which of the two masters had had the honor of trying to capture that young woman's exquisite beauty in oils?

She felt the coach turn and tilt slightly on its springs as if ascending a drive, and Kit suddenly distracted her by gesturing out the window. "Here we are, m'dear. Welcome to Ambergate."

Bryony peered through the glass at the modest but stately white mansion situated atop a grassy knoll. Six blond limestone columns at the front of the house rose up to meet a gently sloped red roof. Long rectangular windows overlooked a verdant expanse of grass and carefully cultivated rosebeds. She spied a gate at the top of the hill, and when the coach paused before it, she noticed the curious golden stones studding the limestone pillars.

"Those are ancient fossils, insects and flowers and such, preserved in amber," Kit explained. " 'Tis how the house got its name."

"What a lovely home you have, Kit."

He beamed with pleasure at her remark. He was proud of Ambergate, which though not on the scale of many grand Tudor manor houses of the day, was a dainty monument to his mother's memory and his own favorite residence.

"Do you truly like it, Bryony?" he asked her. By mutual if silent accord, they had already advanced to a first-name basis during the journey from Town.

"Aye, Kit, I can see why you're loath to leave it for even a day," she declared.

"The queen herself even picnicked here once," Kit said proudly.

Bryony murmured an appropriate comment as the coach passed through the gates and came to a rolling stop. Then Kit moved to exit the vehicle and assist her down. As they alighted from the coach, a pair of little girls who had been playing on the vast lawn came dashing pell-mell toward them with delighted shrieks.

"Papa! Papa!"

Kit turned, releasing Bryony's hand, and knelt there on the drive with a broad grin as the two small bodies impacted hard against his.

"Now, kittens, settle down!" he laughed amidst their smothering hugs. "We've company today, and so you must remember your manners."

At once the little girls were properly abashed, and both stepped back from their father to gaze curiously at Bryony with big green eyes. They had on matching white damask dresses, sashed with wide yellow ribbons, and dainty lace caps perched upon their auburn curls. Suddenly very serious, they curtsied in unison to Bryony, and she couldn't help but smile.

"These little urchins are Anne and Grace," Kit said with corresponding pats on each little head. Then he asked the two girls, "Where's your sister Maggie?"

"In the house, having her bath." Anne, the eldest, answered her father with a terrible grimace. "Mama said my turn's next!"

"As well it should be," Kit replied in a mock-stern tone, winking conspiratorially at Bryony as he rose. "Girls, I want you to meet Mistress Bryony O'Neill. She'll be staying here with us for a while."

Grace scrunched up her freckled nose. "Why, Papa?"

"Why, indeed? Don't be impertinent, Gracie. Just because I said so, that's why."

Kit swept up the smaller girl to ride on his shoulders, as

they continued down the drive toward the mansion. Anne skipped happily along at his side, but Bryony hesitated when she saw a scowling woman standing in the open doorway.

At first, Bryony assumed it must be the housekeeper, for the woman's dark brown hair was pulled into a severe, unbecoming coil at the back of her overlong neck. Her gown was plain gray serge without even a hint of lace or embroidery. But when Kit paused to drop a kiss on the woman's thin cheek, Bryony realized with surprise that it must be the lady of the house.

Ignoring her husband and Bryony entirely, Elspeth Tanner turned on the little girls instead. "Filthy cubs!" she scolded them in a harsh, strident voice. "Upstairs at once for your baths! Isobel is waiting for you."

"Yes, Mama," the children chorused dutifully before they clambered up the stairs. Then Kit's wife turned and regarded their unexpected guest through cool gray eyes. Elspeth Tanner's mouth was pinched white about the lips, and Bryony thought her slightly crooked nose gave her the look of a wet cross hen. There was not a shred of warmth or welcome in the woman's expression, and she meanly took in Bryony's appearance for several seconds before turning on her husband.

"What's this bit of baggage?" Elspeth demanded.

Kit flushed dull red, then said as sternly as he could manage, "Elspeth, this is Mistress Bryony O'Neill. She'll be staying with us for a time, so may I suggest you make haste and ready one of the guest chambers."

Elspeth's mouth opened, and then shut with an audible snap. Without another word, she turned and stomped up the stairs after her daughters, with her skirts clenched in her whitened fists.

"I'm sorry," Kit said wearily to Bryony, before he closed the open door behind them. He suddenly looked like a beaten man, and for the first time she noticed the fine stress lines about his lips and eyes.

"I'm not welcome here," she said.

"Nay." Kit shook his head almost angrily. "You're my guest, Bryony, and Ambergate is my home. There will be no more said about it. 'Tis just Elspeth's way, that's all."

"It would be far wiser, if I returned to the ship."

"As Slade said, that isn't possible right now."

"Why not?" Bryony asked him. "Something more has happened than the fact he suddenly needs to take inventory, hasn't it? Please, won't you tell me what's really going on?"

Kit sighed, fumbling for words. "Elizabeth Tudor is . . . somewhat upset with Slade," he confessed. " 'Tis best if he is left to handle the matter without any undue distraction. I hope you'll trust me in this matter, Bryony."

"Of course," she said quietly, but this revelation was disturbing. Slade was in some sort of trouble with the queen. Over what matter? Her?

As if reading her mind, Kit quickly sought to distract her. "May I show you my home?" Without waiting for a reply, he led Bryony down the main corridor into a charming sunny parlor.

A spiral brick fireplace dominated the room, before which a deep crimson carpet was unrolled to display its fleur-de-lis design. Gate-leg tables of gleaming chestnut wood framed a massive Gobelin wall tapestry, depicting a formal coronation scene in rich shades of blue and gold. There were a number of carved wainscot chairs, and a murrey velvet divan strewn with silk pillows.

"Faith, but it's beautiful," Bryony exclaimed, genuinely awed, and she saw that Kit was pleased.

"I insisted it be kept the same, even after our mother's death. Of course, Elspeth wanted to make changes. She said the stained-glass especially was reminiscent of the Dark Ages."

Bryony glanced at the lovely, crimson-and-green-colored rose motifs set into the plain lead glass windows, and had to disagree. With the sun shining brightly through the glass, the effect was nothing less than magnificent.

"You did the right thing, Kit, preserving the room," she informed her host with a smile.

He smiled back. "Mother always favored this parlor for her embroidery and china-painting. She said the light was best on this side of the house, and she liked to gaze out over her rose garden in the summer."

"What was she like, your mother?"

Kit thought a moment. "Being a Slade—'twas her maiden name, you see—she had the distinctive red hair. But on her, it was just right. Meredith was her name, Merry for short, because she was always so cheerful. Everyone loved her, especially the queen. Mother went to court until she was too old to dance attendance upon Elizabeth Tudor anymore. But even then, she was still one of Bess's favorites."

"And your father?" Bryony was curious, and felt she somehow gained important insight into Slade himself with the answers to her questions.

Kit chuckled. "Ah, that's doubtless where all four of us boys got our tempers. Even though our mother had the red hair, our sire was not one to tolerate nonsense of any sort. Henry was serious, almost grim . . . a typical father of four sons, I should imagine. George has turned out to be the most like him."

"What of the rest of you?"

"Well, there's Slade, of course, the baby Tanner and by reputation the most reckless. And me. Although it's hard to judge oneself fairly, I confess I'm a family man at heart, though I spend a great deal of time at Court."

"There's one more, isn't there? Phillip?"

"Aye. Let's see. Phillip is the steady sensible one. But a bit inclined to be ruthless. He's the ambitious sort, too. Inherited that trait from our father, I daresay. Father would have been proud to see Phillip wed a veritable heiress this month with the queen's blessing."

The mention of marriage gave them both pause. Bryony could not quell other questions that suddenly came to her mind, and her lips.

"And Slade's betrothed," she said, trying to adopt a tone both light and unconcerned. "What's she like?"

Kit hesitated, sensing the undercurrent of pain. Very carefully, he said, "Gillian's not like anyone I've ever met, or likely will again. She's ambitious, too, but to an even greater degree than Phillip . . . and as you must know, she and Slade have been at cross-purposes for the past months."

Bryony's anguished eyes showed a fleeting spark of hope, and Kit silently cursed himself. He didn't dare let this young woman misunderstand his brother's position.

"Gillian will be at Court for a few more weeks, only until the wedding."

"Wedding?" Bryony's whisper raked at his conscience, but Kit managed to nod.

"Aye, 'tis set now for Michaelmas. You didn't know?"

She shook her head almost violently, the lustrous blue black hair flying around her shoulders. He'd never seen such naked pain in another human being's eyes before, and it shook him to the core.

"Sweet Jesu. I'm sorry, Bryony . . . I assumed Slade must have told you," he stammered awkwardly.

"It doesn't matter," she whispered fiercely, moving swiftly to put her back between him and the window. She seemed to gaze over the budding rose garden, but Kit suspected tears had suddenly silvered those incomparable sea blue eyes.

"Go away!"

Slade hadn't intended to snarl when a scratching came at his cabin door, but it was too late to correct his tone. The door opened and a male voice said teasingly, "Why, little brother, if that be the answer to my invitation, then I'll be returning to shore posthaste."

"Phillip!" Surprise and genuine pleasure lit Slade's face, and immediately he closed the ledgers and rose from the chair before his map desk. As the two young men came together in the cabin for a brief embrace, Slade apologized for his sour mood.

"I left orders that nobody disturb me, while I worked on these accounts for Bess. I confess I'm nigh close to tearing my hair out."

"Then I'll gladly help out, seeing as how Kit and George and I also have a stake in your prospects," Phillip replied with a broad grin. Like their mother, Phillip Tanner was perpetually cheerful and easygoing, and like their father he had a financial savvy that Slade envied. As for his wardrobe, Phillip never spared any expense, and today he was clad in dark blue velvet breeches and a silver-paned brocade doublet.

Of the four brothers, Phillip's eyes were soft brown, rather than green. His golden hair was shorn fashionably short, and complemented by a neatly pointed beard. His wholesome good looks had always made him a favorite with the ladies.

"How did your last journey fare?" Phillip inquired. "Down the coast of Africa, was it?"

"Aye, and we had our usual success," Slade said with a chuckle. "Save for encountering a few disgruntled Spaniards, we traveled the coastline in record time." He gestured at the chair he had vacated. "Sit and stay a while, Phillip. We've much to talk about."

His brother nodded his head in agreement, but chose to sit on the edge of the captain's bed instead. Stretching out his long legs, Phillip exclaimed, "It's a pleasure to relax! I've been riding hard since Oxford, in order to finalize the wedding banns and catch up to you. Kit sent a message that you were back."

"He probably didn't warn you about my sudden downturn of fortune."

"Actually, he did." Phillip shook his head. "Bad bit of luck, that, upsetting the queen."

"It wasn't Bess, but rather Gillian who was outraged," Slade explained. His tone was grim. "She called the curs on me when I threatened to move to Ireland and dissolve our plight-troth."

Phillip looked surprised. He glanced to the silver frame resting on the table beside Slade's bed. "But I thought you two were reconciled."

Slade followed his brother's gaze, and his own eyes narrowed when he realized that Bryony had purposefully placed the picture back beside his bed. Walking across the cabin to snatch up the miniature, he said, "No. I vow we'll never be reconciled to Bess's satisfaction. Gilly's not fit to be anyone's wife."

When Phillip didn't argue with him, Slade gave a bitter little laugh, tossing the picture facedown on the table. "I see you've heard rumor of Gilly's infidelities, even so far as Oxford. Yet I shouldn't be surprised. Did everyone in England know she was cuckolding me all this time?"

Phillip was embarrassed. He sympathized with his brother's plight, and thought Slade looked more worn and depressed than he ever recalled seeing him. After a moment of tense silence, he said, "I hope you'll still come to my own wedding this week, up in Beverley."

Slade accepted the change of topic with good grace. "What, so far as all that?" he teased Phillip. " 'Tis a long day's ride even in fair weather."

"Quite a journey, true, but most assuredly worth it. The prettiest women come from Yorkshire, Slade. Wait 'til you see my Faith."

"Once I might have agreed with that, but now I lay claim to further knowledge," Slade quietly replied. "For the bonniest of them all come from Ireland, Phillip, with their wild black hair and bewitching blue eyes."

Phillip's eyebrows shot up, but Slade only shook his head with a laugh and said, "Don't worry, big brother, I'll be there. Go ahead and reserve a spot at St. Mary's for me."

* * *

"You're welcome to come to the wedding with us," Kit invited Bryony for the third time, as he and the Tanner family made ready to depart London that weekend. "I'm sure Phillip and his bride wouldn't mind an extra guest."

Bryony smiled, letting him know she appreciated the offer. But the thought of being trapped in a closed coach with Elspeth Tanner for more than a minute was enough to assure her refusal. In the first twenty-four hours she'd been at Ambergate, Kit's wife had not even acknowledged her presence, much less offered a cordial word or two.

It hadn't been hard for Bryony to decide that keeping to the guest chamber was the easiest course for all concerned. Never mind the fact that she craved fresh air and sunshine, and occasional conversation. She had learned to endure life without kind words at Raven Hall, and this place seemed no different.

Kit was distressed over his wife's treatment of Bryony, but he couldn't force Elspeth to be civil. Elspeth had been less than pleased when a shipment of three large trunks had arrived for Bryony shortly after her arrival. When the trunks were opened, they were found to contain every necessary article of feminine clothing imaginable.

There were gowns of silk, velvet, taffeta, finest linen, and rich damask. Every brilliant hue of the rainbow was represented, though blues and greens dominated the lot, in the shades which best flattered Bryony. Ruffs, puffs, and pickadils dotted the various outfits in the latest courtly styles. There were even several dressing gowns, as well as cloaks, undergarments, shoes, and hose to match.

"Well," Elspeth commented, hands on her flat hips as she narrowly surveyed the contents of the trunks, " 'twould appear this is payment for some sort of services rendered, wouldn't you say, Mistress O'Neill?"

Bryony's cheeks burned at the woman's nasty remark. She

wanted to refuse the trunks. She knew where they had come from. But ever-practical Kit pointed out that she desperately needed clothing and accessories for the days to come. He knew his uncharitable wife was not about to share her wardrobe with their guest.

Bryony was finally persuaded to keep the trunks, but she was bothered by Slade's extravagant generosity. If he thought to apologize somehow by lavishing her with presents, then he was sorely mistaken. She would not give Slade the satisfaction of appearing at Phillip's wedding wearing one of the gowns he had sent. She might still be his prisoner, but she was not his property, nor his mistress.

This time when Kit again invited her to attend the wedding, she said, "No, thank you. I would prefer to remain behind. A wedding is a gathering meant for family, not strangers."

"I told you Gillian won't be there, didn't I? She never comes to family events like this."

"Aye, you mentioned it. But it was not that which decided me. Honestly, Kit, I simply prefer not to go."

He sighed, and then broached another touchy subject. "Bryony, you know I can't leave you alone at Ambergate. All the servants have been given the weekend off."

She knew what he was really driving at, and steeled herself for the blow. Thanks to Kit, it had almost been possible to pretend that she was not a prisoner, but rather an acquaintance visiting for a time. Kit's warm congenial manner and his adorable little girls had even helped her enjoy a few hours here, when Elspeth was away.

"It's not that I don't trust you," Kit continued, "but Slade's entrusted you to my care and keep, and I can't risk anything happening to you. He warned me there might be some who'd seek to whisk you away, in order to use you as a weapon against your father."

Bryony stiffened at that. "As Slade himself has done! Wherein lies the difference, Kit? One jail is much like another, though I confess this one to be more pleasant than most."

At that moment, the children's nursemaid entered the parlor where they were talking. Isobel Weeks was a poor relation who had fallen on hard times, and Kit had generously taken the girl in, when her parents had died and she'd been left without any prospects. She was a plain young woman, clearly favoring Elspeth's side of the family, but unlike her older cousin, she was merry of heart and manner, and the children adored her. She carried a sweet-smelling bundle in her arms.

"Forgive me," Isobel murmured, seeing Kit was occupied. But his green eyes had already lit up at the sight of his littlest daughter, and he immediately held out his arms to take the sleepy little girl.

"Thank you, Isobel. I'll carry Maggie out to the coach. Are your own bags packed for the weekend?"

"Aye, Cousin Kit. They're in the hall."

"Tell Malvers to load them when he's finished with the team."

"Certainly." Isobel bobbed a brief curtsy, then offered Bryony a shy and friendly smile before she slipped away to find the others.

By the way Kit tenderly cradled his tiny daughter, Bryony could tell this red-haired imp was his favorite. Maggie Tanner was clad in a long gown of fine white cambric, daintily embroidered with yellow daisies. Her bright auburn hair was curled in tight ringlets all over her head. She was barely two, and still needed naps. She dozed contentedly in her Papa's arms, while Kit and Bryony finished their discussion.

"I realize you're not a child, Bryony," he said, "but I've engaged a woman to come and stay at the house for the weekend."

She gave a sigh of surrender. "I expected no less."

Kit was clearly unhappy with the situation. "Were it up to me, I'd have Isobel stay with you. But Elspeth insists she can't manage the girls for so much as an hour without her cousin's help. All her shrieking and screaming only makes them more stubborn, you see."

Bryony nodded. "Wee ones, I've found, do best with a firm, but gentle hand. I've never been around young girls before, but I learned my own mistakes with the lads out on the ships. They're quick to take advantage, all children are. But nobody is more trusting and devoted than a child, either, if you treat them right."

Kit wondered at the sudden sadness in her eyes, though he nodded in agreement with the truth of her words.

"I'm afraid we need to leave soon, if we're to make the wedding ceremony in time. The gentlewoman who agreed to come and stay should have been here by now."

"You have my word I won't try to escape," Bryony replied with a wry smile. "Besides, where would I go? I've lost my ship, my life savings, and any shred of dignity I once might have possessed."

"Then you'll agree to stay at Ambergate until we return? Slade would have my head, if anything happened to you."

Bryony saw Kit's worry was genuine. But if she had inherited one thing from her noble Irish ancestors, it was honor.

"Aye," she said softly. "You have my word on it."

He sighed, half with relief, half with regret. "Then I accept your promise, Bryony O'Neill. Though I feel badly that for the first time in many centuries, my beloved Ambergate will serve not as a pleasant country estate, but a jail."

Slade had fully intended to be present at Phillip's wedding with the rest of the Tanner family, but an unexpected summons waylaid him just before he headed north to Yorkshire.

Word came to him via one of the queen's runners that he was urgently needed at Whitehall. The request actually came from Gillian, not Bess, but knowing he dared not defy the queen's ward, Slade sent his regrets to his brother by messenger, before he left for the palace.

Inwardly, he seethed with a cold white fury, but he let no outward sign of it mar his expression as he dismounted inside the royal gates and handed over his steed to one of the stable lads.

This time, he inadvertently found himself wearing appropriate court attire, as he'd already been dressed for Phillip's wedding. The elegant outfit turned female heads, as he strode briskly down the corridors in the direction of Gillian's chamber.

A lace-edged falling band supplanted the huge ruffs Slade detested, and added the only frivolous touch to his clothing. His snow white doublet had full sleeves, which fastened at his wrists with genuine sapphire buttons. The short-sleeved jerkin was crafted from butter-soft blue leather, slashed to show golden panes. His darker blue velvet breeches and blue hose were relatively plain, but showed his well-shaped legs to advantage. His fine Spanish leather shoes were so new they creaked, as he strode past a group of court ladies tittering behind their hands. But with the silver rapier clanking at his side, none dared make an untoward comment.

Slade ignored the whispers, stopping only to demand directions from a startled page. Soon enough he was at Gillian's chamber, where he scratched impatiently at the door. A flurry of activity within the room heralded the opening of the door, and the maid standing there gasped when Slade thrust his way past her without formality.

"Milord!" the servant cried. "This is a lady's chamber!"

"That's debatable," Slade coldly replied, turning to survey the jumble of luxuries within. There were a variety of rich gowns carelessly draped over chairs, and priceless jewels were scattered like raindrops on a dresser and several tables. As the maidservant continued to protest his presence, another female voice shrilled from behind another door, " 'Tis all right, Elinor! It's only my betrothed!"

The sound of Gillian's voice raised the hair on Slade's

neck, and with his rage firmly focused, he brushed past the tiring woman and threw open the door to the inner chamber.

"How dare you!" Gillian Lovelle's breasts heaved above a low-cut violet silk gown as she whirled to face him, and her pale blue eyes sparkled dangerously. Another maid had been brushing out her silvery blond hair, and it cascaded in long loose curls over her shoulders. For just a moment, Slade softened, seeing a shadow of the angelic-looking young woman he had once desired for his wife.

Then the image was shattered as Gillian's eyes narrowed on him. "It took you long enough!" she snapped.

Slade spoke through gritted teeth. "You appear to be in capable hands, madam."

"Aye, no thanks to you! Leaving me here without a word, while you gallivanted off to Ireland."

"I had no idea you favored the notion of a long journey, Gilly. Otherwise I should have gladly made the proper arrangements for you to accompany me."

She gave an indelicate snort. Both of them knew quite well she had no wish to leave Whitehall, even for a day.

Slade was suddenly reminded of missing Phillip's wedding, and his anger returned with a vengeance. Taking a single stride forward, he grabbed Gillian by the wrist and thundered at her, "If you called me here for naught this time, then you shall grandly rue it!"

Unimpressed, Gillian tossed her head. Glancing at her two maids, who hovered in the doorway, she snapped, "Leave us! Slade and I must speak alone." The two servants regretfully departed, lingering as long as they dared in order to overhear more juicy gossip. But Slade trailed them out, slamming the door firmly shut behind them and turning to face his betrothed again.

"Explain yourself, Gilly. I know you called me away from Phillip's wedding on purpose."

"La, don't be so tiresome." She turned to a mirror and absently plucked at the embroidered folds of her gown, twisting this way and that to appraise the view. "I have a matter of some urgency to discuss with you, Captain Tanner."

Slade stiffened, when she uttered his title as if it was the lowest insult she could think of. "It had better be important," he warned her in clipped tones.

"Of course, it is."

Slade saw a complacent smile curve Gillian's rose-colored lips in the mirror. He steeled himself for the worst. He expected another plea for money, perhaps a haughty demand to have first pick from his next cargo, anything but what she said.

"I'm pregnant."

Somewhere in the haze of his shock, Slade finally managed to find his voice. "Congratulations," he replied evenly. "I trust you know who the father is."

Gillian blanched, and two bright spots appeared on her cheeks. She whirled about as if to strike him, then reconsidered. Her breast was heaving with obvious emotion—though of what sort, Slade couldn't tell.

"I'll forgive you for that," she said, "because I know we both lost our heads that night."

"That night?" Nonplussed, Slade stared at her. Then he saw what she was driving at, and an incredulous burst of laughter escaped his lips. "Come now, Gilly. You can't expect anyone to believe that the child—if there really is one—is *mine.*"

She returned an arch smile. "Faith, Captain Tanner, but the other ladies are quite willing to testify to the queen that they have witnessed you tiptoeing into my chamber many a night."

"Then they will also be forced to admit I had to wait in line."

"Bastard!"

"Hardly, my dear. I assure you, my parents were properly wed at the time of my birth. George has the family records at Cheatham, if you want to see them."

Gillian took a deep breath, obviously trying not to scream. "How can you be so cruel to me?" she whispered, in an amazingly quick turnabout, complete with trembling lips and tear-filled eyes.

"Bravo, my dear Gilly. A pity you missed your true calling. You really should have been an actress. You've played me for a fool often enough, doubtless reasoning I was too enamored of the sea and your sweet wiles to suspect what was really going on when I was absent from Court. But word of your little peccadillos has spread, even as far as the Continent."

Her eyes narrowed. "You have no proof."

"Who needs proof? Half the men I've met have already sampled your charms. It could almost be said, m'dear, that you are the national dish of England."

This time, Gillian did slap him. Hard. The crack echoed throughout the room, but Slade didn't so much as flinch. His eyes turned to green ice as he turned to leave. Gillian reached out and desperately grasped his arm.

"But I'm not lying. Look!" Unwillingly, Slade glanced over his shoulder and saw Gillian smooth the loose gown against her stomach. The slight bulge of early pregnancy was unmistakable. His eyes narrowed suspiciously, and she cried, "Aye, it's real enough! Feel it if you wish. *Feel your son kicking inside of me!*"

With a disgusted sound, Slade pivoted away from her. His thoughts were whirling wildly. He didn't doubt that Gillian was really *enceinte,* but whose brat was it? He recalled with sickening clarity the one morning he had awakened in the lady's bed, soon after they had been first introduced at Court, when Gilly still assumed he was a baron. He'd been so drunk he had no recollection whatsoever of making love to her, but now he realized the evidence was damning. When he awoke, they had both been naked, and he remembered Gilly purring about his remarkable prowess.

Was it even slightly possible that a single night of indiscretion three months ago had resulted in this?

"The child is due midwinter," Gillian continued, as if reading his mind. "Count the months, if you like!"

Fists clenched at his sides, Slade said, "I'm not the only man who knew you then."

"You'll have to take my word that you were. 'Tis the only time it could have happened, Slade. And even if you don't believe me, Bess will. If necessary, I'll appeal to her for help."

He spun around in sudden fury. "You little bitch," he snarled. "Why won't you let me be? I've done nothing to you, and yet you insist on making my life a living hell!"

"All I want is a name for my child!" Gillian shrieked back.

"Even the lowly Tanner one? God's teeth, Gilly, that's rich! You didn't think it good enough for you before, yet you would slap it on your bastard child?"

"Your son," she corrected him, protectively cradling her gently rounded belly. In repose, she looked like the Madonna. But Slade was not deceived by her virginal attitude and appearance.

"I wish you joy of what you've done, madam, and everything that goes along with it. For I'm washing my hands of you, this time for good. I'm going to start a new life in a new land, where even your claws can't reach me."

Gillian stared at him in disbelief. "You're jesting."

"Most assuredly not. You may continue to play your revolting little games here at Court all you like, but at least I shall no longer be privy to them."

"You'll come back, Slade," she threatened him. "I'll see to it!"

"Will you?" He shrugged. He turned to leave.

Gillian cursed and lunged after him, clutching at his sleeve. He briskly shook her off as one would an insect, and strode for the door. Behind him, she fell to her knees and screamed, "You'll regret this, Slade! I'll appeal to the queen. You'll pay dearly for what you've done to me!"

Deaf to her threats, Slade threw open the door and stormed out of the chamber. But he was forced to acknowledge the very real power Gillian Lovelle held over him and his family. She could easily ruin them all. And he also knew that until the child was born, he would be haunted by the possibility that for the first time in her life, Gillian was telling the truth.

Eleven

Bryony was out in Ambergate's rose garden, when she heard the clip-clop of horse's hooves coming up the cobbled drive. Paying it no mind, assuming it must be the woman whom Kit had employed to watch over her and the house for the weekend, she continued to walk along the neatly kept rose beds. To her delight, she spied the first flower of the spring, a frosty white bud, half-unfurled. As she bent to inhale its musky scent, she smiled a little wistfully at the memory of her own mother's roses.

Alanna O'Neill had possessed neither the funds nor the time to manage a vast show garden such as this, but her wild red roses had been lovingly tended, just the same. The great prickly bushes still sprawled in an unkempt fashion outside Raven Hall. Nobody had trimmed them for years. It suddenly occurred to Bryony that both her mother and Slade's had loved roses. She wondered what other hobbies the two women, English and Irish, might have had in common. She sighed, realizing she would never know.

Bryony paused in contemplation of a delicate rosebud, when a sharp thorn pricked the pad of her index finger. She would do well to remember the many dangers hidden behind beauty, she reminded herself as she briefly sucked at the wound. Slade Tanner was very comely on the outside, but he possessed great potential to wound her heart.

She turned to gaze in the direction of the sea. To be honest, she had entertained the notion of escape for some time after

Kit and his family had left, but her plans were quickly dashed once reason set in. Where in London could she hope to find sympathy for an Irish rebel, and how on earth would she manage to steal a ship? She did not choose to martyr herself merely for Brann's sake. He would hardly appreciate it. Besides, she had given Kit her word not to cause trouble, and so she would await the family's return.

Meanwhile, unbeknownst to her, Slade was seeing to his own horse in the Ambergate stables, since the stablehands were also enjoying the weekend off. Wearily, he attended his mount and tack, then crossed the expanse of lush lawn leading toward the rear of the mansion. He was tired and dispirited from the ugly episode with Gillian at the palace. It was too late to attend Phillip's wedding now, and so he had sent his regrets. The thought of having Ambergate all to himself for the weekend was appealing. Like Kit, he far preferred the smaller family home to the great estate George maintained at Cheatham.

Slade was walking up the garden footpath when he heard soft humming issuing from behind a tall thick stand of roses. Coming to an abrupt halt, he felt his heart begin to hammer faster. His mother Merry had always hummed similar little ditties as she puttered about her precious garden, and Slade wondered if he were hearing a ghost.

Then he caught sight of a very real hand reaching between two bushes to cup a particularly beautiful red bud, and his own fingers shot out to grasp the flower first. A startled shriek was closely followed by a pair of wide blue eyes peeking through the dense briars.

"Slade!"

Bryony's soft cry warmed his heart. There was surprise and uncertainty in her voice, but also a tentative thread of warmth he could not miss.

Swiftly he walked around the row, having neatly plucked the red rose bud. Bryony turned to greet him, looking lovelier than ever in a crimson-colored silk gown with paned red and silver sleeves. Her raven hair was loose, gleaming with gentle blue highlights under the sun. Her rosy lips parted, but it was he who spoke first.

"Don't speak," he said. "Just let me look at you."

Bryony was trembling so, she couldn't have moved nor spoken if she'd tried. She wildly wondered what Slade was doing there, and what she should do. The mere sight of him, standing before her so tall and handsome in the secluded garden, made her heart race with anticipation and futile hope.

Slade came toward her in a slow saunter which only seemed to emphasize the building tension between them. Bryony regarded him almost warily, confronted with a fresh flurry of emotions, as she gazed once more into those deep green eyes, set like emeralds against his sun-bronzed skin.

The faint stubble of beard on his chin made Slade's face look as if it had been lightly brushed with gold dust. Even in her memories, he had never been more handsome. His white teeth flashed as he raised his hand, gently tucking the short stem of the rosebud behind her ear.

"There," he quietly stated with satisfaction. "That's better. Your hair should always smell of roses."

Bryony blushed, remembering the rosewater bath she had indulged in while on the island. She knew Slade referred to the same incident, when he continued to smile at her in that disarming way.

" 'Tis the Red Rose of Lancaster," he observed. "It suits your complexion, and your gown."

To hide her nervousness, Bryony quickly indicated the white rosebud she had earlier found. "And this one?"

"The symbol of the House of York. I trust you've heard of the War of the Roses?"

She nodded, and Slade expounded, "Henry VII united the two warring factions through marriage. Thus the Tudor Rose was eventually created, a white rose superimposed on the red. Somewhere in this maze of hedges, there is doubtless a lesson to be learned."

Bryony had all but forgotten about roses. "What brings you to Ambergate?"

"Anticipating a weekend away from my ship and routine duties," he replied.

"I assumed you were going to your brother's wedding."

"Aye, but urgent business waylaid me at the last moment." His eyes darkened a bit. "But I'm more curious as to what you're doing here at Ambergate alone. Knowing Kit, he must have invited you along to the wedding."

Bryony nodded. There was nothing she could really offer for an excuse, except to try and explain how she would have felt terribly out of place at an intimate family gathering. Instead, she said, "There was supposed to be a woman here to stay with me, before the family left. But there's been no sign nor word from her yet."

Slade's jaw hardened. "And Kit left you alone anyway?"

" 'Twas not his fault. Your brother trusts me, and I gave my word to stay put," Bryony defended Kit while also pointing out her own loyalty. "I could hardly ask the others to miss Phillip's wedding merely for my sake. Besides, does it appear to you I was making haste to escape?"

Slade had to admit defeat. He was too weary after the confrontation with Gillian to want to argue with Bryony.

"I'm staying the weekend," he announced abruptly.

"Here?" Too late Bryony realized how foolish her question sounded.

"Aye." His lips twitched with mirth. "Does that sit ill with you, Mistress O'Neill?"

"No, of course not. It's your family home, not mine." Bryony fell silent then, a little worried about the unspoken possibilities. She and Slade would be alone for the first time in days. She wondered if he felt the same delicious anticipation welling inside. It was impossible to tell, due to his formal reserve.

Thankfully Slade did not seem to notice her discomfort. "Let's move inside, shall we? It's getting too cool to be outside without a wrap." Bryony nodded, falling into stride beside him on the dirt path. "Can I assume Cook is gone, as well?" he inquired.

"Aye, Kit gave all the servants the weekend off. I assured him I could fend for myself. There's a cold supper set aside, enough for two."

"Good. I'm famished." Slade paused to open the garden gate leading to the rear of the house, ushering her through with an easy grin. Bryony proceeded him through the kitchens by means of the servant's entrance. She went directly to the larder to prepare several large platters of sliced cheese, fresh bread, and meats. She added several jars of pear, peach, and plum preserves, and carried the platters one by one into the dining hall.

Slade quickly made himself at home. He removed his falling band and unbuttoned his leather jerkin as well. To their impromptu feast he added a bottle of sweet fruity wine he had retrieved from the cellar.

"The woman Kit hired will doubtless think this quite a domestic sight when she arrives," he remarked, as Bryony handed him a plate and settled down across the table from him.

"With one exception," she pointedly replied, pausing to take a nibble of the sharp cheddar from her plate. "She'll know at once I'm not Lady Gillian."

The smile on Slade's face abruptly vanished. "That reminds me, Bryony. What did you hope to accomplish by putting her miniature beside my bed?"

"Accomplish?" She shrugged, attempting to look far more unconcerned then she felt. "Naught but to remind you of your sworn oath to another."

"I'll take it upon myself, when I wish to do that," Slade said curtly, spearing a piece of meat and bringing it to his lips. The meal continued in silence for a time, and he seemed to partake more generously of the wine than was his usual habit. Bryony wondered what myriad of unhappy thoughts drove

Slade to indulge in three goblets so quickly. She did not have long to wait for the answer.

"There's been no word yet of the *Alanna Colleen*," he bluntly informed her. " 'Twould appear she's lost at sea . . . or at least, she must be accounted so."

Bryony's throat tightened as she thought of Finn and the young lads she had swept so recklessly into the lap of danger. "It's my fault," she said a little huskily. "I feared the caravel was too light to ride out the storm, but I didn't stop them from going."

Slade suddenly reached across the table and gripped her hand. Her swimming vision focused on the strong brown fingers interlaced with hers. "You mustn't blame yourself, Bryony. In fact, I forbid you to indulge in needless guilt. I was the captain in charge, and so take full responsibility for their deaths."

"Aye," she flung back, "but will it bring them back?"

He simply shook his head, withdrew his hand from hers, and sat back in the chair. "Nay," he admitted. "But there's no call for both of us to shoulder the blame."

A taut silence reigned, while Bryony struggled to bring her emotions under control. Her throat burned with tears, tears she needed and badly wanted to shed, yet could not seem to produce. Was she nothing but a dried husk, then? No. She simply knew that neither remonstration nor tears would bring back the beloved crew of the *Alanna Colleen*.

"Concerning Gillian," Slade said, abruptly changing to another uncomfortable topic. "I told you I did not wish the woman's portrait on display in my cabin."

Bryony dropped her gaze and pretended to concentrate upon her dinner. "Did you set it aside, then?" she lightly inquired.

"Aye, I did. Whatever might have existed between Gilly and myself is long gone. Dammit, Bryony, look at me!" When she reluctantly raised her gaze to his, he continued. "What happened between you and me had nothing at all to do with her. Aye, don't look so surprised. You heard me right. The woman has not taken my name yet, nor shall she ever, if I have my say."

"Then why did you plight your troth with her?" Bryony challenged him, her temper quickly rising.

"One reason, and one only: the queen's request. Or rather, Bess's demand. God's nightshirt, Bryony! Don't look so dubious. Gillian Lovelle has no more love or regard for me than I have for her. In fact, Gilly has nothing but spite and contempt for me and my entire family, and would see us all destroyed, if possible."

"But why?" Bryony demanded.

"Do you truly wish to hear the ugly truth? Very well, then, you shall know all. Gillian is furious with me because we became betrothed, as she puts it, by trickery. You see, she had mistakenly heard at court that I was heir to my father's title. In actuality, 'twas George, my eldest brother, whom Gilly heard discussed. It was not until we were formally betrothed that she learned the truth of the matter. And she has never forgiven me for the misunderstanding."

Despite his grim tone, Bryony had to chuckle. "Did you misrepresent yourself to her?"

"No!" he exploded. "Gilly assumed such nonsense entirely on her own behalf. When she learned I was a mere captain, she could hardly be consoled. To be frank, she was absolutely furious. But since that dark day of discovery, she has apparently reconsidered. 'Twould appear Gilly finds some benefit in wedding a man already married to the sea. Since I am gone much of the year, she sees herself free to continue her dalliances at court. Elizabeth Tudor is truly the one pressuring the match. She seems to think marriage would settle Gilly down somehow."

"And would it?" Bryony asked.

Slade snorted. "Hardly. Lady Gillian—and I do use that title casually—has little patience for domestic scenes, and even less for children. In truth, I doubt we would spend more than a fortnight together in any year."

Bryony did not know what to say. The rage and the pain were reflected so clearly in Slade's eyes, that she could hardly deny the truth of his story. Without hesitation, she reached across the table and clutched his hand in hers. Slade squeezed hers in return, understanding the silent gesture. He sighed deeply with relief.

"Thank you," he said in a low voice. "Thank you for at least listening to my side of this sordid tale."

Bryony swallowed hard, and asked him softly, "What can I do to ease the pain, Slade? Tell me."

He closed his eyes for a second, but when he opened them again they were calm and resolved, like the peaceful green seas of summer.

"Just love me, Bryony. Be with me for these last few hours . . . and then I swear, I'll set you free."

How could she deny such an anguished request from the man she loved? Bryony was not heartless, though she granted she was probably foolish enough as they both rose and she found herself in Slade's arms.

He nuzzled her hair, as if with relief. The red rose fell and was crushed under his heel on the carpet, releasing a poignant fragrance that seemed to swirl about them as they frantically embraced one another, as if trying to make up for lost time.

Bryony clung to Slade with a mixture of emotions: heady relief, the fiercest of love, and secret fear. What madness possessed them both to deny a fickle powerful queen, and each of their cultures? Such is the insanity of love, she marvelled, just before Slade's lips found hers and she lost even that last shred of reason.

Nothing mattered now but the feeling of his strong warm hands clasping her waist, his mouth eagerly feasting on hers, licking the last droplet of sweet wine from the corner of her lips. Laughing softly, Bryony broke free of his embrace and dashed to the base of the stairs leading to her room. She paused with her hand on the silky smooth mahogany banister to look back at Slade with unmistakable invitation. He did not wait long to follow.

Sweeping Bryony up in his arms, Slade carried her with quick and easy steps up to the guest room. Lightly kicking open the door, he padded across the wine-colored Aubusson carpet to the large canopied bed. As he lowered her to the bed, her eyes shimmered brightly with anticipation, and a smile curved her lips.

"Sweet Jesu, you are so beautiful," Slade said huskily, basking for a moment in the warmth of Bryony's gaze. He ached to tell her that he loved her, that perhaps he had even from the first moment those sea blue eyes of hers had locked with his in a silent sensual battle of wills. But what would it gain either of them now, except heartache?

In the gentle stillness of twilight, Slade shed his clothing and came to her with hands outstretched. He waited for her to accept his offer, as without hesitation her fingers entwined with his and drew him down to the bed. Slade knelt on the coverlet for a moment, Bryony's dark hair tumbling over his cupped hands, while his broad thumbs traced the enticing lines of her mouth, and the endearing little curve at the base of her lower lip.

His hands dropped to the laces of her gown, and the hooks and ribbons parted without protest. Even as he gently drew the gown from her, he made each step a slow deliberate seduction, and the banked flames between them began to rise higher and higher.

Slade paused for a brief moment to regard the raven amulet she wore about her neck. He sensed that the gleaming disk reflected the free spirit deep in Bryony's soul, and he respected that. Mayhaps it was mere coincidence that his own hair was the same bright hue as the Irish red gold . . . or perhaps not.

"My sea raven," he murmured, tracing the amulet against the softly beating pulse in her throat. Bryony smiled at the endearment, lifting her eyes to gaze into his with a look that was at once both serene and compelling.

This time, to his surprise and delight, it was she who urged him back upon the lacy coverlet, swinging her long leg over him in order to straddle his hips. The black velvet curtain of her hair fell around them both, the heady scent of the Lancaster rose still lingering in the thick curling tresses. Slade lifted his hands to cup her breasts, gently kneading the satiny flesh in a prelude to love. Yet it was Bryony who was in control this time, clasping her slim thighs against his with a strength which both startled and aroused him.

As she slid slowly down, inch by inch, onto his rigid, silky hot maleness, they both gasped as if in delight of a new discovery. Slade's hands dropped down and gripped her small waist, both to steady and guide Bryony in the sweet undulations which rocked them in fierce unison.

Oh, blessed union! A shattered gasp escaped Bryony's lips as she and Slade became one. Passion suddenly clawed at her with savage intensity, rendering her breathless as she rested her palms flat on her lover's broad shoulders. She gave a sob of pure emotion.

"Aye, love! Aye!" Slade's voice was low and fierce, demanding she succumb, demanding she submit to the pleasure. He clasped her so tightly, Bryony feared she would faint.

She responded with an instinct born and bred from generations of passionate women. As her liquid softness clenched his manroot, waves of ecstasy slammed over them both, and Bryony's head fell back. She flew swift and high on feathery wings of pure delight, keening her relief to the stars. For a moment it even seemed the shadow of a great flying bird fell over them, embracing them briefly in cold swirling darkness. Her eyes flew open, startled. Fear clutched her like an icy fist, but a second later Slade groaned deeply, flooding her with the warm and virile evidence of his love. He seemed to sense nothing wrong. The room spun softly about them, its darkening shadows blending their curves together into simpler lines of black and gold.

Gradually Bryony relaxed and rolled to Slade's side, where she rested her damp cheek upon his. She realized the moisture came from tears, only when he turned to kiss them gently away.

"Sweetheart, why do you cry?" he whispered.

"Because it can never be," she honestly replied, and when he did not gainsay her, she closed her eyes as if to deny the bitter reality morning would surely bring.

But with morning came other surprises. Bryony awoke to find herself alone, and for a stark moment feared Slade had left her altogether. Then she heard the whicker of horses somewhere outside, and the clatter of impatient hooves on the drive.

Sleepily she crawled from beneath the rumpled covers, wondering when and how she had managed to get under the blankets. She crossed the floor to one of the trunks Slade had sent, and drew a silken dressing gown from its depths.

Flinging it around her body, she moved to the window and peered out over the yard. In the drive below, two riderless steeds were hitched to the iron post. One was a big sorrel gelding, the other a dainty gray mare. She drew the curtains back in place and debated her next move. Who had arrived unannounced at Ambergate? Was it the woman Kit had hired, come at long last to assume her tasks?

Bryony tiptoed to the open bedroom door to see if she could overhear any voices in the hall below. There were none. A calm silence reigned over the apparently empty mansion, and more curious than afraid, she finally decided to brave the stairs.

She was halfway down the steps in her bare feet, when Slade stepped out from the banquet hall. Spying her, his eyes lit up, and a delighted grin curved his mouth.

"Good morning, my lady," he said, and proffered her a deep, somewhat exaggerated bow. Despite her mood, Bryony laughed. Slade was elegantly garbed in russet Venetian hose, his leather jerkin collared and faced with red fox fur. The doublet beneath appeared to be buff-colored velvet, with a low pointed waist trimmed with lace. He was freshly shaven, and his red gold hair shone as brightly as his Spanish boots.

Deciding to play along, she bobbed him a mock curtsy in her dressing gown. "Good morn, milord."

"Will you join me in breaking your fast?" he asked her seriously, a hand outstretched in invitation.

Bryony first cast a wary glance behind him. "Are we still alone?" she whispered. She thought of the two steeds tethered outside.

"Indeed we are, madam. After our meal, I intend to enjoy a brisk morning ride. Would you care to accompany me?"

Bryony's instant smile gave Slade his answer. He suggested she might wish to dress before coming down, as the fire in the great hall was unlit, and it was distinctly chilly in the morning room. Bryony agreed and returned to her room in order to select appropriate attire. She pored over the various gowns, until she found one to match Slade's outfit for taste and style.

It was a peach confection, daintily slashed and embroidered with exquisite detail. The long sleeves were fitted at the wrists, trimmed with ivory lace, then puffed and slashed at the shoulders to reveal cream-colored silk panes within. The underskirt was a creamy silk to match.

The wide-spreading taffeta skirts required a French farthingale for support, smaller and flatter than the cumbersome English version, but nearly as awkward to don. The stiff whalebone stays cinched her waist to a mere handspan. It was difficult for Bryony to dress herself without the assistance of a maidservant, but she managed.

Lastly, on went knee-length tailored hose of finest peach silk, with small embroidered bands to match the gown. The sturdy leather shoes Bryony selected would hold up better when riding than flimsy silk or velvet slippers. A soft-crowned Spanish hat of peach and ivory velvet topped off the stylish ensemble. A spray of ostrich plumes tilted rakishly off to one side.

When she descended to the hall at last, Bryony felt almost like the lady Slade had greeted earlier. And when he rose hastily to his feet from the table, his green eyes sparkling with pleasure, she knew she had chosen well.

"I feel as if a goddess of the dawn has consented to join me this morn," he said humbly, as Bryony's skirts whispered across the carpet in his direction. When she stopped before him, he raised her hand to his lips and held it in a lingering grasp.

Bryony's skin tingled at his faintly possessive touch. "I have you to thank for the beautiful wardrobe," she said.

" 'Tis little enough to make amends for everything else," Slade replied. He turned slightly to gesture at the sideboard. "I can hardly replace Cook, but it seems to be passable fare."

There was creamy porridge in two silver bowls, thick wedges of crusty bread, and a selection of ripe fruits and preserves. Golden butter in an earthen jar and slices of plump pink ham rounded out the repast. Bryony chose a little of everything and returned to the table to sate her hearty appetite. Slade had already eaten and watched her with visible pleasure, now and again pausing to fill her goblet with a deep red malmsey wine.

The fare was simple, but delicious. Bryony enjoyed everything on her plate, feeling a bit guilty for eating so ravenously. Her tight stays creaked in protest, when she finally rose to her feet.

"I'll clear the board," she began, but Slade shook his head and drew her by the elbow toward the door.

"Later. Our mounts are doubtless impatient to be off. Have you ridden before?"

Bryony gave an uncertain nod. It was true she had ridden Finn's horse a few times, but she'd never quite mastered the ornery old cobb. She imagined the Tanner stock would be even more high-spirited and frisky. Slade assured her otherwise, as he led her outside and introduced her to the gray mare.

"This is Arabella," he said, as he congenially rubbed the horse's velvety nose. "Let her get the scent of you first, before you try the saddle."

Bryony held out her hand palm-up as he instructed, and let the mare whiffle at her. "It tickles!" she laughed, as the horse's lips gently nibbled her flesh.

"She'll eat your puffs and pickadils, too, if you give her ample opportunity," Slade warned, when Arabella's nose began to roam in search of tasty tidbits. Bryony rescued the lavish lace of her sleeve just in time from the mare's greedy mouth. Slade stepped up to boost her into the sidesaddle, and she found she needed his help to arrange the vast skirts over the horse's rump and sides. Her beautiful gown was going to be quite soiled by journey's end, Bryony ruefully acknowledged. But it was too late to change now.

After seeing her safely settled, Slade mounted his sorrel gelding. They left Ambergate's yard at a slow pace. Sensing Bryony's uncertainty, even knowing Arabella was a good-natured and obedient mount, Slade decided their first outing should be leisurely. But still, it was rather amusing to discover there was something in life Bryony O'Neill had not yet mastered. He teasingly remarked on that fact, as they rode down the gently curving lane towards town.

"Oh, the O'Neill wouldn't keep horses," she breezily explained in her matter-of-fact way. "There was simply no opportunity for me to learn to ride."

"Why?" Slade asked. "Was your father afraid of them?"

Bryony gave a little chuckle, for the first time not hotly denying the Irishman's true relationship to her.

"Hardly," she replied. "He said they were useless beasts, not worth their keep. Favored by *Sassenach* oafs who had nothing better to do than to trundle their—ah—lazy behinds about."

Slade laughed. "He might well be right, from what I've seen

at Court. I rarely get a chance to ride myself. Kit's the true horseman in the family."

"Aye, your brother asked me to ride with him when he returns from the wedding. He said Elspeth has a bad back, and, of course, the girls are too young yet to accompany him."

"Take him up on the offer," Slade urged her. "Kit can instruct you much better in the ways of proper riding than I."

They were riding abreast down the narrow lane now, and Bryony turned her head to regard him a little hesitantly. "Are you certain? I mean, I thought you might be jealous—"

"Of Kit?" He gave a soft guffaw. "Bryony, I have absolutely no fears where my brother is concerned. He's the consummate gentleman, and faithful to a fault. Elspeth may be less than the ideal wife, but it would never occur to him to betray her or the children. 'Twas unfortunate he felt he had to marry Elspeth to hold onto Ambergate. Her generous dowry, you see, was needed to save the property after Father's death. The Crown tried to claim it several times in the past, and if not for Elspeth's money, Kit would have lost his inheritance.

"Though their marriage was never a love-match, Kit has tried to make it up to Elspeth. He has given her everything in his power, and in return asked only one thing: a son to carry on his name. In the beginning, I think, he loved her for the children's sake, despite her nature. So you see, poor Kit deserves a little pleasure out of life. Riding is his one true joy and only escape from dour reality, and 'tis only fitting he should be able to share that pleasure with a friend."

Bryony smiled, relieved by his words. Aye, she would dearly love getting outside on a daily basis, trotting Arabella through the lush green fields and breathing deeply of this fresh spring air. But then she remembered Slade's promise to send her home after this weekend was over. She shot a quick glance at his handsome profile, wondering if he had truly meant it. Should she ask? No, she decided, it would only shatter the beautiful morning, a day she selfishly wished would last forever.

Deep in thought, she did not notice they had reached the end of the lane, until Slade abruptly drew up his mount.

"Shall we head back now?" he asked her. Before them lay the busy road leading to London, clogged with horses and coaches even at the early hour. Before Bryony could reply, an open carriage trimmed with gleaming silver decorations came to a swaying halt in the road, stopping directly before them. She heard Slade swear softly under his breath when he recognized the passenger inside.

Bryony had no time to react. But she recognized the woman's flawless face. She had seen it once before, gracing a miniature. It was the lady Gillian Lovelle, Slade's betrothed.

Twelve

"Slade, darling, is that you?" the blonde cooed out the coach window. But beneath her silky tones lurked pure venom.

"Come on," Slade said in a low voice, nudging Bryony's mount with his knee to get her attention. "We're going back now." He started to rein his sorrel about in the lane, but a sharp comment from the other woman stayed him.

"Don't be a fool," Gillian hissed across the short distance separating them. "I have no intention of reporting your little indiscretion to the queen, dear heart, but 'twould be wiser of you not to parade your whore in public. Gossip is so rife nowadays at Whitehall. It tends to sorely upset Bess."

Slade flinched visibly. But his expression was calm as he regarded his betrothed with a steely gaze. "You will tender an apology, madam," he coolly responded. "Bryony here is my cousin. Surely you have heard Kit speak of her at Court."

Bryony did not know who was more surprised by the easy way Slade delivered the lie—her or Gillian. Her heart felt as if had been suddenly seized in a tight fist. Was Slade always so convincing when he lied? She could see the briefest hesitation in Gillian Lovelle's slitted, pale blue eyes. Then the beautiful woman swept a dismissing glance over her, and turned her attention back to Slade.

"One cannot always be certain," Gillian purred. "I heard rumor of a black-haired wench aboard your ship."

"An obvious mistake," Slade said.

"I am glad to hear it, dear heart. Nothing must come between us and our little family now, *n'est-ce pas?*"

Slade did not respond, except to stiffly touch the crown of his beaver hat. "We bid you good day, madam," he said, reining his horse about. Bryony followed his lead, turning Arabella swiftly in the narrow lane to return to Ambergate. Behind them, Gillian sputtered with anger and indignation for her coach could not easily pursue them. Eventually they heard the creaking of the springs, as the coach rumbled on down the road.

Bryony glanced at Slade. His features were grimly set and furious. She herself was a little shaken, not having expected to encounter Slade's betrothed so soon, if ever. Gillian's exquisite loveliness was indeed marred somewhat by the bitterness about her mouth and eyes, and her caustic manner. Bryony angered as she recalled the woman's snide comment about her position, and then drew herself up short. In the eyes of Elizabethan law, she *was* Slade's mistress.

How could she have forgotten for even one moment that Gillian, not she, was destined to become Slade's wife? Last night had not changed anything. Even Slade had admitted as much, by lying to Gillian about his relationship with Bryony. Cousin, indeed! The falsehood hurt, and even though she could understand Slade's reluctance to identify her to the other woman, her heart still cried out: *He has denied me!*

And somehow it seemed as if the magic of the morning had abruptly shattered into a thousand fragments, and Bryony was left with only a few pieces clutched in her trembling hands.

"Slade," she quietly asked him, "what did she mean about 'nothing coming between you and your little family?' "

He did not answer for a long moment. Only the steady plodding gait of the horses filled the silence. She waited, her hands clenched white on the saddle pommel.

"Gillian is pregnant," he said at last. This was uttered with the same terse indifference he might have used speaking of a mare in foal. "She claims the child is mine."

Bryony felt her legs go weak, and was glad for the support of the saddle. She braced herself for more to come, but Slade offered nothing. The gently waving fields of green blurred before her, and a moment later she tasted the hot salty tears in her mouth. *How dared the day be so beautiful?* she silently railed. *How dare it?*

Bryony did not ask the obvious. There was no need. If the child was not Slade's, he would have swiftly denied it. That left only one possibility, the one she had been secretly dreading all along. Oh, she did not doubt that there was genuine animosity between Slade and the lady Gillian, but he was an honorable man, and would doubtless do right by Gillian. It meant only one thing for Bryony: she had lost him. Had she truly ever had him to begin with? Little wonder Slade had stayed in London. It must have been for Gillian's sake, not hers. She longed to bury her burning face in her hands and give way to the sobs, but pride stiffened her shoulders, and she stared resolutely ahead. If Slade sensed her misery, he said nothing.

The mansion soon loomed above them like a white behemoth, looking far different from the charming country house where they had only recently shared their love. Last night had been so wonderful . . . and yet so terribly wrong! The horses came to a clattering halt in the yard, and the sweet notes of a warbler pierced the silence. The cheery birdsong only made Bryony want to weep. She avoided Slade's eyes as he assisted her down from the saddle. Numbly, she stood before him only by necessity; the mare blocked one avenue of escape, Slade the other.

"There's nothing I can say, is there?" he asked her quietly. Bryony did not want him to see the tears in her eyes, but his anguished gaze forcibly sought hers out. She sensed that he looked for the understanding that had been offered him last night. But everything had changed now, and his resigned sigh a second later seemed to indicate he realized that.

"You vowed to release me, did you not?" she said at last, almost choking with the effort. Somehow she managed to keep her chin high, though her eyes still burned with the unshed tears.

"Aye, Bryony," he whispered. "Though I'll damn myself forever for it."

Her throat ached with the words she longed to say, words of both consolation and castigation, but nothing issued forth. Bryony would always wonder what might have happened next, had the rattling approach of a coach upon the lane not distracted them both from the issue at hand. For a moment, she dreaded the possibility that Gillian had pursued them to the house and intended some further exchange of insults.

But she recognized the Tanner coach instead, far less ornate and much larger to accommodate Kit's growing family.

"They're back early," Slade remarked with surprise, but she couldn't tell if he was annoyed or relieved. His long stride carried him down the lane to meet the coach as it came to a stop. She watched from a distance as the Tanner family disembarked, everyone looking tired and cross from the long journey. The two brothers briefly embraced, and she saw Kit flick a concerned glance in her direction. She was too far away to hear what he said to Slade. She only knew that when Slade turned back to the house with the others, he wasn't smiling.

When Kit's two oldest girls spied Bryony, they shrieked with delight and came running toward her. Bryony could immediately tell Anne and Grace had been a handful on the trip. Both of their white dimity dresses were stained and rumpled, their red curls askew, as they arrived before her babbling breathless stories about the exciting journey north. Behind them tagged Isobel, the proverbial poor relation, looking wan and harassed and carrying Maggie in her arms.

"Here, let me take her," Bryony offered, reaching out to relieve the burden of the sleeping child from a weary Isobel. The young woman nodded in gratitude, too exhausted even to speak.

At that precise moment, Elspeth Tanner exited the coach, flinging the train of her dove-gray gown before her. When she saw Bryony holding her youngest daughter, she stiffened with outrage and said something brusque to Kit. He didn't dignify his wife's complaint with a reply, but left her in order to join the larger group on the drive.

"I imagine you're wondering why we're back so early," Kit said a little mischievously. "Would you believe our staid sensible Phillip chose to elope at the last moment?"

"What?" Bryony exclaimed, glancing over at Slade to see his reaction. He was finally smiling a little. "You mean after all the preparations were made, Phillip and his bride did not show up at the church?"

"Aye, and there was a fair row about it, too," Kit chuckled. "Faith's family accused the Tanners of raising an incorrigible and irresponsible son, and naturally I could not resist pointing out that there had been considerable rumor of—ahem—the good Reverend's supposedly chaste daughter being rather far gone in the family way."

"You mean—" Bryony began.

"Tanner men have never lacked for offspring," Kit said, with a loving glance at his own girls. "Remember, Slade, how Father used to complain he need only look at Mother, should he wish another son?"

"Aye," Slade murmured, looking less amused. Bryony could well understand, after their recent unpleasant encounter with Gillian Lovelle.

Elspeth finally joined them, bustling right up to rudely snatch little Maggie from Bryony's arms. She thrust the child back at Isobel, saying curtly, "Mind your duties, girl, if you wish to keep a roof over your head here!"

Maggie stirred and began to fuss, and Bryony had to hold her tongue as Isobel meekly took the children into the house. Elspeth cast Bryony a triumphant glance before she sailed away. Neither Kit nor Slade had an opportunity to intervene.

"I'm sorry, Bryony," Kit apologized after the other woman had disappeared into the house. "It seems the wasted journey put Elspeth into an even worse mood than usual. She's angry at Phillip for pulling such a stunt, disgusted with Faith for not better guarding her virtue, and, of course, vexed with the children as she usually is."

"I've never approved a man taking a strap to his wife," Slade put in grimly, "but 'twould appear there are a few times when it might be warranted."

Kit laughed at that, though Bryony sensed Slade was half-serious. Then Slade asked the coachman, Jem, to take Arabella back to the stables. He did not surrender his sorrel, though, nor remove the gelding's tack. Bryony realized he did not intend to stay at Ambergate another night. Slade confirmed her suspicions a short time later, when he offered up some excuse about needing to see to his ship and crew.

Kit's invitation for his brother to stay longer was politely but firmly declined. Bryony could only watch as Slade mounted his horse and prepared to leave. Had they been alone, she might have demanded some explanation of his actions. However, she could see nothing but cold resolution in his dark green eyes.

Slade offered only the briefest farewells, before he touched his hat to them and rode off down the lane. Bryony felt herself swaying, and Kit quickly grasped her arm. "Are you all right?"

She merely nodded. Was Slade angry with her, or the whole world? Why had he said nothing of her future, of his promise to return her to Ireland? The questions whirled in Bryony's mind, and she felt both helpless and frustrated.

She also suspected that Kit knew more than he let on. But he simply squeezed her arm in a brotherly fashion, turning to lead her into the house. "Come along. You look like you could use a cup of hot tea, laced with a dollop of brandy. Lord knows I could. That trip seemed endless. Can you imagine what I endured, being shut up for over eight hours in a hot coach with five chattering females? Felt like I was trapped in a pen with a damned gaggle of geese . . ."

Despite herself, Bryony smiled. She liked Kit a great deal.

It seemed he always had a ready balm at hand for her troubled heart.

Life quickly returned to normal, once the Tanner family settled back into their daily routine. Kit was distressed to hear the woman he had hired had never shown up, but was obviously relieved nothing untoward had happened in his absence.

Or so he assumed. The truth came later in the week, in the form of a curt note from Slade, along with sufficient monies for Bryony's return passage to Ireland. When he received the missive from his brother, Kit felt saddened by his duty to inform his guest that she could leave.

He had just begun daily riding excursions with Bryony, and enjoyed his role as riding instructor. She was a quick learner, and had advanced from a trot to a full gallop in less than two days. Already she had traded in the docile Arabella for a more spirited mount with a white blaze like lightning upon his nose. Summer Lightning was the horse's name, a four-year-old colt from Kit's beloved dam, Tudor Lass. Bryony had mastered the spirited steed as easily as she had the sea.

But now their lessons, it appeared, must come to an abrupt end. Kit rode out with Bryony one morning in order to deliver the news in private. He disliked the thought of shattering her lighthearted mood, and so waited until they had covered considerable ground, heading at a canter over the gently sloping hills towards the river.

Summer Lightning was in a frisky mood, tossing his head and prancing, with an obvious desire to gallop. But Bryony restrained him easily, laughing at Kit, who needed all his strength just to coax his own mount to keep to a canter.

Kit had several favorites in his stables, but exercised all the horses regardless. Today he was riding an old brown mare the children called Nimmie. Her full name was River Nymph, but her riding days were all but over. After her retirement from the stables, Kit intended to use the gentle hack to teach his girls to ride.

When they reached the banks of the river, Kit dismounted and helped Bryony down from the sidesaddle. They tied the two horses to a stout willow tree, and collapsed side by side on a grassy knoll to rest for awhile. Spring was in full bloom now. Bees buzzed around them, hunting for the sweet clover in the grass. Birds tittered in the trees, swallows swooped back and forth for insects hovering in the light wind. Bryony was watching the swallows, when Kit unexpectedly dropped something in her lap.

She glanced down at the heavy kidskin purse in surprise. "What's this for?"

"It's enough to see you home, and then some," Kit said. His voice held a note of apology. "A message came from Slade today. He intends for you to keep the clothes, as well."

"Surely he'd prefer Gillian have them. Or is she too petite?"

Kit winced at the anger in her voice, though his brother deserved no less. He decided it was up to him to try and explain Slade's position.

"Bryony, perhaps you don't understand that the queen has threatened to revoke Slade's charter, if he doesn't wed Gillian. He mustn't act rashly now—"

Her head turned, and her gaze sharpened on him. "What do you mean?"

"I mean he would be a suicidal fool to disobey Bess's orders. The whole family stands to suffer from her whims, not just Slade. He's protecting all of us by agreeing to marry Gilly. 'Tis the very reason he's also deliberately distancing himself from you." When she didn't reply, he added softly, " 'Tis also obvious as paint upon a post that you love my little brother. No, don't deny it." Kit raised a hand when she began to protest.

"I suspect he feels the same for you, Bryony. So I don't believe he'd mind my trying to explain things to you. Gillian wants to wed Slade, because of the secure position he offers her in Bess's Court. He may not have a title, but he's a favorite with the queen and comfortably settled. Theirs will be a marriage in name only, I think. But I vow Gillian is ruthless enough to see Slade and all the Tanners destroyed, if he tries to cross her now."

Kit saw the outrage flare in Bryony's beautiful blue eyes, and he quickly spoke again.

"There's nothing we can do. Gillian is the queen's ward, and Bess favors the match. For Slade to defy the queen would bring disaster down upon us all. 'Tis not the end of the world, Bryony. You're a lovely, intelligent girl, and there are other men who can appreciate that."

But Kit's words hit her harder than a fist, and her voice broke on a soft keening cry. "But I love *him!"* she cried, and the pain was so obvious in her eyes that Kit felt obliged to reach out and give her a brief hug.

"I know it hurts. And what can I say except I'm sorry for the both of you? Life dishes up some pretty dastardly things, and yet we all go on—"

Bryony pushed him away and jumped to her feet, flinging the purse of coins aside. She began to pace the grass furiously, neither wanting nor needing his sympathy. "You don't understand, Kit! You're telling me we can never be together, and never is a very long time!"

In the bright sunlight he noticed the dark circles beneath her glistening eyes, and realized for the first time the depth of her grief.

"Aye," he quietly admitted, "maybe I don't really understand. I've never suffered a love like that myself. Perhaps that is even more tragic."

Bryony put aside her own pain for a moment to imagine what it must be like for Kit, living with a cold heartless woman like Elspeth, someone who obviously despised his touch, and even his children. She understood Kit spoke from a different, but equally wrenching experience.

With a deep sigh, she calmed herself and settled down beside him on the grass again. "Kit," she said hesitantly, "if I wished to stay on at Ambergate a little while longer, would you indulge me?"

He looked at her long and hard, with green eyes too similar to Slade's for comfort. Then at last he nodded.

"Only on one condition. That you'll give up any foolish notions about my little brother. Let him go, Bryony, please. For everyone's sake."

She nodded in return. What Kit asked of her was only fair. She would not willingly endanger him or his little girls. But she had discovered in the past few days that she as yet had no desire to return to Ireland. What awaited her there except the O'Neill's certain chastisement, and the painful reality of the deaths of her crew? She was not ready to accept the fact that she would never see O'Grady's merry face again, nor ever lovingly scold her underage crew. Mab probably missed her, just as she surely missed the dear old woman, but right now she could hardly bear the thought of Mab's knowing eyes peering straight into her soul.

For Mab, many said, had the Second Sight. She would know at once what Bryony had endured, see the pain and heartache hidden so carefully behind her smile, where most others could not glimpse it. No, she wasn't quite ready yet to face the old woman. That, along with the bitter reality of her and Slade's empty future, must wait until she could better accept them both.

Thirteen

England, Summer 1578

Spring gradually melted into summer, and due to the increasing heat and crowded conditions in the city, disease soon began to make its annual appearance. Kit took a break from his duties at Court, not wanting to take the chance of exposing his family to any of a myriad of illnesses. Besides the dreaded smallpox, miasma and dysentery were also common. Consumption especially tended to flourish in the damp climate.

As the weather warmed, the Thames began to stink of rotted garbage and the pestilence generated from hordes of flies. Luckily, Ambergate was far enough from the river to avoid the ghastly smells, except when the wind reversed direction.

To avoid any chance of illness herself, the queen had taken to travelling again, visiting whatever fresh country site caught her fancy. For those fortunate—or unfortunate enough—to be honored with a royal visit, the preparations alone were staggering. Large numbers of ladies and courtiers descended upon the hapless residents of Castle Such-and-Such, or many a quaint midland estate, and vast quantities of luggage, furniture, and supplies followed in their wake.

The royal convoy moved slowly, no more than twelve miles a day, giving ample warning to those ahead. But even the most talented chatelaine found it hard to prepare for the onslaught of such noisy, ill-mannered, demanding guests.

Elizabeth Tudor expected a high standard of ceremony, and

lavish entertainments were not optional, but required. Hence, the ever-dutiful, if not overly eager, gentry welcomed their sovereign at the boundaries of each county. The queen waved and smiled serenely from her coach of checkered emeralds, diamonds, and rubies, at the sight of flags waving and the sound of church bells clanging a merry welcome. Most evenings fireworks were set off, and pageants staged for the amusement of the easily bored courtiers.

Thankful to have escaped Whitehall for a time, Kit came home to rest during those few weeks of reprieve. He looked older and more tired to Bryony.

She had never intended to feed so long off Kit's hospitality, but somehow the weeks had trickled by. Though she tried to insist on paying for her keep, Kit refused, and instead asked her to stay on for the children's sake. His girls had taken a special shine to her, as had Isobel, and although Elspeth had made her displeasure with Bryony clear from the outset, at least Kit had a say concerning guests in his home.

During her days at Ambergate, Bryony spent much of the time romping with Kit's three redheaded cubs, and sharing exciting stories of the sea with Isobel in exchange for a few lessons in dressing her hair and Elizabethan manners. Although she knew Kit's wife disliked her and would welcome her departure, it gave Bryony a perverse pleasure to linger on and irritate the ill-tempered woman.

Certainly, Elspeth had made Kit's life a living hell. She constantly carped and complained, not above verbally denigrating her husband before the children. Her snide remarks extended to their guest, too, until, weary of the harassment, Bryony waged a counterattack before the others.

"*I* should never be so bold a hussy as to accept gifts from a man betrothed to another," Elspeth once remarked, very loudly and virtuously at the table.

"Never fear, madam. I cannot imagine you should ever have cause to inspire similar admiration," Bryony replied.

Elspeth was too shocked to respond. Few had dared to challenge her before. But although Bryony had won that battle, she also realized the woman's accusations were true enough. After all, she and Slade had become lovers, and he was indeed betrothed to someone else. That fact made her both an interloper, and a woman of the worst repute. Did she honestly expect him to leave Gillian for her? Would she respect him, if he did?

Whenever she thought of their last night together, her throat tightened. Though Slade had visited Ambergate a few times since his initial departure, he never stayed long. Mostly he played with his nieces, whom he clearly adored, or discussed business matters with Kit in the privacy of his brother's study. Bryony merited only a formal greeting, though their eyes always met and the electricity in the air could have easily started a fire.

During a hiatus from Court, Kit received an invitation to a royal masque. Bryony was again ready to leave, but Kit persuaded her to stay on a week longer, by convincing her that word of the missing *Alanna Colleen* might arrive when many of the queen's captains attended the formal affair.

The September masque was to be held in honor of the Duc d'Alencon, a French contender for Elizabeth's hand in marriage. Kit described the duke as a man half the queen's age, somewhat smallish in stature, with a nose rumored to resemble that of a parrot's beak. Though the poor nobleman was considered to be quite homely, and a disappointing candidate in that respect, he could hardly be faulted for either his impeccable taste in clothing, or his high ambitions with regard to the Virgin Queen.

The masque, Elizabeth proclaimed, was to be based upon the theme of birds. It was said that the young duke had a fancy—or some said fetish—for feathered creatures. The queen was happy enough to oblige his unusual hobby, and ordered her Court to attend the spectacular gala *en force.*

Kit was not surprised to be included in the summons, being an acknowledged favorite in Bess's Court, but there was a very obvious oversight when Elspeth was not named as his partner. He chuckled a little at this, knowing the dislike was mutual between the two strong-willed women. He soon learned that Elspeth would have snubbed an invitation in any case, even though doing so might be considered a form of treason. He immediately cast about for another partner for the masque. The answer, when it came, was obvious—Bryony O'Neill. He put the question to her at once, delighted when she said yes after some hesitation.

" 'Twill give me a rare chance to ask the other captains about the *Alanna Colleen*," she said with visibly growing excitement.

Kit nodded. "But you'll have to be very careful, Bryony. Bess is liable to think you a spy, if she hears wind of an Irishwoman plying her guests with such unusual questions."

"But you said it's a masque, Kit. Doesn't that mean all the participants are in disguise?"

He followed her logic with a slow spreading grin. "Aye, I see what you're getting at. Well, as long as you stay away from the center of attention, she shouldn't pick up on it. But remember, there are spies among the queen's court, too. Be extremely cautious of what you say and do."

"I will," Bryony promised him absently, already turning her thoughts ahead to what she could wear. With Isobel's help, she swiftly decided on her costume, and the bird she would represent.

She would go as Raven, the centuries-old symbol of the O'Neill clan, and thus flout Elizabeth Tudor right beneath her own nose. With the help of Isobel and two of the upstairs maids, she quickly altered one of her gowns into a suitable costume for the event.

All four women giggled and gabbed over their secret project, working far into the wee hours of the morning, after Elspeth and the children were abed. Bryony did not want to risk Kit's wife learning of her design, and possibly trying to thwart her plans. Isobel and the others were sworn to secrecy, and even assisted her with purchasing several eccentric items needed to perfect the outfit. Even Kit was excluded from their project, lest he try to dissuade Bryony.

At last, the first weekend of September arrived, and with it the cooler weather all London had prayed for. The great masque was to be held at Whitehall, recently reopened. The Court's absence for several months had provided a rare opportunity for a thorough cleansing. The queen had deemed the palace suitable for receiving her French suitor with all due pomp and circumstance.

The finishing touches were put to both Kit's and Bryony's costumes, and the Tanner coach was readied for the evening. By design, Kit and Bryony would be among the last to arrive, so as to slip in and blend more easily with the crowd.

Kit already regretted his choice of partner for the night. Not because of who Bryony was, but because he rightfully worried as to how she would fare among so many wolves. He knew what manner of blackguards served Bess on bended knee. Most were base opportunists, fawning courtiers with a shrewd eye for beauty, and a shrewder one for debasement. Many a maid had lost her innocence or her purse to such charming rogues. He feared he might be called upon to defend Bryony's honor more than a time or two tonight.

Watching Bryony descend Ambergate's staircase in the full regalia of her costume, Kit's heart sank even further. Her gown was no less than stunning, crafted from a simple sheath of pure black silk, unencumbered by stiff hoops or even a farthingale. It clung to Bryony's flesh like a second skin, glistening with deep blue highlights to match her hair.

Her tresses had been artfully arranged to resemble a raven's wing, drawn to one side and over her left shoulder in a shimmering curve. Threaded through the ebony locks were genuine raven feathers, at a distance indistinguishable from her hair.

In her right hand she carried a large fan, dramatically fashioned from more raven feathers and generously sprinkled with tiny jet beads. The only color to be seen on her person came in the form of the magnificent amulet around her neck. When it flashed in Kit's direction, he glimpsed the image of a flying raven deeply etched into the gold.

Bryony O'Neill was a dark proud beauty, he thought, like night itself emerging to cast a pall over the sun. Kit took a deep breath, steadying himself as he took her arm. Beneath the black velvet half-mask obscuring her face, he caught a mischievous glint of her sea blue eyes.

"You'll strike them silent," he prophesied.

Bryony laughed. "Just your queen, and then I should be content. Elizabeth has played unfairly with my folk for too long."

Kit took that as a hint of things to come tonight, and shook his head in despair. How had he gotten himself into this?

"I believe we look very well together," Bryony said, admiring his costume as well. Kit was obviously a robin, in his gray-and-black paned trunkhose and a scarlet tuft-taffeta doublet. A jerkin of soft gray leather was fastened over his "red breast" now, but would be removed later at the masque. The winged and stiffened sleeves of his doublet had been slightly enlarged, to effect the illusion of flight.

"I confess I feel ridiculous enough now, but I'm apt to be somewhat consoled once we arrive at Whitehall and I get a glimpse of all the other fools," he chuckled.

They both had chosen dark cloaks to conceal their costumes, but they waited until the excited children had a peek at them before they were whisked off to bed by Isobel. Elspeth had taken to her bedchamber earlier with a headache, and did not appear to wish them farewell, so there was nothing left to do then but go to the palace. Hoping he had made the right decision after all, Kit escorted Bryony to the queen's masque.

Every road to Whitehall was jammed for miles that night.

"Either Bess has invited the entire city to view her latest beau, or we are mistaken and this is actually a funeral procession," Kit jested as once again their coach rumbled to a halt in the heavy traffic. He opened the window and stuck his head out to peer in vain for the source of the delay.

"Can you see anything?" Bryony asked.

"No, but I hear a terrible cacophony somewhere up ahead," came his muffled reply. "I think there must have been an accident of some sort."

Inch by inch they continued on, almost an hour passing before they could tell what was going on. Kit's jest had not been far off the mark. Their driver shouted something back at Kit, when next he leaned out the window. Kit hastily yanked his head back inside and shut the window. For good measure, he yanked the shade over the scene they were about to skirt.

"What is it?" Bryony exclaimed. She could hear weeping and wailing outside the coach, and shivered at the mournful cries of human misery.

" 'Tis the pox," Kit said. "Spreading like wildfire through the East End. They're closing certain streets in Town to try and prevent further deaths."

Suddenly Bryony caught a whiff of a disgusting, acrid smell. "Oh, Kit, not—"

"Aye." He fumbled in a pocket and then pressed a silk handkerchief upon her. "They're burning the bodies."

But even through the sweet cloying scent of ambergris, Bryony still smelled the nauseating smoke of burning flesh. She shuddered, and Kit wrapped an arm around her shoulders in a comforting brotherly fashion. He, too, had pinched his nostrils shut, but breathing through his mouth instead, he felt as if he tasted the fouled air.

It seemed hours before they passed through the area of scourge and reached the palace grounds. By then both of them were considerably sobered in mood, and alighted from the coach with pale faces. Kit's driver, perhaps more used to such unpleasantries, seemed unaffected and even sent them off with a cheery wave.

Bryony clutched Kit's arm to regain her balance. She feared

for a moment that she was drowning in a sea of live bodies. In a daze, she let Kit lead her through a marble hall filled with bright lights and crowded with costumed revelers. It was lushly decorated with hothouse blooms, colorful ribbons, and various works of art.

They were greeted at the entrance to the masque by a pompous fellow dressed as a blue jay, who demanded to see Kit's invitation, all the while discreetly glancing at Bryony's bosom. Finally they were admitted through this gilded portal into another world, and craned their necks in appreciation of the exquisite decorations. From the foiled ceiling floated silk ribbons, fashioned like leaves and flowers. The main gallery had been transformed into a giant mock bird cage, complete with golden ribbon bars running down the walls. Already it was filled with every variety of bird imaginable—all in human guise, of course. Everyone had obeyed Elizabeth's whim, and wore masks and lavish costumes.

Bryony couldn't help but stare at a passing couple, a leggy heron paying court to a dainty hummingbird of a lady. Just beyond them, Kit pointed out an even more ludicrous sight, that of a vulture hovering behind his chosen prey for the evening, a woman dressed as a swan, gliding serenely along with white skirts wide as a hedgerow.

Bryony laughed softly to her partner. "Oh, what I wouldn't give to drop the O'Neill right here in the midst of all this nonsense."

"A crusty old salt, is he?" Kit asked.

"Aye, the worst sort, especially when it comes to the English. He can't stand pomp and circumstance, let alone such pageantry. What would he make of all this, I wonder?"

Within the hour, everyone had moved to assemble before a huge circular stage built in the west wing of the palace. Along the way, Kit had pointed out to Bryony the tilt-yard, cockpit, bowling alley, and tennis court Elizabeth's royal sire, Henry VIII, had ordered constructed during his reign.

Whitehall had originally been known as York Place, and

once belonged to Cardinal Wolsey, the archbishop of York. The king had taken a fancy to it, and, in the straightforward manner commonplace to so many Tudor monarchs, had seized the building and grounds from the archbishop, along with Hampton Court.

Greenwich Palace, where Elizabeth I spent much of her time, had been deemed too small to receive the Duc d'Alencon and his enormous retinue in the proper style, so the Court had returned to Whitehall for the masque and related festivities. The stage and surrounding chambers had been mocked up to resemble a Roman city this night. Soaring white pillars wound with ivy and flowers set the stage for the little *commedia dell'arte.*

Bryony noticed that her and Kit's arrival attracted a great deal of attention. Though Kit wore a mask, his banner of red hair was very distinctive.

"That's not Elspeth Tanner," she overheard one woman whispering to her male partner, as she and Kit threaded past the couple for a better view of the stage.

"Aye," the masked man agreed, in a low speculative Scottish burr. "Elspeth does no' hae a figure like that!"

"Jamie MacNab!" The woman slapped her escort with her feather fan in reproof, before the two moved off and were lost in the crowd. Amused, Bryony looked after them until Kit drew her attention back to the stage and low balcony above it.

The queen and her proposed French consort finally made their belated appearance. As one, the Court gathered below the balcony swept graceful curtseys and low bows of respect to the royal pair. There was no mistaking Queen Elizabeth, though she was a good sport and had donned a brightly spangled mask for the festivities. She had chosen to appear as Peacock.

Over the queen's huge wheel-farthingale, yards of sky blue and green silk flowed into a long train studded with sapphires, emeralds, midnight blue lapis lazuli, and pale blue Persian turquoise. These jewels represented the eyes in the peacock's tail, though genuine peacock feathers had also been arrayed into a fanlike display attached to the padded roll around her hips. Whenever Elizabeth Tudor moved, the entire gown glittered from head to toe. Even her kid slippers were generously stitched with tiny gems and reflected the lights as she pivoted slowly from side to side, acknowledging the hearty accolades of her court.

Against her will, Bryony was impressed by the English queen. Elizabeth Tudor carried herself with such innate dignity, that it seemed she could be nothing else but royalty, born to the throne, as it were.

Beside the Virgin Queen, yet standing in the shadows literally and otherwise, was the Duc d'Alencon. The young man had chosen to don the costume of a most appropriate bird—a mallard duck. Though no doubt his bejeweled bottle-green silk doublet and royal tan trunkhose were intended to impress, his neck was all but swallowed up in an enormous cartwheel ruff; and his short and stubby stature gave him the illusion of waddling along behind Elizabeth, as she moved along the balcony.

Bryony stifled a laugh, watching the sadly mismatched couple making their little promenade. She was apparently not the only one to have noticed the unlikely pair these royals made, for a nearby chuckle caught her attention. She turned and sought the source, and caught sight of a tall man disguised as a Hawk pressing a gloved hand to his smiling lips.

Then several lights were extinguished, so the Court focused all its attention on the stage. The comedy began with a flourish, as a handful of Italian actors skipped out to the bang of a drum. Trained to improvise rather than act, the performers launched into a brazen rollicking spectacle of dances, jests, and gymnastics. Kit whispered in Bryony's ear by way of explanation that although the play always had the same stock characters, they were completely unpredictable. No two performances were the same.

The lead character, an artful maidservant called Columbina, was the only one without a mask. Bryony had never seen a female actress before, and was fascinated by this dark-eyed tease, who played to the audience and her fellow actors with such ease. Columbina led her conspirators on a merry adventure that bordered on the bawdy at times.

For the grand finale, the clownish valet called Arlecchino entered into a mock duel with Capitano, a boastful soldier. The men scuffled wildly on stage to Columbina's shrieks of encouragement, and eventually ended up in two sorry panting heaps, which set the audience to roaring with laughter and approval. Bryony clutched her aching sides, having laughed so hard herself she feared her stays would split. She was sorry to see the play end, and noticed the queen was smiling with pleasure at the success of the entertainment.

Though the play was ended, the night had just begun. Everyone adjourned to the Great Hall, where music was already underway, a ceremonial *danse basse* pacing the entrance of Elizabeth Tudor and the French *duc.*

Kit kept Bryony firmly pasted to his arm. So far she had kept to her promise and stayed silent, content to watch with wide eyes all the other unique birds and their eccentric behaviors. Surely, Kit prayed, he and his beautiful partner would not attract any undue attention tonight. Yet he still felt like a ship boldly sailing into enemy waters with a foreign flag flying on the mast.

He led Bryony into the gliding circle of dancers. For several refrains, the entire Court revolved around Elizabeth and her suitor, though the poor duke resembled nothing so much as a bewildered duck standing in the center of a busy marketplace.

The drama and pageantry were exciting to a young woman who had never even dreamed such events existed. Bryony threw herself wholeheartedly into the celebration, and Kit laughingly restrained her from jumping into a lively gailliard when the music abruptly changed. He quickly drew her to the sidelines to watch the other dancers instead.

Bryony pouted with mock disappointment and waved her fan furiously at her flushed cheeks. "It's so stifling in here! There's not enough air to go around."

"I'll get you something to drink," Kit offered. "Stay put, and don't move a feather!"

She nodded at his stern order, content to stay where she was. But she was aware of numerous male birds gazing speculatively in her direction the second Kit left, and smiled to herself in a secret female fashion which felt totally unfamiliar. She knew her costume was both unusual and striking, and realized everyone at Whitehall was trying to guess who Kit's partner was.

Doubtless some rumor would start to the effect that the family man had a raven-haired mistress. Bryony didn't care one whit for such gossip, and Elspeth would probably pay it no heed. The woman might even be relieved, if her husband turned his unwanted attentions elsewhere.

But Kit's little girls were the ones who needed to be protected. Therefore, Bryony decided, her behavior this night would be exemplary. She turned a cold shoulder to the flirtatious rogues and bold courtiers, who dared to make a move now that her escort was gone. When she caught sight of two men converging in her direction, obviously intending to trap her in a corner, she picked up her skirts and squeezed through the crush of bodies in search of a safer spot.

In the sweltering crowd of revelers she felt a male hand rudely grope her breast, another her thigh. She gasped in outrage, but dared not strike out for fear of hitting the wrong person, or another woman. The tide of joyous celebrants carried her helplessly along, as Bryony struggled to free herself from the crush. She might as well have attempted swimming upstream, for all the ground she gained.

Then at last she was abruptly discharged from the swirling mill of humanity into a side corridor. She gasped with relief and stumbled a little to regain her balance. As she did so, she accidentally bumped into another woman.

"Forgive me—" Bryony began. They both reached to free the long trains of their skirts at the same time, but found them hopelessly entangled. It forced them both to stop and face one another, if only for a moment.

"Clumsy little fool!" the other woman snapped, as she tugged impatiently at the glistening white folds of her costume.

There was something disturbingly familiar about the petite woman swathed in snow white silk. Even her hair was powdered silver gilt, and was dressed with pearls. Bryony had not intended to stare, but the rude manner of the woman perturbed her somewhat. It seemed all too familiar.

The Raven contemplated the Dove for a long moment, until behind the white velvet half-mask a pair of pale blue eyes rose and met Bryony's. They narrowed a second later.

"You!" Gillian Lovelle snarled. "I might have guessed. Obviously Slade's cousin is no brighter than he. Extend your apologies at once, girl! You have surely torn my hem."

"As I recall, my lady, you are the one who still owes an apology," Bryony replied in a voice as cool as a winter wind.

Gillian gasped and made a swift move to strike her rival. Bryony easily blocked the blow with her wrist, though her fan was sacrificed for the cause. The broken raven feathers drifted down to the floor, where the other woman promptly crushed them under her little heel.

"Impertinent chit," Gillian muttered before she turned and swept away. "Best watch your tongue, or I shall see 'tis cut out and fed to Bess's royal mutts!"

A moment later Gillian was gone, their gowns no worse for the encounter. But Bryony remembered the woman's vile threats to see Slade and his family ruined. The queen's goddaughter was a powerful woman here in the Tudor court. What chance did Bryony have to defend herself or anyone else against such vicious acts of revenge?

Her stomach gave a sickening plunge when she thought of something else. Where Gillian Lovelle lurked in the guise of a dove, no doubt Slade himself flew not far behind.

* * *

Slade Tanner stared in disbelief at the figure who had just materialized across the hall. There was no way to ascertain his suspicions yet, but in his pursuit of Gillian, he had seen his fiancée pause for a few moments before a masked woman garbed in black silk.

The slender figure with the generous waterfall of night dark hair, painfully reminded him of Bryony. But he convinced himself that there was no way she could be here. She'd left for Ireland long ago, hadn't she? Kit had assured him as much. Though on the day he heard that Bryony would set sail, Slade felt an ache in his breast that made him more aware of his misery than ever.

Already he regretted having given in to Gillian's incessant whining by coming to the queen's masque. But when the invitations had been sent out, and Gilly had pouted and begged enough to drive any man insane, he had finally surrendered and tried to convince himself that perhaps enough time had safely passed for him to attempt to speak again with Bess.

He hoped once Elizabeth saw how miserable and ill-suited he and Gillian were, she would at last relent. Their arranged wedding was now less than two weeks hence. But to Slade's fury, Gillian had deliberately played the role of the perfect lady tonight, clinging to his arm and gazing up at him insipidly whenever Bess glanced their way.

But when the queen finally retired to her throne to watch the other dancers, Gillian promptly deserted Slade in search of fresh game. He watched her head off in pursuit of a French count she had dabbled with earlier in the Season, one of the duke's hangers-on. Slade intended to interrupt their cozy little rendezvous, and expose them to Bess's harsh brand of justice. Everyone knew the queen had little mercy for maidens who dallied with men beneath her nose. She expected perfect unflagging loyalty from everyone, especially her ladies. Bess was a strict monarch, but fair. Slade was counting on her sympathies, once Gilly's perfidy was revealed.

But he hadn't expected to be confronted with the woman

he loved in the process. He knew without a doubt that the beautiful raven across the hall was Bryony O'Neill, once he caught a glimpse of the amulet about her throat. *Little fool!* he silently railed at her, even as his heart swelled with unexpected happiness and relief. She hadn't left, after all!

Feeling the sudden sensation of a gaze pinning her against the wall, Bryony caught her breath. A quick glance around betrayed nobody visibly staring at her, but the disconcerting sensation continued until she finally spotted the golden-haired Hawk boldly eying her from across the hall.

With a swift glance she took in the long muscular legs clad in tan trunkhose, the tawny velvet doublet embroidered with copper metal thread, and the lace-edged falling band bordering a neck bronzed by the sun. The man's golden hair was partially concealed by a soft velvet cap tipped with hawk feathers. Even though his face was obscured by a tan velvet mask, she knew in a flash why the husky chuckle earlier at the play had caught her attention. It had struck a familiar chord in her memory, and her heart. *Slade!*

The name almost broke from her lips, but not before Kit returned and pushed a goblet into her hand.

"I thought I told you to stay put," he playfully scolded her. "I had a devil of a time finding you."

"What is it?" Bryony asked, dropping her gaze to the contents of the goblet. Her cheeks still burned from the Hawk's intense, unwavering stare.

"Red wine," Kit said. "You look as though you could use it, too. Drink up!"

Watching the couple across the room, Slade felt his insides tighten. He, like everyone else, recognized Kit even in costume. But the note of gladness in his heart was tempered now with the darker suspicion that Bryony might be working her delightful wiles upon his brother.

'Twas ridiculous to even think such a thing, Slade sternly scolded himself, but he couldn't help it. He knew in his heart his brother wasn't one for dalliances; Kit was a reliable husband and devoted father. Besides the fact that Kit simply did not have the same damned weakness for blue-eyed Irish witches that Slade did . . .

But if Bryony had not stayed in England for Kit's sake, then why was she here? Slade knew he must learn the answer, if only so he could firmly exorcise her from his thoughts and dreams once and for all.

Fourteen

One moment Bryony sensed she was being closely scrutinized, then just as swiftly the sensation faded away. She dared to glance in Slade's direction again, but he had melted away somewhere into the crowd.

She tried to quell her pounding heart by exchanging small talk with Kit. She quickly asked him the names and identities of several of the costumed guests, and he obliged her.

"That tall fellow over there, the one dressed as a stork, that's the queen's treasurer, William Cecil."

Bryony smothered laughter behind her hand, watching Cecil stalk the hall. "He even walks like one!"

"And the pretty canary in the corner is one of Elizabeth's maids, Bess Throckmorton." Kit indicated a voluptuous lady whose diaphanous costume of bright yellow silk and feathers descended in a wispy fashion around her.

"She's very lovely," Bryony remarked.

"Aye. The queen likes to surround herself with pretty women. Mayhaps it makes it easier for her to imagine that she, too, is beautiful." Kit spoke in a low voice, obviously not wanting to be overheard.

"Elizabeth Tudor is striking," Bryony said. "She doesn't need to be beautiful." Her gaze drifted again to the ginger-haired woman regally perched on her throne. There was an arrogance of manner and prideful bearing about the Tudor woman that, oddly enough, did not anger Bryony.

Instead, she admired Elizabeth Tudor's backbone, while at

the same time Bryony pitied her present position. As Kit had explained, the queen's advisors all anxiously sought to marry her off, for any unmarried woman—especially a queen—was thought to be a weak and unnatural creature. Bryony felt equally sorry for the poor French *duc,* seated beside Elizabeth upon a raised dais, almost but not quite on the queen's level.

While Elizabeth looked distinctly pleased by the success of her masque, young d'Alencon seemed either bored or distressed by the evening's events. He only nodded or replied abruptly, whenever the aging queen leaned close to murmur something in his ear.

"I predict that match is not to be," Bryony wryly remarked to her own partner.

"I believe you're right." Kit was impressed by her insight. "Francis is a good man, a gentleman, but Bess needs someone with a firm hand."

"Ah, that one won't take to bit nor bridle, Kit. Nor should she be expected to."

His eyebrows rose. "This, coming from an Irishwoman?"

Bryony chuckled. "I'm not defending Elizabeth Tudor, merely making an observation. She fairly radiates strength of character. She's made of sterner stuff than either you or I, Kit. Besides, where is it written that a woman must have a husband to have a meaningful life?"

Kit gave her a look of mock alarm. "The Bible, among other places. Best beware, m'dear. You might be sent to the Tower for spouting such an enlightened ideal."

She merely laughed and slipped her arm through his. "Darling Kit, had you no familial responsibilities here, I'd be sorely tempted to pay my crew to kidnap you, and bring you on board my ship for a lesson in female leadership. Better yet, bring your queen with you. I have a feeling she'd make an admirable understudy for the captaincy."

Kit chuckled. "Faith, I have a feeling you two have dangerously much in common! Both headstrong women entirely intent upon your own courses in life. And why do I also sense neither one of you are willing to listen to the voice of reason?"

"Come now, when have I ever given you any indication otherwise?" Bryony teased him.

"The moment you saw my brother here tonight. Nay, don't bother to deny it. I know it took everything you had for you to stay in one place and not go to him. I'm proud of you for keeping your promise. But remember your word to me, Bryony. Leave him be."

She sobered as well. "Aye, Kit. Let none say an O'Neill cannot keep a sworn oath. But I confess to you, 'tis likely the hardest thing I've ever had to do."

Pausing in the darkened corridor, Gillian Lovelle glanced warily over her shoulder one last time, before she threw herself into her latest lover's arms.

"Cherie," Pierre breathed lustily against her powdered hair, "I thought you had forgotten!"

"No," Gillian replied a bit impatiently, "I was merely waylaid by a clumsy little cousin of Slade's. Doubtless the sly chit intended to tear my gown on purpose. She was jealous of all the attention I was receiving."

The count suddenly laughed, and she stiffened in his arms with annoyance. "What, pray tell, is so amusing?"

"You speak of the mysterious Raven, no doubt. I saw you two collide from across the hall. The Court is all atwitter over her beauty and true identity. But surely you do not believe she is any relative of your betrothed. Rumor holds that Tanner brought the wench with him back from Ireland."

"La, then she must be his mistress. Slade always did have poor taste. It must be his common blood." Gillian gave a little trill of carefree laughter, while inwardly she raged. *How dare Slade humiliate me in this fashion!* But even as she made a mental note to make her wayward fiance pay dearly for his little indiscretion, she lovingly groped Pierre's groin. The

Frenchman groaned when she squeezed him a little too roughly for comfort.

"Ahhh, beloved, you are the sort of woman who never changes. A dangerous lover, and an even deadlier foe. Yet still I crave your kisses." Pierre suddenly took her mouth in a savage kiss. Gillian moaned and rubbed lewdly against him, as he moved to yank the gown down about her shoulders.

"I must love you, my little dove. Let me sample your sweet delights!"

"Not here!" She broke from his embrace to cast another furtive look behind them. "Slade is looking for me."

"Where, then?" Pierre was unperturbed and persistent. He considered Tanner a complete fool, because the captain intended to marry a woman better suited to be a mistress, and also because Slade let Gillian get away with her affairs right under his nose. Had Gillian been his own wife or fiancée, Pierre decided, he would have beaten her black and blue for even glancing at another man.

As things went, however, Gillian made a passionate and interesting mistress, though she was inclined to be greedy, and he'd grown a bit weary of her tantrums. She'd led Pierre a merry chase for nearly six months, remarkable indeed as the count was renowned for his conquests. But then, Gillian was an accomplished tease. She studied her lovers beforehand, and chose them with the same careful consideration one would normally give a prospective husband.

She'd told Pierre that she had no intention of repeating the mistake of her betrothal and getting involved with a man of no account or means. Thus, the count and Gillian's other lovers were all older wealthy men. Some had curious predilections and perverted preferences where lovemaking was concerned, but Gillian cared not as long as they were generous with her. Pierre was the most exciting of the lot, for even at fifty he still had the stamina of a bull.

The Frenchman swiftly pulled Gillian up a narrow spiral staircase, ignoring her halfhearted whispers of protest. The two emerged into a little alcove, lit only faintly from the revelry below, and located almost directly above the queen's throne.

The forbidden thrill was exquisite to Gillian. She gasped with pleasure as Pierre thrust up her skirts, backing her hard against the wall. He unfastened his codpiece just far enough to do the trick, and slammed brutally into her as she moaned and squealed with unabashed delight.

Collapsing against her some minutes later, Pierre's breathing rasped noisily in her ear. Gillian coyly bit his earlobe and begged for an encore, but for once he was not able to perform.

The count weakly withdrew, haphazardly adjusting his red grouse costume. He felt sweat trickling down his brow as he stared at the tousled blonde leaning against the wall. Pierre feverishly mused to himself that never before had he seen a live angel with the soul of a devil.

"Pierre? Are you all right?" Gillian hissed. His dark eyes were glassy, and he almost frightened her with his vacant stare.

"O—oui," he stammered, "it is just that for a moment, I felt a little dizzy." He mopped at his damp brow with his embroidered velvet sleeve, as he turned away from her.

Gillian shrugged and brushed it off as his age. After all, Pierre was no longer a young man. It was a compliment to her that she could exhaust him so quickly, and set his head to spinning. When he glanced at her again, she gave him a wicked smile and reached out to chuck him under the chin.

"Come on, lover, let's have another quick round of fun, before my poor fiance stumbles upon us. And then we'll adjourn to the privacy of your chamber, and you can give me that little diamond bracelet you promised me last month."

Slade lost sight of Gillian during the changing of the dancers in the crowded gallery. Cursing softly, he began to stalk the confines of the hall, glancing into every dark doorway or recessed space. He was aware of several amused glances coming from men he knew had sampled Gillian's charms. It only made him all the more determined not to wear the costume of a cuckold tonight.

But in the process of searching for his wayward betrothed, he ended up on the same side of the hall as Bryony. And when he was within a few feet of her, he could not resist approaching, if only to gauge the reaction in those beautiful blue eyes behind the black mask.

"Good evening, Mistress Bryony." Slade bowed stiffly from the waist, glad that Kit was not there to witness the encounter. His brother had wandered off just moments before, and like the proverbial hawk, Slade had swept down on his prey.

Bryony's temper flared at Slade's crisply formal address. There was not a hint of the tenderness that had existed previously between them, and his eyes were chips of green ice through his mask.

"Good evening," she replied, hoping she sounded as indifferent as he. "Are you looking for someone?"

You know damn well who I'm chasing all about the palace, to the amusement of the entire Court, Slade thought bitterly. No doubt Bryony was among those secretly laughing at his predicament. His fists clenched at his sides as he loudly stated, "I seek my betrothed, madam. Have you perchance seen the Lady Gillian?"

Ohh, how dare he torture me with the fact of their betrothal yet again! Bryony fumed. She deliberately considered the matter a fraction too long. Let the arrogant Englishman think she neither cared for him, nor noticed how lovely Gillian Lovelle was tonight!

"Nay," she mused at length, "I think not. One as unfamiliar with the Court as I can hardly recognize anyone in disguise here, and there are so many bodies milling about." She gave him a sweet smile, which was belied by the daggers in her eyes.

Slade could not mistake her icy dismissal. It only enraged him further. He could not bear to have the only woman he had ever loved treat him this way. Gillian was one thing. He had come to expect her little cruelties and caustic remarks. But they had never penetrated the armor shield about his heart. Bryony's arrows not only wounded, they burned.

Reaching out, he abruptly seized her by the arm. "You have some explaining to do, my fine Irish witch," he hissed against her ear.

"The same might be said for you, sirrah," Bryony shot back, though she was alarmed by his words and the tone he used. But before she could protest, or Kit return from the refreshment tables, Slade spirited her away into a secluded corridor.

He drew her into an empty chamber after checking a number of doors along the hall. Then he released her, turning to face her from across the room and glaring at her above folded arms.

Bryony set down her broken feather fan on a marble-topped table in the corner and glowered right back.

"Why are you still in London?" he demanded.

"Is that what this is all about?" she scoffed.

"Aye. I gave instructions you were to be sent home on the first ship back to Ireland."

She laughed caustically at that. "By whose order, Captain Tanner? Yours? Need I remind, 'twas you who dragged me to your precious England in the first place, with neither apology nor sufficient explanation, then proceeded to throw me upon the mercy of your kin, once you had tired of caring for me."

Slade's stare bored through her, and he obviously was prepared to rebut her accusation, but she swiftly raised a silencing hand.

"Let me finish. You deceived me and used me in the worst way, full knowing the consequences, as I did not. Once you had what you wanted, it seemed you were content to wash your hands of me. Now, tell me, why should I feel obliged to owe you an explanation for anything I do?"

Slade burned with frustration. He wanted to tell Bryony he was sorry, and admit that he had behaved like the worst sort of cad, but the words just wouldn't come. He was so bitter and worn down with the battle of his life, that he looked to vent the bottled rage any way he could.

"Damn, you shouldn't be here!" he burst out, smacking his right fist into a cupped palm as he moved to angrily pace the chamber. "The Tudor Court is a kennel of wolves, looking to devour the innocent."

Bryony gave a soft bitter laugh. "Thanks to you, I'm hardly in that class anymore."

The reminder hit Slade like a physical blow. He winced with the painful truth of her words and paused to gaze regretfully back at her. Damn, why did she have to be so lovely, so fascinating, and yet still so forbidden to him? He'd been forced to watch a hundred other men eyeing her tonight, and it made his blood burn with the need to possess her again. Bryony O'Neill was his! She always would be. Yet the bitter irony was he could never truly possess her.

"I don't know what to say." The confession escaped him in an unhappy rush, and he pressed his palms to his throbbing temples. "I've made such a bloody mess of my life."

The anger in Bryony was immediately swept away, when she saw the genuine agony in his eyes. Behind the velvet mask his green eyes were bright with pain. Stepping forward, she pulled his hands down into hers and held them tightly.

"I'm here for you, Slade," she whispered. "Oh, love, don't you see I couldn't leave you?"

Slade stared at her, a muscle working in his cheek, half-daring to hope and half-disbelieving. He wanted to believe her—Lord, how badly he needed to believe!

"D'you mean it, Bryony?" he asked at last. "Did you stay in England for my sake?"

She only nodded, too upset to speak. Tears drenched her sea blue eyes, the very same eyes he had dreamed about every restless night since their parting. Those endless, tortured nights . . . Slade was tired of them, tired of denying himself, and their love. In a single swift movement, he drew the mask from her face and let it fall to the floor.

"I want to see you when I kiss you," he muttered, drawing her into his arms. His heart soared when he felt her clutch him with equal fervor and lift her lips to his.

This time Bryony did not try to fight the forbidden sensations Slade wrought from her very heart and soul. Neither did she protest when he lifted her upon a low table and swiftly and fiercely brought their bodies into heated conjunction once more. They melded into one figure, fused together by a deep passion so powerful it was impossible to deny.

Trembling, they clung to one another for those exquisite few minutes that both knew must last them a lifetime. Slade's mask had tumbled to the floor as well, and Bryony traced his endearing dimple for the last time. Someone he sensed this intimate little caress was her farewell, for he suddenly gasped and murmured against her flowing dark hair.

"Dear Jesu, I can't let you go," he rasped.

Bryony's eyes burned with brilliant tears. "My love," she whispered brokenly, "oh, my love, you must."

"Let's leave this place . . . run away together . . . tonight."

"Don't be foolish, Slade. Remember the queen." Bryony's words gave him pause. She was serious. "Your family mustn't suffer for our folly," she continued firmly. "This must be the last time we meet." Even though she wanted with all her heart to run away to sea with him, she knew such a foolish act would only see the Tanner family destroyed. Gillian Lovelle was vindictive enough to go to any lengths to force Slade to heel. So Bryony simply clung to him, her words still ringing hollow in the chamber, while piece by piece her heart slowly fell to the floor.

Slade was silent for a long time, stroking her hair as if it could offer him some consolation or the answers they both sought. He knew Bryony was right, that they must deny themselves in order to protect so many others, but common sense seemed so ridiculous when their love and mutual happiness was at sake.

"I'll never forget you, my little sea raven," he said at last, and Bryony knew with a sinking certainty that he had made his decision. Though it was the right one, the only one, it didn't hurt any less. Slade stepped back and looked at her long and hard, his green eyes glittering with unshed tears.

"I'll remember forever how you looked this night, how you felt in my arms now as well as the first time I ever held you," he continued hoarsely. "And all the times in between, when I saw both the fierce raven and caught a few glimpses of the woman within." Gently, he touched the amulet at her throat. "I pray this will protect you when I cannot. For surely you are destined for greater things than I. 'Tis the only explanation I can understand, or accept."

He tenderly kissed her brow then. For a second Bryony feared she would break—and weep, or scream, or beat upon his chest in rage and denial—but deep down inside she was numb . . . she also wore protective armor around her heart . . . for it had been donned the day she was born, by sheer necessity.

"Know in your heart that I am with you always," Slade added as he reluctantly withdrew from her embrace, "but for the sake of my family and yours, Bryony, we must never meet again."

Bryony left the little room with a deep rend in her soul she feared would never be mended again. Slade departed in the opposite direction, pausing only to place one final fierce and emphatic kiss upon her lips. He did not look back.

She smoothed her costume, replaced her mask, and then woodenly returned to the hall, each step a mindless motion serving to only briefly distract her from the secret torment at hand. The colorful dancers and the gay music seemed only a foggy dream now, in which she blundered helplessly about.

Suddenly a hand shot out of the crowd and seized her, and she was abruptly yanked into the arms of a huge albatross.

"Dance with me, little raven!" a voice boomed, and she looked up into a familiar pair of twinkling black eyes.

"Lafleur!" She spat his name like a curse, and the big Frenchman merely roared with laughter.

"Thought I'd forget you, eh, my fine Irish *fille? Non,* Giles Lafleur never forgets an insult, especially when it comes from a lightskirt!"

The room came into sudden sharp focus with the intensity of her anger. Bryony raised her hand to slap him, but the Frenchman lightly batted it aside as he spun her about the room.

"That's better," Lafleur growled under his breath. "I feared your delightful spirit was somehow crushed by *le Capitaine* Tanner! I am glad to see you are no worse for wear after a few nights in his arms."

Bryony sputtered with outrage, and struggled for freedom as Lafleur dragged her gaily about the hall to the plucky strains of "The Frog Galliard." Other couples were staring at them, no doubt marvelling over the ludicrous sight of a giant white albatross clutching a squirming black raven.

"Release me!" Bryony demanded.

"What, and let you fly away so easily? Not this time, *ma petite.* I've news of your family."

Abruptly she ceased her struggling to crane her neck up at him. "The O'Neill?"

"Aye, and your brother, too."

Bryony's mind raced on, wondering what had happened to Brendan since she had left Raven Hall. She desperately wanted to hear how they were managing back in Ireland. But she was well aware that Lafleur was the sort of man who offered nothing for free.

"All right," she conceded with a sigh. "What's your price, Lafleur?"

He chuckled at that. "Now, why would you have such a low opinion of me, *chérie?* I seek naught but the pleasure of your company tonight."

Somehow Bryony doubted that, but she finished the galliard with Lafleur and they left the floor amid a final flourish of dancers. Against all odds some color had returned to Bryony's cheeks from the exertion, and with further surprise she discovered that she was suddenly hungry. She begged Lafleur for a respite.

"Very well," he agreed, clamping a meaty fist around her wrist, "but don't get any ideas about flying away, eh?"

"All I desire is a quick bite to eat," she replied, leading him to the opposite end of the hall where several huge sideboards had been set up, nearly groaning with all the weight of the food upon them.

In keeping with the theme of birds, the palace staff had prepared a luxurious spread fit for royalty. It quite took the breath away upon first glance. The main dish was roast peacock, redressed in all its feathers after cooking. As Bryony and Giles served themselves, they discovered the peacocks were stuffed with glazed orange ducklings, which in turn were filled with curried pigeon. Inside the delicately seasoned squab was a delicious mixture of chopped eggs and hazelnuts.

There were also platters of juicy pink ham and freshly caught trout in aspic. Great golden wheels of hard cheese had also been rolled out on the tables to complement the meats. Thick loaves of bread and silver crocks filled with creamy sweet butter were arranged beside bowls of peaches, pears, and rare sweet strawberries. Sweetmeats and tiny iced cakes rounded out the rich repast. Lastly, a long line of wooden casks had been opened for the occasion, offering a light fruity wine for the women, and a stout mead for the men.

While Captain Lafleur heaped his platter high, Bryony took small choice samples of everything. She hoped by dallying at the tables that Kit might happen by and rescue her from Lafleur's attentions. Glancing about the Great Hall, she spotted at least a dozen robins, but none of them sported a mop of bright red hair, and nobody appeared to defend her honor.

When she and Lafleur took seats at a trestle table set well

apart from the main activity in the hall, Bryony leaned toward the grinning Frenchman and demanded, "Well? What news have you?"

Lafleur tossed aside his mask and finished tearing a huge chunk of bread in half with his hands before he spoke. "What's it worth to you, little girl?"

She gritted her teeth in annoyance. "Damn you, Lafleur, I've no patience for your games. If you have something to say about my family, then say it." She started to rise, but in a surprisingly quick move his big hand shot out and yanked her down again. She landed with a thump on the hard plank bench.

"What's the hurry, *ma petite?*" he drawled as he liberally spread a hunk of rye with butter from his plate. He licked his greasy thumb before sinking his strong white teeth down into the soft bread. "You must play along, you know, if you wish to know your father's fate."

She glanced away in disgust, as he spoke and noisily chewed at the same time. " 'Tis not Brann I'm worried about. Tell me the news of Brendan."

He shook his dark head, swallowing and mischievously wagging a finger at her. "You must pay for information anywhere in the world, wench. I'm no exception."

"Devil take you, Lafleur! I haven't time for this."

"Then you shall never know your brother's fate."

"You're the lowest sort of rogue, an opportunist!"

"Tsk, tsk, little one, 'tis no way to treat the man who likely holds your future in his hands."

Bryony snorted with disdain at that claim. "Oh, all right," she wearily conceded, "what's your price?"

An impudent grin split his face at the question. "That's better, though you could use a lesson or two in graceful surrenders. If I have my way, I'll make *une grande dame* of you yet, Bryony O'Neill."

"God's teeth, Lafleur! I'll endure your presence, but I don't have to take your insults."

He laughed at her outrage. "My price is reasonable enough,

lass. I'll take your word that someday you shall willingly spend one night with me."

His words startled Bryony, even more so when she realized he was serious. She understood he didn't want her company just to play cards. She immediately tried to laugh it off.

"That's rich, Lafleur. Why would you want a skinny-boned bird like me?"

The Frenchman eyed her frankly over the plump leg of a duckling. "I don't know," he said, "but I do. Maybe the thought of mounting *la femme capitaine* is just too exciting for this old salt."

"Be warned: I've no intentions of being conquered by any man."

"Forgive me, little raven, but I think your heart has already been captured," Lafleur said wisely. When Bryony flinched, he chuckled.

"Ah, I've no desire to hurt you, *ma petite.* Merely to discover what *Capitaine* Tanner found so fascinating. I know you yearn for him, *ma doux,* but if things do not work out between you two, perhaps there will be a little room left in your heart for Lafleur, eh?"

"I can promise you nothing."

Giles shrugged as if unconcerned by the possibility. "I see Tanner still holds your heart. But I want your word you'll allow me that one night, if Slade does not offer you more. If you cannot agree to such a trifling request, then you'll not hear the news I have of Ireland."

Bryony tried to think of a way out of this latest predicament. Alarmingly, there didn't seem to be one.

As if reading her mind, Lafleur said suddenly, "Promises come easily to the fair sex, *chérie,* but if you give your word and then back out, I'll know you for *Le Corsaire's* brat."

The reminder of the slur he sought to cast upon the O'Neill name made Bryony redden with outrage and draw herself up. "I've more honor in my little finger than any cursed Frenchman!"

"Oh?" His eyes twinkled at her. "Then . . . ?"

"Aye! You'll have your chance at me, Lafleur . . . *after* you tell your tale!"

Fifteen

Apparently accepting her word as good, Giles finally pushed aside his trencher and moved closer to Bryony.

"I'm sorry," he said, serious for the first time that she could recall. "But all was not good in Ireland."

Bryony's breath left her in a single shattered gasp. "What happened?"

Lafleur hesitated, clearly not certain how to break the news.

"God's nightshirt, speak up! Is it the O'Neill? Brendan? Tell me!" she demanded.

"The old woman . . ." he began at last.

"You mean Mab." Bryony saw Giles nod, but already she had rushed on to her own conclusions. "Sweet Jesu, no!"

"I arrived just as the funeral was taking place. Everyone was there—"

"How? How did it happen?" Bryony threw aside her mask and openly wiped away the fresh tears on her cheeks. How much more could she take in one night?

" 'Twas a fever, O'Neill told me. He mentioned she was very elderly, and there were none who knew how to nurse her properly." Lafleur's voice was oddly gentle all of a sudden. "Who was she, *chérie,* your grandmother?"

"No. Merely the woman who raised me as her own." A ragged sob caught in Bryony's throat. "I should have been there for her! Mab always looked after everyone at Raven Hall, but especially me." Suddenly she remembered Mab's last dire prediction, that they would never meet again on this earth.

Bryony had assumed it meant she herself would be killed or captured by the English. It had never occurred to her that Mab might have foreseen her own death. She shuddered with the depth of her emotion, longing to keen her loss aloud in the old Gaelic way.

"That's the worst of the news," Lafleur assured her. Had Bryony but glanced in his eyes, she would have seen the genuine sympathy written there. "Your brother is fine. He wed a Scottish wench."

Bryony tried to smile through her tears. "Then it must be Glynnis MacDougal. Did you see her? Was she a comely lass with bright red hair?"

Lafleur grinned. *"Oui,* and already she's half-gone with child."

"No!" Bryony gasped, trying to imagine pink-cheeked little Glynnis with a great belly, and her eyes widened in disbelief. "But they've only been wed a few months!"

"And how long do you suppose it takes to make a *bébé?"* Lafleur teased her. "A century?"

Even in her grief, Bryony had to chuckle a little. "Oh, 'tis wonderful news. How happy Dan must be!" Then she mused quietly, "An old life steps aside for each new life to come in . . . that's what Mab always said. And I guess it's true."

"Ah, *chérie,* don't cry," Lafleur said a little gruffly, when her lower lip began to tremble. "From what I hear, the old woman had a good long life, and she was as feisty on her deathbed as she was the day she first came screaming into the world."

Bryony sniffled and nodded. "Aye, that sounds like my Mab. Ornery till the end. But still . . ."

"You'll be glad to hear your father brushed me off, just like you warned Tanner he would." Giles cleverly changed the subject, reasoning it would temporarily distract Bryony from her grief. And it worked. Sudden anger flashed in her eyes.

"He's no sire of mine! I could've saved you the effort of

going all the way to Ireland, but Slade wouldn't hear of it, of course."

"Where is the English rogue, anyway? I need to tell him my news, too."

"I don't know." Bryony decided to speak frankly. "We parted company tonight, Lafleur, and he's given up the idea of settling in Ireland. From now on, I'm a free woman, and I'll thank you to treat me as such."

"Only until I call in your debt," the Frenchman reminded her in a playful, yet ominous tone. "And then for one blissful night, *chérie*, you'll answer to me."

When Slade finally found Gillian, he ordered her to retrieve her cloak from her tiring woman.

"We're leaving," he abruptly announced, daring her to protest as a hundred eyes looked on.

Gillian drew herself up to explode, then quickly thought the better of it. From across the hall, Elizabeth Tudor was keenly observing their exchange.

"Aye," she said, loudly and graciously. "Whatever you say, dear heart."

Slade stared at her suspiciously a moment, then briefly stepped outside to signal his coachman. He was wise enough not to leave Gillian alone, however, and when the expected summons came from the queen, he seized his wayward betrothed firmly by the upper arm.

"You have my permission to simper now all you wish, madam, for the benefit of the Court," he told her coolly.

"Knave!" Gillian replied through clenched teeth. "Your coarse blood is reflected in your manners."

"I shall take that as a compliment, Gilly, if your own behavior is indicative of the nobility."

Furious, she yanked her arm free, only to feel Slade deliberately step on the long train of her costume to pin her in place like a struggling butterfly. She threw an outraged glance over her shoulder, and when he moved aside, she saw the black mark his boot had left on the white silk. Before she could cause a further scene, Slade grabbed her by the wrist and dragged her toward the queen's throne.

By the time Gillian came before Elizabeth's critical eye, however, she had composed herself enough to sink into a deep curtsey. Slade made the queen an elegant knee, as always, and this time the couple felt the warmth of her approval cast upon them both like a warm velvet cloak.

Gazing benignly down upon the pair, Elizabeth said, "You may rise, Captain Tanner. And my dearest Gillian. I am grieved to see you would take your leave so soon."

"The hour grows late, Your Majesty," Slade replied without visible emotion.

"True, but you are always welcome to stay at Whitehall, Captain. You can keep close quarters with your red fox of a brother, can you not?"

Reluctantly Slade inclined his head. "Aye, Your Grace. I am honored by your invitation."

"But still inclined to refuse." Surprisingly, Elizabeth Tudor smiled. She seemed unusually benevolent tonight, but then she was often in a mellow mood whenever lavish attention and attendance was heaped upon her. "Tell us the truth, Captain Tanner. You are far more anxious to be alone with your little Gilly-flower."

As Slade forced a smile, Elizabeth gave a merry laugh and turned to translate for the French *duc* at her side. The homely d'Alencon offered up a lopsided smile, which was all the queen seemed to expect. She reached out and patted his thin knee almost affectionately.

"Ah, youth!" Elizabeth sighed then, eloquently clasping her freckled hands together. "How I envy you all." She paused to look meaningfully at the couple. "Alas, the court grows impatient to hear the wedding banns. Is Michaelmas no longer suitable?"

Remembering Gillian's threats, Slade responded cautiously.

"We did not wish to upstage the duke's arrival, Your Majesty. All England is basking in the light of your good fortune and happiness."

Elizabeth preened like a young girl. "Then I suppose we must all contrive to be more patient. Alas, however, I fear I have inherited my sire's somewhat choleric nature."

And his infamous temper, too, Slade longed to say, but wisely kept silent. At last Elizabeth allowed them to bow out.

"Fare thee well, children. I shall expect to hear joyous tidings very soon."

As the couple took their leave, another pair moved forward to be presented to the queen. Slade's eyebrows rose when he recognized Bryony on his brother's arm. In vain he tried to get Kit's attention, to indicate with his outraged look that he questioned his brother's sanity in presenting an Irishwoman to Bess. Finally noticing Slade's glare, Kit just shrugged, indicating he'd little say in the matter. Elizabeth Tudor herself must have demanded an introduction. Now it was up to Kit to supply a creative story.

Slade had to see what would happen. When he paused, turning to look back at the presentation area, Gillian followed his gaze and quickly realized what was happening. Her eyes narrowed, but she did not argue when he stopped to watch. She, too, was curious as to how the black-haired chit would explain her position to Elizabeth. The queen was no fool. Granted, the wench had a clever costume, but even a mask could not hide a treasonous heart from Bess.

Bryony felt the weight of the Court's eyes upon her, as Kit led her before the infamous English monarch. His steady presence gave her the courage to endure. With Elizabeth Tudor looking on critically, she sank into a graceful curtsey, one she and Isobel had practiced in secret for days. It was also just a shade deeper than the one Gillian had executed.

Elizabeth spoke first. "Very well done, Mistress—"

"Bryony Tanner," Kit smoothly intervened. "A distant cousin of ours."

In the ensuing taut silence, he hastily explained, "Your Majesty is surely aware one of my father's younger brothers settled in Ireland some years ago. Your Grace may also recall recently restoring titles to some lands there for my own brother."

Elizabeth Tudor shrewdly glanced to her advisor, William Cecil, who gave a short nod of confirmation.

"Mistress Tanner has come to visit us for the Season," Kit continued without a ruffle. "She graciously agreed to be my partner this evening, when Elspeth suddenly took ill."

The queen's painted auburn eyebrows arched at that, but she turned and addressed Bryony instead. "You are a fresh face in our Court, m'dear. We always delight in welcoming visitors to our fair England."

" 'Tis my honor, Your Highness." There was no help for Bryony's soft Irish lilt, but at least it was pleasing to the ear. She kept her voice low and respectful.

Elizabeth smiled with airy approval. "I am pleased to see you both took the masque in the proper spirit. What a curious necklace, m'dear. 'Tis most unusual, but very striking. Is't the renowned Irish gold?"

Bryony stiffened a little as she felt the Court's attention shift to her precious amulet. She swallowed hard before she spoke. "Aye, Your Majesty. Thank you. 'Twas a gift from my brother, my only living sibling."

"Are your parents gone?"

Nervously Bryony glanced to Kit. He gave her the briefest nod and a quick wink of encouragement. "A—aye, Your Majesty. Both long gone, to my eternal regret."

Elizabeth keenly observed, "But I see you wear no other jewelry, Mistress Tanner."

"Forgive me, Your Majesty. I was recently informed of another death in my family back in Ireland. Thus I wore black this eve." The story rolled smoothly off her tongue before she could stop it, but Bryony realized she had told a half-truth anyway. Mab certainly counted as family. And she saw her story was credible enough, when Elizabeth Tudor nodded gravely.

Before she and Kit were dismissed, however, the queen motioned Bryony closer. Elizabeth twisted a cabochon-cut ruby off her right little finger, and handed it to Bryony.

"Every lady deserves a new bauble now and then, don't you agree, m'dear? Take this now as a small memento of your visit to my Court, and wear it in good health when you cease to mourn."

Bryony was surprised to feel her eyes suddenly mist. This unexpected if somewhat gruff kindness took her completely off guard. "I shall treasure it always," she murmured, then lightly kissed the queen's outstretched hand.

When Bryony was finally dismissed, she turned, still flushed with emotion and heady with triumph, to face Slade, standing only a few feet away. Their gazes met and locked, and in a flash she read the approval and praise written there.

Well done, my love.

But the precious moment passed all too swiftly, and she and Kit moved into the cold dark night alone.

It seemed as if a door slammed shut on his life, when Bryony disappeared from view. Slade stared after his brother's departing coach as he and Gillian awaited their own driver further down the lane.

Noting the direction of his gaze, Gillian maliciously remarked, "Your cousin certainly seems to have Kit groveling at her feet."

Slade turned and gave her a coolly measuring glance. "Careful, Gilly. It almost sounds as if you are jealous of the favoritism Bess showed the girl."

She snorted with disdain. "A mere Irish wench! Obviously out of her element here, and plain as a pikestaff to boot."

"But worthy of a queen's ring," Slade reminded her.

"Think you Bess was being generous for no reason? La,

on't forget I've been at Court for nigh a decade now, and I ell know how Bess's devious mind works. She was simply etting a trap for the little chit."

Something in her carefree manner made Slade uneasy. Was : true, did Bess suspect Bryony's real identity?

"What kind of trap? And why?" he demanded, unable to ide his irritation and concern from Gillian.

She smiled archly at him. "Why, is that worry in your voice, ear heart? Methinks you show a mite too much concern over distant cousin!"

"No games, Gilly. Tell me what you know," he growled un-er his breath.

"Oh, very well," she huffed. " 'Twas clear to me Bess did ot believe the girl's story at all. I watched her face as they poke, and Bess was suspicious of the chit's true motives. And s doubtless you already know, she distrusts the Irish. Bess nly gave Bryony the ring because if she proves troublesome, nd the queen desires to question her, she can turn around and ccuse her of theft."

It sounded more like a plot Gillian would dream up, but lade knew Elizabeth Tudor was both intelligent and devious. Ie had heard of others tempted into treason under similar cir-umstances. Most had their lives ended on the block. He felt is blood turn cold.

"But the whole Court saw Bess give Bryony the ring."

"Bryony, is it now?" Gillian asked archly, then suddenly urned cruel. "You wear your foolish heart on your sleeve for ll to see, Slade. You have much to learn about Court and eeping clear of gossip. Be warned, I'll not tolerate such un-avory rumors after we're wed. 'Tis obvious to everyone you unger after your brother's new whore."

The coach pulled up to a sudden halt before them, forcing lade to bide his time. But after he handed Gillian inside, and he was comfortably seated and looking at him expectantly, e briefly enjoyed his own revenge.

"Lady Gillian," he loudly announced, clearly enough so both

the driver and several others overheard, "You reek of rutting. Therefore I will rent another coach for myself, while you reflect in private on your scandalous behavior."

Before Gillian could screech her outrage, he slammed the door shut and stalked off to cool his heels.

It surprised Gillian somewhat that she not only felt rage at Slade's brutal remarks, but a genuine prick of jealousy at the thought of him loving another woman. Not that she wanted him herself—nay, 'twas not that at all—she was simply vexed at the notion he wanted someone else. It was clear he had somehow become ensorcelled by that damned Irish witch.

Gillian was forced to admit she had grown somewhat lax in tossing him crumbs of affection. She quickly decided she must do a better job of drawing him up short. Just like stallions, men needed a cruel bit, tempered at times with juicy tidbits to keep them coming back for more. Slade's behavior during the masque had been alarming indeed. If Elizabeth had not been present, she sensed he might have abandoned her altogether. 'Twould not do, Gillian fretted. Not at all! She had managed to keep Slade in line for well over a year, and she must not let him get ahead of her in the game now.

But how to curb his growing defiance? The answer surely rested with the Irish girl. Thoughtfully Gillian tapped at her teeth with the ivory handle of her fan, as she sat reflecting upon matters in the coach. There must be some way to effect the chit's downfall without casting suspicion upon herself. She must work up her courage to speak to Bess, to plant the seeds of doubt and suspicion in her godmother's mind, and carefully nurture them to fruition. Bess was much more than a temperamental monarch. She was a deadly enemy, and a damned clever woman. Gillian was forced to be careful, too, lest she find herself embedded in a coil of her own making.

Within a few minutes she decided upon her next course of action. She would immediately retire from Court to Dovehaven, the little country estate Bess had selected for her and Slade. The move would please Bess immensely, and also make her far more receptive to Gillian's future plea for an audience. The marriage was less than two weeks away now. After the wedding, Gillian would summon the Irish girl to Dovehaven as well, and somehow contrive to have the servants stumble upon her and Slade together, *inflagrante delicto.* Gillian would then rush back to London in tears, with ample proof of Slade's perfidy.

Gillian already knew what the Virgin Queen would think. What she was counting on was one of Bess's irrational rages. Like her father before her, Henry VIII, Elizabeth Tudor had a vile temper which, oddly enough, was often provoked by real or imagined secret trysts among others. Henry Tudor had beheaded two queens because of wild accusations of adultery and incest; he had sent Cromwell stumbling to the block under similar ridiculous charges. Under both Tudors, many an innocent party had been accused and sentenced, if not to death, then to eternal disgrace.

This was Gillian's greatest fear. All she knew was life at Court, and its licentious, ofttimes bawdy nature had always appealed to her adventurous spirit. She had taken her first lover at twelve, a besotted court page, and after a quick succession of stableboys and riding masters, she had progressed to the more sophisticated and generous gentlemen of Bess's Court.

Still, she knew she flirted with disaster whenever she cuckolded Slade. Gillian did not believe he would inform Bess of her habits, as the queen was fiercely loyal to her mother's memory, but it would be dangerous to underestimate the queen's intelligence network. Bess had spies everywhere. Gillian was usually careful to meet her lovers outside the palace, but once in awhile the temptation to couple right beneath her monarch's nose was overwhelming. Tonight had been one of those rare times. Poor Pierre! He had not been able to fully appreciate the thrilling interlude.

Idly, Gillian wondered what had happened to Pierre, after

she had snatched the diamond bracelet from his sweaty palm and flounced from his apartment. He had collapsed upon his bed, not even bothering to pursue her.

Gillian had felt insulted at the time. Now she speculated that perhaps it was only the dysentery making its nasty rounds. A few cases had popped up lately, as it made its predictable annual return. She made a private vow to avoid all her lovers for a few days. She had important work to do, and needed her full wits about her.

The dowry house Elizabeth Tudor had granted her ward was far too small for Gillian's liking, but here at least she ruled with an iron hand. Dovehaven was a charming manor house, fashioned in an L-shape and crafted of dark red brick. It derived its name from the adjoining dovecote on the south side of the house. By the time Gillian set up satisfactory residence along with her staff, another week had passed. Michaelmas was Tuesday next. With a thought for that, Gillian sent an urgent message to Slade. He had not returned to Ambergate for some reason, instead staying aboard his ship.

There were still plans to be finalized, as far as the wedding was concerned. Bess had insisted on a ceremony at Canterbury Cathedral, not far from Dovehaven, to be followed by a formal court affair at nearby Deal Castle. Even in the matter of her own wedding attire, Gillian had little say. Her godmother had sent a heavy, candlelight-colored satin gown, liberally embroidered with lace and tiny seed pearls. It was a gorgeous confection, but to her chagrin Gillian discovered it was much too small since her last fitting. Luckily, her tiring woman Elinor was swift and handy with a needle. The waist and bustline of the wedding gown were discreetly let out to afford Gillian breathing space, and a better disguise for her pregnancy.

On the day Slade was due to arrive at Dovehaven, Gillian

bathed and chose her outfit with care. She donned a voluminous blue velvet gown, that dipped low enough in front to expose the twin suns of her rosy areolae. That ought to distract Slade, or any common fellow, she thought with glib satisfaction. The underskirt was pale blue silk, embroidered with asters in silver thread. Lastly, she draped several long strands of ivory pearls, Bess's wedding gift to her, around her neck to distract attention from her rounded abdomen.

The babe was due in less than five months now. Gillian had deliberately starved herself to fend off any rumors at Court. Only Slade, one other person, and Elinor, her faithful maidservant, knew of her condition. Once the wedding band was safely on her hand, Gillian would not bother to hide her belly anymore. But she dared not trifle with Bess's temper at this stage in the game.

Pregnancy had wrought awful havoc on Gillian. Instead of lessening as the months wore on, her nausea seemed to be getting worse. In the past few days alone, she had retched half a dozen times. Her justifiably famous, creamy white skin had begun to turn scaly in spots and itch like St. Elmo's Fire. Even her lovely fingernails had ugly streaks on them now. Gillian hated her condition, but was also aware it was simply a means to an end.

At least her silvery blond hair was still her crowning glory, and it had grown thicker and shinier during the past few months. For Slade's visit she dressed it in a single lovelock, letting it dangle enticingly over her shoulder. Gillian studied the final results in the pier glass of her bedchamber, and smiled. Slade would never convince anyone he had been driven to another woman's arms—especially that plain-faced Irish chit's—by her own lack of charms. The courtiers all agreed Gillian Lovelle was beauty personified, and her nickname at Court (one admittedly coined amid sly smirks) was Aphrodite.

Thinking ahead, Gillian ordered her new cook to prepare all of Slade's favorite dishes. But when he finally arrived at Dovehaven, he was not so naive as to accept the warm welcome without question. When Gillian actually met him at the door, he was immediately suspicious.

Slade studied his fiancée's flushed cheeks and bright eyes, and decided that Gillian was either heady with wine or triumph, or perhaps both. She chattered about the fresh country air and how she hardly even missed Court.

"Did you bring me any new baubles from Town?" she wheedled Slade, as she clung to his arm and drew him to the table set with steaming platters of ham, roast capon, and even an iced bucket of raw oysters.

"You have more than enough finery, Gilly," he gruffly responded.

She pouted, then ventured coyly, "I hear tale you are not quite so uncharitable where others are concerned."

Something in her sly manner pushed him over the edge. He freed his arm from her grasp and curtly ordered, "Explain that remark, madam."

Gillian tossed her head. "I know you've been keeping that Irish wench as your mistress," she said, startling him at last into a guilty flinch. "Well, who is she, in truth, some peasant's brat or dairymaid you've taken a fancy to? Nay, I suppose not, for the clothes you bought her were far too fine to be worn about the farm!"

She raised her voice to a shrill pitch, so it carried all through the halls and hopefully upstairs, the better to reach all her servants' straining ears.

To her surprise, Slade did not deny it, nor even ask how she had learned of Bryony. They both knew servants gossiped endlessly, although in this particular instance Gillian had an entirely different source.

Slade said shortly, "Will you begrudge me one pleasure, Gilly, when you are apparently determined to take your own wherever you find it?"

"Whoreson!" she snarled.

Slade shrugged, enraging her further. "Call me what you

like, but it won't change the fact of what you are. And be careful of how you slander others, madam, lest someday the same be said of you—or your child."

"Our child," Gillian corrected him, protectively moving her hand to her stomach. When he merely lifted a dubious golden brow at her, she cried, "You'll regret this one day!"

"Aye, of that I've no doubt. But you, too, shall learn a different sort of regret, when you take your place in our nuptial bed. For if it's children you want, Gilly, I'll gladly give you a dozen in as many years."

She shrieked with horror at the thought. "Nay!"

"Aye," he continued savagely, "you'll perfect the art of spreading your legs for me, as you have for so many other men! I intend to keep that little belly of yours well furrowed and planted, for if I get nothing else from this marriage, I shall have sons from you. In other words, m'dear, you shall be nothing more than my broodmare in the years to come, and if you think reasonably upon it, you will realize you have been in training for nothing less."

"Bastard!" she screeched at him. " 'Tis nothing less than a cruel threat with which you intend to frighten me."

Slade gave a humorless chuckle. "The tables have turned, Gilly. In less than a week, I shall be your lord and master, under both God's and man's law. If I choose to beat you, I can. Your body shall be my legal property, to use or abuse as I see fit. Neither Mother Church nor Godmother Queen will gainsay me.

"You know Bess has given us this remote estate in Kent, because we are expected to perform for her like royal lapdogs. Indeed, I hope you do enjoy the rarefied country air as much as you claim, Gillian, because this is where you'll do your duty by me, and give me many sons. 'Tis where you'll live for the rest of your days, and likely where you'll die."

She shook her head furiously. "I won't leave Court!"

"Ah, but hasn't your dear godmother told you yet? I'm afraid you've already been dismissed, m'dear. Your clever scheme has assured you will no longer be a maid of honor, but rather a simple housewife on a placid country estate."

Gillian trembled with fury. "My whole life is ruined, and 'tis all your fault!" she spat at him.

"I see. But I confess I've forgotten how I managed to wheedle Bess into burying us together here in the country."

Ignoring his sarcasm, Gillian redirected her attack and lashed out again. "The queen shall hear of your abuse, mark my words! And Bess won't take kindly to hearing tale of your Irish whore, either."

"Abuse, is it, when you've been openly cuckolding me ever since we met? You've had so many lovers, Gilly, I myself have forgotten all their names. Who was it this week, just Count Andre, or perhaps the entire queen's guard?"

When she flushed bright red, he continued ruthlessly, "And speaking of your dear Pierre, I regret to report he died suddenly at Whitehall last week."

Gillian blanched. "You're lying!" she gasped.

"What reason have I to lie? Of course, he was old, and so succumbed more easily to the pox."

"The . . . the pox?" she stammered, horrified.

"Aye. Died stark raving mad, the poor fellow. No doubt after spreading it to all his ladyfriends first." Slade noticed her sudden pallor. "Why, what's wrong, my dear? You look rather wretched yourself."

Gillian abruptly clapped her hands to her mouth. "I must . . . must get some air!" came her muffled cry. Without another word, she whirled and rushed from the hall.

Sixteen

Gillian awoke from her nightmare with a violent start. She sat bolt upright in bed, shivering and drenched with sweat. All night long, Slade's words had rang through her head amid tortured visions. Pierre dead . . . from the pox! And then she remembered in agonizing detail how strangely her lover had looked and acted, and the nonsensical words Pierre muttered as he mounted her at the queen's masque.

She whimpered when she raised a hand to her forehead, and felt the fever burning there. Her limbs felt like they were stuffed with lead, aching and heavy. Her back throbbed fiercely, and she thrashed under the covers in a futile attempt to ease the severe pain. Surely it was just the babe. The pox was a fickle thing, and never before had she succumbed, even when surrounded by sick and dying courtiers over the years.

But if it was the babe, she realized, then it was far too soon. Having never experienced labor before, Gillian was frightened. But she had heard other women complaining about the agony of childbirth, and especially the lower back pain. She had had three abortions herself, at the hands of an experienced hag, but knew it wasn't the same thing as true labor.

Gillian quickly thought of Doreen Haymaker, the widow she had hired to manage Dovehaven. One of the servants had mentioned Mrs. Haymaker's skills with poultices and herbs. Surely the woman could do something to ease the pain for her, or at least attempt to stop the early labor.

Gillian tried to crawl from her bed. But it was too much effort, and with a weak gasp she collapsed against the sweat-soaked pillows. She was completely exhausted. The servants slept upstairs and would never hear her feeble cries for help. She could not even reach the bellpull from where she lay. She knew she must endure until morning, when Elinor came again to tend her.

Slade had abruptly departed after giving her the brutal news of Pierre's death. His last words were that he would be at the chapel Tuesday next, as ordered by Bess, but beyond that, Gilly must expect no more of him. For a moment, she almost regretted forcing him into matrimony. But then, the news of the count's death had upset her greatly. She nearly cried over Pierre, then realized with a characteristic pang of annoyance that he had not bothered to provide for her before he so thoughtlessly died.

So, the count's vast estates would go to his wife, a French shrew who would not take kindly to having to deal with her husband's mistress. Perhaps, Gilly mused, as she slid in and out of her feverish state, she should plead her belly and blackmail the French bitch into supporting her and the child. It did not matter that the babe was not Pierre's. Who could prove otherwise?

Late the next morning, Elinor discovered her mistress prostrate in bed and wracked with pain. She immediately recognized the signs of fever, and like Gillian, assumed premature labor had begun. She ran to find Mrs. Haymaker, all the while babbling hysterically that Lady Gillian was dying. The large, competent older woman lightly slapped Elinor's cheek to bring her to her senses.

"Get 'old of yerself, chit. 'Twill do yer lady no good to weep and wail about the 'ouse. Now go upstairs to me room and fetch the knitted brown satchel from the chair. Bring it to 'er ladyship's room."

"Aye, mum." Elinor bobbed a frantic relieved curtsey and dashed off.

Mrs. Haymaker calmly assembled a tray containing a bowl of broth and a pitcher of water, and trudged up the stairs to Gillian's chamber. She entered without fuss. She was, after all, the new housekeeper, and had some small authority here.

At first she did not suspect anything unusual was afoot. Lady Gillian was semiconscious and all the signs for childbed fever were there. When Elinor returned with the satchel, Doreen assembled her little bottles containing various dried herbs upon a table. She took a pinch each of Black Haw, Skullcap, Valerian, and Cramp Bark. Dropping the bark, roots, and leaves into a small mortar and pestle, she ground them thoroughly and then handed the pestle to Elinor.

" 'Ave Cook boil this in water over the fire for a count of fifty. Then pour it into a cup and bring it back to me."

The young maidservant looked relieved. "You can help milady, then?"

"Aye, though 'tis likely she's lost the child already. Send an urgent message after Captain Tanner. 'E left early this morning, and 'as a right to know what's 'appening."

Elinor nodded, still clutching the stone pestle, and then rushed out of the room. Mrs. Haymaker turned back to her patient. There was little she could do for the fever, but let it run its course. She could ease her lady's discomfort, however. As Gillian moaned and thrashed, the housekeeper dipped a cloth in the tepid water in the pitcher and gently swabbed the flushed face upon the pillows. Over the next hour she coaxed her mistress to drink several cupfuls of water along with the broth and herbal decoction. Gillian was on the verge of delirium now, but obediently parted her dry lips to gulp the liquids thirstily.

But when Mrs. Haymaker finally examined her patient's abdomen, she found no signs of labor. Alarmed, she realized that even the herbs could not have worked so quickly. She drew back the covers, lifted Gillian's nightrail, and gasped at the sight of the small red weals covering her patient's legs.

When Elinor came into the room, Mrs. Haymaker ordere her sharply, "Stay away! Leave this 'ouse at once."

"What is it?"

" 'Tis the black pox," came the grim reply. "May God 'av mercy on our souls."

Slade was halfway to London when the messenger sent fron Dovehaven caught up with him on the road. He sent the la on ahead to notify his crew of his delay, and then to Ambergat with the curt message that he was returning to Dovehaven t tend his ill fiancée. He curbed his first uncharitable impuls to leave Gillian to her fate. If she was miscarrying his chil as Mrs. Haymaker claimed, then he owed her some small al legiance.

When Slade arrived back at Dovehaven, he was shocke to find the house and grounds abandoned, all except for Mrs Haymaker. Even Gilly's tiring woman, Elinor, was nowher to be found. Slade confronted the housekeeper in the hal and demanded to know why all the servants had left thei posts. He was totally unprepared for the news which greete him.

Mrs. Haymaker did not waste time on pleasantries. " 'Ti the black pox," she informed him matter-of-factly. "I've 'a it meself, so I stayed on to nurse 'er ladyship." She indicate her badly scarred skin beneath the generous freckles. "I sen the others away until the blight passes."

"Good thinking, Mrs. Haymaker," Slade praised her, the quietly asked, "The babe?"

The woman just shook her head. "Ye should leave straight away, sir. This is a marked 'ouse now."

But it was getting dark, and Slade was weary from his trav els. He proposed to stay over at the other end of the house fo one night. He was genuinely concerned about Gillian, thoug he could not deny her passing, should it come, would free hir from a sentence worse than death.

"How is she?" he asked Mrs. Haymaker later that evening.

The big woman shrugged. She looked clean and capable, and he relaxed a little believing Gilly was in good hands. "We won't know fer a few more days yet, if the blisters break. 'Twill be the first test of what's to come. Captain Tanner, I do wish ye'd ride on to safety. I'll not 'ave another sick soul on me conscience."

" 'Tis said that miasma carries the plague," Slade said. "The air here in the country is fresh and clean. Gilly must have contracted the pox whilst in London. Surely there is no real danger to others now."

Mrs. Haymaker shrugged her massive shoulders. "There are no servants left to tend yer needs, sir."

"I can fend for myself for a few days. Go back to your mistress. My thanks for your devotion to Lady Gillian."

"Och, sir, don't thank me. I'm 'appy enough to 'elp out when I can."

He was silent a moment. "Tell me the truth, Mrs. Haymaker. Will Gillian live?"

She looked at him directly. "Some do, some don't. The bloody pox is surely the Devil's own 'andiwork. But be warned, likely either way 'er ladyship will no longer be a beauty. Can ye live with that?"

"Aye," Slade quietly replied. "But can Gillian?"

Two days later, exactly as the housekeeper had predicted, Gillian's fever suddenly broke, and for awhile it appeared she would recover without incident. She was lucid, though weak. But nobody had thought to cover the pier glass in her room. Her rising shrieks woke Slade and brought Mrs. Haymaker running.

"Sweet Jesu, my face!"

The housekeeper discovered Gillian staring in the mirror with a look of horrified fascination. Her once flawless complexion was blistered with great red papules, as the dreaded pox marched on to the next stage of infection.

"Don't look, milady," Mrs. Haymaker scolded her, quickly moving to drape a length of material over the glass.

"Move aside!" Gillian shouted. Her silvery hair was matted to her skull, lank and damp from oil and perspiration. Her eyes bulged wildly from her head. "Get that monster out of my room!" she screamed, hurling a pillow at her own reflection in the mirror.

Slade entered a moment later, halting on the threshold and coming no further, so as not to risk infection. "What the devil's going on?"

But Mrs. Haymaker didn't need to say a word. The source of Gillian's rising hysteria was obvious. Slade recoiled with shock at the sight of the creature in the bed. Gillian resembled nothing so much as a skeletal ghoul, with a grotesquely distended abdomen. When she snarled at the housekeeper, he could see the open sores in her mouth. At a loss for what to do, he looked to Mrs. Haymaker for help.

"Come now, milady," the housekeeper said calmly, and Slade had to admire the large woman's bravado as she tossed the sheet over the mirror and went to Gilly's bedside. "I've a nice cup of 'ot tea for ye 'ere. 'Twill 'elp ye to feel better."

"Where's Elinor?" Gillian crossly demanded. She seemed to have no memory of the past few days.

"Hist now, she's busy downstairs, and ye need yer rest. Ye've been sore ill, milady." Mrs. Haymaker bustled efficiently about the room, seemingly immune to the stench of vomit and excreta, which made Slade's stomach roil. Yet the housekeeper had managed as best she could, changing the linens and Gillian's nightrail twice daily. She turned now and gave him a reassuring nod. Gillian seemed to have calmed at the sound of Mrs. Haymaker's crisp authoritative voice.

Slade left the women and wearily retired to his room to pass the night. Sometime later he awoke to a terrible stench and maddened laughter, as Gillian crawled under the bedsheets beside him. She tried to kiss him, and with a reflex of disgust Slade shoved her away, provoking a scream of fury from her cracked bleeding lips.

The ruckus woke Mrs. Haymaker, who had fallen into an exhausted doze in a chair by Gillian's bed. The housekeeper came rushing into the captain's room just as he snarled, "If the pox does not kill you, madam, then so help me God, I shall!"

But Gillian was beyond reason and only cackled wildly at Slade's threat. Some of the angry pustules on her skin had broken, and were weeping a clear yellow pus. Gillian fought furiously as Slade and Mrs. Haymaker pulled her from the bed and dragged her back to her own room. Slade held Gillian fast against the tick mattress as she spat and struggled, while Mrs. Haymaker hurriedly tore strips of cloth from her own petticoat to bind the younger woman's hands and feet to the bedposts.

At last the other two fell back, exhausted. Gillian gradually lapsed back into feverish muttering and then unconsciousness. Mrs. Haymaker's eyes quickly filled with tears.

"Oh, Captain Tanner!" she gasped. " 'Tis all me fault for fallin' asleep! I never thought she could leave the bed on 'er own; weak as a lamb, she was."

"You mustn't blame yourself, my good woman. You've cared for the Lady Gillian for nearly a week now without respite. You're worn to the bone. We simply must find someone else to take a turn. It may as well be me."

Horrified, she pressed a fluttering hand to her ample bosom. "Mercy, I couldn't let ye nurse the lady, Captain 'Tis women's work. Besides, ye must not become ill yerself."

"If 'twas meant that I be spared, then so be it," Slade wearily replied. "But you cannot continue to bear this great burden alone, Mrs. Haymaker. Gillian has already done her worst tonight. The final outcome is up to God."

* * *

Two more days passed, and Gillian's condition did not improve. She miscarried a stillborn child on the third day. Saddened, Slade saw to the burial of the tiny, perfectly formed boy in Dovehaven's cemetery. The fresh mound seemed so out of place amid the weathered stones and markers of those who had lived here so long ago. He realized he must inform the queen of the events at Dovehaven, and beg her leave to postpone the wedding further. Gillian was in no condition to travel, and though Mrs. Haymaker assured him the worst had passed, there was still the chance of infection spreading to others.

Knowing Elizabeth Tudor's fear of disease, one which bordered almost on paranoia, Slade felt confident enough to send a message to Deal Castle, where Bess and her Court had already traveled in anticipation of the wedding. He warned everyone not to come. Then he sat down to pen a hasty note to Kit, realizing his brother would doubtless be worried after his first missive had arrived.

After Slade finished up his correspondence, he rose and stretched the knots from his shoulders and back. A troublesome ache had begun in his belly, and he wondered if the meat he had eaten for dinner had not been salted enough, and therefore spoiled. By necessity, the meals of the past few days had been skimpy hasty affairs. He could not complain, as the food was still better than many a night he'd spent at sea.

He suddenly felt exhausted. Gillian was a terrible patient, who screeched and fought her caretakers at every turn. He and Mrs. Haymaker had begun to take twelve-hour shifts. While one tended Gilly, the other slept like the dead.

Wearily Slade trudged up the stairs to his room, deciding he would somehow figure out a way to send the messages in the morning. Right now the bed looked too damned inviting. He yanked off his boots and collapsed against the bolsters. Unconsciousness hit him like a huge black fist.

He awoke to dry heaves in the night. With an angry oath for the spoiled meat, he grabbed the chamberpot just in time to catch the contents of his stomach. His forehead was cold, and yet he was dripping with sweat. He was so bloody thirsty. He pushed the reeking chamberpot to the far corner of the room and blundered about to light a taper. Then he carried it downstairs and on the high board found a decanter of malmsey wine, and thirstily downed several goblets in a row.

The noise he made roused Mrs. Haymaker, who came down to see if he was ready for his shift. One glance at the captain told her her greatest fears had come true. Gently but firmly she pried the goblet from his shaking hand.

"Ye must lay down," she ominously ordered him.

Slade's glassy green eyes registered no comprehension. "I've urgent messages to send," he muttered, sounding drunk. He took a single wavering step towards the door, and by some miracle she saved him from falling.

"I'll send the messages, Captain," the housekeeper rapped out. "Get ye upstairs to bed."

Slade didn't argue. He was too sick. Mrs. Haymaker helped him up the stairs, and the moment his head hit the pillow, she rushed back downstairs and grabbed up the messages left on the desk from the night before. Without even bothering to seal either of the two with wax, she swept up her cloak from the stand in the hall and rushed out the door.

Bryony watched Kit's face go pale as he read the note from his brother, and Mrs. Haymaker's cryptic message scrawled at the bottom. "Dear God," he rasped. "Gillian has the pox. And now Slade is sick, too."

"Nay!" The terrified cry escaped her lips as Kit's knuckles turned white where they clutched the parchment.

"Gillian lost the child two days ago. Mrs. Haymaker says here Slade started the rash last night. She asks us to pray for the household."

"I'll do more than that," Bryony vowed, swiftly moving to

retrieve her cape from the stand in the hall. When she returned to the parlor, she said, "I'm going to Kent to help Mrs. Haymaker. I can do no less for the man I love."

"Sweet Jesu, Bryony, 'tis madness! We're talking about the black pox!"

"I know. But when Dan and I were small, our nursemaid, Mab, saw us through what she called the little pox. She said 'twould protect us from all the other kinds."

"It sounds like old wives' superstition to me," Kit argued. But he saw the futility in trying to stop her. There was a fierce determination reflected in her eyes.

He sighed. "I can't let you ride that far alone. And the carriage would be too slow. I'll tell Jem to saddle Queen's Folly and Summer Lightning."

"Thank you, Kit." A ghost of a smile touched her lips. "But you know I cannot let you into that house, for the girls' sakes."

He nodded in understanding. " 'Twill at least ease my conscience to see you safely there. I'll go tell Elspeth of our plans. We must leave now, if we're to be there before nightfall."

When Bryony and Kit arrived at Dovehaven, both were breathless and weary from a journey which had been made over hard-packed dirt roads at a flying pace. But neither of them hesitated in attending their duties. While Kit kept his word and did not enter the house, he did ride on to the nearest village in an attempt to recruit any other folk who might have survived the pox and could help with the onerous nursing tasks.

Meanwhile, Bryony relieved Mrs. Haymaker for a few hours and set about tending the two patients. The sight of Slade, so weak and wracked with pain, immediately put her own stomach in fearful knots, but she attended to his and Gillian's basic needs and then diligently set about burning the soiled laundry and clothing out in the yard.

While she was still outside, Kit returned from town with a

husky peasant girl on the back of his horse. "This is Nelda," he said, lowering the girl to the ground. "She's had the pox."

Bryony took one glance at the girl's pitted face and callused capable hands, and nodded with relief. She then ordered Kit to return to Ambergate and await further news. He was obviously reluctant to leave, but to her relief he didn't argue. She then had Nelda help her move the patients, so she could strip and burn the soiled sheets from their beds. Then the two women lowered Slade and Gillian one at a time into a cool tub of water, scrubbed their skin, and washed their hair. Even with Mrs. Haymaker's best efforts, they were filthy from the blight.

When both patients were clean and their open sores dabbed with soothing liniment, the women slipped Gillian into a fresh nightrail, Slade into a nightshirt, and both of them back into bed. It was no easy task, especially handling Slade, though Nelda was stronger than many a man. Mrs. Haymaker awoke in time to help the other two half-drag, half-carry him back to bed. She nearly wept with gratitude for their help.

" 'Tis Divine Providence what answered me," she sniffled.

Bryony assigned Nelda to tend Gillian, who was in the final stages of the disease, but she knew Slade still must surmount the worst, and she was determined to be at his side. Already in the delirium of fever, he had cried out her name several times, and with an aching heart she cradled his burning hand to her breast and silently wept.

The night passed for them both in a blurred agony. On the second day it seemed Slade's fever had miraculously broken, but Bryony remembered Mab's warnings about the deceptive nature of the pox, and so would not let him out of bed, no matter how convincing his arguments. Though she and Brendan had only been six when they had contracted the little pox, she remembered how Mab had tended them with firm but comforting diligence. Somehow, whether by Mab's secret potions or the simple power of prayer, they had both emerged from the blight alive and without scars. Bryony knew that was extremely rare, at least where the black pox was concerned. Already she could tell Gillian's skin was permanently flawed.

Curiously, Slade's betrothed never asked what Bryony was doing there, and did not seem to comprehend what had happened to her. Like an infant, Gillian meekly allowed herself to be bathed and fed, staring vacantly out the window most of the time. Sometimes she roused, but usually only to pick at the scabs on her face and limbs. Any attempts to prevent her from doing this resulted only in violent struggles and screams, so the other women agreed they would leave her be.

Nelda was convinced Gillian Lovelle was possessed by a demon. Mrs. Haymaker was inclined to be more practical. " 'Tis the brain fever," she said matter-of-factly. "It 'appens sometimes with the pox."

"Will her wits recover?" Bryony asked.

The housekeeper did not answer her, one way or the other.

As Bryony had feared, the scourge returned with a vengeance in a few hours, and Slade was again writhing and drenched with sweat. She asked Mrs. Haymaker and Nelda to hold him still, while she dribbled a cup of water against his chapped lips. Very little made it down his throat, and her fears multiplied when his skin became nearly as hot and red as the angry rash upon it.

"Is there no physic nearby?" she fretted aloud.

Mrs. Haymaker nodded. "Aye, there's old Dr. Mills in Deal. 'E says the only remedy for the pox is bleeding and purging of the bad blood."

Bryony shook her head. "It's not his blood which is sick, Mrs. Haymaker. The fever will kill him first. We must cool him off somehow!"

"I can sponge down his body, mum," Nelda offered.

"That will help a little, but it's still not enough. He's burning up!" Bryony suddenly had an idea. "Is there anyone nearby who keeps ice in the summer?"

A light slowly dawned in Mrs. Haymaker's eyes. She began to look excited. "Aye, dearie. Old Jack 'Unter cuts blocks from the River Stour in winter, and sells them all year round."

Bryony turned to Nelda. "Do you know where this fellow lives?"

"Aye, mum. I can run straight to his house from here."

"Can you ride?" When Nelda nodded, Bryony said, "Even better, then. Take my horse instead. He's down in the stable now. Be careful, girl, for he's a spirited cob." She drew a golden coin from her bodice, one of a handful Kit had slipped her before he left, in order to pay for Nelda and the housekeeper's services.

The girl's eyes widened at the sight of the sovereign. Nelda had never seen, let alone held, a coin of such value.

Bryony said sternly, "I'm counting on you to bring back as much ice as you can. A small cart would be even better. Maybe this Jack Hunter can loan you one. Buy as much as you can with this, and the rest is yours."

Nelda nodded. Bryony did not believe the girl would abscond with the horse and money, but her instincts were all she had to go on. After Nelda left, she returned her attentions to nursing Slade. Mrs. Haymaker checked on Gillian and reported that the young woman seemed to be improving. At least she had begun to take some interest in food again.

To Bryony's relief, Nelda soon returned, not only with the cart and horse, but Jack Hunter himself. The thin, stooped, elderly little man even helped her carry the buckets of ice up to the bedchamber. Jack explained to the women that he had survived a bout of the pox when he was young. And he had the scars to prove it.

He and the others watched with curiosity as Bryony wrapped chunks of melting ice in clean linen, and packed them close against Slade's body. She covered him in the cooling blocks, leaving only his head exposed. He had lapsed into unconsciousness from the raging fever, and so there was no concern he would throw off the ice, at least for awhile.

Jack Hunter scratched his wiry head and swore in frank amazement. "Faith, it never occurred to me to keep ice for this," he said. "I sell it mostly to those at Court, when they visit Deal Castle. The nobility use it in their drinks, and for fruit ices in the summer.

" 'Ow do ye keep it from melting?" Mrs. Haymaker asked.

"I stack it in a hole way underground, covered with straw and wood. 'Tis surprising how little melts before winter comes again." He seemed vastly pleased by the notion of having another market for his efforts.

Bryony proved as generous as she was clever. She fetched another sovereign from her bodice, and pressed it on Jack Hunter before he left. He was so impressed, he did not even insult her by biting the coin to prove it was real.

Then she gave another gold coin to Nelda. The homely young girl's eyes filled with surprise, and then spurted tears when she realized the whole thing was for her.

"Oh, mum," she cried. "Yer far too generous!"

"Nonsense," Bryony said curtly. "Most would have run off with the coin, or horse, or both. You deserve a reward for your faithfulness, Nelda." She then turned to tend Slade again, dismissing any arguments.

Seventeen

One morning, as the first faint blush of dawn crept over the eastern skies, Slade's fever settled for the final time. Drowsing in a chair at his bedside, Bryony awoke with a start, not sure what had disturbed her. Her gaze immediately focused on the face of the man she loved.

She knew in an instant that God had heard her anguished prayers. Slade's countenance was suddenly serene, his brow damp, but cool to the touch. She lifted his hand and one of the deep-seated scabs fell away from his palm, revealing the new pink skin underneath.

A sob broke from her dry throat. She trembled with emotion, as she laid a kiss upon his pale drawn cheek. As tears of relief and exhaustion rolled down her own face, she happened to glance out the window. A single white dove suddenly burst from the dovecote toward the east, its frosty wings sharply outlined against the spreading sunrise. It was almost as if the scourge itself had finally surrendered and took flight, she thought.

She rose from the chair and quietly drew a fresh sheet over Slade's unconscious figure. She did not wish to disturb him. He would need plenty of sleep in order to regain his strength. Yet she marvelled as she examined his skin, that he seemed to have emerged relatively unscathed from the virulent disease. Only a small scar above one eyebrow attested to the terrible battle of the past few weeks.

Bryony went downstairs with the intention of finding a

handful of fruit or quarter of bread to ease her hunger pangs. But she found herself too weary even to glance through the kitchen stock. She knew she had lost too much weight herself in the past days. Her weariness now seemed to reach her very bones. She had nursed Slade for well over a week, with only brief snatches of food or sleep. Nelda and Mrs. Haymaker had tended to Gillian, and relieved her when they could. It took all three of them to subdue Gillian, however, whenever the young woman was taken with one of her mad fits.

Bryony found Mrs. Haymaker with her head resting upon her plump arms. They were folded across the kitchen table, as she snored away like All Saints' thunder. Bryony did not want to wake the poor woman, but she knew a message must be sent to Ambergate, and one to town to retrieve the staff.

She gently shook the housekeeper's shoulder. When Mrs. Haymaker awoke with a tired groan, Bryony told her the good news.

To her surprise the big woman broke down and cried, giving great gulping sobs of relief. "God bless ye," she fervently exclaimed, grabbing Bryony's hand and pressing it to her lips. " 'Tis all yer doing, Mistress Tanner. Without yer 'elp, I never could 'ave managed so long."

Bryony had told Mrs. Haymaker that she was related to the Tanners, if only to spare them all unnecessary questions and upset. She smiled wearily at the woman. "You and Nelda did as much, if not more."

"Och, but we'd 'ave never thought of using the ice as ye did. I vow it saved the good captain's life! Too bad we did not think of it before 'er ladyship's pretty skin was ruined."

"How is Gillian?" Bryony asked.

"Better now. I've given her a posset of 'erbs to 'elp her sleep. Nelda agreed to stay with 'er, while I caught a bit of rest. She's a good girl, that Nelda Simms."

Bryony agreed. "Perhaps Lady Gillian can find a position for her here, after . . . after she and the captain are wed," she finished lamely.

Mrs. Haymaker didn't seem to notice her discomfort. She fairly beamed at Bryony. "Aye," she said happily, " 'tis a fine idea, Mistress Tanner. Nelda would make a good chambermaid. And I could use another girl 'ere in the 'ouse. I'll ask Lady Gillian when she's well."

Bryony smiled again at the woman and left with the excuse that she needed to bathe and change her clothing. In her haste to depart Ambergate, and by virtue of the fact her horse had only two saddlebags, she had brought only two changes of clothing with her. Only one remained. She had chosen the plainest of the gowns Slade had given her, but still, it had been hard to see such lovely materials ruined.

In the privacy of a guest room upstairs, she filled the round oak tub with water she had laboriously hauled up in buckets the day before. It was cold, but she was far too anxious to be clean to care. She stripped off her soiled gown and undergarments, and climbed into the water with a bar of harsh lye soap she had found in the larder. She scrubbed her skin until it looked as raw as it felt. Lastly she washed her hair, gasping as the icy water trickled over her back and face.

Finally she climbed shivering from the tub to dry herself and slip into fresh silk stockings and clean underthings. The remaining gown was light brown velvet, trimmed with a darker braid. The underskirt was plain cream silk. The gown had a cloak to match, lined with dark rabbit fur. Bryony tossed it around her chilled shoulders and fastened the frog clasps.

Feeling somewhat restored, she left the chamber just in time to overhear a shrill female voice coming from Gillian's room. She immediately crossed the hall and discovered that Gillian was awake and viciously castigating Nelda about something.

Spying Bryony in the doorway, the patient's lips curved in a visible sneer. "So," Gillian said, briefly breaking off her attack on poor Nelda, "my husband's whore has come to gloat over my misfortune."

Bryony was startled. Clearly Gillian was perfectly lucid now, as evidenced by the unwavering murderous glare fixed on her rival. Bryony quickly gathered up the shreds of her dignity, as Nelda seized the opportunity to flee to safety somewhere else.

"Captain Tanner is not your husband yet, my lady," she reminded Gillian in cool tones.

"Aye, but he soon will be. Never presume 'twill not be so," Gillian said in a threatening vein.

"I was not aware I ever had," Bryony replied.

"Your coming here is clear enough. Brazen slut! You will come to regret meddling in our lives, believe me."

Unwilling to argue with a woman who was missing her wits, Bryony turned to leave. She was startled by the sight of Slade in the hall, wavering slightly, but otherwise determined to stand. He had somehow managed to dress himself, and though he was thin and pale and his shirt only halfway laced, he still managed to project a fierce countenance as he brushed past Bryony into the room.

"You little bitch," he began without preamble, as he advanced on an equally startled Gillian in the bed. "How dare you attack Bryony in such a manner. She nursed us both back from hell's gates! She saved your miserable life, you wretched woman, and you owe her your eternal gratitude, not condemnation."

Gillian quickly rallied under his attack. "How do you know 'twas her intention to save me?" she suggested slyly. "I caught her sneaking into my room last night. Surely the wench planned to put a pillow over my face."

"Christ's bones, madam, have you heard nothing I said?" Slade roared. "Bryony saved your life! Had she wished to harm you, she had more than ample opportunity while you lay dying, and ranting like a madwoman all the while."

"Aye, I lay dying in this house and you summoned your whore to nurse me!" Gillian snapped back. "If that is not cruel, I do not know what is." Seeing Slade's expression darkening, she added in a silky voice, "Mayhaps I am mistaken. Perhaps she is your brother's whore instead, and you and Kit simply share her on occasion."

Slade stared at her, as if unable to believe another human being could be so venal.

"My God," he rasped, "you're a heartless creature, Gilly. You've energy enough to assassinate Bryony's character, but have not even mentioned the babe you prattled on about for so many weeks. Where is your motherly grief?"

The woman in the bed squirmed a little, pinned in place by his flaming green eyes. "Well," she said petulantly, "it isn't as if we can't have other children."

At her flip retort, something visibly snapped in Slade. He stormed over to the pier glass that Mrs. Haymaker had so considerately covered, and yanked down the sheet with a flourish. He gestured to Gillian's reflection.

"I don't think you'll be spreading your legs for any man now," he brutally pointed out, then turned and limped from the room.

Bryony followed, just in time to catch him by the arm in the hall before he fell. Sweet Jesu, he was so thin! Slade's muscles could hardly support his weight, and even as she steadied him, she raged at him, "You belong in bed! The pox is nothing to toy with."

" 'Tis over," he said flatly, and at first she thought he referred to his illness, but then she was not so certain. He suddenly turned on her. "Why did you come?" he demanded. "You exposed yourself to unnecessary danger."

She was astonished by the anger in his voice. "I had to come. There were no others who could help, and Mrs. Haymaker was exhausted. She could not care for two patients all alone—"

"Jesu!" Slade exploded. "You little fool! Is there no sense at all in that pretty head of yours? You could have died! You still might!"

His words roused in Bryony an ire she had hoped never to feel again. " 'Twas love which brought me here," she bitterly retorted. "A foolish misplaced love! For I see now that nothing has changed; you see me only as a willful child, a wayward waif who must needs be corrected, often and sternly!

"But I tell you for the hundredth time, Slade Tanner—I am a woman grown, and under my right of free will choose my own actions—foolish or otherwise—and accept the full consequences as they come. If I choose to risk myself to save another, that is my choice; when I came to the aid of the ill and the weak and the weary in this house, I did so knowing I might possibly jeopardize myself in the process.

"But I see now I was wrong. Not in saving you, for I shall never regret that, but in assuming you would ever come to understand that I am one of the rarest of all creatures on this earth, a woman with both heart and mind! If you cannot accept one, then I do not offer the other. Aye, I am relieved you are recovered, and Gillian also. Never did I desire her death, not even for a moment. But 'twould appear to me now that you two are well suited, after all. She is naught but a vain, selfish, vicious child, and you are accustomed to treating all women as such. I bid you both good fortune and godspeed. Never fear; never again will I darken your path."

"Bryony—" Slade began, both shocked and enraged by the speech she had delivered, but she whirled away before he could catch her, and he was far too weak to pursue her.

"Bryony!" he shouted once more, furiously, then more desperately, but her skirts had long vanished around the corner, and to his frustration he felt his knees slowly buckling beneath him in the hall.

Within Gillian's chamber, the woman in the bed was still gazing mesmerized at the hideous creature reflected in the glass. Never had she seen such a monster, a harpy straight from the churning depths of hell! The creature stared back at her with narrowed bloodshot eyes. Tangled pale hair like a silver shroud framed a distorted face, pitted and scarred with open sores and angry red scabs.

Gillian reached from her bed and grabbed a nearby vase. As the mirror shattered explosively into a million tiny fragments, she buried her face in the pillows and screamed until she could scream no more.

Bryony rode as far west from Dovehaven as she could, and as fast as she dared along the dirt and roughly cobbled roads. Summer Lightning carried her without complaint at a reckless gallop she hoped would clear her mind of the painful memories of the past few months.

As the miles dropped behind them and sanity gradually set in, Bryony slowed her tired mount to a blowing walk. But it also meant she was forced to think again. She had never thought herself capable of hurting so deeply. She had naively believed her scarred heart was safely sheltered. Had she learned nothing over the years? The O'Neill's emotional abuse had apparently been just a preamble for the misery to come. *Ah God!* she silently railed at the heavens. *Why was life so unfair?*

Angrily she wiped away a few stray tears on the back of her hand, concentrating fiercely on the carriage ruts in the road. It did not occur to Bryony to worry about highwaymen, or bandits, or men of ill repute waylaying her on the way to London. She was so very, very weary. The horse's plodding gait nearly lulled her to sleep over the next few miles. She did not realize the animal had stopped to graze along the roadside, until a nearby voice startled her from her light doze.

"Madam? Are you ailing?"

The polite inquiry came from a young man atop a big bay gelding. In one swift embarrassed glance, Bryony took in his rich green velvet doublet and breeches, fine cloak, and the golden chains about his neck.

"Nay, I fear my mind was wandering," she murmured, groping for the reins which had slipped out of her hands.

He frowned, this explanation obviously not suiting him. She

noticed he was dark-eyed and golden-haired, a comely Englishman with arresting features.

"Have you come from Canterbury?" he inquired, looking a bit perplexed as he eyed her winded horse.

She flushed a little. "No. My steed is very spirited, and I but sought to curb his friskiness with a hard run."

"He looks familiar to me," the young man said, and Bryony stiffened, wondering if he intended to imply she was a thief.

Then he added good-naturedly, "You must have entered him in the races before. I'm afraid I'm a bit too devilishly fond of the races myself. You're missing a lovely one this weekend at Epsom. I should have gone, but alas, my new bride tends to pout when I am gone overlong." He offered her a brilliant white smile. "Right now I'm headed to a place called Dovehaven. D'you know of it?"

The name so obviously startled Bryony that she knew she could no longer avoid his curious questions. "Aye," she replied. " 'Tis where I hail from even now. You're Phillip Tanner, aren't you?"

"What the devil!" he exclaimed with surprise. Then he had the grace to flush at the inadvertent oath. "I apologize, madam, but you have me at a definite loss. Have we met before?"

"Nay, sir. My name is Bryony O'Neill. I've just come from nursing patients at Dovehaven."

Phillip merely nodded at her words. Obviously he assumed she was a servant of some sort. No well-bred lady would venture upon such backroads alone. "I'd heard Slade was ill, and thought to see if I could help the household in any way. How does my little brother fare?"

"He is weak, of course, but overall he came through it very well. I believe the infection has lifted. But I would caution you not to enter the house, if you have not endured the pox yourself."

Phillip assured her he would not. "Our brother Kit sent me a message, and I had to come. But two weeks have passed since word of Slade's illness, and we had no news. I volunteered to ride over and check on the household. Not that I'll be much help, but our family always supports one another through such trials. Lord Tanner, our eldest brother, has promised to send a carriage from Cheatham Manor full of foodstuffs and clean bedding."

Bryony was relieved, knowing those at Dovehaven would be well cared for now. But she also felt a prick of envy at Phillip Tanner's nonchalance when he spoke of his family. How he obviously took it for granted that they would always be loving and supportive of one another! She wondered what it would be like to be surrounded by such devotion. It was a bitter pill indeed to realize she would never know.

She murmured, "I fear I must beg your leave, sir. I must press on to London posthaste."

"By yourself? Is there no manservant to at least escort you there?" Phillip shook his golden head with exasperation. "Whatever was Slade thinking?"

"He is still too ill at present to think clearly," Bryony replied. But she had to smile at the outraged chivalry in Phillip's voice. He bore a faint resemblance to Slade, but his proud bearing and chauvinistic manner were very similar.

" 'Twas sheer stupidity on my brother's behalf to send a single female off to Londontown without an escort," Phillip grumbled. "I see I must tend to the completion of your journey, Mistress O'Neill."

"Nonsense!" she retorted a bit more sharply than she intended. Her wounds still smarted from Slade's patronizing words earlier. "I'm nearly there now, and you've many a mile to go yet. Darkness falls soon upon us. Move on, Master Tanner, and rest assured of my safe arrival in Town. I'm no aristocrat to be waylaid by the likes of cutpurses or rogues."

Phillip frowned at her, his brow creased with worry. "I like it not, Mistress O'Neill," he said severely. "Were I not so anxious to aid my brother's household, I should insist upon escorting you to your family's hearth in Londontown. You say 'tis not far?"

"Just around a bend or two," she replied evasively.

"I like it not, but you seem a capable sort. You sit a horse as one born to the saddle, Mistress O'Neill. Very well, then godspeed to you." Phillip Tanner touched the brim of his plumed hat and set his heels to his mount. He was off with a burst of speed that startled her, his horse's shod hooves clattering noisily upon the cobbles into the distance. For a moment, Bryony smiled after him. Were all the Tanners neck-or-nothing riders? It appeared so!

Then she sobered and nudged Summer Lightning back onto the road with weary resignation. Only a few more leagues to go, and she would be free of Slade Tanner and his family forever. She wondered why she wasn't jubilant at the thought.

It was nearly twilight when Bryony finally found herself at the outskirts of London. She estimated she had just enough time to make it to the river before total darkness fell. Crossing London Bridge, Bryony's horse halted in the glut of traffic, and she gazed longingly down over the swirling waters of the Thames.

Too many days had passed since she'd walked a deck. The familiar ache was beginning again in her belly. She might not have Slade Tanner, but she still had the sea. It was fickle, too, blowing fair weather and foul, but at least she knew it would always be there for her.

A rough curse from a cart driver behind Bryony caused her to start, accidentally tapping her horse in the ribs. The gelding would have bolted recklessly, but she quickly gathered him up and brought him under control. Luckily she had learned to become quite a passable horsewoman during her stay at Ambergate. She owed Kit much for his hospitality. Aye, she vowed, she would send him some valuable trifle as thanks one day, if her fortunes ever improved.

Summer Lightning trotted gracefully down from the bridge on the other side, and they rode down on to the port of London.

At the wharf the gelding stopped, snorted, andtossed his head, as if to say he understood her need. Bryony gazed hungrily at the rows of barges lining the river. She knew the greater ships lurked in the distance, just beyond the mouth of the Thames. For a moment, she longed to fling herself down into the nearest skiff and row for all she was worth to escape England and its pain. She almost wept from sheer frustration. But she also knew she was tired, and out of sorts. Now was no time to plan her future.

As she breathed deeply of the salt tang, her eyes alighted on a longboat tied some distance down the quay. The light was poor now, but Bryony was almost ready to swear she gazed upon one of the *Alanna Colleen*'s longboats. She remembered the caravel had distinctive longboats of Portuguese design. Although there were probably hundreds of similarly styled ones in Portugal, she was certain they were relatively rare in England.

Hoping against all hope, she touched her heels to the horse, and he broke into a brisk ringing trot along the docks. As she moved closer to the elusive longboat, other craft and various cargo stacked on the quay obscured a clear view of the vessel. Ignoring the randy whistles and catcalls of the seamen she passed, Bryony guided her mount deeper and deeper into the murky fog near the river's edge.

She didn't dare trust any of the motley sailors to row her out for a better look at the longboat, but the docks extended far enough so that she thought surely she could get close enough to tell for certain if it belonged to the *Alanna Colleen*. Then her horse came to an abrupt halt. Someone had seized the gelding by the bridle, and on reflex she leaned down in the saddle and blindly struck out in the fog.

"Mon Dieu!" a man swore roughly in ringing tones as her hard little fist connected with his head. Bryony's wrist was knocked aside, and as she prepared to battle for her life, the fog parted and a familiar beetle-browed face glared up at her.

"I assumed you came to keep your oath to me, *chérie,* not knock my teeth out!" the man growled, rubbing his jaw.

Torn between relief and dread, Bryony snapped, "You flatter yourself, Lafleur! I'm here on business, nothing more!"

"And what do you call our arrangement, *ma jeune fille,* if not business?" he replied with a toothy white grin. "Ah, perhaps you prefer to think of it as pleasure. I know I do."

"Hah!" Bryony scoffed at him, giving the reins an abrupt jerk and freeing the bridle from his hand. She felt the gelding's muscles tense as he prepared to run, but before the animal bolted, Lafleur had dragged her down from the saddle and crushed her against his broad chest.

Her fists began to beat a steady tattoo upon him. The Frenchman merely chuckled at her puny attempts to get free, until she folded her fingers tight and swung a fist again at his bearded jaw. She caught him squarely on the chin, and Lafleur sputtered in pain and outrage, but did not let her go. She cried out.

"Hold!" came a disembodied male voice from the swirling mists. His Irish accent was nearly as thick as the fog. "Release the wench, you rogue!"

"Mind your own damned business," growled Lafleur.

" 'Tis me business whenever I stumble across a lady being abused," the voice replied, and a stout figure swaggered out of the fog beside them, one hand confidently on the hilt of a foil at his side. Immediately Bryony recognized that endearing craggy face.

"Finn!" she cried, tearing free of Lafleur and flinging herself into the arms of the startled young man. She was gratified to feel them close quickly and protectively around her.

"By all the saints!" Finn swore softly, setting her back from him a moment later. His surprised gaze swiftly traveled over her from head to toe. " 'Tis our own Bryony O'Neill, and dressed like a fine *Sassenach* lady to boot!"

Behind them Lafleur sputtered with indignation. "Watch your hands, Irishman! That's my woman there!"

"Is she, *señor?*" inquired another male voice, this one silky with deadly intent as he stepped from the fog beside Finn. "Would you care to debate the issue with me?"

Bryony turned and saw Diego Santiago gracefully weighing a fine dagger of Damascus steel in his brown fist. She had the satisfaction of seeing Lafleur redden at the challenge.

"These are two of my able crew." She couldn't resist taunting the Frenchman, if only a little. "They would defend me to the death. Can you say the same of your men?"

Giles eyed her with surprising good humor. "You're a damned bold *fille,* Irish, and you've played Lafleur for a fool one too many times. But perhaps I underestimated you from the beginning," he grudgingly admitted. "No woman earns such loyalty without cause."

Bryony turned to the other two men with hope written all over her face. "That's *Alanna*'s longboat I spied nearby, isn't it?"

"Aye," Finn O'Grady laughed, "but thanks only to the grace of God, and one hell of a captain!"

Diego modestly accepted the compliment. "I could not have done it without you and the lads, O'Grady. *Señorita* O'Neill trained her crew well."

Lafleur was listening to all this with pure amazement. "I would have a word with you," he said to Bryony at first opportunity.

Diego answered his request with a thin smile. "But not today, eh, *mi amigo?* Run along now." The wiry little Spaniard ominously slapped the cold steel of his dagger against his open palm for emphasis.

"Wait. I would hear what he has to say." Bryony thought she'd detected a new note of respect in the Frenchman's deep voice. She was curious to know what he was thinking.

Lafleur shook his head. "Not here, little tigress. There is a pub nearby, where we might speak in private. Your friends are welcome to join us, provided they mind their manners."

Bryony grinned while her two crewmen scowled up at the

big Frenchman. "What say you, lads? If this ruffian will treat us to some ale to wash the dust from our throats, I'll gladly hear him out."

O'Grady shook his head and sighed. "I'd not trust this one with me own rosary, Cousin, but I'll go along for the sport of it. We've quite a tale to tell you ourselves."

"Aye," Diego put in, "and *Capitan* Tanner, as well. Where is he?"

Bryony's smile thinned a little, but she said cheerfully enough, "That, too, is another long story. Let's not let Captain Lafleur's coin burn a hole in his pockets, men. I've a terrible thirst, and if he'll sate it for free, I'll swap tales with you till the cock crows."

So agreed, Lafleur led them all to the nearest tavern, where Bryony also paid the last of her own coin to a reliable lad to return Summer Lightning to his master's stable. She sent no message to Kit, but a simple thanks for the loan of his horse.

Inside the relatively quiet and smoky atmosphere of the pub house, the four of them took seats at a rough plank table.

"You first," Bryony said to the others, reaching for her brimming tankard of cool ale laced with foam. Lafleur nodded to the other two men, indicating they should go ahead.

"As you can see, we survived the storm after all," Finn began with a merry air. "After the ships were separated, we sailed out of a fog bank some hours later to find ourselves staring down the cannon of a Spanish galleon."

Bryony plunked down her tankard. "What!"

Now it was Diego's turn to pick up the tale. *"Si,"* he continued with an ear to ear grin, " 'twas quite an exciting time! We were blown so far south by the storm, that one of King Philip's ships plundering the Welsh coast happened upon us."

"As you can imagine, Cousin, we had no chance," Finn said. "We were immediately boarded and seized in the name of Spain and her king."

"Holy Mother of God! What next?"

With a twinkle in his dark eyes, Diego proceeded, "Of

course, I generously offered to interpret for my fellow countrymen."

Bryony's eyebrows rose, as did Lafleur's. "Indeed?"

"Si, and I quickly assured *mis amigos* that I had already commandeered the caravel for His Majesty King Charles . . . long dead these many years! What could they say? A solid black ship had sailed out of a deep eerie fog right across their bow. She bore no guns, her hold was empty, and her only crew a handful of children." Diego slapped the table with open mirth. "Ah, you should have seen them shaking in their boots, *señorita!"*

Finn, too, laughed at the memory. "Sure, and that's the truth of it! Diego had them running scared, peering down into our hold, crossing themselves like crazy. And after a wee while, 'twas obvious they believed his story about us being the ghosts of the dead. I just kept me mouth shut and let Diego do the talking. The Spaniards finally decided the *Alanna Colleen* was a ghostly vessel carrying poor souls to Purgatory, and they left us quicker than a whore the morning after."

"Where did you go then?" Bryony asked, chuckling.

"The ship was in sorry shape, she was," Finn said, sobering. "Her sails were shredded, her foremast snapped from the storm. Diego sailed us far north as Wexford, but it took many a day." He hesitated then, admitting, "In the while, Cousin, I'd stumbled across the money you left in the cabin. I had to use it all for repairs and provisions, so she'd sail again."

"That's what it was for," Bryony reassured Finn, patting his callused hand resting on the table. "I'm glad now that I was harebrained enough to leave it behind. Tell me: are the rest of the lads safe?"

"Aye, and most of them fit to be sailors now. 'Tis amazing, Cousin, what our little adventure did for the lads. Not a hand lost, and all of them want to sign on with us now."

"So what are your plans, Irish?" Lafleur interrupted quietly, looking at Bryony with his piercing black eyes. "Do you crawl back to Tanner, or salvage a few shreds of pride and return to the sea from which you were spawned?"

She stiffened under Finn's and Diego's curious looks. They did not know yet what had happened to Slade, but now was not the time to try and explain.

"What's your proposition, Lafleur?" she countered calmly. "I assume you have one. But be warned, if it's a ship's doxy you seek, the tavern wenches here would be far more suited to such a life than me."

He grinned with defeat. "I've an honest business proposal this time, *ma petite.* For you and your loyal friends here. The thought of Spanish riches tempts this old sea dog's soul. One ship is not enough anymore to capture a great Spanish galleon. But with two . . ."

Bryony's eyebrows rose. "And you dare to call the O'Neill a pirate?"

"Bah, wench! 'Tis called privateering, when it is the enemy! Even Bess looks the other way when Spanish ships are sacked. Think of the treasure to be had!" Giles's eyes took on a devilish gleam, as he twisted the black tails of his drooping moustache. With a quick glance he saw that Diego was interested, O'Grady looked appalled, but since Bryony was the one who ultimately had to be convinced, he turned his sights on her.

"You'll be beholden to no man, if you join me, lass."

"Not even you?" she dubiously inquired, then took a sip of her ale with an air of cool disinterest.

"Lafleur finally sees he is no match for you, Irish. You thrive on danger and conflict as much as any man. *Oui,* don't deny it! I've seen the fire in your eyes more than once."

But now those same eyes were veiled to him as Bryony gazed down into her ale. "What's the split?" she quietly asked him.

"Fifty-fifty. We sail under the plain black. We seek no letters of marque from Bess or France, and both our crews are sworn to secrecy."

It was tempting. Bryony could not deny it. And she knew

she badly needed to restore the funds she had lost to the *Alanna Colleen*'s repairs. She glanced at the other two men. Finn looked uncomfortable with the idea, but she knew he would go along with it at a word from her. Diego Santiago was the one she worried about. She wondered how he truly felt. Besides being a Spaniard by birth, he was also loyal to Slade Tanner, and might betray them. She said as much aloud.

Diego looked hurt. "I have ten mouths to feed at home, *señorita,*" he said frankly. "I bear no loyalty to Mother Spain, though she be the land of my birth, and this much *Capitan* Tanner also knew. If he will not be sailing again for a long while, I cannot afford to wait."

Bryony considered his words a moment, and then nodded. She raised her tankard in a salute to her three companions.

"Then here's to our future, men. For if we can't find wealth and renown, then we'll damn well take it instead!"

Eighteen

Autumn 1578

For almost two months, Bryony O'Neill and her crew followed in Lafleur's experienced wake, capturing lone Spanish vessels along the English or Welsh coastlines, and generously unburdening King Philip of his gold, jewels, and precious cargos. All the goods were either sold or smuggled off through Lafleur's channels. After what was usually a short but furious battle, the remaining Spanish sailors were not harmed, but either set adrift with plenty of provisions, rowed ashore to laboriously pick their way back home, or ransomed.

Legends quickly sprang up about the fierce bearded French pirate and his mysterious wench. Though she wore breeches and boots like any man, the Spaniards could not quite believe Bryony ruled her own vessel. So they dubbed her *La Francis Joven,* the Frenchman's Woman. She sailed in a smaller black vessel, one as swift and deadly as a cat. The name scrolled across the bow, *Fiach-muir,* was indecipherable to them.

Sometimes she lured a Spanish ship to its fate by flying the half-flag of distress, and when they went to her aid, the Frenchman would suddenly swoop down upon them in his larger galleon like a vulture. Other times, the *Fiach-muir* would trick a Spanish vessel into chasing her, darting in and out of the rugged coves, until the Spaniards became overconfident and trapped her against the coastline rocks, only to find themselves in turn trapped by the French pirate on the other side.

Talk of the daring privateers was soon rife across Europe. King Philip was furious, and ordered extra guns mounted on all his ships. He was certain Elizabeth Tudor was somewhere behind these bold attacks. While it was true the English queen was known to grant letters of marque upon occasion—legalizing plunder of Spanish vessels—Elizabeth herself was both bemused and amused by the rumors drifting through her court that she was responsible, and somehow secretly financing the venture. Moreover, it did not take her long to figure out the name of one of the mystery ships.

" 'Tis Gaelic," she informed her current favorite, Sir Christopher Hatton. " 'Twould appear I have at least one loyal subject among those unruly Irishmen," she sourly concluded.

"Woman, Your Grace," Sir Christopher politely corrected the queen in his bored courtier's tone. " 'Tis said to be a mere slip of a wench, striking such terror into the heart of the Spain."

Elizabeth looked interested. "Aye, Christopher? Is she also said to be fair?"

Aware of his monarch's infamous jealousy, he cautiously replied, "Not uncommonly so, Your Majesty." He quickly changed the subject, asking, "What does *Fiach-muir* mean in the Gaelic, Your Grace?"

"Muir means the sea, I know. *Fiach* refers to some sort of bird. A raven, I believe. I must consult with some of my Irish lords, Christopher. I confess my curiosity has been sore roused."

One warm day in late October, the privateers seized a galleon destined for Madrid, and found its hold to contain nothing but fine Barb horses brought from the Turkish wars and destined for King Philip's stables. Disgusted, Lafleur ordered the entire useless lot pitched overboard, but Bryony intervened and convinced him the unusual cargo would bring a nice profit.

One particularly gorgeous golden stallion with a pale mane and tail she earmarked for her own purposes.

While Lafleur made arrangements to have the others shipped and sold in various private French and English markets, Bryony had the golden stud sent anonymously to Ambergate, along with a bejeweled saddle and tack. She knew Kit Tanner could not refuse such a beautiful creature. His one weakness, other than his daughters, was fine horseflesh.

Perhaps Kit would assume the horse came from the queen. Elizabeth Tudor was known for bestowing such valuable and frivolous gifts upon her favorites. Bryony convinced Lafleur to make an anonymous gift of six pure white mares to the queen, as well. She chuckled at the thought of all the confusion when the purebred animals arrived back in London.

It was November before they finally ceased terrorizing King Philip's ships. The weather had turned foul, and Bryony and Lafleur agreed they had far more cargo now than markets in which to sell it. Spring would bring renewed opportunity, but for now, they were all weary, and the men anxious to get home.

Although it felt so blessedly right to be walking the decks of a ship again, Bryony was forced to acknowledge she was lonely. There was nobody to share in her triumphs or her profits, and although no men could be more devoted than hers, it was a far stretch from the captaincy to the crew.

Lafleur, she knew, had never given up hope that she would eventually succumb to his twinkling charm. She found she could not despise the great bear of a Frenchman, no matter that his hands still wandered upon occasion. The two often stayed up late gambling or swapping exaggerated tales of their narrow escapes. But never did they become lovers, and sometimes Bryony wondered why.

The answer occurred to her one night after she and Lafleur finished dicing in his cabin, and he shooed her off with a brotherly smack on the behind so he could get some sleep. *She still loved Slade.* Somehow Lafleur must have sensed it, or seen it in her eyes. He was willing to wait until she came to him of her own volition.

But Bryony knew that would never happen. However much she admired the Frenchman for his generous spirit, his devil-may-care attitude, even his fierce and loyal love for the sea, he was not the man for her. She felt for him the same sort of casual affection she felt for Finn O'Grady, or Brendan. The thought of her brother made her suddenly and unexpectedly homesick for Ireland. All her crew had plans for their time off until they sailed again in the spring, except for her. She wondered what had happened at Raven Hall since Mab's passing. Surprisingly, she no longer felt any fear at the thought of confronting the O'Neill again.

When she and Lafleur agreed to part company until the spring, O'Grady and the other lads were delighted to hear they were going back to Clandeboye. All except for Diego, who had requested he be returned to London and his family. Lafleur saw to it that the little Spaniard got home safely, with plenty of booty for his reward. Diego had been invaluable as a translator, whenever they seized and boarded the Spanish ships.

Bryony did not know what she expected to feel as the newly christened *Fiach-muir* sailed boldly into Clandeboye Cove one gray November afternoon. The emotions that gripped her, however, were a shock. She felt as if a great burden had been lifted off her shoulders for the first time in her life. Not merely because the ship's hold creaked satisfactorily beneath her with the weight of Spanish treasure, but because for the first time she boldly sailed her own vessel without apology, without hesitation, into her old enemy's territory.

She was not surprised to find the O'Neill in a fury, when she and the others reached Raven Hall. As her crew dropped away one by one to reunite with their kin and families, she soon found herself alone with Brann in the stone tower house.

"I suppose you expect me to think you're such a clever bitch, stealing back the ship you stole from me in the first place!" Brann thundered by way of greeting, as Bryony faced him in the Great Hall with her hands squarely planted on her hips.

"I care not one whit what you think of me," she retorted flatly. "I've only come back for Brendan's sake, and to pay my respects at Mab's grave."

The O'Neill's gaze narrowed on her. "You killed Mab, you reckless little brat! Drove her to grieving so badly, she took ill and died."

"From what I hear, no one could even be bothered to nurse her!" Bryony snapped back. "After all the years that devoted old woman gave the clan, that was her thanks in the end!"

" 'Twas your fault," Brann muttered. "You were the one who ran off and left her, not me."

"Mab knew I was born to a destiny at sea. She did not try to turn me from that path, like you did."

Brann visibly bristled, but couldn't deny it. "Well," he said grudgingly, "I've never denied you've a ken of the sea. But provoking the *Sassenach* navy against me as you did will not soon be forgiven."

"Navy?" Bryony gave an incredulous laugh. " 'Twas one measly ship, old man, and you couldn't handle her! And as for forgiveness, you never let me live down Alanna's death, so why should this be any different?"

She watched the O'Neill purple with emotion. He moved toward her as if he would strike her down where she stood, but she noticed his knees shaking. With shock Bryony realized that he was no longer hale and hearty, this once-powerful man who had ruled her childhood and her nightmares.

For as long as she could remember, Brann O'Neill had carried himself with the proud bearing of a brawny seaman. Yet now she saw those great shoulders were bent, his big finger shaking uncontrollably as he pointed at her.

"Don't speak of Alanna, ever! She was no mother of yours, Changeling, for you came from the fairy folk!"

"Did I, now?" Bryony's eyebrows shot up. "Don't tell me

you still believe your own poisonous rot? You're a fool, old man, every bit as big a fool as Mab ever said you were. *I'm the spitting image of you, and you damn well know it!"*

Bryony whirled and stormed from the hall, having won the last word for the first time in her life. Outside it had begun to drizzle, and the soft green hills were wreathed with mist, dark clouds winging in with the promise of more rain to come. A cold wind bit at her, and she tugged up the standing collar on her new velvet fur-lined cloak, then wrapped it more snugly about her.

She walked to the mound of dirt underneath a great spreading oak east of the tower. This late in the year, there were no flowers for Mab's grave, but Bryony knelt beside the marker and ran her callused fingers over the cold gray stone.

"Lord, old woman, how I miss you," she said in a choked voice, as the hot tears surged up and slid down her cheeks. "How could you just up and leave me like this? I had dreams of a fine house someday, where I could take care of you, as you always cared for me. Now I have the means, Mab, but none to fill the rooms. Would you sentence me to rattling around a great old house by myself? Ahh, damn!"

Bryony fumbled for the top hook on her snug breeches and sighed with relief when the pressure eased. Somehow during all the excitement of the past few months, she had still managed to put on weight. But then, she and Lafleur had eaten like kings whenever they captured a well-caparisoned vessel. She would soon work off the extra pounds again.

Her brow furrowed as she said a last loving goodbye to Mab and finally rose. She moved to gaze out over the cove from the nearby cliff. Today the sea was in a foul mood, reflecting the angry sky. The white-capped waves dashed restlessly against the worn rocks of the cove, as she walked the length of the cliff.

Bryony had not gone far, when nearby shouts caught her attention. Turning, she watched as the tiny figure of Finn

O'Grady scrambled up the hills after her. She moved to meet him, as he burst up over a ridge to the cliffside path.

"Bryony, come quick," he cried.

"What is it?"

"Just look." Finn led her to where an overlook afforded a better view of the open sea and the channel leading into the cove. She didn't know whether to curse or cry, when she saw the familiar vessel bearing down on them.

"O'Grady, do you recognize that wretched ship?"

Finn was not surprised by the bitterness in her voice. He had learned only a little of what had transpired between her and Slade Tanner, but it was enough. Bryony was a fine woman, a brave lass, who deserved better than a faithless *Sassenach*.

"Aye," he said with resignation. " 'Tis the Englishman again. I wonder what he could be wantin' with us now?"

"What, indeed?" Bryony muttered, turning and striding back down the path. Each long stride was a preoccupied one. They both knew Slade Tanner was not here on a social call.

By now the O'Neill had also sighted their unwelcome visitor, and had called together the clansmen. They arrived at the hall bearing everything from swords to shovels, their collective expressions reflecting outrage and hate.

As Bryony approached, she overheard Brann briskly instructing the men on the rules of warfare on his land. "Anythin' goes," he said. "Kill as many of the cursed *Sassenach* as you can, lads. They'll do the same to us, if given half a chance."

Nods and angry murmurs showed approval of his plan. These proud Raven clansmen were willing to die rather than give up one inch of precious Irish soil.

Bryony tensed when she saw the *Silver Hart* had already dropped anchor, and a longboat was being lowered into the cove. Minutes later a single figure climbed nimbly down the rope ladder and took up the oars. *God's bones!* she swore under her breath. Was Slade such a half-wit that he would sail alone and undefended into the enemy's midst?

Pushing through the cluster of her furious clansmen, Bryony reached the O'Neill. When he turned and glared at her with narrowed eyes, she said, "There's only one man coming in. You'd best hear what he has to say, before your bloodthirsty henchmen strike him down!"

"Bah! I know what the *Sassenach* cur has to say, and I won't be hearin' it," he thundered. " 'Tis Raven land, and were the bloody bitch-queen herself to swim across the channel and kiss me dirty feet, I'd still kick her in the arse and throw her fancy English drawers into the drink!"

The men roared with laughter at his witticism, but Bryony only snorted with disgust. "Make a fool of yourself on your own behalf, O'Neill, not anyone else's! The only ones who'll pay for your stupidity are these men and their families. And who'll look after them, when you're rotting in the ground beside Mab and your precious Alanna?"

She stormed off down the path to meet the incoming longboat, and Brann cursed long and loud after her. After a moment's hesitation, Finn O'Grady joined his cousin, gaining jeers and catcalls from the other men for what they saw as his misplaced loyalty.

"Holy Mother of God, Bryony, what are you going to do?" Finn breathlessly demanded as he caught up to her.

"I don't know yet. But at least I owe it to Slade to warn him, before that pack of wild animals back there tears him apart, limb from limb."

Finn shook his head unhappily, but stayed by her side as the longboat came closer and closer to shore. When Slade's features were clearly visible, Bryony felt her heart leap in her chest. Never for a moment had she forgotten a single detail of that handsome face, though she had cursed it many a night in the privacy of her own bed. Even in the rain, the red gold sheen of Slade's hair was clearly visible and brought back a flood of warm memories. She had to restrain herself from stepping forward when he came ashore at last.

Slade jumped out of the longboat, and Finn helped him to pull it farther up onto the beach. When Slade straightened, his dark green eyes went at once to Bryony, and her lips parted in an involuntary little cry.

He looked like he'd been through hell in the past months, one far darker than the pox alone could afford. His face was thin, his cheekbones far too prominent. But his eyes were the same, those blessed bright green eyes, softening now to the color of the rain as he came toward her.

"Bryony," was all he said, his voice roughened by the emotion lurking there.

"Why are you here?" she blurted out, acutely aware of the O'Neill and his men observing their exchange like eager predators.

"I'll take that to mean I'm not welcome."

"Nay. 'Tis just you are in grave danger. I cannot guarantee your safety, nor that of your crew."

Slade smiled at her then, such a slow and carefree smile that the ice around her heart melted, just a little. "I had to see you again, Bryony. Or should I say sea raven? 'Tis rumored a fearsome black bird rules these waters, you know."

"The *Sea Raven* prefers warmer waters, those closer to sunny Spain," she innocently replied. "Surely you did not come here merely to chase the stuff of myth and legend?"

"No." Slade had to admire her calm. He had heard naught but endless tales of the bold wench who seized Spanish booty upon the high seas, and when one rumor told of the golden amulet about her lovely neck, he had known the fate of Bryony O'Neill these past months. "I would never betray you," he assured her. "But there's something between us still that needs to be settled, once and for all."

"Then you're not here to claim Clandeboye again?"

"If 'twas land I wanted, I'd have stayed in Kent. The queen granted me Dovehaven after Gillian's death."

Bryony gasped at this unexpected news. "How? Gillian seemed to survive the pox."

Slade shrugged. "I don't really know what happened. So many days passed in a haze back then. I just remember I was on my ship at the time. Bess had already agreed to postpone the wedding until after Twelfth Night. By the time I got the message from my brother George and returned to Dovehaven, 'twas too late. According to Elinor, Gilly's maidservant, her mistress simply slipped away in the night, without pain. They had buried her even before I arrived."

Bryony's eyes filled with tears at his words. Gillian Lovelle had hated her with a passion, even accused Bryony of trying to murder her, but now all she could feel was grief and deep pity for the woman.

"She was so unhappy," she murmured. "Poor Gillian."

"She was mad," Slade stated without rancor. "Gilly never fully recovered from the brain fever. But I'm not here to talk about her. I'm here to see your father."

"You mean the O'Neill?" She was shocked again.

"If he's your father," Slade teased her. "Can I rightly assume he's the black-browed giant over there, buzzing about like an angry wasp?"

Bryony nodded, reaching out to restrain him when he made as if to move in that direction. "Don't be a fool! He needs no excuse to kill an Englishman, and he's worked up his men into a lather at the sporting idea of it!"

" 'Tis true," Finn chimed in for the first time. "They'd like nothing better than to tear you asunder."

"Not without cause," Slade remarked. Then he matter-of-factly freed himself and began striding up the sandy beach toward the crowd of tense angry Irishmen.

"Oh, merciful god!" Bryony swore under her breath. She rushed after Slade, just as the O'Neill and his men fanned out to confront the approaching Englishman. Her clansmen looked a menacing lot, most weighing various blunt weapons in their rough-hewn hands.

Slade came to a stop several feet away, and had the courage or audacity to laugh. "Call off your dogs, O'Neill! I'm not here for your bloody land. You're welcome to it."

"What then?" The O'Neill suspiciously spat.

Slade offered up a winning smile. "Why don't you be gracious enough to invite this weary traveler inside your hall to find out? I've a mind to sample Irish hospitality. 'Tis said it even outstrips that of the French. But if it makes you feel safer, bring your dogs along, too."

At the suggestion he was a coward, the O'Neill scowled and puffed out his chest. "I've nothin' to fear from one scrawny *Sassenach!*"

Minutes later the two had vanished into Raven Hall, and the doors thudded securely shut behind them. The O'Neill clansmen muttered and milled about outside, and Bryony herself stared in outrage at the locked doors. She had not even been invited in! What business could those two possibly be discussing, which did not involve her? And who did they think they were, that they could dismiss her so lightly?

"Come along, O'Grady," she snapped at her cousin. "We'll not stay where we're not wanted. And I'm of a mind to visit Brendan and Glynnis up at Ballycastle. With the O'Neill safely occupied for the next hour or so, I don't think he'll miss the *Fiach-muir.*" She cast a sour glance at the hall as they walked away.

"Aye, Finn," Bryony added, "the dashing Captain Tanner had best pray he can match us Irish for our silver tongues and quick dancing, or I've no doubt we'll return to find a heap of English bones being picked over by the hungry ravens!"

Slade restrained his amusement at the O'Neill's rigidly formal behavior inside his own hall.

"Have a seat, milord," the gruff Irishman invited him, in a voice heavily laden with sarcasm. Brann indicated one of the wooden benches placed beside the high board. "I pray you'll overlook the humble home of a poor serf like meself!"

Slade glanced around the stone tower house. Aye, Raven Hall might be humble by Tudor standards, with rushes rather than carpets upon the floor, but the rushes were clean, and he caught a mouth-watering whiff of freshly baked bread from the kitchens.

Brann gestured curtly to an attractive, flaxen-haired young woman standing in the shadows. Slade had not seen her there at first. "Fetch us two ales, Aileen lass. I've an uncommon thirst."

Silently and obediently the girl fled to the kitchens. Looking fondly after her, Brann said, "I found her at Dublin market last fall. Proper grateful, she was, to be spared the bed of the lecherous old man her da would have her wed. Aileen cared for her father and five brothers wi'out complaint for ten years, so Raven Hall is an easy task for her, and we're both content with the bargain. I've even a notion to make the wench an honorable woman someday. What d'you think, *Sassenach?*"

Slade didn't reply. He was still looking around, impressed with what he saw. Lining the walls were any number of curious items, including a brace of rusted swords and shields, and a torn and faded standard that looked very old. The standard resembled the one he had first seen flying from the *Leprechaun*'s mast, a screaming raven on a crimson ground, though the crimson had long since weathered to pale pink.

O'Neill followed his gaze and gestured to the standard. "That," he said, with slow and deliberate menace, " 'twas granted to me great-great-grandsire, Fergus O'Neill, by the king of Tir Eoghain, when he brought down a field of twenty *Sassenach* singlehandedly. Have ye heard of the ballad of Niall Mor O'Neill?"

Slade levelly met his adversary's gaze. "I doubt it."

"Then listen well, Englishman;

Ireland is a woman risen again
from the horrors of reproach . . .
she was owned for a while by foreigners,
she belongs to Irishmen after that."

"A charming little ditty," Slade idly remarked, while Brann glowered at him, obviously spoiling for a fight. "But it should ease your mind to know I'm not here to claim your land, O'Neill. In fact," he continued, withdrawing from his leather jerkin a scroll of parchment, "with the queen's permission, I hereby return to you all rights to Clandeboye and Raven Hall."

He handed the parchment to the dumbfounded O'Neill, who made no move to unroll or read it. Instead, the big man's fist tightened on the scroll, nearly crushing it. "You're soft, Englishman," he muttered. "I'd not have let it go so easily."

"I ask only one thing in return, O'Neill. Your daughter's hand in marriage," Slade said.

The Irishman visibly tensed, and his ruddy face reddened even further, if such a thing was possible. The two were nearly a match in size. Brann was bigger, but Slade was taller. They squared off now in the center of the hall, anger and tension hanging like a thick bank of fog between them.

At last Brann growled, "I have no daughter."

Slade was startled, until he remembered Bryony's insistence that O'Neill had never publicly acknowledged her. Could it be true? He laughed in outright amazement, enraging Brann even further.

"Finish stating your case, Englishman, or by God I'll have me men haul you out and flay you alive on Irish soil! Then, before I throw your bloody carcass to the sharks, I'll cut off a sweet memento for the Tudor bitch-queen, if you have anythin' between your skinny-shank legs to send her!"

"Oh, I don't think there's any question of that, O'Neill, for 'tis obvious enough I've managed to plant a seed in your daughter's fertile field."

Slade's remark caused the O'Neill's mouth to open and shut with an audible snap. Brann reacted with pure emotion. His meaty fist swung out to catch his adversary on the jaw, and only with lightning-quick reflexes did Slade manage to duck and avoid the brutal blow.

"That's more like it!" Slade chuckled softly. "Defend the virtue of your daughter like a proper father!"

Realizing what he'd done, Brann froze and stared at the amused younger man. " 'Tis true?" he croaked. "You've gone and spoiled the Changeling?"

Slade didn't respond. Let Bryony's stubborn sire sweat a little more.

"Well?" the O'Neill demanded.

"Have I your permission?" Slade countered.

"She'll have no dower from me!"

"Very well. But may we at least have your blessing?"

The O'Neill chewed thoughtfully on the inside of his unshaven cheek for a long moment. At last he grunted, which Slade took for approval.

"I love your daughter, O'Neill," he continued, "and you'll never know what a stubborn, high-spirited, wonderful woman she is, until you accept her as your own. In fact, she's very much like you. For all the hell you've put her through, Bryony's still fiercely loyal to the Raven clan."

For just a fleeting moment, Slade thought he caught a spark of emotion in the O'Neill's gaze. Then Brann nodded shortly and the sharp gaze of the raven returned, pinning Slade to the wall.

"Aye," he growled, "go fetch the wench. I'll find Father O'Leary. No O'Neill of Clandeboye will be born outside o' wedlock!"

Nineteen

By the time a truce had been called between the two men, Bryony was already long gone on the *Fiach-muir.* When the ship was safely in the North Channel, she motioned Finn to her side.

"It should be an easy trip, for all the rain," she said. She had chosen to take only a skeleton crew on the short journey, as she knew how homesick the lads had been. Finn had insisted on coming along, as she'd known he would.

"It feels good to be on the water again," her cousin replied with a frank grin. "Just a day ashore, and already I was losin' me sea legs!"

Bryony laughed at the truth of that. "And me my iron stomach! Is it just me, Finn, or is the channel unusually rough today?"

He studied her with concern. Bryony did look slightly green, and he'd never known her to have a weak constitution.

"Why don't you go below, lass, and let me take command for awhile. We'll be there in a few short hours. A bit of sleep is probably all you need."

Bryony didn't argue, but moved to the small aft cabin and arrived just in time to catch the contents of her stomach in a chamber pot. She spent the rest of the trip being sick. When she wasn't on her hands and knees over the pot, she lay weakly in the bed, not moving until O'Grady finally came below to inform her they had dropped anchor in Rathlin Sound. She didn't even protest when he helped her up, so she could clean herself up and change her clothing.

After she shooed Finn off, ignoring his worried protests, Bryony eased herself into a new outfit with a grimace. It was only one of the many fripperies plundered from a Spanish ship, and had doubtless been intended for some wealthy contessa's wardrobe. She didn't fancy the loose style of the gown, but none of her breeches seemed to fit anymore. And her roiling belly could not bear the pressure of tight hooks or laces right now.

She donned a simple chemise over which went two petticoats, one of wool and one of fine white linen. The gown's underskirt was silver silk, embroidered in black silk. The dress itself was soft scarlet velvet with a wide, low, square bodice trimmed in pearls. The wide cuffs on the sleeves frothed with silver d'Espagne lace.

When a little of her dignity and her color was restored, Bryony went above decks. As a wave of bright sunlight flooded over her, she had to quell the sharp urge to rush to the rail and retch again.

"God's teeth, O'Grady!" she irritably greeted her cousin. "I thought the lads had learned to keep the ship on an even keel now, at least when she's anchored down!"

Finn's eyebrows rose. He could barely feel the planks shifting under his feet. The sky and sea were as clear as a bell now. They had left the stormy weather in Clandeboye.

"There's the welcoming party," he said to distract Bryony, pointing to shore. He was relieved to see her break into a huge smile, when she recognized her brother and his new wife waving at them.

After relieving the crew, Bryony let Finn row her in. He scarcely landed the longboat when she climbed ashore and was immediately smothered in hugs and kisses by Brendan and his bride, Glynnis. Bryony had met the girl before, but she couldn't help but gasp at the sight of this full-blown, red-haired little rose, ripe in the late stages of pregnancy. Being a petite lass, Glynnis had no room to grow but outward.

"Faith, I see you've been well occupied since my departure," she scolded her brother in cheeky tones.

Brendan grinned. It was obvious how proud he was of Glynnis, as he hovered over his deceptively delicate-looking wife.

"Sure, and we heard tale you had a few adventures of your own, Bry," he said. "We worried something terrible, when we'd heard you been seized by the queen's navy and sentenced to death."

" 'Twas a bit exaggerated," Bryony said, turning to look over the modest little homestead with an approving eye. "What matters is I'm here now. I want to see this fine farm of yours, Dan, everything from the fields and crops to the wee cradle awaiting your son."

"How d'you know 'twill be a son?" Glynnis asked.

"Just look at how high you are carrying. Mab always said boys are carried high like that. I never knew her to be wrong." Bryony sighed, saddened anew by the reminder of the old woman's absence. "I'll never forgive myself for not being here for Mab, when she needed me."

"Don't be foolish," Brendan said. He stepped forward and gave her a comforting hug. "Ah, Bry, she knew her time was near. Glynnis and I asked her to come and live with us, to care for the coming babe, but she refused. Mab wouldn't leave Raven Hall. 'Twas her home, she said, where she herself was born and raised. In her last breath she cursed the O'Neill for denying you your birthright."

A tremulous smile touched Bryony's lips. "Did she think I was dead when I left Ireland?"

"Nay, never. She told us you were simply following your destiny, which had been written in the sea and the stars long before you were born. Like you said, Bry, Mab was always right."

A moment of respectful silence fell between them, and when a soft gust of wind suddenly rustled her skirts, Bryony felt as if Mab had somehow given her a sign. A gentle reassurance that she would always be there, watching over them all.

"I'm so glad you came," Brendan said to his sister later that day, while he worked to repair some broken harness inside the house. "I wanted you to see our home, and how happy I am now."

Bryony was helping Glynnis prepare the evening meal inside the little white-washed cottage with its thatched roof. She paused in scrubbing vegetables, and turned to face her twin.

"I can tell, Dan," she said softly. "This home is full of love and laughter, and I'm envious of you. It's good to know life can sometimes be fair."

"What can we do, Bryony?" Glynnis asked, hearing the note of sadness in the young woman's voice. "Would it help if Dan spoke with the O'Neill on your behalf?"

Bryony shook her head. "Oh, 'tis far too late for that. Mab tried for years, and all for naught. Anyway, I've come to accept it."

"Have you, now?" Brendan challenged her, and saw his sister visibly tense. "Bry, I defied him and won my right to happiness. You can do the same, if you truly want to."

"But there's nothing I want from him," she lied.

"What about the *Alanna Colleen*? I don't want her, I never did, and what's more, you were always the sailor I never was."

"She's the *Fiach-muir* now, and anyway the O'Neill has no claim to her. I can buy her a hundred times over with the booty Lafleur and I earned sacking Spanish ships. O'Neill will ask a high price, I'm sure, but I'm prepared to meet it."

"He'll have to come through me first, and that's no small task now," Brendan vowed as he tossed down the mended bridle on the table. "He owes you something, Bry, and though a ship is damned measly compensation for the devilish way he's treated you all these years, I'll see to it with my fists, if I have to."

Bryony didn't doubt his threat, as her twin had grown quite large from so many months of hard manual labor. Brendan's arms were thickly corded with sinewy muscle, his hands big and blunt, farmer's hands now.

She smiled at him. "Dan, I appreciate your support. But I want to settle things with the O'Neill myself." She felt a sudden wave of dizziness, and Glynnis quickly clutched her arm.

"Feeling faint?" the little redhead asked her.

"Aye. I guess I'm more tired than I thought."

Glynnis took her hand. "Come lie down in our room," she ordered. " 'Tis no wonder you're worn to the bone; you've been through a great deal of excitement lately."

After Glynnis O'Neill saw her sister-in-law comfortably settled in the master bedroom, she returned to the main room.

"Is she all right?" a worried Brendan asked his wife.

"Of course. 'Tis perfectly natural for a woman to feel a bit faint, when she's breeding."

"Aye, I know she's been—" Brendan began, then came to a sputtering halt. "What!"

Glynnis gave him a faintly superior look. "I suspected as much the moment I saw her, Dan. I don't know your sister all that well, but 'twas obvious to me her face is fuller, and she has a glow about her skin and eyes. That dizzy spell just confirmed it for me."

"God's nightshirt!" he swore softly, so Bryony wouldn't overhear. "It can't be. Bryony? But how . . . who?"

"*How* is something you should know perfectly well by now, my dear husband," Glynnis teased him. "But as to *who,* only your sister can say . . . if she's of a mind to."

Brendan thought hard and fast. There was only one man who had been alone with Bryony for any length of time, and since Brendan knew her as one not easily charmed by strangers, the answer seemed fairly obvious.

"Devil take him!" He shot to his feet cursing roundly. "He'll rue the day he seduced my little sister!"

Before Glynnis could stop him, Brendan charged out of the house like all the proverbial hounds of hell were at his heels.

Out in the field, Finn O'Grady was visiting with a neighbor, Tully MacQuillan. Neither noticed the human maelstrom headed in their direction, until Finn happened to glance up and see Brendan.

"Danny boy!" he called out merrily, waving a hand in invitation and not comprehending the black rage twisting his cousin's features.

"Danny boy, is it, you lowlander scoundrel!" Brendan shouted as he came to a halt right before Finn.

Instinctively Finn's hands balled into fists. "You'd best have a reason for talkin' that way to me, sodman!"

"Aye, I have reason aplenty. Starting with the fact you've hurt my sister beyond repair, you scurvy dog!"

Finn's dark eyes flashed at the insult. "What manner of tale have you been hearin'?"

"Bryony didn't have to say a word, O'Grady. 'Tis written all over her face."

"What is?"

"Lord! I ought to kick your lily white arse just for askin'!" Brendan swore explosively, already on the verge of swinging.

Tully hastily stepped between them. "Easy, lads. What's this all about?"

"You'd better ask him!" Finn said, pointing at Brendan.

"Nay, Tully, ask the weasel here why my sister's good enough to bed, but not to wed!"

Finn's jaw dropped with obvious shock. "What are you sayin', Danny?" He digested the news for a moment, then murmured under his breath, "So that's why she's such a poor sailor now."

Unfortunately Brendan overheard. His indignation peaked. "You do know! So that's the way of it, eh, O'Grady?" His ham-sized fist suddenly closed around the smaller man's arm.

"Mind, you're only our second cousin, so the Church will have no qualms about it. Aye, you'd best sing the banns right now, knave, for in less than an hour, you'll be a married man!"

When Bryony rose after a short nap, she felt much better. She found dinner bubbling merrily away over the hearth, but the rest of the house was deserted. Then she overheard something outside. It sounded like a heated quarrel was underway. Wondering what was happening now, she went outside to see.

She was surprised to see her brother physically hauling a protesting Finn O'Grady back to the house. Glynnis stood nearby, watching the men and wringing her freckled hands.

Bryony stepped out in the yard to confront them. "What happened?" she demanded.

Brendan was puffing from the effort of dragging poor Finn around. "You don't need to worry, Bry," he gasped out. "He'll make an honorable woman of you."

She reddened slightly. "You'd better explain that remark right quick, Dan, before I get angry."

He shuffled his feet a little in the dirt. " 'Tisn't as if I'm tryin' to interfere, but it's my place to look after you now, since the O'Neill won't. And I'll be damned before I let some rogue make free with your reputation."

Bryony just stared at him. Glynnis motioned her back into the house, while to the men, she said sharply, "Quit your tomfoolery and get back to work. We'll call you when dinner's ready."

None of them dared to dispute the feisty little redhead. But Brendan never let go of Finn's arm, and the two Irishmen matched glares as Tully MacQuillan tried once again to play peacemaker.

Inside the house, Bryony waited for Glynnis to join her, and then pounced like a wet cat. "Was that about what I think it was?"

Glynnis had the grace to flush. " 'Tis all my fault," she

confessed. "I happened to mention to Dan that you were with child."

Wide-eyed, Bryony looked at her sister-in-law. "No, it can't be," she whispered, then slowly sank down into a chair to support her trembling knees. She recalled all of the strange symptoms she'd been having for the last month or so.

"When did you last bleed?" Glynnis asked her gently.

"August, I think it was. Ohhh, God's foot!" Bryony swore, and clapped her hands to her mouth in mixed disbelief and shock.

"Then you're three months' gone already," the other young woman sagely remarked. "Did it never occur to you to wonder?"

"No . . . it never did. Sweet Jesu, what will I do now?" Bryony gasped.

Her sister-in-law quickly rushed to embrace her, murmuring, "Don't fret, love. 'Twill be all right. You can stay here with us, as long as you need. There's plenty of room. Why, we'll raise the bairns together! And Dan can use Finn as an extra hand in the fields—"

Bryony suddenly remembered poor O'Grady's plight and laughed outright. "Oh, Glynnis, Finn isn't the father!"

The redhead's eyes widened with shock. "He isn't?"

"No, you silly goose. 'Tis a man you don't know, and the only one I've ever loved." Bryony's smile abruptly vanished.

Glynnis drew herself up, prepared to be outraged. "Did he desert you when he found out?"

"He doesn't know either, anymore than I did until just now. I left him instead. And save your breath, Glynnis. We're not meant to be together. To begin with, he's not even Irish—"

Bryony got no further than that when there was another uproar outside the house. Expecting to find a full-blown brawl underway, both women rushed out and stopped in their tracks in the yard.

Storming up the seaside path, with Slade Tanner and Father O'Leary in tow, came the O'Neill of Clandeboye.

* * *

"I've taken matters into me own hands, as you can see," Brann said to the startled women. He then turned to the elderly priest in his black cassock, who was panting from the steep climb. Father O'Leary was no longer young, but he had baptized, married, and buried almost four generations of O'Neills. No other man would do for the job. Besides, O'Leary was willing to waive the wedding banns, considering the urgent circumstances and Brann's past generosity to the Church.

"Well, Father," the O'Neill said brusquely, "there's the bride, and here's the groom. Get on with it, man."

Bryony strode forward with a sputtering noise. "Just a moment! How dare you tell me who to marry!"

"Aye," Brendan put in, pushing Finn O'Grady before the others. "Here's the scoundrel who's responsible, the one who'll take Bryony to wife, if he knows what's good for him!"

Confusion erupted as the two prospective bridegrooms were hotly defended by their champions. Bryony happened to glance at Slade during the squabbling, and stiffened when he winked at her. She couldn't deny he looked dashing in his russet velvet doublet embroidered with gold thread, fastened over a snowy white shirt lavish with lace. His matching breeches were piped with gold thread also, the stockings black to match his gleaming boots. His golden hair had long since dried from the rain, and glistened with soft auburn highlights.

But his obvious levity over the situation was simply too much. Gritting her teeth, Bryony brushed past the arguing Irish mob; nobody but Slade seemed to notice her departure. She didn't know where she was going, only that she had to escape such rampant stupidity! She was furious and flustered, and still more than a little shocked by what Glynnis had said inside the house. And the O'Neill! How dare he show up like this, dragging Slade and Father O'Leary to the altar like some outraged sire. *Precious little, too late!* she fumed.

Skirts bunched in her hands, Bryony fled to the nearby

copse of oaks. She ran until her breath rasped and the tears had dried to tight streaks on her cheeks. Then she collapsed against a tree, biting her knuckle to quell the urge to cry. The crunch of dry leaves startled her from her reverie. Whirling about with surprise, she confronted Slade.

"Why did you follow me?" she lashed out at him.

"Bryony, we must talk." Slade looked so serious and yet so handsome, as he propped his foot on a fallen log a few feet away. It took every ounce of pride and self-control she possessed not to go to him. Her arms ached to embrace him again, her fingers itched to caress that golden hair, if only one last time.

"I came to Raven Hall not to claim the land, but to claim you as my bride. That's what I wanted to ask you earlier, but I wanted to do it right and secure your father's permission first."

"My father? Bah! He's no father of mine," she spat.

"You're making a mistake," Slade said quietly. "I think the old man truly regrets how he's treated you. He just doesn't know how to say it. That's why he came here today. 'Tis important to him to stand at your wedding."

Bryony tossed her head. "Who says I'm getting married?"

Slade smiled, momentarily disarming her. "I hope you are. Will you consent to be my wife, Bryony O'Neill?"

His voice was deep and yet gentle. Bryony looked away for a moment, fiercely studying the red and golden leaves of fall, the same colors as his hair. Everywhere she turned there were reminders!

" 'Tisn't that easy," she said at last. "There are too many things left unsettled."

"Do you refer to my previous troth? Gillian is gone," Slade said.

She shook her head. "Not Gillian. Another lady stands between us now, the *Fiach-muir.* For I'll not give up the sea, Slade. Not for you, not for the Devil himself, if he was to ask me!"

"I'm not asking you to surrender the water, Bryony. Long ago I realized that's why I love you so much. You're the only woman who will ever understand my calling, the only wife who could ever participate in a life at sea with me." Slade moved toward her, hope and excitement making his green eyes gleam. "I'm proposing we sail together, Bryony. I'll seek release from Elizabeth's charter, and we'll start our own trade company, headquartered here in Ireland or in Kent, wherever you wish."

It was so tempting! Bryony gazed at Slade, her heart pounding in her chest from exertion and something else she was still afraid to recognize. "I . . . I don't know," she stammered. "Slade, you don't know everything about me, where I've been these past months, what I've done—"

"La Francis Joven," he said, and saw her stiffen. "The Frenchman's Woman. Aye, love, I know 'twas you. The moment I heard tale a bold Irish wench sailed the Bay of Biscay with naught but a pagan amulet protecting her pretty neck, I knew my sea raven had followed her father's path of flight after all."

" 'Twas not piracy!" Bryony countered hotly. "We were privateers, and *your* homeland profited from it, Englishman!"

When Slade merely chuckled, not about to argue, she drew herself a notch taller. "Another thing. I was not the Frenchman's mistress. Aye, the Spaniards thought it made for a spicier tale but never did the Frenchman's shadow fall across my bed!"

"It doesn't matter," Slade said, and Bryony sensed that he didn't completely believe her, but was willing to let it pass. "The past is gone, sweetheart, and we can start afresh." He came close enough to brush back a loose tendril of hair from her cheek.

"Ah, Bryony, how I've missed you. Give me your hand, love, your hand to kiss now, and hold in troth forever." Slade raised her hand to his lips, all the while gazing into her eyes. A magical spell seemed to settle over them in the little copse and unexpectedly Bryony's fear and anger melted away in one fell swoop.

"Aye," she finally heard herself say, her voice hushed and breathless and very faint, as if coming from a great distance away. "I will, my love. I will!"

When they returned to the house and told the others the news, the cheers exploded around them, the loudest coming from Finn O'Grady, who suddenly found himself a free man.

Glynnis immediately offered the use of her own wedding gown, and then rushed Bryony into the house to see to hasty last-minute preparations.

When Glynnis opened her dower chest and promptly unfolded a glistening mound of material, Bryony gasped. "Oh, tis beautiful!"

She reached out to reverently touch the heavy, winter white satin skirts, and gossamer tulle sleeves, sheer as a spider's web. The underskirt was embroidered with small pink pearls and trimmed with Scottish rose point lace.

"My mother and five sisters helped me sew on it for nigh a year," Glynnis said proudly. "I'm glad 'twill not go to waste, but see another young woman blissfully wed."

They tried the gown on Bryony, and it fit perfectly, all except for being a trifle short in length.

"Wait!" Glynnis cried, running for her sewing box. "I can let down the hem; 'twill only take a moment."

A second later someone hammered on the door. "Better hurry!" Brendan called out. "Both crews have rowed in, and the good Father is beginning to enjoy his ale!"

With a final flurry, Bryony was ready for the ceremony. Glynnis left her at the last moment to take her place outdoors. For November, the Irish weather was surprisingly mild and warm. The sun glistened across the bride's raven hair as she made her appearance, and those assembled fell silent.

Bryony lent truth to the old tale that every woman is especially beautiful on her wedding day. The lacy white gown suited her darkness to perfection. A misty veil descended over her loose hair, just reaching her fingertips.

There were no flowers for the bride, but Bryony needed none, for her radiant smile slanted across the assembled guests like a shaft of golden sunshine.

She started to move down the path the others had cleared, forming two lines on either side of her. Bryony was halfway there, when someone else joined her. She bit her lower lip hard with unexpected emotion, when the O'Neill took her hand and firmly slapped it upon his arm. Brann led his daughter before the priest and then handed her over to her bridegroom.

"Be good to her, Englishman, or you'll answer to me," the O'Neill said gruffly, before he turned and walked away.

"Courage, love," Slade whispered to Bryony with a playful wink before he, too, turned to face Father O'Leary, tucking her hand comfortingly under his arm.

Bryony was glad for the veil. Tears were sliding down her cheeks. But she managed to speak the necessary words, in Latin and English, and then traditional Gaelic, her voice surprisingly clear and strong, her heart quietly soaring.

At last Slade lifted the veil to kiss her. He trailed a finger gently down her moist cheek, before he took her lips in a long, sweetly possessive kiss. There were whoops and cheers from the appreciative onlookers. Then he took her arm again, and they both turned to face the smiling guests.

"My friends, and my new family, may I present to you Madam Bryony Tanner.

As the merrymaking immediately commenced, with Father O'Leary standing first in line for another round of ale, Slade seized the opportunity to sneak his new wife around the corner of the house, out of sight of the others.

"You've made me the happiest man on earth, sweetheart. Except for one thing."

Bryony's stomach dropped. "What?"

"When will we ever be alone again? And how the hell am

I supposed to get you out of that dress, with all its damned hooks and knotted laces?"

Bryony started to laugh. Trust Slade to think of something like that! Then she sobered, as she suddenly remembered the other small detail she had yet to share with her husband. His keen gaze immediately registered something troubled in her expression.

"What is it, little raven? Are you feeling poorly?"

"No, Slade, not poorly. Just . . . with child."

His eyes did not widen with surprise as she expected. Instead, he chuckled low. "Aye, I wondered when you would get around to telling me. There was no doubt in my mind, once I saw you at Clandeboye."

"Did everyone know but me?" Bryony stormed, shocked to find herself bursting into tears. "Sweet Jesu, not more tears," she hiccuped.

Immediately he gathered her into a comforting embrace. "Babes tend to make women weepy, sweetheart. Or so I've heard it said. 'Twill pass in a few months, and then just like spring, you'll feel restored again, and have a feisty little Tanner in your arms to show for it all."

"Oh, Slade, I love you!"

He couldn't help but grin, for Madam Bryony Tanner was weeping quite conspicuously, as she finally spoke the words he had longed to hear ever since they met.

Twenty

It had been a glorious honeymoon. Slade awoke with a smile on his lips, turning on his elbow to gaze down at the woman sleeping beside him in the captain's berth. His beloved wife. Not only in title, but in his heart as well. At last he felt complete, and only one thing now remained to see their happiness made secure.

He knew he must seek release from the queen's charter. Deserting Elizabeth Tudor without permission was high treason. Though he and Bryony had already secretly mapped out their strategy and proposed trade routes under their own name, using both the *Silver Hart* and the *Fiach-muir,* Slade knew he would be foolish to attempt even a single voyage without securing his freedom from Bess first. Word would quickly trickle back to her, if he did not return to England within a reasonable time.

In his eyes, he had two choices, neither of them appealing. He could leave his wife with her kin in Ireland, while he went to ask Bess's license, or he could take Bryony to Kent and reestablish a household at Dovehaven. He had instructed Mrs. Haymaker to close down the estate after Gillian's death, and the house was barely habitable since many of its furnishings had, by necessity, been purged by fire.

But Slade knew he would worry about Bryony's health during such a voyage. The Irish Sea was notoriously rough in winter. Even though she seemed born to walk a deck, so far this pregnancy had not set well with her. Perhaps because it was her first. Although in the mere two weeks since their wedding, she had blossomed even more, if such a thing were possible. Her stomach seemed settled, and she was visibly pregnant now, plump as a little partridge hen. How she hated it, whenever he teased her about it! Slade chuckled aloud, and Bryony awoke and stretched luxuriously. She offered her husband a warm sleepy smile.

"Good morn, my love."

She always greeted him thusly, and Slade rewarded her with a deep and thorough kiss.

"Good morning, my lady wife," he said. "What manner of meal takes your fancy today?"

She thought a moment. "Curried eggs and fresh bread dripping with honey," she promptly replied. "I've a devilish craving for sweets nowadays."

He laughed, and tenderly patted her rounded little belly. " 'Tis not so surprising, madam, since you already show the results of many such meals."

Her tongue darted quickly out. "Ooh! You might acknowledge your own responsibility, sirrah." Bryony ruefully glanced down at her swelling abdomen. She felt so fat, and only four months gone with child! But as Glynnis had assured her, some women were large from the start. She looked like a damned blue whale!

"I can't help it I'm so hungry," she said crossly as she sat up and reached for her satin wrapper. "What truly vexes me is that soon I'll not be able to wear any of those fine Spanish gowns I took such a pleasure in pilfering!"

"Tell me what you need, Bryony. We'll send for a special tailor and a seamstress to make you a new wardrobe for your confinement."

Unexpectedly she shuddered. "Confinement! I hate that word, Slade. As if I was some unsightly sea cow to be hidden away, so as not to offend the tender sensibilities of men!"

He laughed and pulled her into his arms, slipping his warm hand inside the wrapper to tenderly cup a ripening breast. " 'Tis fine by me should you choose to go naked the entire time sweetheart," he murmured as he kissed her neck. "In fact, I daresay I would delight in the opportunity to share your confinement in the privacy of our bedchamber . . ."

She had to smile as she drew Slade's head up to hers. "English rogue," she whispered playfully, before sealing the wor with a quick kiss. "Send for your damned tailor, then. I'll no have it whispered Mistress Tanner has a miserly husband."

"Madam," he reminded her in a fiercely possessive tone.

She giggled. "Madam sounds so old and dignified! As if a mere Irishwoman could aspire to English nobility."

His brow furrowed in disapproval. "Please don't mock you heritage, sweetheart. You must be as proud of it as the O'Neil is, for the child's sake."

"The O'Neill is far too oft a braying jackass," Bryony sighed, "but aye, if it pleases you, husband."

Slade was not deceived by her lowered lashes and sudde submissiveness. He gave her a firm swat on the behind, an when her eyelashes flew apart and her beautiful sea blue eye suddenly snapped sparks, he laughed with delight.

"That's better. While I'll be the first to admit that Irishwomen are a fiery stubborn lot, they surely outshine thos pale English roses any day."

At that moment there was a scratch at the cabin door, an Slade waited until Bryony had scrambled back beneath th coverlet before calling out, "Enter!"

Young Rusty Todd came in, staggering beneath the weigh of a great silver platter filled with a rich assortment of foods Grinning ear to ear, the cabin boy eased it down on the tabl across the room.

"With Master Hiram's compliments, Cap' n."

"Let's hope our new cook is as familiar with the galley a he is the end of a yardarm," Slade said with a twinkle. H reached to the bedside table and tossed a coin at the lad. I one smooth move Rusty caught it, bit it, and neatly deposite the coin inside the pocket of his leather jerkin.

"Thank ye, Cap'n Tanner."

Bryony inquired, "And how does Lord Rumple fare, Rusty?"

The boy's smile faded. His voice was suddenly sad. "Och, I've seen no 'ide nor 'air of 'im since London, missus. I've searched the ship fore an' aft, but 'pears me old moggie is gone."

"Perhaps he found a lady friend in London," Slade suggested. "Toms are known to be fair weather friends, lad."

"Aye," came the unhappy reply. Rusty left them then to break their fast in privacy.

"I'll send a message to Dan and Glynnis," Bryony said after the boy had gone. "Their farm cat just had a passel of kittens, and I'm sure they won't miss one. I think I even spied an orange tabby among the lot. Finn can choose a kitten for Rusty when it's weaned."

Slade smiled at his wife's thoughtfulness. He knew Bryony would make a wonderful mother, for all her independent ways. But the mood in the cabin had sobered sufficiently for him to broach another sore subject.

"It's time for me to petition the queen," he said. "Without her blessing, we'll find buying and selling in any European port all but impossible."

Bryony knew he was right, but she felt her temper flare. "Why can't we just sail under our own colors?"

"Because Bess would soon hear of it and be furious. Never underestimate the long arm of my queen, love. She would quickly seek her revenge on us both. Without formal release from her charter, I would, in essence, be committing treason."

"Even though she suspended it at Gillian's request? I can't believe the Tudor bitch would be so fickle."

"Ah, but she is. And Bess may not take kindly to the news of our marriage, either. 'Twill doubtless come as a shock."

"As if a grown man needed permission to marry!" Bryony exclaimed with typical indignation.

"Aye, sweetheart, I know it sounds daft to you, but Bess is

a very domineering person. She wants nothing important to occur in her kingdom without her express knowledge and consent."

"Then we shall present a united front to Elizabeth Tudor, and beg her indulgence. Though 'twill try my temper sorely to do so."

Slade hesitated a moment. "I believe it would be best if I returned to England alone for such a purpose."

"What!"

"Hear me out, love. There's the babe to think of now, and I won't risk you both on the voyage. I think it would be far more prudent if you stayed with the O'Neill or your brother for a few weeks, until I've secured Bess's approval for our plan. Then there will be no obstacles to beginning our new life together."

" 'Tis already begun!" Bryony exclaimed, indicating her rounded abdomen. "You cannot leave me here, Slade. I refuse to be put out to pasture like some pregnant mare! Let us go together and plead our cause before Bess. She may be more inclined to reason, if she sees our need for haste."

"More likely she will be enraged," Slade said gently. "Elizabeth Tudor is a very moral lady, my love."

"And I am not?"

"I did not mean to imply that at all—"

"Oh! Did you not!" Angrily Bryony threw back the coverlet and climbed cumbersomely from the bed, clutching the wrapper over her heaving breast as she turned to face him. "It suddenly occurs to me you've shown no undue happiness over the fact that you are soon to be a father, sir!"

A shadow crossed Slade's eyes, suddenly darkening them.

"I'm happy," he said so abruptly she could not quite believe him. "I'm happy, Bryony, because you are, and I love you so damned much, that nothing else matters but the fact you are my wife. Never will there be any question as to the child's surname. You have my word on it."

Something in his tone angered and confused Bryony. A niggling suspicion began to grow in her head and heart, as she stared into his calm green eyes.

"You don't believe me," she whispered, comprehension slowly dawning as she pressed her palm flat against her throat. She felt her own pulse pounding furiously. "You don't believe the babe is yours."

"It doesn't matter, Bryony," Slade repeated evenly. "We both made our mistakes. I'm not the sort of man who excuses male behavior, and condemns a lady under similar circumstances. I love you, sweetheart, and the babe shall be as much mine as it is yours."

She was silent for a terrible moment. Then, "Damn you to hell, Slade Tanner!" Bryony shouted. "Or mayhaps, I should damn you to your precious England instead. For in my mind, and in truth, they are surely one and the same!"

"Bryony—" He would have leaped from the bed, but she whirled on him so ferociously that he almost shrank back.

"How dare you!" she said in a low, frighteningly calm voice. "How *dare* you equate me with your former betrothed, that faithless *Sassenach* snake! Aye, I see you did not believe me at all, when I told you in the forest that day that I was not the Frenchman's leman. But never for a moment did I imagine you believed me so low as to pass off a bastard as my husband's heir! Very well, then, Captain Tanner. Crawl back to Court, to your precious bitch-queen, and whine as much as you like of your new bride's perfidy. But never, ever come crawling back to me, because that is one door which shall be forever closed and bolted to you, Englishman!"

Bryony pulled on some clothes, then whirled, and stormed from the cabin. She slammed the door so fiercely, it shuddered in its frame. Moments later Slade heard her ordering the crew to row her in. He made no move to leave the bed, but sat there in agonizing silence for a very long time with his head clutched in his hands. Dear God, what had he done?

* * *

"Quit pacing, girl!" the O'Neill irritably ordered his daughter, a week or so after the *Silver Hart* had departed for England.

Bryony had taken up residence at Raven Hall in her ol chamber, for although Brendan and Glynnis had invited her t come north, she sensed she would be intruding on their privacy. For all they were expecting a child any day, they ha only been wed eight months. Newlyweds desired and deserve time alone. Besides, Bryony knew she would not feel comfortable there, between Dan's constant lectures and Glynnis' pitying looks.

The O'Neill's acid remarks were not much better. Ever sinc Slade had left, Brann had gotten in many a pointed jibe.

"Buckle up, wench," he blustered at her now, not about t admit that the sight of Bryony sniveling about the hall ove the past week tugged at his frayed old heartstrings. "The Englishman will be back, mark me words. He's too calf-eyed ye to stay away for long."

His taunt hit a tender spot in Bryony, and she rounded o him with a virulent oath. "You old goat, what would you kno about love?"

The O'Neill just looked at her for a long hard momen "Plenty, I should think," he replied, "for I loved your mothe beyond death, and still do to this day."

Bryony didn't know what shocked her more, the admissio that Brann O'Neill could love at all, or the fact that at lon last he referred to Alanna as her mother. Their gazes met an locked, and in that instant she knew the old man asked he forgiveness, though the words would never cross his lips.

"Tell me," she said softly. "Tell me how you two met."

He gave a slow grin at the recollection. "We met at th Donnybrook Fair in Dublin Town. Alanna was there with he da, sellin' vegetables and whatnots from a rickety old stand

Her da was a farmer near Edenderry, y'see, which probably explains your brother's fancy to work the land."

Bryony was fascinated, and even put aside her own misery for the moment, to take a chair across from him at the high board. Propping her elbows on the table, she said, "Go on."

"Well, I walked up there to get a better look at that pretty slip of a blond colleen, and what do you know, but she turns up her nose in the air." Brann chuckled at the memory. "Oh, I reckoned meself a fine figure of a man in those days, with plenty of coin in me pockets to jingle. And here was this proud wench, lookin' the other way on purpose. Why, it riled me so sore, I stormed right up and stole a kiss from those sweetly pursed lips, while Alanna was still gazin' to heaven right past me."

Bryony grinned, despite her mood. "And what did she do?"

"What else? slapped me, o'course, and packed quite a punch for such a scrawny thing, too." Brann rubbed his beard in absent recollection. "But oh! the fire in those bonny blue eyes. I knew right then I must have her, even if'n I had to kidnap her to do it."

"How did you bring Alanna around?"

The O'Neill snorted. "I didn't! She would have nothin' to do with me without a silver claddagh on her hand, turned 'round the proper way to show she was a wedded wench. Nay, lass, it took me nigh a good year of formal courtin' to get your mum to surrender to me charms."

"Where were you married?"

"At Edenderry Church, for her da was dyin' at the time. She wanted him to see her settled to a man of means. She didn't want him to worry, here or in the hereafter. Alanna was like that, God assoil her gentle wee soul."

Bryony saw his eyes misting over. No wonder he resented Alanna O'Neill's death, for he had loved her so much. And though he had been wrong to blame a babe for it, she somehow understood the depth of the despair he felt. For she suffered from something similar herself now.

"You never remarried," she said quietly. "Did you never wish to, if only for heirs?"

Brann surreptitiously wiped at his eyes with the back of his hand. His voice was still rough and thick. "Nay, not even for more sons. Alanna was me soul mate, as old Mab used to say. Once her light left me, I was surrounded by darkness, and I stubbornly refused to look for another light." He hesitated, glancing almost shamefacedly at Bryony. "I was very bitter, girl, from that day forth. You know that . . ."

"Aye," Bryony said abruptly, not sparing his feelings. "You were beastly to me, and Brendan, too. I won't ever forget those years, but at least I understand a little of how you felt, and with that much, maybe someday I can begin to forgive."

It was the most he could expect, and the O'Neill knew it. With a tremulous smile, suddenly looking very old and tired, he extended a huge hand over the table and placed it upon his daughter's.

The O'Neill was right about one thing. Bryony was worried about Slade. Oh, she was furious, too, and hurt beyond measure, but these emotions seemed to fade into the background as the weeks passed and there was no word from him. It was not that she expected Slade to return soon, if ever. But she had always trusted her instincts, and the troubled, violent dreams she had of late and the constant, unbidden flashes of Slade's face in her mind, almost drove her wild.

She brooded upon the meaning of her dreams and dark fancies, and wondered if he had met with a terrible accident, maybe death. No! Her heart cried out with surprising agony, and in that moment she realized she still loved him.

Loved a man who would sooner think the worst than trust the woman he claimed to love, a man who had not apologized for his cruel assumptions, and yet generously offered to accept her child as his own. Damn him! Bryony silently fumed. Why would he not leave her in peace, even in her dreams?

"That's the brat in your belly," the O'Neill said matter-of-factly, when she told him of her nightmares. "Alanna always had terrible dreams, when she carried you and Dan."

"Did she? Of what?"

He was silent a moment. "She dreamed of dyin', and of failin' to give me the son I craved so mightily, a son who would follow in me footsteps at sea. And on both counts, she was right in the end."

"So the Sight is true," Bryony said thoughtfully. Suddenly she went to him and took his burly hand in hers. "Oh, Da, I'll never forgive myself if I don't go to England and find out what's happened to Slade. If I'm wrong, he can curse me for it, though not as loudly as I'll curse myself."

He grunted, but was secretly pleased by the fact that she had finally taken to calling him father after all these years.

" 'Tis just a breedin' woman's fancies," he scoffed. "The *Sassenach*'s brat has softened ye, chit."

She smiled. "Perhaps a little. If Changelings can be softened." Brann started to scowl, then realized she was only jesting and gave a grudging smile in return. He knew she was too much an O'Neill to waver from her course. She would go, with or without his approval, and so he gave a curt nod.

"This time, take our best men as crew, not those useless brats you claim are decent pirates. Bah! I won't believe it, 'less I was to see it with me own eyes."

"Then you have my permission to captain my next Spanish venture," Bryony replied with a twinkle in her eye. "I'll likely be confined to childbed, worse luck, and come spring, King Philip's rich galleons won't wait. Just think of it, Da—enough gold plate to festoon Raven Hall, stone by stone, yards of damask and lace and fine Spanish velvets, Ceylon rubies and rare Siamese sapphires, and everything from Mallorcan pearls to Seville oranges to amuse your women."

Brann's dark eyes gleamed as he threw back his silvered head and laughed uproariously. "Aye, there's no question about it, Bryony O'Neill. You're me own greedy get, and damned if

I'm not just proud and greedy enough in turn to take you up on your generous offer!"

Bryony sailed from Clandeboye on the last day of November. A moody gray sky was reflected in the choppy waves of the Irish Sea. Freakish storms had already been reported up and down the coast; some squalls had been severe enough to wreck light craft upon the rocks, while one ship had simply vanished.

But there was no room in her mind for such concerns, as Bryony paced the decks of the *Fiach-muir* again. Her thoughts were all of Slade. Thankfully, her bouts of *mal de mer* had passed as her pregnancy advanced, and she once again felt at home upon the sea.

Finn anxiously watched over his cousin as she took command during the rough crossing. By necessity, Bryony had given up wearing breeches, and instead donned a split skirt of ruby-colored velvet. She looked magnificent with a gold embroidered bodice fastened over a white blouse, frothed with Carrickmacross lace. Her dark hair was caught back casually on either side of her heart-shaped face with Spanish mother-of-pearl combs.

But Finn could see the worry etched into her features, and sighed with his own misgivings. He had tried to get Bryony to delay her crossing until the child was born, or Slade returned, but he was forced to agree that the Englishman had been gone far too long to bode well.

The winds hinted at a hard winter to come. The caravel bucked and plunged in the icy gray green waves, as spirited as any green-broke filly. Bryony did not seem disturbed by the creaking timbers the crew tried not to reflect their fear as the waves became rougher and deeper.

A day later they sailed into the relatively sheltered Strait of Dover, and there the sea subsided into deceptively mild fits. Pleased by the time they had made, Bryony rewarded her men with two days' shore leave and a fistful of doubloons each. Then she rowed in with the crew, suspecting nothing amiss even when the port master came to meet the longboat.

"Madam Tanner?" the man stiffly inquired after Finn had helped her onto the docks.

"Aye?"

The port master motioned to the men behind him, and suddenly Bryony and her crew were surrounded by a contingent of the queen's guard, dressed in the Tudor green and gold.

"What is this?" Bryony demanded. "What manner of buffoons are you to accost a captain and her crew without cause?"

"Your questions will be answered in due time, milady," said the captain of the guard. "Come peaceably, lest we are forced to take sterner measures. Do you understand?"

Her startled nod was all he required. With a single word from Bess's henchman, Bryony and all her crew were seized and placed under arrest in the name of the Crown.

Slade awoke on the fourth week of his imprisonment, and was greeted with the sober presence of the Secretary of State. Walsingham had never responded to his demands for an audience until now, so he was somewhat surprised to find the man looming over his cot.

"Good morning, Captain Tanner." Sir Francis greeted the prisoner with a thin smile, reminding Slade of a ferret. Walsingham's sense of humor matched his colorful garb, for he had none of either. Clad head to toe in black, he was a militant Puritan who took his role as Elizabeth's protector very seriously. Walsingham had even been playfully nicknamed "Spy" by the queen herself.

" 'Tis a lovely fall day outside," Sir Francis idly remarked, as if it was every day he found himself standing in a prisoner's cell.

"Is it?" Slade responded warily, coming quickly to his feet rather than allow this damned vulture to continue hovering over him. "I could hardly know, Walsingham. My cell has no windows."

Ignoring the remark, the secretary shuffled through a thick sheaf of papers in his hands. "Ah, let's see. You have been brought up on a variety of charges, Captain Tanner, and your case is being considered by the council now."

"God's blood, man!" Slade exploded, forgetting for a moment his precarious position and succumbing to the rage which had been building in him for nearly a month. "Then am I to finally learn what falsehoods have been brought against my name?"

The other man pursed his lips in warning. "I will be brief, Captain. You have been accused in the wrongful death of Elizabeth Tudor's goddaughter and maid of honor, Gillian Lovelle. The evidence is really quite damning, sir. I have no doubt there is enough here to convict you of the murder of your estranged betrothed."

"Estranged?"

Walsingham primly brushed at a speck of dust on his robes. "Ah, rumors still fly wildly at Court as to your stormy relationship with the fair Lady Gillian. 'Twas a well-known fact, Captain Tanner, to which I bear personal witness, that you and the lady quarrelled publicly on many occasions."

Slade shrugged. " 'Twas also well known, Walsingham, that Gillian spread her legs wide for any man who cared to ask. Do you also claim personal knowledge of that fact?"

The secretary stiffened. "Sir! I will thank you to remember I am a married Christian man."

"That means little enough at Court. Did you send my message to the queen?"

"Aye," Walsingham replied shortly. "Her Majesty ordered it destroyed without reading a single word. I must warn you, Captain, the facts I have uncovered here and in Kent make it most unlikely you will escape execution. Therefore, in view of that fact, I am prepared to be charitable. In exchange for a full confession, I shall plead leniency for you, and offer a more merciful end. Instead of torture or beheading, you shall succumb to the *peine forte et dure*."

Slade paled. That particular form of death consisted of crushing a man slowly, by adding the weight of several stone each day, until the agonized victim finally expired. The only real difference between beheading and the death by stones was that if a man were removed to Tower Green to be executed, all his holdings were forfeit to the Crown. The estate of one who died by pressing, strangely enough, could be passed on to his wife and heirs.

Slade also recalled Walsingham's expertise with the rack. He knew the secretary had taken unabashed pleasure in torturing several of the conspirators recently caught during the Babington Plot. Sir Francis was convinced the Catholics constantly schemed to effect Elizabeth's downfall, and so was particularly merciless when it came to punishing those he suspected of conspiring with the enemy. Had Walsingham somehow learned of his wife's identity? Slade was not a Catholic, but Bryony was. It would be just like Bess's Spy to twist such an incidental fact to serve his cause.

"Will you not confess here and now, Captain Tanner, and save us both a tiresome inquest?" Walsingham urged him.

"No. For you to suggest that Gillian Lovelle was murdered is one thing, but to accuse me of it, is quite another."

Walsingham irritably cleared his throat. "Nobody is suggesting anything, my good man. The queen's coroner has definitely attributed the cause of death to poisoning, and the evil agent as salvarsan." He riffled the papers in his hands for emphasis, as if to impress Slade with his painstaking work on the case.

"My lord Walsingham," Slade said impatiently, "if you are so well informed as you would have me believe, then you doubtless know my betrothed was gravely ill. She contracted the black pox from one of her lovers, and suffered horribly. 'Tis not so unusual for one in such agony to take small doses of salvarsan for relief."

The secretary pounced. "Ah, but one would hardly place it in their own food, so as not to be noticed! If the lady was indeed so indisposed as you claim, she would not be up and about, baking berry tarts!"

"I still insist upon my innocence. I would far prefer to take my chances at trial rather than make a false confession."

"Very well," Walsingham curtly responded, and turned to leave. Then, almost as an afterthought, he laid his trump card on the table. In silky tones, he said, "What a pity, Captain Were you not so stubborn, I might have arranged a last meeting between you and your wife, recently arrived in our fair city."

When Slade stiffened, the other man corrected himself with mock embarrassment. "I refer, of course, to your Irish Catholic wife, whom you wed without the queen's knowledge or consent."

"Walsingham, you bastard, if you so much as touch Bryony—"

The secretary made an expression of distaste. "You misunderstand my intent, Captain. I simply think the queen and her council would be most interested to learn how you came to wed an Irishwoman so shortly after the Lady Gillian's sudden death. Also how your bride came to be in a—ahem—state of such obvious delicacy, after only a month of married bliss."

Slade wanted nothing so much in that moment as to strangle the old crow. Walsingham was openly threatening to hurt Bryony, if Slade did not confess! And who knew what hideous tortures the man had up his sleeve.

"I swear by heaven, Walsingham, if you harm my wife, I'll indeed become the dreaded murderer you espouse me to be, and I'll begin with you as my first victim!"

Slade had the satisfaction of watching the secretary hurry away to bang on the heavy wooden door for the guard's attention. When the bolt was drawn and his freedom assured, Sir Francis risked one last poke at the man in the cell.

"I understand you are distraught, Captain Tanner, and hence not thinking clearly. You shall be given twelve hours to choose your path. But be warned; either way you cannot win. And consider: when you are gone, who will protect your pretty wife then? Good day, sirrah!"

Twenty-one

When morning dawned, Bryony was already fitfully pacing the apartment where she was sequestered at Whitehall Palace. She had been given no chance to explain her circumstances or ask any questions, but simply removed to this chamber and placed under lock and key.

Her crew, fortunately, had been released after it was determined they knew nothing of whatever intrigue was boiling behind these palace walls. But Bryony had not even been questioned, when she might have had opportunity to obtain a few answers of her own. Instead, she was hustled off and locked away.

'Twas an outrage! she fumed. Did Elizabeth Tudor think she could get away with treating innocents so shabbily? Granted the apartment was not mean; it was well furnished and would have been pleasant under any other circumstances. There were plush Turkish carpets on the floor, beautiful tapestries graced the cold stone walls, and a soft clean featherbed, should she wish to rest.

But Bryony had been unable to sleep. Wild with fear and worry, she had spent most of the night beating on the thick wooden door and shouting until she was hoarse. But her only visitor was a servant, who came to bring fresh water and food and empty the chamber pot.

The maidservant would not speak to her, but Bryony could tell the girl felt sorry for her, when she received the choice portion of a plump roasted capon and a handful of fresh fruit

"I demand to see the queen!" she confronted the girl when she returned that morning to perform her duties. Frightened, the chit dropped the bowl of porridge and fled from the chamber. Bryony threw up her hands in exasperation. It was a good thing she wasn't hungry, for the servant didn't return. Under normal circumstances Bryony would have starved herself to get a reaction from her jailers, but now she had the babe to think of, and needed to keep up her strength.

Not much later in the morning, the door opened again with a flourish. This time Giles Lafleur strode in as if at home on familiar territory. The Frenchman looked rakishly handsome in a dark blue velvet outfit edged with silver braid. He quickly closed the door and leaned against it, raising a finger to his lips and giving the shocked Bryony a cheeky grin.

"So, the sea raven has been caged at long last," Lafleur said, obviously amused.

"God's breeches! How did you get by the guard?"

"Simple, *chérie.* A well-greased palm works wonders."

She shook her head, still stunned by his appearance. "But how did you know I was here?"

"I make it my affair to know much about you, little girl. I spied your ship and went to inquire as to your whereabouts. Your crew was in an uproar, and O'Grady told me what had happened. *Ma petite capitaine* captured by Bess Tudor!"

Bryony ignored his laughter. "The English witch had me seized the moment I rowed ashore. And for what? So she could lock me up and throw away the key? I have no idea why I'm even here."

"Ah, but I do." Lafleur waggled a finger at her. "You are her key to wringing a confession from *Capitaine* Tanner."

"Slade? Then you know what's happened to him. Tell me!"

With an obliging grin, her former partner provided a hasty but thorough recollection of the past few weeks. Bryony grew paler and paler during Lafleur's recitation.

"How did you hear this, Giles?" she demanded.

"Such talk is rife all about London, *ma petite.* Some enterprising courtiers are even placing bets as to which way Slade will choose to die."

She shuddered. "He could not have killed Gillian! She died from the pox."

"Did she?" Lafleur mused. "Many are saying she survived the blight, only to succumb to *L'homme jaloux.*"

The jealous man. Had Slade been jealous of Gillian's peccadillos? Bryony had believed he accepted his faithless betrothed, just as he excused what he assumed was her own affair with a notorious French privateer. But then she remembered the fury in his eyes at the queen's masque, when he had stalked the Great Hall end to end, looking for Gillian.

A cold draft seemed to ice her very bones. Was Slade capable of murder? No! It was impossible. Yet, of all those who knew Gillian Lovelle, who hadn't wished to strangle her at one time or another? The woman had been little more than a venal bitch, lacking any sort of conscience or compassion.

Bryony's shoulders slumped with defeat, and Giles moved closer, wanting to comfort her, but resigned to the fact that she would probably reject him again. She was so very lovely for all her weariness, looking somehow softer than he recalled. He had not been able to get her out of his mind since the day they had parted company on the high seas.

"Giles," Bryony rasped, her eyes glistening like wet sapphires as she gazed up at him, "I beg of you, help me to get in to see the queen! How can it be done?"

He shook his head and suddenly became serious. "I must advise against it, Bryony. Bess is absorbed in other matters at the moment, most notably the Earl of Leicester's marriage to Lettice Knollys. She is likely to tear off your pretty head."

"I don't care! Can't you see I must do whatever I can to save Slade?"

She did not see the flash of pain in Giles's dark eyes. "Do you love him?" he roughly demanded.

"Aye! He is my husband now, in the eyes of man and God alike, and the father of my unborn child."

So that explained her new softness, Giles thought. In that moment he realized whatever small chance he had once had with Bryony O'Neill, was forever gone. He gave her a wry and, although she did not know it, resigned smile.

"I may be able to help you, *chérie.* I still have some small influence at Court from my old days. And as long as Slade is kept here at Whitehall, there is a chance."

Her heart beat faster at his words. She would do anything to save Slade. "How?" she breathlessly asked.

"I have a few friends. Not many, but enough. We might be able to create enough of a diversion to occupy the guards, while Tanner is spirited away. Of course, it will be very dangerous."

She nodded her understanding. "But you will try?"

Giles gave a philosophical French shrug. "What have I to lose, but my charming head? But this will also be very expensive. I will have to buy many loyalties."

"I understand. All my money and valuables were left aboard the *Fiach-muir.* Help yourself to whatever you need. Tell O'Grady his mother's name was Fiona, so he'll not question my will in the matter."

Giles nodded. "I must hurry. I could afford to buy only a few moments with you." He strode swiftly forward, raising her hand to his lips. *"Adieu,* my sweet Bryony. I will treasure the memory of our sailing days forever."

He pulled her into his arms, giving her a firm and thorough kiss. Just as abruptly he set her free again. There had been no time to struggle, but even if there had been, Bryony would not have done so. For she sensed Giles Lafleur was saying goodbye to her, in the only way he knew how.

Suddenly the chamber door was flung wide open, startling them both.

"What's going on in here?" a gruff voice demanded.

It came from a heavy-set man in a crisp Tudor gold and

green uniform. His thick Cornish accent bristled with outrage, as he stared at Bryony and the Frenchman.

With a Gallic curse, Lafleur turned to flee. But not before a brace of guards had appeared to block his escape.

"How did this rogue get in?" the captain of the guard asked Bryony.

"I don't know," she honestly replied. "Please, sir, he meant no harm."

" 'Tis Jeb Desmond to ye, milady. I'm the night watch." The big man turned and narrowly eyed the defiant Frenchman who was caught up on either side by his guardsmen. "Ye'll answer for this," he ominously told Lafleur. "Her Majesty ordered no harm was to come to this young lady."

Elizabeth Tudor thought that much of her, at least? Bryony suddenly saw her chance, and flung herself at Desmond with her hands clasped in an eloquent plea. "I beg you to take me to Queen Elizabeth, good sir! I have valuable news to impart which I'm sure she is most anxious to hear."

Desmond was startled and took a step backwards. "So ye claim, wench! Why, do ye know how many ask to see Her Grace every week? They're lined up for leagues, they are!"

"Aye, I'm not surprised, for your generous and good ruler is surely predisposed to kindness, Captain Desmond. Her Majesty was even so thoughtful as to comment upon this simple bauble of mine on a previous visit to Court." Bryony drew the raven amulet over her neck, removing it for the first time since Brendan had given it to her. She handed it now to the wide-eyed captain of the guard.

"Please offer it to the queen with my warmest felicitations and inquire if she might also recall the arrival of six pure white horses a few months ago. Say only that a certain loyal subject seeks her audience, a lady once known as *La Franci Joven.*"

Accepting the amulet with obvious reluctance, Desmond nodded. "I'll pass on the message, milady," he dubiously said. " 'Tis right odd, though, and I can't guarantee she'll listen."

"That's all I ask. Please just try."

With a baffled nod, Desmond turned to go. He paused before Lafleur with a final ominous word.

"Like as not ye'll see the rack for this, laddie. Lucky for ye that Walsingham's too busy torturin' others right now to start on ye just yet. But mark my words, ye'll have yer turn, or my name isn't Jeb Desmond."

Whistling a sprightly tune, Desmond and his men left then, but not before Giles had slipped Bryony a quick and encouraging wink. That irrepressible Frenchman! Did he truly believe there was still a way out of this coil? With Lafleur went her last chance to save Slade's life. And quite likely, Bryony realized with a sinking heart, her own as well!

To Bryony's surprise, she was summoned to appear before Elizabeth Tudor less than a day after sending the amulet and her regards. Having fully expected Desmond to pawn the jewelry himself, she was both pleased and nervous at the prospect of facing the queen in person.

She knew she had only one chance to plead Slade's case. Yet her only outfit was crumpled and stained from wear, and though she restored her hair as best she could, she realized she looked less than presentable. Surely the queen did not expect her female prisoners to look fashionable! She hoped not, for if Bess Tudor was going to have a fit about her appearance, there was likely little to be gained by begging for Slade's life.

Two guards came for Bryony, and she fell into an uneasy silence as she walked between them. They did not subject her to the humiliation of manacles, though she was aware they had the power to do so.

The queen's receiving hall was some length from where the prisoners were kept, and it took a good half-hour to navigate the many stairs and hallways. But at long last Bryony stood before a pair of gold-chased double doors, which led into the queen's antechamber. Her stomach in knots, she was forced t wait further while one of the guards slipped inside and an nounced her arrival to whomever presented such news to th regent. Then she was subjected to a tiring hour-long wait, be fore the doors swung open at last, and she was guided inside

Elizabeth Tudor had chosen to retreat to her throne, rathe than meet her supplicant on equal footing. She gazed loftil down upon the younger woman, as Bryony came forward an made her obeisance in the form of a deep graceful curtsey.

She had no way of knowing Elizabeth was in an exception ally foul mood, having recently learned of her beloved Robin secret marriage a year ago to her own cousin, Lettice Knollys Robert Dudley had experienced the queen's fury over his de ception, and so had been wisely absent from Court of late ordered to retreat to his manor at Wanstead. The earl's absenc pained Elizabeth greatly, and she was so devastated by hi faithlessness that Slade's similar appeal had fallen not only o deaf, but angry ears.

When she was granted permission to rise at last, Bryon lifted her gaze and studied the queen. Elizabeth Tudor wa wearing a sumptuous gown of pumpkin-colored velvet, whic parted in front to reveal an orange silk stomacher. Her hug sleeves were slashed to show matching cloth of gold insert webbed with golden thread. The queen had chosen jewelry t complement her attire, several large baroque pearls on bot hands which matched her earbobs, a square golden citrine, an a smoky topaz cut in the shape of a heart.

A high, fan-shaped lace ruff rose stiffly behind Elizabeth neck, framed by her ginger-colored tresses. Lying upon he pale freckled bosom was another magnificent citrine set i gold filigree. It scattered golden pinpoints of light all abo the receiving chamber, whenever she moved.

"La Francis Joven, I presume?"

Elizabeth's voice was tart and dry, and Bryony could nc tell whether she had met with disapproval or not. The woman gray eyes reflected no emotion.

"Aye, Your Majesty. Thank you for agreeing to see me."

The queen sniffed sharply. " 'Twas not so much my desire as my curiosity, madam. I confess I wished to see what manner of wench is bold enough to both sack Spanish ships, and wed a man of this Court without his regent's permission. Worse yet, an Englishman accused of murdering his betrothed wife."

Bryony inwardly bristled even as she calmly replied, "I know you are dismayed by these events, Your Majesty. I, too, was both shocked and saddened by the news of Slade being accused of your goddaughter's unfortunate death. I will not waste your time any further by confessing I am here to beg a boon from you."

"A boon, madam? Mayhaps the captain's life, or is't his pockets you wish to plunder?"

Bryony flushed. The little cruelty was deliberate, and when she glanced up she found Elizabeth staring fixedly at her abdomen. The queen looked unusually pale, and her eyes were dark with violet half-moons beneath them. Bryony could not know her pregnancy was but a bitter reminder to Elizabeth of her own fallow loins and empty bed.

"I beg your indulgence, Your Grace," she said, submissively lowering her gaze. "I but came to plead for my husband's life, as he is clearly not guilty of the grievous charges lodged against him."

"Faugh, madam! Think you not any mortal man would put away his rightful betrothed, if he took a fancy to a scheming doxy? Yea, Mistress Tanner, you play the innocent now, but I see you have known a man without benefit of wedlock yourself, and are bold enough a jade to parade such evidence before the eyes of my Court!"

The unexpected attack only served to inflame Bryony. She promptly forgot about her vow to stay humble, no matter what it cost her. "Aye, Your Majesty," she snapped back, "I but seek to save the father of my unborn child, and therefore cast myself upon your tender mercies. 'Tis foolish, perhaps, to expect a Virgin Queen to sympathize with the plight of a young mother, but nevertheless I bare my soul and my belly to your judicious eye."

Elizabeth gave an indelicate snort, angrily thumping her bejeweled scepter upon the platform where her throne rested.

"How dare you plead your belly to me, you common Irish tramp! Only because of your condition shall I spare you from immediately being removed to the Tower for your foul impertinence!"

"Aye, impertinent women try you sorely, do they not, Your Grace?" Bryony could not resist a final sweet retort. "Witness for one the convenient death of the impertinent Amy Robsart."

Her words had the same effect as a slap to the face of the aging queen, who whitened with outrage and then purpled with fury at the reminder of such evil gossip. It was common knowledge in her realm that Elizabeth might have earlier married the Earl of Leicester, Robert Dudley, if not for the strange circumstances of his first wife's death. Many had suspected Dudley of murdering poor Amy to get her out of the way. Some even whispered of Elizabeth's encouragement in the matter. Whatever the truth, Lady Dudley's suspicious death had made it quite impossible for the queen to ever marry her Sweet Robin.

Elizabeth Tudor's bitter grief and rage over this fact now drove her over the edge. Half-rising from her throne, she thundered, "Guards! Remove this Irish adder from my path!"

To Bryony she added, "Be warned, madam, should I ever spy your shadow in my Court again, I shall see to it your waspish tongue is first removed, and that you are then cast into a dark pit among your own kind!"

Bryony knew the irrational queen meant every word of it. There was nothing she could do but drop her gaze and execute another curtsey, this one far sharper and shallower than the last. As she backed slowly away from the throne, a brace of guardsmen burst into the chamber and grasped her firmly on either side.

"Remove that baggage!" Elizabeth shrilly ordered them.

Bryony was swiftly hustled away from the enraged queen's sight. She was returned to her prison apartment, left to await with dread every passing moment, knowing each was yet another second closer to the hour Slade would meet his end.

The day of Slade Tanner's trial dawned cold and gray, a sheet of rain clouds hanging in the east, as if to forbid the rising sun. The captain was roused from a fitful sleep by his jailer, who curtly instructed him to dress. Slade rose and, after a hasty toilette, he fastened his forest green broadcloth coat over an ivory-colored frieze doublet, topping woolen knee-length breeches of matching green.

He had no intention of being hauled up for public spectacle looking unclean and unkempt, so he had bartered earlier for a bath and shaving instruments. Almost anything could be bought in prison, short of freedom. Better meals and even access to friends or relatives could be had for a price. Slade had taken advantage of the system. He had just enough coin to meet with all three of his brothers, and persuade the guard to allow him a change of clothing. His dashing appearance outside of Whitehall later that morning was enough to arouse considerable comment from the gawking courtiers and wide-eyed ladies en route.

Slade's trial was to be held at Westminster, the traditional site of many a sentence of doom. The prisoner and his four guards rode in silence, ignoring the rowdy spectators along the way. There was much pushing and shoving and shouting, as onlookers jostled for position to get a glimpse of the infamous Captain Tanner.

At last Westminster Hall loomed before them. Slade dismounted, squared his shoulders, and went unprotesting into the custody of yet more grim-faced guards. He was hustled through a back gate to avoid the curious crowds out front. Inside, a dank stone staircase lit only by flickering torches led to a Spartan cell, where he would be kept alongside other prisoners until his case was called.

As was customary, Slade would remain totally ignorant of the proceedings, until he was challenged to refute the accusations before the King's Bench.

He had scarcely settled on the flea-ridden, sour-smelling straw mattress, when a familiar dark shadow fell over his cell. Slade's eyes narrowed as he recognized Walsingham pausing on his way to court. In his hooded black robes the secretary resembled Death hovering over his chosen victim.

" 'Tis not too late yet to change your mind, Captain. Really, I would recommend the *peine forte et dure.*" Sir Francis licked his thin lips with anticipation. "I would be honored to plead your case and execute the sentence, as well. 'Tis truly an art form of sorts, and it is said I have a finesse for it."

Slade's eyebrows rose like twin swords in the smoky orange glow of the torches. "I am sure you would enjoy such a spectacle, Walsingham. But you shall kindly forgive me if I don't offer myself as a willing sacrifice into your hands? For I confess I have heard, sir, that you not so much delight in hearing a man repent of his sins, but rather in watching him die a ghastly death by inches."

The black robes stirred angrily at that, and without another word Walsingham was gone. Slade realized he had just sealed his own fate, for he knew the secretary would now stop at nothing to see his head roll upon Tower Green.

The Minister of State had managed to seal Mary Stuart's fate less than a month ago. If he could sentence the mighty Queen of Scots to die, how could a mere commoner like Slade Tanner hope to divert the sadistic desires of a pompous ass like Walsingham?

Bryony felt terrifyingly close to fainting in Westminster's Great Hall. It was packed to capacity with restless bodies. Aside from the five justices presiding beneath the royal Tudor oat of arms, and the officers of the court seated at a green aize-covered table, it was standing room only in the hall. She, t least, had been given benefit of a hard bench, where she ould move more easily before the bar, should her testimony e demanded.

Jeb Desmond, her kindly jailer, had seen to it that she could ppear presentable. Not only had he magically secured a bath or her, but even a maidservant to clean her clothes and dress er hair. Bryony had no idea she looked tragically lovely, and nany men eying her in the court chamber thought with relish hat the captain's soon-to-be widow would need a new protec-or.

The crowd stirred with interest when the Minister of State inally made his appearance and stated the nature of the day's earing. Lesser cases had been waived, so the charges against Captain Tanner might be heard. One of the clerks writing the olls stood and pronounced the charges one by one. They in-luded high treason and murder. Bryony took a deep breath o keep from fainting. Her gaze took in the fact that the queen erself was notoriously absent, and she acidly thought to her-elf that perhaps Bess was not brave enough to witness such ridiculous spectacle in person.

After the opening statements, the first to approach the bar vas the royal coroner. A fishy-faced fellow with a shock of vhite hair, he ambled up before the justices and bluntly stated is findings. Gillian Lovelle's death, he said, had surely re-ulted from a philter of slow poison in her food. The agent vas without a doubt salvarsan, of the red variety. The motive? He grinned a little ghoulishly and stated he would leave that p to the King's Bench to decide.

Walsingham then rose and proceeded to paint a portrait of Slade as a selfish womanizer who sought to free himself from is devoted loving fiancee, so he might marry, in Walsingham's vords, "An upstart Irish wench." Bryony had to bite her lower ip so hard it bled, to keep from jumping up and shouting that the minister was an outright liar. Why, he made it sound as if Gillian had been on par with the Blessed Virgin!

Much of the morning droned on with similar outrageous statements. Walsingham soon had everyone nearly bored to tears with his rambling tirade. His witnesses were actually quite few. When the court recessed for the midday meal Bryony escaped outside for some fresh air. The captain of the guard, Jeb Desmond, stayed securely at her side.

For some reason the gruff Cornishman had taken a liking to Bryony, and she had teasingly offered him a position on her ship, if she ever obtained the freedom to sail again. Desmond stood protectively beside Bryony, making threatening gestures at those who catcalled or tried to distress her in any way. He also insisted she accept a bowl of stew with lamb and rice, and a small goblet of watered wine to sustain her strength.

When the trial resumed, Bryony was relieved to see Slade at last brought in. A physical ache slammed through her as she observed her handsome golden-haired husband, making his way through the crowd. Slade was marshalled in chains, as were most prisoners who appeared before the bench. Yet his broad shoulders were not bowed despite the fact that he was flanked on either side by ushers with staves, who looked as if they could wrestle dragons, and win.

Slade was prodded forward before the five justices. He glanced around the room, and for a fleeting moment, he met Bryony's eyes. His darkened with outrage to see her there, and she in turn tried to send a silent message of love and hope in the few seconds before he looked away again.

The room hushed as Walsingham took the floor again and read off the name of the next witness: Mrs. Doreen Haymaker. With obvious reluctance, Dovehaven's former housekeeper assumed a stance before the bar and answered the secretary's questions in a nervous too-loud voice.

Poor lady, Bryony thought, watching the large woman who had so bravely confronted the pox, now quavering and flushing under Walsingham's hard scrutiny. He queried Mrs. Haymaker ıthlessly about the state of affairs at Dovehaven, how often ıe had overheard Slade and Gillian quarreling, even if she ad ever seen or overheard them making love. With sly insinution he led her toward an inevitable conclusion, confusing Irs. Haymaker so thoroughly that after awhile she ceased anwering him, and merely gestured helplessly in reply.

"My good woman, you must reply in a clear voice!" Valsingham ordered her. "How else is justice to be served? Iow, recount once again for the court what you heard Captain anner say to his betrothed the night he himself caught the ox."

The housekeeper's lips began to tremble, and tears spilled own her pockmarked cheeks, highlighting the old white scars n her skin. With a swift apologetic glance to Slade, she stamıered, "He said to her, milord . . . he said, " 'If the pox does ot kill you, madam, so help me God . . .' "

"Aye?" Walsingham pressed her brutally. She had trailed off ıto soft weeping. "What did he say?" he thundered.

" '. . . s—so help me God, I will.' "

The onlookers gasped and murmured amongst themselves, vhile Walsingham's small eyes glittered with triumph. "Thank ou, Mrs. Haymaker," he smugly concluded.

She continued in a sob-choked voice, "Och, but sir, 'twas aid in a fit of anger, not—"

"Thank you." Walsingham rudely cut her off with a mencing stare, motioning for the ushers to escort her out. He ırned to the five justices. "Next witness, my lords: Elinor urt, former tiring woman of the deceased . . ."

The day dragged on endlessly. To Bryony's surprise, the secetary did not call her to testify, perhaps because he suspected he would not fluster as easily as Mrs. Haymaker and the other imple country women. All three of them sobbed out their pologies to Slade after the prosecution was finished, but by ıen it was too late.

Walsingham had twisted their stories so cleverly, that he had ainted quite a vivid picture of two lovers carrying out a des-

perate plot of revenge, not only against Gillian Lovelle, bu
the Queen of England, as well.

Slade was the last to state his version of events; to his credi
he appeared cool and unruffled. His hard gaze remained a
fixed to Walsingham the entire time.

"You must acknowledge, Captain, that you wanted your be
trothed out of the way in order to marry your Irish mistress!"
the secretary shrieked in his face at one point, when Slade
stubbornly refused to admit to Gillian's murder.

" 'Twas well known Gilly sought her pleasures wherever
she would," Slade replied. "I simply decided to avail myself
of a similar freedom."

Several men in the hall were seen to squirm a bit at Slade's
remark regarding Gillian's appetites. Walsingham deliberately
ignored them. He made pointed reference to the fact that Gillian was one of Elizabeth Tudor's maids of honor, and the
queen did not tolerate any such philandering in her Court. His
statement provoked a ripple of low laughter throughout the
room. Walsingham flushed angrily, and brought his case to a
swift conclusion.

Now it was up to the five royal justices to decide upon
Slade's guilt or innocence. Bryony desperately wondered how
they were leaning. It was impossible to tell by their stern coun-
tenances. Few men would dare to cross the powerful Walsingham, she suspected. But did that mean they would condemn
a man to die, even if convinced of his innocence?

There might be hours or days before their decision was
handed down. With grief weighing heavy in her heart, Bryony
was led from the Great Hall by Jeb Desmond, back to her own
version of a cell, where she would keep a silent vigil until she
learned her beloved's fate.

Twenty-two

Exactly one week after Slade's trial, the verdict was proclaimed from the King's Bench at Westminster: Guilty of intent to kill, of precipitating murder against a loyal subject of the Crown, and also of high treason against Elizabeth Tudor. Slade was to be executed at Tower Green, preferably before Christmas and Twelfth Night, so as not to spoil the festivities.

Only because of his brother's pleas was Slade to be spared the rack or other tortures. Walsingham was quite disappointed by this provision.

Kit, Phillip, and George each demanded to be allowed to visit the youngest Tanner, but all three were denied their petitions, nor were any of them allowed to submit any latent testimony on Slade's behalf. Slade's brothers stubbornly set out anyway, determined to bring the facts to light.

While George Lord Tanner and Phillip combined their legal expertise to search for flaws in Walsingham's case, Kit journeyed posthaste to Dovehaven to comb over the scant clues left there. They all agreed they were probably overlooking some very obvious evidence, which might serve to overturn Slade's conviction. But they were unable to unearth anything. Walsingham and his cronies had been very deft and thorough in destroying any evidence that did not suit their cause. Even the deceased woman had been quickly cremated and buried, ostensibly to prevent further spread of the pox.

When Bryony heard the verdict, she was devastated. Though she had been freed shortly after Slade's trial on the grounds that a pregnant woman could not be tried, she would again be subject to arrest and imprisonment after the child was born. Therefore, Jeb Desmond urged her to flee England at the first opportunity. For some reason the stout Cornishman also believed Slade was not guilty, despite all evidence to the contrary.

" 'Tis best if ye leave London right quick," the captain of the guard said gruffly, to cover his own emotions upon hearing the proclamation of death. "Don't let Walsingham have second thoughts about it, milady. He's a right wicked man, he is."

But Bryony shook her head, fiercely rejecting freedom now that it was offered her. "I must stay," she whispered. "Is there any chance I would be allowed to go to my husband?"

"In the Tower? Nay, lassie. Ye must put such a notion from yer head, and carry on. There's the little lad in yer belly to think of now."

"To be raised without his father? If that dark day should come, Jeb, I'll make the Crown rue it! For my son will be a Tanner, too, and I'll never let him forget it. And mayhaps someday I will have my own revenge on Bess Tudor on the Irish Sea!"

Alarmed, Jeb saw by the ferocity in her eyes and voice that she meant it. He shook his grizzled head in sorrow, over what a dismal future this one sad hour had wrought.

Less than three days later Slade Tanner was taken by barge downriver to the Tower. Again it was a windswept and rainy December day. But this time no crowds had gathered to see the captain escorted to his new harsher quarters.

The procession crossed beneath Tower Bridge, and when the barge was docked, Slade startled those few present by walking through the Traitor's Gate with his head held high. There was no sign of faltering in either his stride nor his gaze, and he glanced up at the forbidding gray stone structure without visible emotion.

The central portion of the fortress, and the oldest, was the White Tower. It had originally been built by William the Conqueror, ironically one of Slade's own ancestors, in 1078. I was also where Elizabeth Tudor had spent much of her childhood, a prisoner of her own half sister, the Bloody Queen Mary.

Slade was led through St. Thomas's Tower over the wide deep moat. He could see the block which had been set upon the Tower Green so that he might observe his fate and ruminate upon his alleged follies. The Yeoman Warder joined the procession at the Main Guard house. Slade was then removed to Beauchamp Tower, which had also seen many famous and infamous heads come and go. He quietly jested to his jailers that at least he would be in excellent company. Both Lady Jane Grey, Queen of England for only nine days, and the courtly poet Sir Thomas Wyatt had once gazed out from within these same high stone walls.

Inside his prison quarters, Slade's manacles were removed, and he was advised he could attend morning mass at the chapel of St. Peter ad Vincula, if he wished. Then the Yeoman Warder and his guardsmen promptly departed. After the great wooden door slammed shut and locked, Slade went to the narrow window to gaze down upon Tower Green. He had an excellent view of the block and the parade ground, where the queen's witnesses and the rowdy crowds would observe the grisly spectacle of his death.

When darkness fell, Slade witnessed the Ceremony of the Keys from a distance, watching the yeoman warder's bobbing lantern proceed across the Tower Green and then disappear for a moment, as the man went to lock the ancient doors of Byward Tower. Then the present arms were given by his escort, and the Tower was pronounced closed until dawn's first light.

Slade had been relatively calm until that moment. For some reason, the night watch's call sent shivers up his spine. For he realized in that sober moment, he would never leave this place alive.

* * *

Dinner came in the form of a small roasted capon, severa slices of honey-cured ham, and lamprey cooked in galytene sauce. There was raisin bread, boiled cabbage, and two rosy winter apples, baked and swimming in Devon cream. Slade ate more heartily than he imagined he could under such circumstances. He finished off the surprisingly tasty fare with the half-skin of red wine that had been left.

The dinner hour also brought another unexpected visitor Slade had just polished off the wine, when the sound of the key grating in the lock once again disturbed his solitary brooding. He glanced up in surprise from the small table where he was sitting, and watched in amazement as a familiar figure strode into the tower chamber, looking mightily aggrieved.

"Mon Dieu!" Giles Lafleur proclaimed, whirling on the young guardsmen who had trailed him in and who stood there looking somewhat sheepish. " 'Tis too dark in here by half *garçon.*" He snapped his big fingers impatiently. "Another torch, quickly."

Lafleur took the torch the bewildered guard offered him flipped the younger man a coin, and then shooed him out and firmly closed the door. Slade watched the proceedings in utter amazement, then slowly got to his feet, while the Frenchman stuck the extra torch into an iron wall sconce and briskly dusted off his hands.

"There! Never complain that you do not have friends in high places, *Capitaine* Tanner." Giles turned and offered the bewildered prisoner a broad grin. "Though whoever though the day would come when Lafleur would end up bribing his way into a prison, rather than out, eh?"

"Lafleur, how the hell did you come to be here?"

"Come now, *mon ami.* No time for questions. We must say our fond farewells, *n'est ce pas?"*

Slade gave an ironic smile. "Then you're not here to rescue me, as I'd hoped?"

Lafleur grinned. "Ah, but I fear I'm in every bit as deep a predicament as you. You see, I was caught visiting your little raven. She did not betray me, but alas, one of the guards I had bribed felt his palms itching too soon. He offered me up, and so I found myself seeking Bess's mercy."

Slade was confused. "Why on earth would you ask to be taken to the Tower, Giles? Surely your crime did not deserve so terrible a sentence."

The Frenchman chuckled. "Of course not. Petty criminals such as I are usually offered up to Tyburn Hill. We do not usually merit royal attention at all. But your queen took notice, when word drifted to her that I was none other than the infamous *Le Francais Corsaire.* English Bess granted me this one request, to say goodbye to an old friend. Then I will be granted my freedom, on the condition I resume harassing Spain for her benefit."

"You!" Slade stared hard at Lafleur, who stood there calmly straightening his wide velvet cuffs. "So you are the one responsible for sacking Spanish ships alongside Bryony. I should've guessed! Rumors at Court were rife about the infamous French privateer, and his equally notorious wench."

Lafleur's eyebrows raised slightly at the caustic tone to his old friend's voice. "Rumors are known to be wrong."

"Aye, but not this time!" Slade swore savagely under his breath. "I can hardly countenance it. My old friend, Giles Lafleur, and my own wife!"

"Bryony was not your wife then," Lafleur reminded Slade in a low growl, "but even so, her eyes never once strayed from your bed to mine. Aye, Bryony O'Neill refused my ardent attentions, not once, but many times! Her heart holds only room for one man, you great English idiot!"

"But the babe—" Slade began.

"Is yours. Ah, how I wish I could claim otherwise, *mon ami!* For nothing would give me greater pleasure than an excuse to snatch that Irish firebrand from your ungrateful arms. *Mon Dieu!* I know that England has bred up many fools, but you deserve to be crowned king of them all, Tanner!"

Slade stared at his old friend, half in rage and half in hope.

Lafleur was a notorious womanizer. He liked to brag that he had conquered most of Europe's petticoats. But if it was true that Giles and Bryony were lovers, Slade knew the hot-blooded Frenchman would have promptly set her up as his mistress, and provided for the child. Instead, Lafleur had let Bryony go. Back to Ireland and the man she truly loved . . . the father of her child.

"God's blood!" Slade swore. "What a fool I am. 'Tis too late now to beg Bryony's forgiveness . . . and so I leave her with the cruelest accusation of all to remember me by."

Giles regarded him sadly. *"Oui,* my friend," was all he said.

With unintentional irony, the morning of Slade's execution dawned fair and bright. But for the chilly air, it would have been a perfect day for a picnic. The crowds gathered early to spread out blankets and set out their repasts. A royal execution was always a fine excuse to miss a day of work, and today was no exception.

As he took the customary last rites following mass, Slade's mind was elsewhere on this crisp December morn. He had not been surprised by the guilty verdict, as Walsingham had produced enough evidence to damn a saint. But he regretted the pain his own actions and this ending would cause Bryony. He had made his brothers and Giles Lafleur promise to look after her. He left the chapel with tears trickling down his lean cheeks. Not for himself, or even his immortal soul, but for Bryony and the child he would never know.

Bryony was up hours before dawn on the *Fiach-muir,* where she had taken up residence after leaving Whitehall. From her wardrobe she selected a black velvet gown, whose full skirts were piped with black silk and sparkling jet rosettes. The underskirt was also black silk, though unadorned. She left her ebony hair loose to spill in long curls down her back. She made no attempt to disguise her pregnancy; indeed, she wished to rub it in the Crown's face. Elizabeth Tudor was rendering her child fatherless, and must face that fact.

She took only a black cloak to shield her from the cold December breezes, and then Finn rowed her in. Her cousin was silent and grim, his own grief restrained by her icy calm. Bryony was falling to pieces inside, but she would not give this damned England nor its people the satisfaction of seeing her weep. Slade must also see she had the strength to support him in the end.

Tears glittered in her eyes like tiny diamonds, as she stepped off the barge to pass through St. Thomas's Tower. Bryony paused to fiercely rub them away, before she and Finn moved into the public eye. She sought to distract herself by gazing around the lawn at Tower Green. It was surprisingly well kept. There were even rosebeds, though the flowers were long since gone. The biggest surprise of all were the pet ravens, which were kept by tradition in the yard. Their deep raucous cries made Bryony shiver, as she hurried through the crowd with Finn hovering protectively at her side.

She was soon forced to face the gawking onlookers and the gruesome sight of the wooden block which had been laid out several days before. She came to an abrupt halt, swaying a little as she clutched Finn's arm.

From the window of the Beauchamp Tower, Slade saw his wife enter Tower Green. He cursed and hurried to finish dressing. Giles had managed to smuggle him in an outfit worthy of a prince. It seemed a final bitter jest on the Tudor Court Slade so despised.

He hastily donned the rich black velvet doublet paned with gray silk and generously embroidered with silver thread. There were breeches and boots and stockings to match. The somber colors were very striking with his fair coloring, but Slade didn't pause to glance into the small looking glass Lafleur had brought. He merely tied his red gold hair neatly back with a black velvet ribbon, and declared he was ready.

When Slade was escorted by the yeoman warder down to

the yard, many in the throng stopped to gape with regret, seeing such a fine figure of a man going to meet his end. He paused before a dark-haired woman wearing matching black velvet, and it was enough to bring a sudden hush upon the onlookers. For these two were clearly lovers beyond the grave and when she threw her arms around his neck and clung as if she would force him to carry her to the block, too, several women watching them openly wept.

"Ah, love, you shouldn't be here!" Slade chided his wife before she cut off his gentle tirade with a fierce kiss.

"And leave you alone to your fate?" Bryony murmured thickly through her tears. "Nay, Slade, I intend to watch your every step, and soundly curse the Tudor bitch with each one. She will live to regret this day, I swear it!"

"Swear only that you will look after our child, and raise him to be a Tanner to make me proud," he said. Their gazes met, his warm and loving, and in that instant Bryony knew Slade believed her. She ached to tell him she had already forgiven him. Nothing mattered now except their love. But before she could speak, he kissed her firmly upon her sun-warmed hair, and gently withdrew.

"Fare thee well, my little sea raven. Know that I love you now, and always will."

The onlookers murmured with discontent. His strong voice had carried to the ends of the yard. And many lunching upon Tower Green that day, suddenly lost their hearty appetites.

"Please, you must listen, Your Grace! Only this once, if never again, but there is no moment to spare!"

Elizabeth Tudor raised her gaze from the parchment she had just finished signing. It was the royal order for execution. She pressed it with her seal, and then Walsingham snatched it from her fingers and scurried off before Kit Tanner could persuade her to grasp the nature of his plea.

"Master Tanner," she said sharply, "you presume a great deal of my patience of late!"

The queen looked regal and magnificent, her cloth-of-gold skirts paired with an emerald green velvet bodice trimmed with pearls. She was wearing a large diamond tiara, and her ginger hair was elaborately puffed over hidden pads. Rouge had obviously been used to restore some color to her pale skin. She gazed upon her former favorite with obvious exasperation.

"They are waiting upon m'word at the Tower," she added.

"Aye, for the very purpose of doing a wrong which might yet be prevented!" Kit remained upon one aching knee, since she had never given him permission to rise. Bess was still very angry over Gillian's death and Dudley's secret marriage, and it showed in her every action.

Elizabeth Tudor toyed with her feather pen a moment more, then set it impatiently aside in the ink bottle. With an exaggerated sigh, she said, "Very well, Master Tanner. What last trifling request do you have on your brother's behalf?"

"Just one thing, Your Majesty. That you agree to hear the words of a woman who was not allowed to speak at Slade's trial, one who can cast a truer light upon the circumstances of Gillian's death."

Elizabeth's gray eyes narrowed. "Do you seek to detain the Crown from due justice, sirrah?"

"On the contrary, I but seek to save my brother and your reputation. For if the shocking truth should come out later, it may not speak favorably of Your Majesty."

Elizabeth, always obsessed with her public image, looked alert at that. "You have five minutes, no more!"

"Thank you, Your Grace." Kit rose with her permission and hurried to bring the witness before her. The queen gazed with interest upon the toothless old hag who cackled up at her, an elderly crone apparently neither frightened nor impressed with the notion of meeting her liege.

"Who is this person?" Elizabeth demanded.

"Her name is Elsie Hobbs. She practices the healing arts

in the little village of Deal. She is the one who sold Gillia the red salvarsan, with which she poisoned herself."

Elizabeth's eyes widened. "Is't true, old woman?" she de manded.

The hag raised her bulbous nose an inch higher. "Aye, Yo Grace. She was worried she 'ad the lues, and so I sold 'er 'alf-packet of it meself."

Elizabeth frowned. "The lues?"

Clearing his throat, Kit supplied, "The French disease, You Majesty. I believe the royal physicians have dubbed it syphilis after the old poem by the same name. 'Tis often treated wit salvarsan. 'Twas the tale Gillian used to buy it for herself."

"Quite a lady, that one! Heh-heh!" Elsie Hobbs chortled.

Appalled, Elizabeth rose from her throne. "Why would Gil lian commit suicide?" she demanded. " 'Tis a mortal sin!"

"Aye, Your Majesty, but so is a flawed face here in our crue Court. 'Twas noted by every witness at the trial that Gillia lost all semblance of beauty to the blight. She could hardl bear to live with pockmarks, after being likened to Aphrodite." Kit took a deep steadying breath. His heart was pounding har for more reason than this.

"I know you wish to believe Gillian was a moral righteou lady, Your Grace. But there is something else I must need add to the sordid tale, something I would inform you of i private."

Curious, Elizabeth motioned for the Hobbs woman to b dismissed, and when the cackling hag had left, Kit Tanner tol his story. The queen listened without saying a word, thoug ultimately her gray eyes filled with shock and then tears. Whe he was finished, Elizabeth Tudor hastily summoned her guar and ordered that her fastest barge be readied, so that she coul travel to Tower Green in pursuit of true justice.

In his final moments, Slade's voice rang out clearly acros the green yard where both people and ravens flocked.

"God Bless Our Majesty, Queen Elizabeth," he declared, "for though I never dreamed to come here as a criminal myself, I pray you bear me witness that I am no traitor! I was ever the queen's man, and always shall remain so. Thus, it ends."

"No!"

A broken scream carried across the yard, and Slade glanced back to see his wife struggling wildly in Finn O'Grady's restraining arms. When Bryony found she could not succeed, she sagged in defeat to the ground, her dark skirts puddling about her knees. She keened wildly at Finn's feet.

Slade was careful not to look at Bryony again as he approached the block, lest his final resolve fade. He walked up to the executioner, where by tradition he quietly pardoned the masked man for the grisly task he must complete, and also paid a half-crown head tax. Just as he knelt, a great shadow fell over the block. So dark it was for a moment, that Slade thought a cloud must have passed over the sun. The executioner hesitated, and then they both heard an excited babble rise from the crowd.

"Lor'!" he heard a nearby woman gasp. "What was that?"

"A ghost!" one man cried, and another exclaimed, "Nay, 'tis just the mighty shadow of all the birds, rising as one."

And indeed it was. Something had disturbed the dozens of ravens settled upon the yard and trees, and they all rose, and circled the block three times in eerie silence. They vanished over the Tower walls just as several shouts from the restless crowd brought the proceedings to a halt.

"Hail, the queen's barge!" Cupped hands passed the word like wildfire. Hands gestured frantically towards the river. "Her Majesty arrives!"

Heads craned about, and an excited murmur arose from the spectators gathered on Tower Green. Impatient with the delay, Walsingham once again flourished the signed death warrant in the executioner's face.

"Be done with it!" he ordered the fellow. "The queen mus
not be exposed to such unpleasant affairs of state!"

The burly henchman hesitated just long enough for a cr
from the barge to drift through the gates.

"Halt the proceedings! By Her Majesty's decree!"

For a moment Walsingham looked as if he might wrest th
axe from the executioner and complete the act himself. The
he saw Elizabeth Tudor's pinched expression as she entere
the yard, and he wisely slunk away and vanished into th
crowd.

Slade quickly rose to his feet and faced the royal entourag
from Whitehall with bewilderment and relief. Elizabeth's arri
val caused her people to clear a path for her as if they wer
so many sheep, and like a haughty lioness, she proceeded di
rectly to the block. In the shock of seeing his queen in person
Slade forgot himself, and received a gruff but playful rebuk
from Elizabeth Tudor.

"La, Captain Tanner, have you forgotten so soon the fin
manners my dear Meredith taught you?" she asked. "I shoul
expect a graceful leg at least, for saving such a pretty hea
from the block."

At once Slade flushed and dropped to one knee. "I humbl
crave your pardon, Your Grace," he murmured. "And as al
ways, you have my eternal devotion."

The onlookers waited with baited breath, while the quee
mused upon his words. With a husky little chuckle, Elizabet
Tudor finally extended her beringed hand to be kissed. Onc
that was accomplished, she bade him rise.

"There have been some new facts come to light in this mat
ter, Captain Tanner," she announced. "Therefore, the Crow
has decided that you shall be retried upon these charges i
view of new evidence."

Scarcely daring to believe his good fortune, Slade inquire
"When, Your Majesty?"

"I would prefer the matter be settled shortly. Then, Go
willing, our good minister shall be content to let you retir

from service to the Crown, and enter into private trade as you apparently desire."

"And you, Your Grace? Are you agreeable to the notion of allowing me to pursue a new course?"

Elizabeth glanced meaningfully at Bryony, and gave a sharp little sniff. "Faith, 'twould appear to me you already have, Slade."

When she used his Christian name and he saw the smile playing about her lips, Slade realized he'd been granted a reprieve. But how had it come about?

Those questions could be answered later, Slade decided. For all that mattered now was that he could spend one more precious moment in Bryony's arms.

Twenty-three

Winter 1578

The very same day he won his freedom, Slade and Bryony prepared to depart England for a new life together. The testimony at Slade's second trial had gone very differently. The proof Elsie Hobbs had offered and the corroboration of several of Gillian's previous lovers, was enough to silence Walsingham forever.

Slade realized that he owed his life to his brothers. Because of their diligent efforts, they had uncovered Elsie Hobbs and exposed Gilly's paramours. Now he was a free man, ready to set sail in search of good prospects and even greater fortune.

He and Bryony traveled to Ambergate one last time to say farewell to Kit, who had especially gone out of his way to assist Slade in his hour of need. They were surprised to find the house in an uproar, and Elspeth gone. She had left a curt note informing Kit she was returning to her family in Cornwall, and intended to seek an ecclesiastical divorce from him as soon as possible.

While such *divortium a mesna et thoro* separations—commonly referred to as "bed and board" divorces—were occasionally granted, neither party would be free to remarry. In effect, Elspeth Tanner had just doomed Kit to the likelihood of never obtaining a legal male heir.

Bryony joined Isobel upstairs to help her comfort the confused children, while Slade joined Kit in the study.

"What happened?" he demanded, as his brother poured them both generous snifters of his favorite pear brandy. "Was there some serious problem of which I was unaware?"

Kit gave a short laugh. "My life with her was nothing *but* one long problem, Slade. Elspeth detested the girls almost as much as she detested me. Of course, she has no claim to the children under canon law, but just to be careful, I have demanded her family formally relinquish them in writing when Elspeth obtains her divorce."

"On what grounds does she seek divorce?" Slade demanded. "You have been nothing but an exemplary husband. You have never starved or beaten her, and the law is quite clear that a man may do either or both, if a wife proves irascible. Elspeth has certainly acted thusly ever since I have known her. She has insulted, scorned, and publicly ridiculed both you and our family. She has tread on the thin ice of treason at Court functions. I have seen her slap the girls and Isobel quite viciously at any number of gatherings. I confess I do not know how you managed to keep from throttling the woman all these years."

"Neither do I," Kit admitted. "But Elspeth gave me three beautiful daughters, and for that I cannot fault her."

"Daughters, aye, when you needed sons," Slade replied. "Who will inherit Ambergate now? You know that under the decree of the Church, remarriage is not possible for either of you now."

Kit nodded. He was obviously still rattled by his wife's abrupt desertion, and spoke slowly and heavily. "I have decided to deed over Ambergate to you, Slade," he said, "with the one provision, of course, that you will see to my girls' dowries and finding worthy husbands for all three of them, if something untoward should happen to me."

Slade was startled. He did not like the undercurrent he heard in his brother's voice. "Don't talk like that, Kit. This will soon pass, or at least the shock and upset of it all. Mayhaps Elspeth will even change her mind."

Kit shook his head and took a deep gulp of the brandy. His

green eyes were strangely veiled. He was not at all the carefree fellow Slade was used to seeing. Something else was amiss, something dreadfully wrong. Had he loved Elspeth so much, then? Granted, the woman was a cheerless viper, but if Kit honestly adored his wife, Slade would not fault him for taking her back.

Seeking to change the subject to a happier one, he said, "I wanted to thank you again for finding Elsie Hobbs. Her testimony literally saved my life."

For some reason, Kit did not smile back. "You have precious little to thank me for, brother," he replied.

Slade laughed a bit uneasily. "What's this? False modesty from Bess's favorite silver-tongued courtier?"

His mirth swiftly faded, when he realized Kit was serious. One more look into his brother's eyes, and he felt an icy frisson of fear he could not explain. "My God, Kit. What's wrong?"

Briefly Kit closed his anguished eyes, not speaking for almost a minute. Then, slowly, he said, "I blame myself for everything, Slade. The whole bloody mess could have been prevented, if only I wasn't such a damned coward . . ."

Slade frowned, confused. Was Kit still speaking of his wife? Then he felt every muscle in his body tense with anticipation, as the other man continued his confession.

"I didn't intend for it to happen, god knows, but a man can only take so much, and after ten years of hell with a cold nagging bitch for a wife, he cannot help but take comfort wherever 'tis offered . . ."

Slade said nothing, letting Kit unburden his soul at his own pace. He waited silently even as his gut contracted with pure emotion, expecting another leaden blow.

"It just happened," Kit blurted, raking his hands through his bright auburn hair. "One night last spring, when Elspeth and Isobel and the girls had gone north to visit her side of the family." His voice trailed off for a moment, then resumed with a softer cast.

"Gillian came to Ambergate. I confess I had been drinking

rather heavily, sitting before the fire here with a bit of warm brandy to ease my loneliness." He forged on abruptly, not daring to glance at Slade. "And then suddenly Gilly was here. No promises, no questions, no demands. Not yet, anyway . . ."

"How long, Kit? How long did it go on?"

His brother still refused to look at him. Instead Kit took another fortifying gulp of brandy. "Long enough. And every single time, I damned myself the morning after. Oh, God, you can't imagine how I did!"

"Aye, I think I can."

Kit was not to be assuaged. He had to get the rest of the story out before it drove him mad. "Gilly came to me several months later," he continued in low voice, "and told me about . . . about the child."

"Sweet Jesu."

Kit nodded, his handsome features contorted with agony. "Aye, the babe was mine, Slade. There is no doubt at all in my mind, and Gillian assured me 'twas so. She threatened to tell Bess, Elspeth, and bloody England itself, if I didn't keep her expenses paid at Court. What could I do? I could stand to lose Elspeth, Lord knows, but what about the girls? I couldn't bear the thought of them being taken from me. And Gillian convinced me she would bear me a son . . . the heir I've always wanted. I've damned myself a thousand times for agreeing to Gilly's evil scheme, but I was desperate. As long as I paid my dues in a timely fashion, she kept quiet.

"Somehow my own darker side convinced me that you would be a good father to the lad in my stead. And . . . and if by some chance the lad had red hair, I reasoned, 'twas common knowledge it runs strongly on our mother's side of the family. Nobody would suspect a thing."

"Dear God." Slade sank down into a chair, staring up at his brother with both amazement and shock. Curiously he felt no anger, though perhaps the emotion quivering in Kit's voice had served to allay it. "What else do you have to tell me?" he asked.

"Nothing more, except I feel like a despicable human being. Do you know what it cost me to keep silent, Slade, especially when you were so ill? And when I heard Gilly lost the babe, my only son, I wanted to weep aloud and scream and rail to the heavens above at the unfairness of it all. I nearly told you everything then. But I selfishly thought it would still work out in the end . . . Sweet Jesu, how little I knew!"

Kit's explosive oath was followed by a calmer tone, yet one more frightening for its obvious despair. "I kept telling myself over and over that someday I'd confess to it all, and openly claim Christian Tanner as my son." A bitter smile twisted his lips. "Aye, I'd already named him, that wee little scrap of flesh, while still he slumbered in his mother's womb. Foolish and presumptuous of me, wasn't it?"

"Nay," Slade said, " 'tis no less than I've come to expect of the generous brother and father I know."

As Kit's shoulders began to visibly shake, Slade rose from the chair and hugged his brother hard.

"I didn't love her!" Kit was suddenly sobbing. "I was just too damned weak . . . and I wanted my little boy so badly . . . !"

"I know," Slade soothed, his own deep voice husky with emotion. He was devastated by the depth of Kit's grief, yet also set free by the knowledge just imparted to him.

"I forgive you, Kit," he said without hesitation, sensing that was the only absolution his brother required. "And I understand everything, though I wish you'd come to me earlier. We've always been so close."

"I had to protect the girls," Kit said, wiping his face on his sleeve and stepping back to compose himself. "I wouldn't let them be hurt for the world. And to that end I used you, Slade. If you never forgave me, you would be perfectly justified, I know."

"Kit, you've paid the price of your folly a hundredfold. We both suffered from Gillian's cruel whims and games. There's no need to continue her legacy of hate now. I don't think you girls would ever profit from the truth anyway. What good would it serve?"

His brother nodded gratefully. "What about Bryony?"

"I love and respect my wife a great deal. I know she wouldn't betray your secret to anyone on earth, and I think it might ease her own conscience to know the truth. The memory of my betrothal and the death of the babe still haunts her. 'Twould be a kindness to offer Bryony the same peace we both have now."

Kit nodded. "I'd like to tell her myself, with your permission. I owe that wife of yours a lot, you know. She was the first true female friend I've ever had."

Slade smiled and reached for the decanter of brandy. "Then may I propose a toast, brother?"

"Certainly." Kit raised his glass with alacrity. "What to?"

Slade thought a moment. "To Christian Tanner," he said, quietly but firmly, "and his father. And to each of our bright futures." He filled each snifter to the rim with the sparkling golden liqueur. As they raised their glasses in unison, he added, "And to the ladies that will make it all possible: Lady Luck and Bryony Tanner."

"Here, here!" Kit said, and over the rims of the snifters the brothers' green eyes met. In that moment Kit knew his secret was forever safe, and Slade realized there was no limitation to his life's ambitions. For he had his ship, the sea, and a loving wife. What more could one man ask?

Epilogue

Raven Hall, Ireland
October, 1579

"Da! You mustn't! You'll only spoil them more," Bryony protested.

"Nonsense," the O'Neill told his daughter gruffly, scooping down a huge hand on either side of his rocking chair to catch a grandbaby. Plopping a wide-eyed twin on each knee, he be gan to rock and bounce them briskly to the sprightly tune o "Bold-eyed Bess."

Across the hall the twins' exasperated mother and thei equally amused sire watched the unlikely proceedings. Thei girls were as different in temperament as they were in looks On Brann's left knee, five-month-old Katherine Alanna gaze up at her singing grandsire with typical Irish indignation. Sh was obviously quite put-out to have been snatched away fron her exploration of the floor. Kat suffered having her silky blacl hair petted by the old man, but when his singing turned int more of a tuneless bellow, she quickly supplied her own un happy howls.

By contrast, Erin Meredith was quite content to stare up a her grandpa's ruddy face as he crooned the raunchy ditty. Sh flirted with him with her big gray green eyes, and dimple prettily when he rumpled her coppery curls.

"Enough already!" Bryony went to fetch her daughters. " won't have you teaching them that sort of blarney, old man!

"And why not?" Brann blustered. "They're half O'Neill, aren't they? 'Tis high time they learned a few native ballads."

"Native, aye, but tavern songs? Would you have your grandchildren growing up believing brawls are the order of the day?" she scolded him.

Brann laughed. "And who's to say they aren't, in Ireland?" Reluctantly he surrendered his granddaughters, watching as Bryony settled one infant on each hip.

"You're an old mother hen, that's what you are," Brann grumbled at his daughter. He wouldn't admit how his own eyes had misted at the first sight of the twins, just after their birth in the same chamber where his wife had died. He had cast his gaze heavenward, and silently thanked God and a beloved angel named Alanna for these two little precious packages sent from above.

With a sigh, he said to Bryony, "I suppose you'll be takin' an old man's joy away now, and sailin' to England again."

"Old is right," Bryony countered. "Since when have you given up the sea? Why don't you come along this trip, and make yourself useful? I could sorely use a nursemaid."

Brann scowled at her jest. "My bones are gettin' too old for that sort of nonsense, girl. In fact, I'm even thinkin' of taking your brother and Glynnis up on their offer to move north to Ballycastle."

Bryony's mouth dropped open. "You'd leave Raven Hall?"

"Leave it? Bah! I'd sell it to me own kin." Brann playfully winked at his son-in-law across the room. "For the simple price of an English sovereign to place over me eyes when I'm dead."

"Why do I get the feeling you're not speaking of coins?" Slade said wryly, rising to relieve Bryony of one of the twins.

The O'Neill just grinned. "I've a hankerin' to go north anyway, and rest me old bones a spell. Besides, who's going to make sure Dan raises wee Derry like a man? Until you get a son on me girl here, he's the only O'Neill heir."

"Any sons of ours would be Tanners anyway," Bryony pointedly reminded her father. "We agreed to honor the girls' dual heritage with their names, but a boy must needs follow his father's line."

Brann quickly indicated his opinion of that. "Hah! Likely any girl-brats you throw will have more mettle in 'em than any of Danny's lads!" He chuckled again when he saw both of the twins watching his every move with alert bright eyes. Erin Meredith, Merry for short, was her grandpapa's darling, while little Kat's emerald green eyes hinted at plenty of trouble to come.

"Och, she's going to be a spitfire, that one!" Brann predicted, pointing a finger at the dark-haired baby who promptly scrunched up her tiny nose. "I've seen that look before. Best get ready now, Englishman!"

Slade grinned and rose to the challenge. "Both my daughters will, I hope, follow their mother's admirable example, and become women of high spirits and sharp minds. 'Tis why we've taken them along on each journey so far."

"And?" The O'Neill demanded of their progress.

"Kat was born to the sea, as I suspected from the beginning," Bryony said with a fond glance at the dark-haired infant propped on her hip. Then she smiled just as lovingly at the gurgling redhead in Slade's arms. "I think our little Merry prefers the land, though. I predict she'll be the one to dance in Bess Tudor's Court someday."

"Not without her father present!" Slade put in, quickly and protectively.

Bryony smiled at her husband. "We'll see they have a proper upbringing, love." She turned and eyed her father sternly. "Which does not include learning the second chorus to 'Bold-eyed Bess'!"

"Haven't I heard that in a pub somewhere?" Slade mused.

"Have you?" O'Neill blandly replied. He winked at his son-in-law, asking, "Off again to foreign shores, eh?"

Slade nodded. " 'Tis the last trip before winter sets in, I promise. I sincerely hope our little adventures are over fo awhile. Right now I'm craving the simple but satisfying life of a family man."

"Then you'll stay at Raven Hall?" the old man asked them hopefully.

"After we get back from London, aye." Slade glanced at his wife. He could see the new warmth with which she regarded her father. "I think, though, that it might be a bit of a rough trip for the twins, don't you agree, love?"

Bryony caught on and slipped a quick wink to Slade. "Aye, it might at that. Mayhaps we can leave the girls with one of my cousins."

"Now, now, no need for that," O'Neill quickly put in. "Why, I've got a way with the wee ones myself, don't you think?" As he spoke he motioned for them to return his granddaughters to their rightful throne, his big lap.

When the twins were happily settled again, Slade took the opportunity to draw his wife outside into some rare Irish sunshine. Outside the hall, the sky was clear and piercingly blue, and the last roses bloomed in scarlet profusion against the weathered gray stone walls. At the same moment they both reached to pluck a red bud, and smiled at each other as the memory of another rose in another garden suddenly came to mind.

Slade asked her softly, "Are you happy, Bryony Tanner?"

"Aye, very happy, all except for the thought of leaving the twins for a time."

"They'll be better off here, and I think 'twill please the old man to no end to have some company for a few weeks." Slade reached to touch the gleaming amulet at the base of her throat. "I think we owe Bess our thanks in person for her generosity, sweetheart. After all, she didn't have to send the amulet home for Kat's christening, nor set aside Dovehaven for Merry's dowry."

Although they had christened their second daughter Erin Meredith at birth, within a few weeks she had been nicknamed Merry for her sweet disposition, just like Slade's mother before

her. And when Elizabeth Tudor had learned of this, she ha
been touched enough to grant the country estate to her ne
little goddaughter.

Bryony agreed it would be a wise idea to thank the queen then asked him, "Are we going to visit your brothers, too?"

"I doubt it, love. I daresay we'll be too busy to even spar them a simple hello!"

"Not even Kit?" Bryony was worried about Slade' brother, especially since Elspeth's unexpected death from th influenza, while in Cornwall. At least the girls still had Isobe Weeks, and they adored her, for she had been more of mother to them from the beginning than their own had eve been. Bryony knew that devotion was returned in full mea sure. She wondered if Kit fully appreciated the quietly loya young woman, who had lived beneath his roof all these year at Ambergate.

"Well, perhaps a quick hello to George, Phillip, Kit, an their respective families, and then we'll be back," Slade sai "I'm in quite a hurry to get my own wife home again, an start on that son the O'Neill's so worried about."

Bryony stepped into her husband's embrace with a laug "What makes you think I want any more of your ornery chil dren, Slade Tanner?"

"Because of whatever attracted you to their ornery sire i the first place! Now, look at me, madam." When her beautif sea blue eyes slowly raised to his, he growled low in his throa "Woman, you are incorrigible. If you don't stop looking at m like that, we'll have started on the next Tanner before we eve leave for England!"

"And would that be such an outrage, sirrah?" she tease him.

Slade only briefly considered it. "Nay," he decided, liftin his wife and swinging her around in the bright fall sunshin He set a marked stride for their nearest ship, the *Fiach-mu* while nearby the shadow of a great black bird traced lazy sp rals above the shimmering blue water, riding lower and low upon the gentle trade breezes, until the sunlight splashed pure gold across its ebony wings, and bit by bit, it slowly vanished into the sea.

Dear Reader,

I've always loved the great drama, romance, and pageantry of Tudor England. I think if I could choose any time frame to ive in, I'd pick that splendid era of discovery!

I constantly strive to bring you unique exciting tales, each one woven on a rich historical tapestry. I hope I've succeeded with *Sea Raven.*

Slade and Bryony are very dear to my heart, and so are Kit Tanner and his three redheaded imps, Anne, Grace, and little Maggie. Look for Kit's story to appear this summer in Zebra's *Angel Love* Collection.

Then, in early '97, Zebra and I will bring you *Fire Raven,* he continuing adventures of Kat Tanner, Slade and Bryony's ldest daughter. The second novel in my Raven Series is set n Wales and England, and once again you'll meet magnificent Elizabeth I, and a whole host of colorful Tudor characters.

As always, I love hearing from readers. Please feel free to write me at: P.O. Box 304, Gooding, Idaho 83330. If you in- lude a SASE, I'll be happy to return a specially autographed SEA RAVEN bookmark.

Also look for these other Zebra Books by Patricia McAllis- er:

GYPSY JEWEL
MOUNTAIN ANGEL
FIRE RAVEN (March '97)

and be sure to watch for a novella appearing this summer n Zebra's *Angel Love* Collection.

JANELLE TAYLOR

ZEBRA'S BEST-SELLING AUTHOR

DON'T MISS ANY OF HER
EXCEPTIONAL, EXHILARATING, EXCITING

ECSTASY SERIES

SAVAGE ECSTASY (0-8217-3496-2, $4.95/$5.95

DEFIANT ECSTASY (0-8217-3497-0, $4.95/$5.95

FORBIDDEN ECSTASY (0-8217-5278-2, $5.99/$6.99

BRAZEN ECSTASY (0-8217-3499-7, $4.99/$5.99

TENDER ECSTASY (0-8217-5242-1, $5.99/$6.99

STOLEN ECSTASY (0-8217-3501-2, $4.99/$5.99

FOREVER ECSTASY (0-8217-5241-3, $5.99/6.99

Available wherever paperbacks are sold, or order direct from th Publisher. Send cover price plus 50¢ per copy for mailing an handling to Penguin USA, P.O. Box 999, c/o Dept. 17109 Bergenfield, NJ 07621. Residents of New York and Tennesse must include sales tax. DO NOT SEND CASH.

JANE KIDDER'S EXCITING WELLESLEY BROTHERS SERIES

MAIL ORDER TEMPTRESS (3863, $4.25
Kirsten Lundgren traveled all the way to Minnesota to be mail order bride, but when Eric Wellesley wrapped her in hi virile embrace, her hopes for security soon turned to dream of passion!

PASSION'S SONG (4174, $4.25
When beautiful opera singer Elizabeth Ashford agreed to car for widower Adam Wellesley's four children, she neve dreamed she'd fall in love with the little devils—and with thei handsome father as well!

PASSION'S CAPTIVE (4341, $4.5
To prevent her from hanging, Union captain Stuart Wellesle offered to marry feisty Confederate spy Claire Boudreau. Littl did he realize he was in for a different kind of war after th wedding!

PASSION'S BARGAIN (4539, $4.5
When she was sold into an unwanted marriage by her fathe Megan Taylor took matters into her own hands and black mailed Geoffrey Wellesley into becoming her husband instea But Meg soon found that marriage to the handsome, wealth timber baron was far more than she had bargained for!

Available wherever paperbacks are sold, or order direct from th Publisher. Send cover price plus 50¢ per copy for mailing an handling to Penguin USA, P.O. Box 999, c/o Dept. 1710 Bergenfield, NJ 07621. Residents of New York and Tennesse must include sales tax. DO NOT SEND CASH.